Soray

Also from Bloomsbury
by Celia Rees

Pirates!

Sovay

CELIA REES

BLOOMSBURY

First published in Great Britain in 2008 by Bloomsbury Publishing Plc
Published in the United States in 2008 by Bloomsbury U.S.A. Children's Books
175 Fifth Avenue, New York, New York 10010
Scholastic paperback edition published in 2009

The Library of Congress has cataloged the hardcover edition as follows:
Rees, Celia.
Sovay / by Celia Rees. — 1st U.S. ed.
p.   cm.
Summary: In 1794 England, the rich and beautiful Sovay, disguised as a
highwayman, acquires papers that could lead to her father's arrest for treason,
and soon her newly awakened political consciousness leads her and a compatriot
to France during the Revolution.
ISBN-13: 978-1-59990-203-6 • ISBN-10: 1-59990-203-6 (hardcover)
[1. Social classes—Fiction. 2. Sex role—Fiction. 3. Robbers and outlaws—Fiction.
4. Great Britain—History—1789–1820—Fiction. 5. France—History—
Revolution, 1789–1799.] I. Title.
PZ7.R25465Sov 2008   [Fic]—dc22   2008004779

ISBN-13: 978-1-59990-395-8 • ISBN-10: 1-59990-395-4 (Scholastic paperback)

Typeset by Dorchester Typesetting Group Ltd
Printed in the U.S.A. by Quebecor World Fairfield
2 4 6 8 10 9 7 5 3 1

For Catrin

Sovay, Sovay all on a day
She dressed herself in man's array
With a brace of pistols all by her side
To meet her true love, to meet her true love, away she'd ride

As she was riding over the plain
She met her true love and bid him stand
'Stand and deliver, young sir,' she said
'And if you do not, and if you do not, I'll shoot you dead'

He delivered up his golden store
And still she craved for one thing more
'That diamond ring, that I see you wear
Oh hand it over, oh hand it over, and your life I'll spare'

'From that diamond ring I would not part
For it's a token from my sweetheart
Shoot and be damned, you rogue,' said he
'And you'll be hanged, you'll be hanged then, for murdering me'

Next morning in the garden green
Young Sophie and her true love were seen
He spied his watch hanging from her clothes
Which made him blush lads, which made him blush lads, like
    any rose

'Why do you blush, you silly thing
I thought to have that diamond ring
T'was I who robbed you all on the plain
So here's your gold, love, so here's your gold and your watch
    and chain

'I only did it for to know
If you would be a man or no
If you had given me that ring,' she said
'I'd have pulled the trigger, pulled the trigger and shot you dead'

Traditional ballad

CHAPTER I

May, 1794

Sovay rode out early while the dew was still wet on the grass. The grooms had not risen when she stole from the stables, and thin layers of mist wound themselves round her horse's legs like skeins of discarded muslin as she crossed the bridge over the lake. Once she was away from the house, she spurred her horse to a gallop, crouched close to his neck as she took the old green road through the forest and up on to the common. There, she took up station at the crossroads, positioning herself in a grove of young birch, ready for the London coach, certain that he would be on it. Then she would expose him for the lecherous, double-dealing, false-hearted, despicable, craven little villain that she now knew him to be.

They were engaged and he had betrayed her with a chambermaid. Even the thought of him filled her with shaking fury.

'Not the first he's ruined, neither,' her maid, Lydia, had told her, giving her a look. With no mother, and only an invalid aunt to advise her, Lydia had taken some aspects of Sovay's moral guidance upon herself. Well, she needn't worry on that score. Sovay had not been that much of a fool. Not quite.

Her anger was mixed with a restless impatience. Where was the coach? She wanted this over. Her horse sensed something of her agitation and stamped and pawed, his shoes ringing on the stony ground. She patted his neck and whispered in his ear to quieten him. The air was full of the sweet musky scent of broom and gorse. *When gorse is out of bloom, love is out of favour*. She remembered her mother telling her that. It must have been a long time ago. She plucked a sprig of yellow broom and fixed it to the brim of her brother's hat, her mind going back to the revenge she would have. She would make him beg, she would make him crawl and plead for his life. If he failed the test she was about to set for him, she would shoot him dead.

The crack of a driver's whip, his shouts and curses, the crunch of wheels and the labouring snort of horses broke into her thoughts. She spied through a veil of shifting leaves. There was no other traffic in any direction. She pulled down the black mask that she'd worn at last winter's masked ball and pulled up a green silk kerchief to hide the lower half of her face. The coach creaked almost to a halt at the crest of the rise, the horses sweating after the steep hill. As the driver drew back his whip to urge them onward, Sovay drew her pistols and walked her horse forward.

'Stand and deliver!'

Her words were whipped away by the wind, swallowed by the great open space of the common. She repeated her demand, making her voice deeper, more commanding, and the guard raised his hands into the air while the driver reined the horses in and lowered his whip. Her heart beat harder when she saw that they obeyed her. She kept one pistol upon them and used the other to rap on the door of the carriage.

'Out. All of you out!'

Two passengers alighted: James, looking pale and frightened, and another young man. He was well-set, with a fresh, ruddy complexion, a little above her brother's age, about four and twenty. He was in no hurry to get down from the coach and seemed neither worried nor discomforted by this interruption to his journey, and his self-assurance unnerved her. Sovay trained her pistol on him as she ordered the two to part with their valuables and place them in the saddlebag that she threw down to them.

While James sprang to follow her instructions, the other one showed more reluctance, but soon she had divested both of their watches and their gold.

'Still I want one thing more,' she said, addressing James. 'That diamond ring that I see you wear. Hand it over and your life I will spare.'

She could feel her hand shaking when before it had been steady. This was the test she had set for him. The ring had been given as an expression of true love in an exchange of tokens. He had sworn to die rather than part with it. If he gave it to her, then all the doubts she harboured, all the stories that she had heard about him, were true. James did not hesitate; he was struggling to free the ring from his finger, spitting on his hand to work the band loose. She changed her aim and her hand shook no more. She didn't need to make James beg and crawl. He was doing that of his own accord. He had fallen to his knees, squeezing tears from eyes shut tight in prayer, his clasped hands shaking in supplication.

'Hold your fire, highwayman,' the fair young man said as she pulled back the hammer.

He took the ring from James and brought the bag over to her, slinging it in front of her saddle. She holstered one of her pistols and he dropped the ring into her outstretched hand. The stone flashed in the sun.

'He has given you everything.' The young man looked up at her. 'What more could you want from him? Small hands for a highwayman,' he added and smiled as if he knew her secret.

He was quick. He read her intention in an instant. His eyes still on her, he threw up her arm as she squeezed the trigger. James screamed but the shot missed. The horses reared and shied in their traces so the driver had to struggle to stop them from breaking away and the coach from overturning. Sovay used the confusion to make her escape. She had business back at the house.

◆━◆━◆

Sovay suppressed a sigh of impatience as the painter bent to his painstaking work. She tried not to move, as she had been instructed on numerous occasions, although she was afire with anticipation. She and James had an assignation at their usual trysting place in the garden. He would arrive; he might even be waiting for her now, with no idea that she was the highwayman who had stopped him on the road. Perhaps he would not even refer to it, preferring to keep his recent humiliation to himself. Perhaps she would let him pretend for a time, certainly she might do so, before she made a play of noticing the absence of the ring. The very thought of that made her tremble and Jonathan Trenton gave a moue of impatience.

'How many *times* do I have to ask you?' he said without looking up from the tiny brush strokes he was making.

Sovay murmured an apology and stared out at the garden behind him. She had never wanted to sit for this likeness. It was entirely Papa's idea. He had also chosen the artist. A coming young man who had studied under the late Sir Joshua Reynolds. Papa liked to encourage artists early on in their careers. Sovay disliked Trenton. His voice was high-pitched and whining, his manner fussy and overbearing. She sensed that the antipathy was mutual, although he said little to her, except to scold.

The portrait was almost finished and he was glad of it. This was a good commission and he'd been paid in advance, but he had to travel up from town to take her likeness and these were dangerous times. Highwaymen prowled the roads, preying on all comers, even poor painters, and there was unrest in town and countryside alike, sparked by the terrible events in France. He was not of a cowardly nature and would happily have braved the danger, if he had enjoyed the work, but the young woman standing before him had not proved to be the easiest of subjects. The girl possessed a definite dark beauty, a quality he would like to capture, but her face had a sullen cast, her expression a mask that gave nothing away.

Except for today. There was a flush to her cheeks, a heightening of colour. He applied an extra touch of rose madder. Something had happened to change her gaze from stony indifference to restless animation. He exchanged brushes to add tiny sparks of white and ultramarine to her slate grey eyes. She either stood with such stillness that he was hard put not to paint her like a statue, or she would not keep still. This morning she was inclined to fidget. She had something in her hand. She kept fiddling with it, turning it through her fingers. Something gold and round.

'What is that you are holding?' He would refrain from scolding, but she knew not to introduce variations in habit or accoutrements to their sessions.

'It's a watch.' She turned the face to him.

He grunted, dismissing it. A watch would hardly fit in with the way he had chosen to portray her. Something else caught his interest. She was wearing a ring on the middle finger of her left hand. What on earth had possessed her to do that?

Her hand moved and the diamond flashed in fragments of refracted light as a shaft of early afternoon sun struck through the window that opened from the garden. Her head turned slightly, her eyes moved as if to see past him and through the billowing curtain. There was someone out there waiting for her. A lover, he guessed. The source of her agitation? A further wash of madder across her cheeks seemed to signal the answer.

'You may go,' he said.

She stepped out of her pose and came towards him.

'Have you finished?'

'A little more to do,' he shrugged. 'But the real answer is yes.' She made to pass him, her mind already in the garden beyond the window. 'Do you not want to see yourself?'

She stopped and looked directly at him. A frank gaze, challenging and insolent, as direct and unwavering as if she was a young man.

'The real answer is no. I do not like to look at myself.'

The painter laughed. 'All women like to look at themselves, young or old.'

'Believe me, Mr Trenton, when I say that I do not. I did not want this likeness. I only sat for you to please Papa.'

'Even so . . .' To his annoyance he found himself wheedling, almost pleading. It was suddenly important that she should approve his work.

She stepped past him to look at her portrait. He half smiled, waiting for her to be caught by the spell of her own beauty, cast by the skill of his portraiture. He had seen it many times before. The dress that she wore for the sittings glowed against her skin. The fine white muslin had been difficult to paint but he thought that he had caught the right gauzy lightness. The girl was seventeen, but the style of dress chosen by her father was flowing and loose fitting, more suitable for a younger child. The scarlet sash, that Sovay had chosen to wind round her waist, went some way to lessen the impression of innocence. Trenton stood back examining his work. The white and the red showed off her dark beauty to perfection. He had caught her on the cusp, at the moment of transition from girl to woman. Even with that sullen smoulder, she might never be lovelier . . .

'You are a great admirer of your own work, I see.'

The irony of her tone brought the blood to his own face.

'An artist is only as good as his subject,' he replied with a bow.

'Smoothly said,' she smiled, and her whole face changed. He wished they had time to start over again.

'What do you think?' Suddenly, it was important for him to know.

'It is fine work. You are a good painter. But . . .'

'But what?'

'I do not like to look at myself, as I said. Now, you really must excuse me.'

With that she left him for her assignation in the garden, running as fast as the goddess, Diana, the classical persona he had chosen for her. He went to the window, peering through the curtains, hoping to gain a glimpse of this young man who had so captured her attention, but she soon disappeared past the great cedar tree and into a tunnel of trees that sheltered the Terrace Walk. The young leaves were at their most beautiful: the deep bronze of copper beech blended with delicate golds and the palest of greens to show like a scatter of coin against the dark gloss of the evergreens. He turned back into the room and packed the colours away in his head as he began to assemble his things. He would finish the portrait in his Covent Garden studio. He would put her in a pastoral setting, something a little wild: woodland in early summer, with a lake perhaps and mountains in the background. He liked to add a touch of the allegorical. His favourite for young women was Flora, goddess of flowers, youth, spring and fertility, but that would hardly do here. She had to be Diana, the huntress. He would give her a bow and a canine companion, perhaps a stag caught in a thicket. He grunted with satisfaction. That would do well and it could all be done in the safety of London.

Sovay ran along the Great Terrace, propelled by fury. She was late, but that did not matter, let him wait. She had turned the diamond round so it bit into her palm. She held the watch curled tight in her fist. He was lucky she did not have pistols with her, or she would finish what she should have done earlier.

When she reached the Oval Pavilion, their preferred place of meeting, James wasn't even there. She refused to sit on the stone bench inside the semicircular stone shelter. If she did so, she could not fail to notice the entwined initials carved on the round table, circled by a heart. Even looking at that wretched seat made her want to vomit. Sometimes when they met, in pursuit of greater privacy, they would mount the curving stairway that led to the little 'prospect' room. Sovay fought to control shuddering waves of fury and humiliation. They would not be going there any more.

She paced up and down, her gown brushing the grass, ready to show the watch and the ring, ready to confront him, but first she would taunt him, pay him out for his betrayal. She slipped the watch and the ring into her pocket. She would enjoy watching him squirm.

He arrived full of apologies, with tales of having been set upon on the road by a band of rogues. He had been ready to put up a fight, but the craven nature of his travelling companion meant that they'd had everything taken from them.

'Even the ring I gave you?'

'Even that.' He held his hand out, fingers spread. 'As you can see. I pleaded with the ruffians, but they would have killed me.'

'But it was a token of my love for you.' She looked at him, her large eyes full of hurt and accusation. 'You said you would rather die than part with it.'

'I was set upon, I told you!' He stepped forward, as if to kiss her. 'Come, love, let us not quarrel.'

Sovay turned from him. 'Even so . . .'

She stepped away. He made to follow, his face full of persuading. He was pretty rather than handsome, she realised now, with the kind of sweetness of face that might cause a young girl to lose her heart; but his pale blue eyes were set rather too close together and there was weakness in the chin, petulance in the set of the mouth. How could she ever have found him in the least bit attractive? He did not look his nineteen years. The skin on his cheeks was petal smooth and looked as if it hardly saw a razor; his powdered curls were as soft as a child's.

She turned, withdrawing her hand from her pocket. His eyes grew wider and the blood rose in his cheeks to see his watch dangling from her fist, his ring on her own finger. She threw his gold on the ground before him. He stepped back, hands up, as if to block out the sight of the glittering coins.

'It was you!' he said, and blushed even further, but all the time his eyes grew colder and it was not long before he rallied.

His father had been keen on the match in the beginning. There was wealth in the family, passed from mother to daughter. 'She'll come in for a pretty penny when she is twenty-one,' his father had told him, his eyes gleaming as if he could already see the gold spread before them, but circumstances had changed. He would use the news to mask this humiliation. He was lucky to escape her. There had always been stories. Especially about her mother's family, that their wealth was based on pirate gold. It had been expedient to ignore them. Until now. The whole family was tainted. Today's behaviour confirmed it. A girl who would dress as a highwayman and rob a coach in broad daylight, who would want such a one for a wife?

'The watch I would like returning,' he said, 'but you may keep your ring. I have no use for it. That is what I came to tell you.' He looked skyward as if recalling the words he had rehearsed. 'It is all over between us, Sovay. We can no longer be affianced. Your father is little better than a Jacobin spy and will shortly be arrested. My family cannot continue an association with anyone who shows anything less than complete loyalty to His Majesty.'

Sovay stared at him, trying to make sense of the words coming out of his mouth.

''Tis true, Sovay!' James exclaimed, unsettled by her continuing silence. 'I've heard your father speak sedition on very many occasions. Speaking against the King and the Government. You cannot deny it.'

'I certainly do!' Sovay turned on him. 'He has *never* spoken against the King! He's for reform, of course, but that's a very different thing.'

'I heard it with my own ears at his very table! There is no point in defending him. As for your brother!' James shook his head. 'When he was last down from Oxford, I'd never heard such wild talk. It was enough to get a person arrested, if not convicted.' He hooked his thumbs in his waistcoat pocket, no longer the least bit disconcerted. 'Your family is bound for disgrace. Scandal hangs about you like a bad smell. Well,' he demanded. 'Do you have *nothing* to say?'

Sovay shook her head. Tears of fury were welling up in her eyes and she could not trust her voice. She could hear his father, Sir Royston, behind the words that he had uttered. How could she ever have considered this, this *puppy* worthy of her?

'In that case . . .' He groped for the watch that was no longer in the pocket of his fine waistcoat. Sovay, who loathed sewing above anything, had punctured her fingers to pepper pots embroidering the primrose yellow and dove-grey silk with little pink knots of flowers. A labour of love. One of her few attempts to do the kind of thing other girls did and it had all been for nothing! She turned away, trying to control herself, lest he interpret her tears of rage for something else.

How had she ever felt anything for him? She had been flattered by his attention; that was the truth of it. He was much sought after, considered a great catch, and Sovay had enjoyed feeling superior to every other girl in the neighbourhood. She had persuaded herself that she truly loved him. It was obvious that she had built up an edifice out of nothing and now it was tumbling like a child's pile of bricks. Her brother, Hugh, had always thought him a shallow, cowardly fellow, in thrall to his father; Papa was the one who had persuaded her into it. Although he disliked his pompous neighbour, he had thought that the marriage might be an influence for good. Once they were married, so his reasoning went, Sovay could educate James and Sir Royston into new, more enlightened ways of thinking. As if they would listen to her!

Sovay loved her papa, and respected him, but sometimes his ideals got the better of him. She had an uncomfortable feeling that she had been part of one of his schemes for improvement. He had treated the young man as if he was already his son-in-law and had spent many hours discussing ideas with him: new methods in farming and land management, as well as science, philosophy and the politics of the day. James had listened with every show of attention, encouraging him, drawing him on to make more and more radical statements. Her father had gone along with it, always so trusting, seeing the good in everyone. Sovay now saw that it had all been for one purpose: to get him to compromise himself. Who was the spy here? She turned back, ready to accuse him, but James was already walking away.

'You may keep the money,' he said over his shoulder. 'If what I hear is correct,' he added, his voice cold with ominous warning, 'you may have need of it.'

He did not stoop to pick up his gold and she would not touch it. The coin was left where it settled. Someone would have a lucky find.

She watched him go, all the while seeing his arms thrown up, seeing his back arch, imagining him falling, the rich, red blood spreading to stain the oyster silk of his brocade jacket. If she'd had a gun with her, he would already be dead.

CHAPTER 2

Sovay walked back through the gardens towards the house. Some of her anger had dissipated, but not all. She was glad to be rid of him, better to discover now what a spineless coward he was, what a traitor, but she was annoyed at the way he had trounced her. How he had managed to recover so quickly from his initial embarrassment and *still* behave as though he were superior. If she were a man . . . but then if she were, the situation would hardly have arisen.

Her mind drifted back to the morning. How she'd enjoyed the feeling of being in her brother's clothes. They were a little too big for her. She'd had to belt the breeches tightly into her waist and wear two pairs of socks to stop her feet sliding about in his boots, but she had been able to stride free of encumbering skirts and restricting corsets, to ride astride instead of side-saddle. She liked the heaviness of the pistols by her side, the heft of them in her hand. And when the coach stopped, when she saw James' face, when everyone did *exactly* what she said. She had been taken with an excitement, an exhilaration that she had never before experienced. Even the memory made her heart beat harder. She feared to admit how she had felt. Even to herself.

Her anger towards James returned with still greater force, although part of that was fury with herself for being such a gull, for being taken in so easily, but the insult against her was nothing compared to the things that he had said about her father. Was it malice? Her father and his were hardly the best of friends. They disagreed violently about most things. Sir Royston objected to her father's new ways. He made no secret of his opinion that Sir John Middleton mollycoddled his workers, building them cottages and paying them more than others could afford. Her father would argue that he could do so because his farming methods were successful, but Sir Royston objected that it made it difficult for other landowners who preferred to stick to the old ways. It was true that her father was of a reforming frame of mind, interested in changing other things besides methods of farming, but did that make him a spy? And how did James know? The accusations had to come from his father. Sir Royston was an MP and had the borough in his pocket. He hardly ever attended Parliament but he made it his business to be close to those in power. There could be truth in what James had told her. Papa was from home at the moment. In London on business. Did he know what was being said against him? If not, she must find a way to get word to him. Sovay quickened her step towards the house.

'Miss, Miss!' Lydia came running towards her. 'You're wanted. There's a visitor. What happened?' She asked in an excited whisper as they walked back to the house.

Sovay showed her the ring. Lydia's green eyes widened and she smiled like the cat she much resembled.

'So who's the visitor? Mr Trenton, the painter?'

'No,' Lydia shook her head, 'he's left already. A

stranger. Steward Stanhope sent me to find you.'

In her father's absence, William Stanhope was in charge of the running of the estate, but family duties fell to Sovay. Aunt Harriet, of course, was nominally in charge of the household but she'd be no help. A self-proclaimed invalid, she dosed herself with toddies laced with laudanum, which kept her almost permanently confined to her bed.

'He's waiting in the library.'

'Thank you, Lydia.'

The young man was examining her father's books when she entered the room. He was so absorbed that he failed to register her presence and Sovay stood in the doorway watching him. He was of medium height and solidly built with little affectation as to his dress. His curly fair hair was undressed, carelessly tied back with a black ribbon. His boots were muddy and his broad back strained the dark cloth of his coat. When he stretched up to reach down a volume, the material across his shoulders threatened to split and his hand showed square and tanned against the pale spines of the books. He browsed like a scholar and was dressed like a gentleman, but he reminded her of Gabriel Stanhope, the Steward's son, who was more at home in fields and woods than in a drawing room. She wondered if he had come to see her father on farming business. People often came to consult him about his methods, but in that case why had Steward Stanhope not dealt with him?

He turned, volume still in hand, as if aware of her scrutiny.

'Oh,' he said. 'Forgive me. I didn't realise I had company . . .'

He faltered, but not from confusion. He recognised her immediately, as she did him. He had been on the coach that very morning and had witnessed her excursion as a highwayman. Sovay momentarily found herself speechless. He rallied more quickly than she did.

'I was just admiring your father's library. I envy him this.' He held up the volume that he had taken down from the shelves: Rousseau's *Social Contract*, a 1762 first edition. 'He has a marvellous collection.'

Sovay looked round the room, seeing it with a stranger's eye. The shelves were stocked from floor to ceiling with books on every possible subject. The walls were studded with chronometers and barometers. Globes and astrolabes stood about on the floor. Cabinets held stuffed birds and animals, samples of rocks, minerals and fossils. Every surface was crowded with bits of machinery, brass-crafted devices for generating this or measuring that.

'Yes, he is interested in many things,' she said, just as several clocks chimed the hour in a jangle of sound from the musical to the sonorous while others wheezed and whirred to catch up. 'Clocks being one of them,' she added through the din.

He laughed. 'Excuse me, I have not introduced myself.' He came towards her, hand extended. 'My name is Virgil Barrett. You must be Miss Sovay Middleton.'

He took her hand. She expected him to bow and kiss it, as James would have done. Instead he shook it, as if she were a man. His clasp was strong, his skin warm and dry. Sovay returned his grip and took her hand from his.

'I am delighted to meet you, Mr Barrett. May I enquire as to your business?'

'I have come to see your father, but I understand that he is from home at the moment.'

'That is correct. He was called away quite suddenly. You have missed him, unfortunately.'

'I was afraid of that.'

He began to pace the room, still clutching the book he had taken from the shelves. Could he trust her? The lives and freedom of many, even her own father, could depend on that decision. She was very young, and appeared to be demure, but had he not seen her, masquerading as a man? A highwayman at that? He was sure it had been her. He'd know those eyes anywhere, and there had been murder in them. He'd seen it in the eyes of others. He'd been just a boy, but he had served in the War of Independence. He'd seen it then. The life he led now took him into considerable peril. He had seen it since. Such dangerous behaviour suggested a wild, headstrong nature hiding beneath that modest exterior. She was a long way from ordinary; such an action took nerve and courage. He turned back, having decided. Such qualities fitted these extraordinary times.

'Are you from the West Country?' she asked, to fill the silence. She found his manner, his dress, even his accent hard to place.

'No,' he laughed again, a rich sound in the ticking room. 'I'm a citizen of the United States of America.' He smiled, his teeth white and even, and spoke the words with evident pride.

'Oh I see. My father calls your nation *a beacon of liberty in a dark world*.'

'And so it is! We do not have kings and lords ruling over us. We do not bow the knee. We make our own laws and live in freedom.'

'Not all of you,' she said. Abolition was one of her father's many causes.

'Not all, it is true,' he replied, divining her meaning, 'but I did not come here to debate slavery with you.'

'Why did you come, Mr Barrett? I am curious to know.'

'Do you know where your father has gone? Do you know what called him from home?'

'Not exactly, but he has many interests, as I have said, and is in touch with a great many people all over the country. He often travels to visit one group or another. I believe he was going to London to meet with some men who have asked for his help.'

'Well, I must tell you,' his brow creased into a frown, 'the men he was going to meet are subject to orders of arrest, if they haven't been taken already. That is likely why they contacted him. He is also under suspicion and subject to such an order, as are many others.' He looked around and spread his hands in a gesture of helplessness. 'I looked to warn him but I was delayed on the road. My horse went lame. I had to take the coach . . .'

She turned away so he could not see her blushing. Her actions seemed even more irresponsible and prankish in light of the trouble which faced her now.

'I have to warn you of imminent danger. There is someone coming here, a Bow Street runner with a warrant and evidence against him.'

'But my father is not here!'

'That does not matter.'

'And what are the charges?'

'Probably the lesser charge of sedition. Speaking against the King and the Government. Once the warrant is in the hands of the magistrate, your father will be arrested as soon as he appears.'

And the magistrate was Sir Royston. He would be happy to oblige. His son, James, would supply the evidence. She had heard the very word on his lips not half an hour since!

'What will happen?'

'If he is found guilty? Imprisonment. Even transportation.'

Her father did not enjoy the best of health. A death sentence, either one. The guilty verdict was a foregone conclusion. Who would doubt a magistrate's son?

'The lesser charge, you said,' Sovay looked up into his troubled blue-grey eyes. 'What is the greater one?'

'It is possible he might be charged with treason . . .' Virgil lowered his voice, as if he feared that they might be overheard.

'Treason!' Sovay hugged herself, suddenly chilled, as if the shadow of great events had fallen across Compton, blotting out all light and warmth from the sunny library. 'What would happen if he was convicted?'

'The sentence for treason is to be hanged, drawn and quartered. The punishment has not changed.' He paused. 'And . . .'

'And?' Sovay shuddered and turned away, wishing to hide her agitation. Was that not bad enough?

'If your father was convicted of treason, his lands and property would be forfeit.'

She turned back. And who would benefit from that?

Sir Royston, no doubt. All her father's work would come to nothing. His workers and cottagers would end up as miserable as the wretches who worked Sir Royston's land, the Stanhopes turned out in favour of that weasel of a Steward the Gilmores employed. It was not to be borne.

She had been aware of dark clouds forming, but had no idea that the storm was so near. If only she had paid more attention to her father's preoccupation. He had given up his beloved experiments. His day book and his nature journal had lain unopened for months, the surfaces in his workshop and laboratory had gathered dust while he had spent all his time in here, writing tracts and engaged in endless correspondence. He believed so completely in the rightness of his cause: Reason, Liberty, Equality. These truths had been dinned into her since she was a child, so much so that it seemed strange to her, and her brother, that others did not share them. The Revolution in France had been welcomed in their house with rejoicing. Her father had planted a liberty tree on Compton Dassett village green and the anniversary of the Bastille falling had been the occasion, last year, for a celebratory dinner which had been attended by like-minded friends from across the county, members of the Monday Society who met on the first Monday of every month to discuss science and philosophy. They had toasted 'The Patriots of France', 'Tom Paine' and 'The Rights of Man' but they had also toasted 'King and Constitution', she remembered distinctly. Her father believed absolutely but he was not disloyal. He spared little thought, however, for the danger that his ideas brought with them, and even then his concern would always be for other people, never for himself. All this had been going on in front of her and she had hardly noticed, too preoccupied by that wretch Gilmore. Virgil Barrett must think her very shallow. She would find a way to make up for it now.

'This man. This Bow Street runner. When will he come?'

'I would say that I was a few days ahead of him, no more than that.' He hesitated. 'I would stay and help you if I could, but I ride north. He carries a sheaf of warrants and evidences with him and there are others I must warn. May I trouble you for a horse? I will not get far on the spavined nag I was offered at the inn. Also . . .' He hesitated, not knowing how to put this. 'I find myself without funds and,' his fingers went to his empty waistcoat pocket, 'in need of a timepiece.'

Sovay coloured. This was as near as he'd come to mentioning it, but all through their interview she'd been intensely aware of their previous meeting on the road.

'Of course.' She went to a drawer in the bureau. 'Here's gold for you and a watch and chain.'

He pocketed the money in a jingle of coin and examined the watch carefully.

'This is very like my own watch,' he said with a smile. 'Very like indeed!' He opened the back and examined the maker's mark. 'Made in Philadelphia. What a coincidence! Who would credit it?'

'Who, indeed!' Sovay laughed, despite her embarrassment, grateful to him for so deftly defusing the tension between them.

'My father's collection includes items great and small,' she said. 'Now let us find you a suitable horse.'

'Thank you.' He took her hand again and this time he kissed it. 'I hope that our next meeting will be under happier circumstances.'

'So do I.'

Sovay smiled. She found that she liked him and hoped that they would meet again. She went with him to see that he got his new mount and that he had all he needed for his onward journey.

Virgil thanked her and rode off, glad to feel a good horse under him. A pretty girl. No, pretty did not do her justice. She was both less than that, and greater. Her good looks verged on beauty. She looked small as she stood on the steps to wave goodbye to him. She was very young to be facing alone the forces that were gathering round her, ready to snuff out the flame of liberty that had burnt so bright in that pleasant house. He checked his horse, half of a mind to go back to help her, but he merely lifted a hand in salute and spurred his horse on. It was his duty to warn others of the danger they faced, before it was too late.

❖

Sovay could settle to nothing and knew that this restlessness would not be dissipated until she had found her father and got word to Hugh in Oxford. She prowled the empty rooms and everything that she saw was suddenly newly precious to her.

It was all in jeopardy, for if the house was seized, everything would be cast on the bonfire, or sold and dispersed. And why? For what reason? She looked up at the portrait that hung above the fireplace. Her father had a kind face, his mouth quirked at the corners as if he could not resist smiling and his dark eyes shone with intelligence. Plainly dressed, as always, slightly overweight, the buttons on his waistcoat straining a little, he looked very much the gentleman farmer in his buff-coloured coat and breeches, and his neat, light brown wig. It was a proud pose before his beloved Compton, his gun at his side and a dog at his knee. Sovay felt deep affection as she looked up at him. He was a good man, generous, kind to his tenants, always willing to listen, to help those in need. Why should he be punished? Because he had an enquiring mind? Because of what he believed? He believed in reform, certainly. He believed that all men should be able to vote in secrecy and that parliamentary seats should not be in the gift of men like Sir Royston, but was that sedition? Was that treason? Were all who believed such things to be silenced?

Sovay slowly mounted the stairs, surveying the family portraits which looked down at the hall. Her mother as a young woman, dressed in the elaborate spreading skirts of twenty years ago or more. She was wearing a beautiful gown of pale pink satin, ruched and sewn with bows and bunches of lace that looked like overblown roses. She was sitting in a bower, roses of the exact same pale shade growing all around her. Sovay sighed. Her mother died when she was five.

She turned at the top of the stairs and went into her mama's drawing room. Sovay seldom came in here. She found it hard to bear. Although her mother had been dead for twelve years, her father insisted that there were fresh flowers arranged and that her tea things were laid just so. A collection of miniatures were grouped on the wall to the side of the fireplace:

Sovay and Hugh as children. Hugh at about seven or eight had been a pretty child, with his high colour and blond curls, but he could never be mistaken for a girl. His collar and necktie were askew and there was a careless, unruly fall to his hair and the look in his eyes suggested a mischievous, rebellious nature. Sovay had been younger, not more than three or four. She remembered nothing of the sitting or the artist. The dark, solemn-eyed girl, with a bow in her hair, could be a stranger, although she did remember the puppy she was clutching to her. Hugh and Sovay together, a little older, dressed as Harlequin and Columbine. Sovay smiled, remembering how Hugh hated that portrait and was always hiding it. Their mother had commissioned the likenesses as her illness worsened. She kept them by her bedside, as though she could take their images with her.

The last oval frame on the wall did not contain a painting at all, but a coil of her mother's curling dark hair. Even encased here, and after all these years, it had not lost its lustre. Sovay turned away, eyes stinging with fresh tears. She could see that hair, lovingly dressed and combed by Mrs Crombie, spread over the pillow, arranged around her mother's white, white face, whiter than the pillowcase.

Sovay wiped her tears away and returned to the landing. It was up to her now to find a way to secure this household, to keep Compton from harm. Who would not fight for their family's name, for their honour? Who could criticise her for doing so? She descended the stairs having decided upon a course of action.

CHAPTER 3

So Sovay's career as a highwayman began. She felt no fear. She was filled with a steely sense of purpose and each time brought a fresh rush of excitement as she rode out and challenged the drivers to 'Stand and deliver!' She loved the anticipation as she waited on those bright summer mornings, surrounded by the song of lark and linnet and the heady scent of broom and gorse. Each day, she cut a fresh sprig for the luck it brought her. Certainly, she had experienced no mishap so far. Each time had gone as smoothly as the first, although she had encountered no runner or anything like one, just ordinary travellers. She did not relish taking their jewellery and money, since that was not her intention, and was careless in her larceny. If a passenger was poorly dressed, or was travelling in the boot at the back, or on the roof, she took nothing from them. She treated ladies with great courtesy, bowing, kissing their hands, and leaving them their rings and lockets.

She did not keep the riches she gained. On her way home, she cast them away, dropping coin on the paths the children took out to the fields to scare birds, leaving gold on the heath to be found by poor furze-cutters, casting silver over hedges into cottagers' gardens. All this, along with her swagger and gallantry, meant that every day that Sovay rode out her legend grew and the stories about her spread. She was named for the sprig of broom she wore on her hat. The mysterious Captain Blaze.

She was just about to leave the stable, on yet another expedition, when a hand grabbed her leg. Brady stayed steady, but Sovay nearly jumped out of her stirrups.

'Where are you off to, Missy, on this fine summer's morning?'

Gabriel Stanhope, the Steward's son, stood looking up at her. He was grinning in a way that she found most infuriating, and showed no sign of letting her go. Indeed, his grip on her boot tightened as he waited for his answer.

'Nothing to do with you. Let me go!'

She had known him since they were children, babies even. They had grown up together. There had been a time when she had considered him as much her brother as Hugh. The three of them had been inseparable, running wild in the woods and fields. She had cried herself to sleep many a night, jealous of the friendship between Hugh and Gabriel, and would have done anything to win his regard, but now they were grown up and things had changed between them. They were still friends and she held him in great affection, but that did not extend to him ordering her about as though they were still seven and ten.

'I'll come and go as I please,' she said, 'and ask no leave of you.'

'Oh, will you now? Dressed like that? It's a dangerous game you play, Miss Sovay. They are talking in the inn about a new gentleman of the road. Only a slip of a chap, quite a charmer, but reckless and daring by all accounts. Someone has christened him Captain Blaze, for the yellow cockade he wears.'

He nodded towards the sprig of broom still on the brim of her hat from her last ride out.

'Have they?' Sovay settled back in her saddle. 'Captain Blaze, eh? I like that.'

'It's not a joke, Sovay.' He looked up at her. 'I hope this madness has nothing to do with that fool Gilmore. He got taken down t'other day, by all accounts.'

'That was different. Now I have another purpose. Much more serious.'

She leaned towards him, breathing in his familiar smell of hay and horses and tack room leather. His thick red-golden hair was wet where he had sluiced himself with water. His sleeves were rolled up; his shirt was open to the waist, as if he had just finished washing under the pump in the yard. He hadn't had time to shave. The copper glint of stubble dusted his cheeks. She looked down at his broad face, burnt brown from working in the fields with the men. His wide brow was creased with worry, his blue eyes clouded with concern.

'There's trouble coming, Gabriel, and I'm going to stop it. You have to let me go!'

He did so with reluctance and as she rode off all he could do was stand and gaze after her. He had no way of preventing her departure. She was daughter of the house. He strode into the stable, thinking to ride after her, bareback if need be. He knew the way she would take through the woods and out on to the common, knew the place she would stand and wait. He should stay here. There was trouble brewing. Rumours of revolution were sweeping the country, fuelled by events in France. The King and Country movement had started up again with a vengeance, with its demands for oaths of allegiance and its persecution of any known to be of a radical persuasion. Sovay's father was not popular with everyone. He held extreme views on almost everything and the changes made on his estate had not been liked by all. These could be enough to bring him under attack, get his house ransacked. It had happened in other places.

Gabriel saw his duty clear. He should stay here. Anyway, it was probably too late to stop Sovay now. What she was doing was madness, but she was brave and determined and would not be deflected. He had always admired her for that. She could ride and shoot as well as any boy, but she was heading into unknown danger. He could not help but worry for her. She was headstrong and stubborn with a temper on her which could eclipse any sense of caution. He remembered her and Hugh from when they were children. If you know someone then, you know them for life. They could throw a veil over their true natures: Hugh with his learning; Sovay with her lady-like accomplishments, but he remembered different. Mad, the both of them, competing with each other, neither with any sense of danger. He had got them out of scrapes without number, lied for them, taken the blame for them, suffered many a beating and never minded because he loved both of them in very different ways. Would he hang for her? That was the question now.

He went to the tack room for his cloak and hat and took the blunderbuss down from the wall. It was an old-fashioned weapon, kept in case of intruders, but it was loaded and effective at close quarters. Beside, he didn't have time to find another. He knotted a kerchief to pull up over his face, jumped on Belmont, the horse he had been about to put between the shafts of the hay cart, and galloped for the moor.

❖➤◆◄❖

Once up on the common, Sovay plucked a fresh sprig of broom. Captain Blaze. She smiled at the name as she inhaled the musky scent from the bright yellow flowers. She fixed the sprig to her hat with a diamond pin that she had acquired from some young fop and tucked some into Brady's bridle.

She stationed herself at the crossroads, adjusted the black eye-mask and green kerchief and loosened her weapons. Soon, she would pick up the sound of hooves on the flinty road.

The horses slowed as they toiled up the long hill, but as soon as they reached the summit, the driver cracked his whip, ready to make a speedy descent. Sovay rode out and the horses shied but showed no sign of stopping. A guard sat next to the driver, weapons at the ready, another sat at the back. The coach company was taking no chances after the recent rash of attacks.

The guard took aim as the coach swept past. Sovay felt the heat of the ball as it just missed her cheek. The driver yelled, and his long whip curled out again to lash the rumps of the sweating horses.

'Stop!' a voice called out from below her. 'Do as he says!'

Sovay glanced to the side to see that another had joined her. He was similarly disguised in hat and

30

travelling cloak with a scarf pulled up to hide his face, but he was riding a heavy horse and wielding an ancient musket.

'A clod on a carthorse,' the driver spat over the side. 'If I ain't seen it all. Get out of my way!'

'Carthorse he may be,' Gabriel answered, 'but he'll have your rig over in a second.' He waved the blunderbuss. 'And this'll blow a hole right through you. Do you want to try either one?' The guard at the front looked nervous. The piece was ancient, but it could cut a man in two. 'Throw your weapons down, both of you!' Gabriel shouted as he rode up to join Sovay who had her own gun trained on the guard at the rear.

A large face appeared and the window was filled with a man's bulk encased in a Bow Street runner's red waistcoat and blue jacket.

'What's the delay?' he shouted up. 'Drive on! Drive on, you scoundrel! Shoot the villains, you cowards!'

The guards ignored him, throwing their weapons down. Gabriel nodded to Sovay, who rapped on the door of the carriage. The passengers alighted one by one.

'Damned dogs!' the man in the red waistcoat shouted up at the driver and guard as he got down. 'In it together, I shouldn't wonder!' He brandished his staff at them. 'I'll find out if you are, you can wager upon it, and I'll see the two of you hang alongside 'em. See if I don't! You'll not get a thing from me.'

He turned to Sovay, his small eyes filled with malice. She walked Brady up to him and pointed her gun inches from his head.

'All the better reason to shoot you then,' she breathed

down to him. At the click of the hammer, oily drops of sweat broke from the coarse pores of his face.

'I carry nothing of value.'

'What is in the wallet?'

'Documents, merely. They have no worth!'

'I'll take it anyway.'

'No, you won't!' He brandished his staff as if to strike her arm as she reached out towards him.

'Drop it!' Gabriel commanded. 'Or I will blow your head off!'

The stick clattered to the floor as the man stared into the wide mouth of the blunderbuss.

'Give me the wallet,' Sovay reached down for it. The runner showed every reluctance but a cocked pistol could be very persuasive. He handed the wallet over. It weighed surprisingly heavy.

'The rest of you,' Gabriel turned his gun on the cowering passengers, 'hand over your valuables. Do not try our patience further or we will kill you all.'

Sovay threw down her saddlebag and the terrified travellers hastened to comply.

Sovay collected the bulging bag and Gabriel trained his gun on the runner.

'Hand me the staff,' he shouted down at him. 'Quick about it!'

The man was unwilling to obey, but valued his head. Gabriel took the stick from his hand and used it to urge his horse away. Sovay followed, spurring Brady to a gallop, crouching low over his neck in case the guard decided to let off another shot or two. They did not slacken their speed until they reached the margin of the forest.

Gabriel unscrewed the brass handle of the hollow

staff and read the paper rolled up within it.

'The fellow was a tipstaff. This is a warrant for your father's arrest.'

'Give it to me!' Sovay took it from him and prepared to gallop for the house.

'Wait!' Gabriel took hold of Brady's bridle. 'I find this action you're taking hasty, Miss Sovay, very hasty. Not to say downright foolish. Posing as a highwayman could get you hanged!'

'Then you would hang alongside me.'

'I could not let you act alone.'

'At any account, how could they prove it? A female highwayman? Who'd believe it?'

She laughed and spurred her horse, her face flushed with such recklessness that Gabriel's fear for her deepened.

They were on the track for home when a boy darted into their path. He did not look at Sovay, thinking her a stranger. She had removed her mask, but still wore her scarf high, as if to keep the dust from her nose and mouth.

'Mr Gabriel! Come quick! There's men coming up the drive to the house.'

'Men? What men?'

'I dunno,' the boy shrugged. 'They ain't troopers, nothing like that, but some of 'em got uniforms. They got poles and pikes and say they're for King and Country. They're shouting that Master's under arrest and they're here to see justice done. Sir Royston's at the head of 'em.' His young brow wrinkled. 'Your father's up the far cornfields. We been searching for Miss Sovay and she's nowhere to be found, so your ma says to find you!'

'How many are there?' Sovay asked, forgetting her disguise.

The boy looked up at her, curious, head cocked on one side, as though the stranger was suddenly familiar, then he shook his head.

'Dunno rightly,' he answered, 'but a goodly few.'

'All right, Jack.' Gabriel reached in his pocket for a penny. 'Find as many men as you can. Tell them to meet me in the yard.'

The barefoot boy scampered off, clutching the coin tight in his hand.

'We'll take the guns from the gunroom and any other weapons we can muster,' Gabriel said to Sovay. 'You stay inside. I'll gather the men in front of the house.'

'I will not!' Sovay turned on him indignantly. 'D'you think I'm going to hide like a vixen in a covert? I'm going to confront him. He can do nothing without a warrant.' She reached over and clasped Gabriel's hand. 'Together we'll see him off, and his rabble.'

◆►❋◄◆

After some swift work by Lydia, Sovay appeared immaculately attired in a dove-grey lady's riding habit. She held a whip in her hand and stood at the top of the steps in front of the grand portal staring down at the men massed before the house. Lydia was behind her, clutching a large steel bodkin with which, she'd announced, she was prepared to do considerable damage. Cook stood with Lydia, rolling pin at the ready. A grim-faced Gabriel stood with his men. They made two lines in front of the house. The first rank carried firearms, those behind carried whatever they could find, old swords, pikes and halberds, taken down from the walls of the hall, otherwise whatever they were working with at the time, but hayforks, billhooks, sickles and skinning knives made formidable weapons.

For the most part, Sir Royston's men were similarly armed. Some were in uniform. He had raised a troop of Volunteers, kitting them out at his own expense. Their uniforms had been designed by James, who was riding at the front of the ragged column, splendidly dressed in blue and cream, as proud as a captain of hussars, with one hand resting on the silver hilt of a sword, a plumed cap upon his head, a quantity of gold on each shoulder and tasselled braid across his chest. He looked ridiculous. Sovay heard a snuffle of suppressed laughter from Lydia and would have joined in herself had the situation not been so grave. Sovay surveyed the forces ranged against them. The men from Sir Royston's estate were for the most part quiet, as if they didn't want to be there but had no choice; the rest, who appeared to have been swept from every tavern in the town, were far more vociferous but for the most part drunk. Sir Royston himself was at the head of them all, his bulky figure balanced on a fine bay horse. He went to ride right up to the house, but when Gabriel's men closed ranks and stepped forward, he reined his mount back.

'What do you want here?' Sovay's voice rang out and some of the shouting subsided, replaced by leering and jeering. 'What right have you to trespass on my land?'

'It's not your land, but your father's and he's subject

to arrest,' Sir Royston shouted back at her. 'We are here to see justice done.'

'Arrest?' Sovay feigned shocked surprise. 'On what grounds?'

'Sedition and treason. Now get this rabble out of my way.'

He made to breach the line again and the crowd surged after him, bellowing 'Sedition', 'Treason' and 'Justice done'. Gabriel let off a warning shot above their heads and the furore died down.

'My father is not here. You know that. So I ask again, what is your business?'

'We are here to search the house, seize seditious materials.'

'Do you have a warrant?' Sovay knew very well that he hadn't, since the warrant was in her pocket. She stared back at him, interested to see what he would do now.

'I expect one within the hour,' he said.

'But you do not have one now, so you will not pass, or set one foot in this house. I will remind you once again that you are trespassing. On *your* land, many a man has lost his leg to a mantrap, or his life to a spring gun, or been transported for life for doing just that.' She looked to the crowd behind him. 'You men. Before you move against my father, remember the mercy he has shown to those who have appeared before him on the bench. How many men has he saved from transportation? From the rope itself? You come here shouting for justice; my father has always shown justice and fairness in his judgements. Tell me, is that not true?'

The jeering and shouting turned to muttering

between them. Sovay knew she'd hit home with some of them, at least. Most of the rabble from the town had good reason to be grateful to Justice Middleton. He was known to be lenient and fair. There were looks cast in Sir Royston's direction. Unlike some.

Not everyone felt that way. The Volunteers were not tavern sweepings, they were law-abiding citizens, in the pay of Sir Royston.

'Enough of this parleying,' James yelled, looking to them to support him. He spurred his horse forward and they surged after him. 'Let us clean out this nest of sedition.'

He was close enough to ride his horse at Gabriel and rush him before he could take aim and fire. Sovay feared for Gabriel, knowing he would not give way. She did not want blood shed on either side, but James seemed set on a course of violent action. Sovay stood her ground, square in front of the door. She had a pistol hidden about her and would not hesitate to use it if he got any nearer. He went to draw his sword but he fumbled the elaborate hand guard of the sabre and had trouble drawing the long, curved blade from its scabbard.

'Have a care you don't cut yourself!' Sovay shouted at him. 'Until you know how to use it, I suggest you keep it in its sheath!'

Her words were greeted with laughter by those who heard her. James' charge came to nothing as he twisted in the saddle, flushed with rage, struggling with his sabre and in danger of unseating himself.

'As I said, Sir Royston, come back when you have a warrant. Until then, I demand that you leave my estate.'

At a nod from Gabriel, the Compton men advanced. Already many at the back of the crowd were melting away. William Stanhope was coming up behind them with men from the far fields, armed with stout sticks, sickles and billhooks. Caught between two determined forces, the rest turned tail. They had come to make trouble, perhaps do a bit of looting. They had not come to fight.

'I'll be back, missy.' Sir Royston's beefy slab of a face darkened still further. 'Next time you will not be so lucky.'

❖

When Gabriel came back from seeing Sir Royston's 'army' off the estate, Sovay had already left.

'Gone?' he asked Lydia. 'Gone where?'

'To London, to find the master.' She was throwing clothes into a bag. 'I'm to follow on the next coach.'

'She's riding?'

'Yes,' Lydia looked shifty. 'She took Brady.'

'She's dressed as a man, isn't she?'

Lydia's bottom lip stuck out in petulant defiance, but she didn't deny it.

'I know what she's been doing, Lydia.' Gabriel shook his head with impatience. 'And don't doubt that you've been helping her.'

'She said it would be quicker.' Lydia busied herself with her packing. 'A quicker way to travel and she was less likely to be bothered . . .'

'And you didn't try to stop her! You are older and should be a good influence. You should have shown more sense.'

'You know what she's like, Mr Gabriel. Once she's

38

made her mind up. She won't listen to no one, so how's she going to listen to me? Besides, I admire her for it. Did you see the way she saw off Sir Royston?' Lydia's green eyes gleamed with admiration. 'Like a young queen, she was, defending her territory. With no *men* here to help her. What is she to do?'

Lydia looked at him with just a hint of mutiny. Whatever her feelings for Gabriel might be, she would not betray her mistress. Gabriel had done his part to shield Sovay from her own folly, but such reasoning would be lost on Lydia. With a sharp tongue and decided opinions, she was not beholden to anyone. In her eyes, Sovay could do no wrong. As if she had even tried to stop her! They were both as bad as each other.

Gabriel left her to her packing. She had been hankering to go to London this long time. Now she would get her wish. Her and Sovay, the both of them, needed Mrs Crombie to keep them in order. The old housekeeper was in charge of the London house. They would not play so fast and loose with her about.

Sovay did not lack for courage, that he would admit. She'd seen off Sir Royston and his pike-waving rabble. She'd played them like fish and never shown a flicker of fear, and now she was off again, dressed as a highwayman. What the devil was possessing her? At least, she would not lack for money, Brady had not been unsaddled and the bags bulged with stolen gold from her earlier escapade. He packed a satchel, his course decided. It was pointless going after her. She had too much of a start and there was no knowing which road she would be taking. He would leave his father to guard Compton and go to Oxford; tell Hugh what was happening here. They could go to London together and make sure that Sovay got into no more trouble. The master had to be warned, Sovay was right about that, but she should have left it to Hugh to decide the best way to do it. Perhaps Sir John already knew about these forces gathering around him. Perhaps that is why he had gone from home: to draw trouble away with him, as a bird seeks to lead a predator away from its nest. If that is what his hope had been, then he had failed.

CHAPTER 4

Events in France had triggered a general alarm across the country and more than once Sovay had to pull Brady into hedgerow or farm gate to make way for bands of men on the road, brandishing makeshift pikes. Sometimes they shouted, demanding to know if she was for 'King and Country', but generally they ignored her, taking her for a gentleman, and one well armed with pistol and sword.

She was intent on travelling fast and wanted to avoid inns, but she was hungry and thirsty and Brady was tiring. He needed rest, water, and a bucket of oats if he was to go on until nightfall. She saw a farm, just off the highway, and hailed the farmer's wife who was out in the yard.

The woman readily offered the simple hospitality often shown to travellers.

'I can give you bread and cheese,' she said. 'And there's fresh milk in the dairy, if you'd like some, young sir.'

Sovay dismounted and replied that she'd be glad of anything and was more than willing to pay for what she was given.

The farmer's wife would not hear of it. She instructed a boy to look after Brady and pointed Sovay towards the dairy.

Sovay had been riding hard and the cool of the dairy was welcome. A young woman left her butter-churning and handed her a pail of milk. Sovay drank deep, wiping her mouth on her sleeve. The young woman seemed in no hurry to go back to her work. She was a fine-looking girl, with large blue eyes, the colour of cornflowers, and a slow, lazy smile. Her cheeks held the flush of a damask rose and her simple dress, cut low, showed the flawless, creamy skin of her neck and shoulders.

'You are a pretty young fellow. Where are you off to this fine summer's day?' She rolled her sleeves higher over her rounded arms.

'London,' Sovay replied.

'I'd love to go there,' she sighed and sidled closer. 'They say 'tis full of opportunities. A girl could make her way there, I shouldn't wonder. Care to take me with you?'

'Oh, no.' Sovay smiled and shook her head. 'I can't. I have but one horse, and intend to travel fast.'

'Fast, eh?' The girl laughed, showing neat white teeth. 'Well, if that's the case, perhaps I can interest you in something else? I have strawberries and cherries, sweet and ripe.' She winked, her plump fingers playing with a long, fair ringlet that had escaped from her cap and had fallen across her bosom.

'Where?' Sovay looked around and could see no evidence of fruit of any kind.

The girl laughed and shook her head. 'You are a slow one and no mistake! Well, if milk is all you want, perhaps you'd care to pay me for it?'

'Of course.' Sovay reached into her pocket.

'Not with money, silly,' the girl was very near now, 'I meant with a kiss!'

Sovay moved back out of her reach. This pretty

milkmaid had been flirting with her! All that talk of strawberries and cherries. She had meant something else entirely! Sovay blushed in spite of herself and bowed low to hide her confusion. She clearly had much to learn about what it was like to be a man.

'I'd love to oblige,' she said, taking the girl's hand and kissing it. 'But fear I cannot dally.'

With that, she stepped smartly away, blew her another kiss from the door and made her escape with as much swagger as she could command.

❖➤✖◄❖

No sooner had she rejoined the highway than a carriage approached at speed, the coachman shouting for her to 'Get out of the road!' and forcing her to pull up sharp or else be spilled into the hedge.

She bent over Brady, patting his neck, steadying him down, talking sweetly in his ear as she urged him back onto the highway. All the while, a hard knot of anger tightened inside her. She might have fallen. Brady might have been injured. Such behaviour was not to be countenanced. How dare he drive her off the road?

By the time she had settled Brady, the coach was almost out of sight, but she knew it. James Gilmore had boasted often enough about the elegant chaise that their family owned, with its dark blue lacquered paintwork, high, slender-spoked wheels painted in black and gold, the very latest in springs and suspension, pulled by two fine sporting horses, perfectly matched and mettlesome.

She imagined Sir Royston rocking inside the carriage, intent on who knew what meddling business.

Her fury redoubled. He had plotted against her family, sent his son to spy on them, brought that rabble to invade her house and terrorise her father's people, and now he'd nearly run her off the road! She had not intended to play the highwayman again but she spurred Brady on, cutting across an expanse of rolling heathland, determined to teach Sir Royston a lesson.

She had found a deserted stretch of road at the top of a slight rise, just as the carriage was coming into sight, and waited until it was almost upon her before she rode out.

'Stand and deliver!' she shouted, pistols held high.

The coachman hesitated, then thought better of it. He brought the horses to a halt.

Sir Royston's head emerged, demanding to know what the devil was going on. When he saw Sovay, his eyes widened.

'What have you stopped for, you damned coward!' he yelled to his coachman. 'On. On!'

The driver raised his whip and looked as though he would obey him. Sovay let off a shot and he put it down. She trained her other pistol on Sir Royston.

'You!' she shouted. 'Out of the carriage!'

Sir Royston emerged, his broad face mottled like spoilt beef.

'Fill it.' Sovay threw a saddlebag down to him. She cocked her second gun. 'All you have!'

'Will I? Be damned.' He smiled and his small eyes gleamed malice. 'I know that horse, and I know your secret, missy!'

He made a lunge for Brady's bridle, which caused the horse to rear and kick him in the chest. Sovay had to fight hard to retain her seat as the coachman took advantage of the sudden turmoil to reach for the weapon he kept in the box at his feet. Sir Royston lay winded and gasping, while the coachman loosed off a shot at Sovay.

Brady shied and the ball went wide, but the coachman had another gun ready and his second shot was unlikely to miss. Sovay wheeled Brady away and trained her own gun at the driver. The shot missed but he loosed the reins in panic. The highly strung horses, maddened by the loud reports, bolted, overturning the carriage.

Sovay rode off, spurring Brady across country. That had not gone exactly as she would have planned it. Any satisfaction she might have felt at leaving Sir Royston roaring in the road, his beautiful coach spilled in a ditch, was eclipsed by the knowledge that her secret was out. James must have told his father. She would deny it, of course. Who would believe such a preposterous thing? Nevertheless, doubts set in and, however much she might have relished seeing Sir Royston rolling in the dust, she knew him to be a dangerous enemy who would find a way to use her secret against her.

◆►✖◄◆

She judged it better to keep off the road until nightfall. Her ride across country took her out of the way, distant from any sign of habitation. The day was turning towards evening, with mist thickening from the valleys and the last light from the setting sun a gleam of yellow in the western sky, when she saw smoke rising in a drifting grey haze. The town was tucked in a fold in the hills, strung out along the ribbon of the road. She adjusted her hat, pulling the brim down to shade her face, and realised that she was still wearing the sprig of broom. She removed it quickly, casting it into the hedge, before riding into the town just as the first lights were showing in the windows of houses and cottages. She was tired, so was Brady. It was time to find somewhere to rest.

She rode Brady through the gate of an inn and jumped down. Men emerged at the echoing sound of the horse's hooves on the cobbled yard and Sovay threw the bridle to an eager young lad with curly brown hair.

'Look after him well,' she slipped the boy a couple of coins, 'and there will be more in the morning.'

The boy nodded, pocketing the money quickly before any of the others saw it. Sovay turned to go into the inn, pulling her scarf up and her hat down over her eyes. The low-ceilinged parlour was noisy and crowded, the stone-flagged floor slick with spilt beer, the air wreathed with curling pipe smoke and reeking of onions. She called the landlord away from his duties. At first, he said the inn was full. She drew out her purse and pulled out a handful of coins. When he said that she might have to share, she showed him more gold until she got what she desired. It was not as if she wanted for money.

She had to wait while the present tenants were evicted, but the guineas bought her a room to herself at the front of the building where she could watch the street. The curtain round the bed was thick with dust, the sheets and bolster were none too clean, but there was a fire to cheer the room and take off any chill, and the food was quite edible. She was hungry, having eaten little all day, and soon finished the plate of roast beef, potatoes and cabbage, mopping up the gravy with a hunk of bread. When she had eaten, she ordered more candles and a jug of wine. After these were delivered, she gave orders not to be further disturbed. She drew the only comfortable chair up to the fire, poured wine, and settled down to examine the contents of the wallet that she had stolen from the tipstaff.

She found a quantity of papers, letters and such. At the bottom of the wallet was a large leather purse containing gold. That would account for the unaccustomed weight. Money was not what Sovay had expected, and there was a great deal of it. More guineas than she had ever seen before. She reached in, the coins slippery as fish between her fingers, and tugged out a wad of folded paper. The thin white sheets were in denominations that made her feel light-headed. She pushed them back into the purse and pulled the strings tight. When she had taken to highway robbery, it had been for her own particular purposes. She cared not a fig for the gold she took. It was a nuisance more than anything. What to do with it? Booty like this presented her with an altogether bigger problem.

◆➤◼◀◆

Meanwhile, downstairs in the inn parlour, her fame was growing. Cledbury was a small town where nothing ever happened. The locals took considerable interest in the travellers who came their way. They were puzzled by the horseman not wanting to join them and intrigued by the amount of money he was carrying.

'Purse full of gold,' the landlord reported, chuckling over the amount of money he had extracted for the room.

'He's that handsome,' Emily, the inn servant who had served 'him', told Betty the barmaid. 'Slender as a reed, with lovely, long hair, shiny as silk, like one of them cavaliers. He's ordered extra candles, and all. Why d'you think that could be?'

Betty couldn't guess, and neither could Emily. They were distracted from their speculations by news from the stables. Merrick, the lad who had been given care of the horse, had found something of such great import that he could not possibly keep to himself. A sprig of broom.

'Found this twined in the horse's bridle,' he breathed, full of awe as he held up the wilted yellow flowers. 'I reckon it's that Captain Blaze!'

News that the gentlemen of the road had gained a dashing new recruit had spread quickly from turnpike to turnpike along the highway used by the stage coaches, and Merrick immediately gained everyone's attention.

'Ah!' Jeremiah Berrow spoke up from the chimney corner. 'I heared he was about. Stepped off the road, bold as you like, begged a cup of milk at Harrison's Farm. Paid for it with a kiss. So young Jenny that works there told Jem the carter.' The old man gave a wheezy chuckle. 'She didn't have no kisses for Jem, though.'

'He banged up that fancy coach and all,' Merrick added.

Sir Royston's carriage had limped in that afternoon and was at the coachbuilders being repaired, Sir Royston being forced to continue his onward journey by stagecoach.

There was more discussion as to whether the mystery traveller presently upstairs was, indeed, the highwayman in question, and if he was, what should be done about it. After some talk, they came to the general conclusion that nothing should be done. Gentlemen of the road were held in sneaking admiration and, besides, they were always well-armed and known to be of a ferocious and violent disposition. As Cledbury had no constable and the watch was next to useless, no one in the Saracen's Head suggested challenging the fellow.

There was another stranger present, sitting on his own in the far corner. Digby Clayton specialised in anonymity and no one really noticed his small, shabby figure in dusty black clothes and cheap, ill-fitting wig. He kept his own company, nibbling at a plate of bread and cheese and sipping his half-pint tankard of small ale. He said very little and drew scant attention from his fellow travellers, or the natives, but without ever seeming to, he was taking a keen interest in the discussion, noting everything that was said and by whom. His lips moved very slightly as he submitted each assertion to the lexicon of his memory. Days, weeks, months later he would be able to recite every utterance word for word. It was a valuable skill. He would nip out later to see the lad about the nag that would take him on his journey south. While he was in the stables, he'd take a look at the mysterious gentleman's horse. You can tell a lot from horses.

Upstairs, the object of their speculation was reading through the sheaf of papers contained in the wallet. She was thorough and careful in her study, reading each sheet with attention. Some were in French. Her knowledge of the language was adequate enough to interpret that these were from agents reporting on events in Paris. She put those to one side and began to sift through the rest, placing each one on an appropriate pile in a system of her own devising.

There were warrants, letters, affidavits and reports of meetings from all over the country. The statements were signed with initials, *D.C.*, *D.P.*, *J.E.*, *L.C.*; single names, *Sykes*, *Oscar*, *Warner*; or soubriquets, *Dave the Hat*, *Tom Spitalfields*, *John the Missionary*. She assumed that this was because of the need for secrecy. Some were original documents, while others had been transcribed from some other source in small, neat, spiky writing. Some pages were marked with initials or an *X*. She took these to be oral depositions. Some of the statements were written in a fine, educated style, others were near illiterate. Among the papers, she had found the names of her father and his friends, the members of the Monday Club, and similar groups up and down the country. These men were doctors, ministers of religion, scientists and manufacturers. Respectable in anybody's estimation, and yet they were being spied on and treated as though they were revolutionaries. Letters from them had been opened, the contents transcribed, their interest in other groups carefully noted, their more radical utterances recorded to be used against them. Evidence had been gathered with painstaking care. Others had suffered the same treatment: printers, booksellers, shopkeepers, shoemakers, weavers, men from every occupation, women, too. There was nothing to link these people, except a love of liberty.

One statement had merited her special attention. It related to her father and was signed, *J.G.*

> *I have dined at C— on many occasions and have frequently heard JM speak sedition. He said in my hearing: 'I am no politician, but I have a strong hatred for tyranny and believe all men are born free. The Bourbon King acted the despot and kept the French people enslaved. He got what he deserved. The same fate should await any monarch who treats his subjects in a similar way.'*

Sovay stood and paced the room. *J.G.* stood for James Gilmore, she was sure. He had been set to court her by his father in order that he might spy on her papa. She shuddered now to think of the kisses, the intimacies she had shared with him. To be *used* in that way . . . It was all she could do not to screw the paper up and throw it into the fire, but she resisted the temptation. She must not let her feelings cloud her judgement. She flattened the sheet carefully and put it on the pile that had to do with her father and those connected with him.

At length, she finished her reading. She sat back in her chair, trying to make sense of the information contained in the closely written documents. These were the *evidences* that the American, Virgil Barrett, had spoken of, destined to be delivered all over the country. Sovay allowed herself a small smile of satisfaction, those named could sleep safe, for a little while at least. But for how long? A log fell in the grate, the candle sputtered, she looked round. If they were surrounded by spies, then who could be trusted? She sat for a while staring into the fire, then she carefully gathered all the papers together and returned them to their leather wallet, doing up the latches.

She still did not know what to do about the money. Somehow, taking the papers did not seem like true robbery. Money was different. That was real larceny. You could hang for it.

Sovay yawned. She would worry about that tomorrow. The wine and the fire were making her sleepy. She had not realised how tired she was. Dust showered down from the stiff curtains round the bed and she surveyed the grubby coverlet with distaste. A look at the stained sheets sent her back to the chair. It was not very comfortable, but at least she would avoid the bedbugs. She finished the wine and settled down, using her coat as a blanket, but sleep would not come to her. Her mind was full of questions and speculations. Where was her father? How would she ever find him? Did he know of the dangers surrounding him? And who were all these people with strange names and mysterious initials? This shadowy network had to have a centre. She felt a presence here. Some of the reports were distant and formal, but in others fear fairly oozed off the page. Who was the spider at the middle of this web? What would he do when he found the wallet had been stolen? He was undoubtedly powerful and very likely ruthless. What would he do if he found out who had taken them?

She fell asleep with none of the questions answered, and awoke to find the cold, round barrel of a gun pressing up against her chin.

CHAPTER 5

When Gabriel reached Oxford, he went straight to Hugh's college in a side street off the Broad. He looked up at the tower with its crests and coats of arms, splashes of colour on the honey-coloured stone. There was no one about and the oak door in the arched gateway was closed. Gabriel stepped across the cobbled road, which was not much more than an alley, and hammered on the door. There was no reply. The thickness of the wood muffled his mightiest thump.

He stepped away, wondering what he should do, when a small door set within the greater magically opened and a young man dashed out, gown flying. Gabriel moved briskly and was in the gatehouse before the creaking door could close.

'Yes? Can I help you?' The porter issued from his lodge, intent on protecting the college from an obvious interloper. He could tell, as soon as the man stepped through the door in the outer gate, that the fellow had no right to be here. He was wearing a good coat, a gentleman's boots and breeches, but he did not merit civilities. His build was broad and muscular, his face and hands were tanned and he was wearing the broad-brimmed hat of a countryman. 'State your business, man. I haven't got all day.'

Gabriel coloured under the man's insolent stare and aggressive manner and turned his offending hat round in his hands.

'I am Gabriel Stanhope,' he said. 'I have an urgent message for Mr Hugh Middleton.'

'Who are you? *Friend* of his?' the porter asked with a sneer as he retreated into his lodge.

'I am the son of the Steward at Compton.'

'That right?'

The man did his best to dismiss Gabriel and busied himself, putting letters into pigeonholes. The room was little more than a cubbyhole, panelled in wood, lined with shelves and drawers, all with labels. A wall of keys, also labelled, jingled as he brushed past them, intent on small tasks. A fire smoked and glowered in the corner. It was like the man's kennel.

'I've got an urgent message,' Gabriel repeated.

'So you said.' The porter remained bent over his sorting. 'What makes you think you will find him here?'

'I believe he attends this college,' Gabriel explained patiently. Was the man simple?

'Attend*ed*,' the porter corrected him. 'You won't find him here. Mr Middleton is no longer a member of this University.' His tone was as ponderous and solemn as if he was the Rector of the college and he looked up from his urgent sorting to see what effect this news had on the young countryman. 'He was sent down at the end of Michaelmas Term.'

'Michaelmas?'

'Christmas to you.' The porter smiled satisfaction at Gabriel's ignorance.

'I know well when Michaelmas is,' Gabriel replied. 'It's a deal of a long time ago, that's all. What had he done to merit this punishment?'

'Put his name to a seditious publication.'

'We knew nothing of this . . .'

The porter smiled again, relishing Gabriel's confusion. 'Dare say he didn't want his father to know. If that is all, I have work to do. The college is private property. Only open to members of the University. You are trespassing. Go before I have you arrested.'

Gabriel stood, cheeks burning, the hand on his hat trembling, trying to control his anger. If he had been a gentleman, his treatment would have been different. He would like to take the man by the scruff of his scrawny little neck and ram his pointy nose into one of the pigeonholes that were so commanding his attention. How dare a man like that assess his worth by his clothes, his station in life? He looked through the inner gate and glimpsed a world forbidden to him and his anger burned still deeper. Not for the likes of him. Never would be. Even the servants could treat him like dirt.

Just then, a slightly built, pleasant-looking young man in a full gown stepped out of the shadows into the light, deepening Gabriel's humiliation still further. He must have witnessed the whole encounter. As soon as the porter saw the newcomer, his demeanour changed completely. He bustled out of his lodge with a beaming smile on his face.

'Mr Fitzwilliam! How can I help you, sir? This man is leaving.' He gave a sideways jerk of the head towards the door.

Fitzwilliam looked at the two men, his intelligent, pale hazel eyes assessing the situation. He ignored the porter and came towards Gabriel.

'Gabriel Stanhope, isn't it? Gerald Fitzwilliam.' He shook Gabriel's hand warmly. 'We met at Compton. I don't know if you remember? I came down with Hugh one summer from school? You took us shooting in the woods. What on earth are you doing here? Come.' He ushered him towards the great wooden door of the college that led to the street. 'There's an inn nearby. We can talk there.'

The porter wished Mr Fitzwilliam a very good afternoon and held the door for him. The young man walked out as though the college servant wasn't there, talking to Gabriel all the while. Gabriel had to catch the door to avoid a bang on the nose, but this time, he was not angered by the discourtesy. Don't you see, he wanted to say to the man, all this is no more for you than it is for me. When you get old, if you get sick, they will cast you aside like a worn-out shoe. A horse would be put out to grass. You will not be so lucky.

The porter went back to his lodge and shut the door. A visitor from home asking for Mr Middleton? That might be of interest. He'd been directed to keep an eye on certain students, and Mr Middleton was definitely on that list. There were others in the University who could report on what was said in meetings, private discussions and conversations, but his job was just as important. Any visitors had to report to him and mail, in and out, went through his lodge. He was adept at opening and resealing letters and it wasn't unheard of for items to go astray. Any interesting content was forwarded to an address in London and the payment he received was a welcome supplement to his paltry porter's salary.

The two young men found a place on a settle at the far end of the dark, narrow tavern. Fitzwilliam ordered ale.

'Have you eaten?' he asked, his smooth, bland face full of concern. 'Can I order you some food? The rabbit pie is particularly fine. They are famous for it.'

Although he was hungry, Gabriel declined the offer of food. He was still smarting over his encounter with the porter. The way he'd been treated took the edge off his appetite. The muscles in his jaw bunched as the scene played again in his head. He did not appreciate the way he had been served. *All men are created equal.* But he had not been treated in that way. Not at all. He had heard it said so often. Before, the statement had been just words to him. Now he felt their true meaning. The real significance of all the other words he'd read and heard poured over him now, acting upon him as acid etches metal.

'What are you doing here?' Fitzwilliam asked to break Gabriel's brooding silence. 'Why do you need to find Hugh?'

Gabriel told him of the trouble that had come to Compton: the threat of arrest to Sir John. He left out Sovay's outrageous behaviour but said she'd gone to London in search of her father and emphasised the need to find Hugh.

'He needs to know how things are at home. We must find his father. We have to warn him of the danger that he's in, the forces threatening him.'

Gerald Fitzwilliam listened with interest and a convincing display of sympathy. He was one of Hugh's oldest friends. They had known each other from school and Hugh had followed Gerald to the same college. Gerald was older, a Fellow, but the two had remained firm friends despite the difference in their ages. Fitzwilliam was most concerned to hear what had happened and that Hugh had not been seen at Compton since Christmas.

'He did not mention that he had been sent down?'

'No. Not a word. He did not seem troubled when he came home after term ended. He seemed his normal self. What did he do to merit such punishment?'

'He and some other students published a pamphlet extolling the Revolution in France and arguing that the British people should rise up against tyranny in a similar fashion. College took a dim view, I'm afraid.' His light brown eyes flickered amusement. 'Hugh was summoned before the Rector and sundry senior Fellows. He owned to authorship but would not repudiate and would not name the others involved. The whole matter was referred to the Proctor, who questioned him further.' Fitzgerald shrugged his narrow shoulders. 'And young Hugh was told to pack his bags.'

'Where do you think he might be?' Gabriel asked. Having put away his own dark thoughts, he was seriously worried now about Hugh's apparent disappearance.

'You've heard nothing from him?'

Gabriel shook his head. 'We thought him here, or in London with friends. He often doesn't write for months on end.'

'I really don't know, then. I thought he was safe at Compton with you. I sincerely hoped so, at any rate.'

Fitzwilliam paused, brow creased. 'He did say that he wanted to . . .' He shook his head. 'But even he's not mad enough to have done that. I just took it for hot-headedness.'

'Took what for hot-headedness?' Gabriel asked. 'What did he say he wanted to do?'

'He said he wanted to go to France. To Paris. To join the *citoyens*. To take part in the Revolution.' He paused. 'What you have told me concerns me, concerns me greatly, but we can do little at this late hour. Now, are you sure I can't tempt you to a plate of rabbit pie? I know I could do with some and I'm sure you could after your long ride. I suggest we find you a room for the night and take the early coach to London in the morning. It is my intention to join you,' he said, in answer to Gabriel's look of surprise. 'Hugh is my friend, too,' he added, his pale hazel eyes suddenly serious. 'I'm concerned for him, his family. There's nothing much to keep me here at the moment. Finding him sounds an infinitely more interesting prospect than Greek translation.'

CHAPTER 6

Sovay opened her eyes.
'Don't move,' a quiet voice commanded. 'Leastways, don't move quickly.'
The gunman stepped back and brought a lighted candle close to her face. She tried to see beyond the halo of light but could only make out the dark shape of a man. A velvet sleeve, a lace cuff, the gleam of rings on the hand that held the gun. Apart from that, nothing.

'I wanted to see what manner of cove thought to set up against me.'

'And what do you find?' Sovay kept perfectly still, staring at the gun trained on her.

'An interesting kind of cove, indeed.' Her coat had slipped. He used the barrel of his pistol to part the loosened ties of her shirt. 'One I hadn't thought to see.'

Sovay looked at the empty holster hanging up on the door. He had taken her pistol. She took another from under her coat and aimed it at his midriff.

'What kind of highway man would I be,' she asked, 'with only one pistol? Drop your gun, sir, or it will be the worse for you.'

His eyes held hers for a further moment; he seemed to come to some kind of decision.

'I'd call you a sneaking kind of a fellow, hiding a second weapon like that.' He laid the pistol on the table and held his hands high, 'And one full of surprises.'

She reached forward, flipping open his coat with the barrel of her gun.

'Lay down that one,' she ordered. 'That one, too.'

He had a veritable arsenal under his jacket.

'Are you going to check my boots?' He took the cork out of the bottle and poured himself some wine. 'You're not going to kill me.'

Sovay kept her gun trained on him. 'Don't be so sure.'

'You're not the killing kind. Shall we declare a truce?' He laughed and bowed with a flourish. 'Captain Jake Greenwood at your service.' He sat down in the chair opposite. 'Now, would you care to tell me who you really are and what you think you are up to.'

Sovay told him as much as she thought he needed to know about herself and her background. When she had finished, he smiled.

'Well, Miss Sovay,' he said. 'And what led you to take up a life on the road?'

'I did not do it for gold and silver.' Sovay thought it better not to tell him about her unexpected find at the bottom of the wallet.

'So you deprive some poor cove like me of a living!' He laughed, then his expression became more serious. 'Then why?' He regarded her with curiosity. 'Only a fool with a gallows wish would take up such a life for the thrill of it. I can't think of a quicker way to get yourself hanged. And I think you no fool, Sovay.'

'The first time, it was a private matter.'

'And the other times?'

'A different private matter.'

'So did you find what you wanted? Did you settle this, ah, private matter to your satisfaction?'

'As a matter of fact, yes. Although I fail to see what it has to do with you.'

'That is where you are wrong. Whatever it is you took is valuable to someone. He wants it back badly. You would be advised to get rid of it as soon as you can. The roads are being watched, extra patrols are out, anything like that is bound to affect us all.'

'How do you know? How does he . . .'

He shrugged. 'News travels fast on the road. The individual in question has spies everywhere.'

Sovay had made an enemy. The same man who had sent the tipstaff to arrest her father, who had collected all the evidence against him. The hair prickled on her scalp at the thought of him turning his attention on to her.

'Who is he?' she asked.

Greenwood paused, as though considering whether it was wise to tell her, then he said, 'His name is Dysart. He casts his net wide and has many in his pay, large and small. There will be a reward for information given.'

'Is that why you are here? To rob me and claim the reward?'

'No,' he shook his head. 'I have no liking for his kind. I was just curious, that's all. Now, who knows of your disguise?'

'Gabriel.'

'Who's he?'

'The son of our Steward.'

'Can he be trusted to keep quiet?'

'He helped with the robbery.'

'So we can presume yes, unless he wants to hang by your side. The fewer who know the better. Any more?'

Sovay thought hard. There was the American. She had almost forgotten that he knew. And now this highwayman. And the Gilmores. What had possessed her to hold up Sir Royston's carriage? That was foolish. She had allowed her judgement to give way to recklessness. She could see the wisdom in the highwayman's words. When she had first ridden out, she had not been seeking thrill or adventure, but she had become more and more enraptured by those very things. The excitement and danger had kindled emotions that she had never before experienced. She had never felt so alive as she did up on the heath, hearing the creak of the wheels, the snort of the horses as a coach drew nearer, seeing the surprise on the faces of those she confronted, knowing her own life could be over in an instant but sensing their fear was even greater. But she saw now that she had ventured into unknown regions. The ground was quaking beneath her, threatening to pull her down.

'I assume you are going to London,' the highwayman was saying. 'I go that way myself. We should leave. Now.' He parted the heavy curtains. 'It is nearly dawn. The skies are clear. A fine morning, although it won't last. We should be going before the inn is stirring.' He stood to the side of the window and peered out. 'There's no knowing who may already be about.'

'Why should I go with you?' Sovay was still not sure that she should trust this man.

'Why not? It is safer to ride with a companion. The road is a dangerous place. There are all sorts of bad characters on it. Surely you know that?'

He grinned at her, his teeth white in his tanned face. His strong, even features had just the right edge of rugged manliness and there was an insolent smile in his dark blue eyes. He was undoubtedly a handsome man and he knew his attractiveness to women. His upper lip was marked by the thin line of a moustache, which made him look like the King in a pack of playing cards, and he wore his long, dark chestnut hair loose to his shoulders. It was as though he'd missed his time by a hundred years. He had chosen his clothes with care, with exactly the right kind of show and flamboyance. His plumed hat lay on her bed; he wore a silver and black cut velvet jacket and quantities of lace at his cuffs and throat. He looked every inch the dashing highwayman: tall and straight limbed in buff-coloured breeches and thigh high jackboots turned down to the knee.

His horse was as fine as his owner. A beautiful dark bay with a refined, chiselled head, a slightly dished face and the high tail carriage that spoke of Arab blood. Sovay expressed her admiration as she led Brady out of his stall.

'Yes,' he laughed, 'he's a good horse. I took a fancy to him one day on the Newmarket road. Some young gentleman had a long walk home. You have a remarkably handsome grey. Fine head on him.'

Brady shied away from his stroking glove. Sovay put a hand on his dappled neck to calm him.

'He's a splendid horse all right, but too distinctive, too identifiable. You've got a lot to learn, and no mistake.' Greenwood helped her up into the saddle, and then mounted himself. 'We must stable him as soon as we get to London, or he will give you away.'

◆►◆◄◆

A curtain twitched up in the top gable window at the front of the inn. The room was cheap and small, but it was perfect for its occupant's purposes. It was high, near to the sky, and it gave a good view of the arch that led out of the yard, as well as the road before it.

Digby Clayton was an early riser. Only the owls are up before Digby, was one of his sayings. He watched the two of them ride off together down the London road and then sat down to write on a slip of paper. When he had finished, he folded the paper over, and over again. Then he opened one of the narrow cages he carried in his saddlebags and took out a bird. He crooned to it, caressing the iridescent feathers on the back of its neck, and then stroking it gently under the throat as he attached the note to a band on the bird's leg. He opened the window and, with a few final soft words of encouragement, he let the bird go.

The pigeon sat on a chimney pot for a few moments, head cocked, and then it took off, circled once above the red roofs of the town, and flew off south for London.

CHAPTER 7

As Sovay and the highwayman went on their way to London, Gabriel met Fitzwilliam in the yard of the Mitre Inn.

'Why don't you travel inside with me?' the young don said as he surveyed his fellow passengers. They looked a dull lot. 'You can tether your horse behind. The weather is promising to turn inclement and I could do with some good conversation.'

The sky threatened rain and, as he spoke, the first heavy drops began to fall. Gabriel did not relish the thought of a soaking, so he readily agreed. The coach took the new London road up Headington Hill and on to the capital. Despite Fitzwilliam expressing a need for good conversation, he was soon asleep. Gabriel watched the unfamiliar countryside go by and wondered how his horse was faring. Travelling in the carriage was uncomfortable and he would have made much greater speed on horseback. He wondered if he had made the right decision, but was as soon as fast asleep as his companion.

Gabriel was woken by the guard blowing his horn as they approached the White Hart, the last inn before London. The coach came to a halt in the yard and he stepped down, glad to be out, although even with both feet on solid ground, he still felt the rocking motion of the carriage. The passengers were directed to a dining room, while the guard checked his weapons and the driver saw to the change of horses.

The dining room was towards the back of the inn. The fee for dinner was half a crown, the price included in the ticket. A long table had been set out for the passengers, with bread, knives and a scattering of forks on a cloth that had served at least another sitting, maybe more, judging from the stains upon it. The passengers took their seats and various dishes were brought out and spread along the board. The food was plain, but there was plenty of it. They only had twenty minutes and Gabriel was hungry. He set to with a will, even though the scalding broth burnt his mouth, the steak was tough, the boiled mutton more fat than meat and the potatoes floury on the outside and hard within. His companion ate with rather less relish, but declared it 'Not half bad. No worse than we get in college.'

The guard's horn summoned them back to the coach. Gabriel elected to ride rather than travel inside. He disliked the motion and the stuffy interior of the carriage. The guard was relieved. He could use another pair of eyes and Gabriel looked as if he might be a useful man in a fight.

'Look to your weapon, sir. Make sure that it is primed and ready for use,' he advised as they prepared to set off. 'The next stretch of road is lonely and much infested with highwaymen and robbers.'

❖

'This is a likely spot.' Greenwood drew off the road. 'Now you can learn something. The way narrows, see? Trees crowd close. The road is ill kept. It's been raining and the ground is always sodden.' He pointed to numerous pools and meres. 'I will position myself here where the coach has to slow to negotiate the marshy ground. You go to the top of the rise, keep yourself well hid, and whistle when you see the coach coming.' He grinned at Sovay. 'You can whistle?'

'Yes. I can whistle,' Sovay replied. 'But why are we doing this?'

They had ridden through driving rain and she was wet and miserable. All she wanted to do was get to London as soon as possible.

'Because I'm a highwayman,' he explained patiently. 'It's my occupation. You aren't turning gutless on me, now? You have already done enough to hang twice over. What difference will one more excursion make?'

'No, I do not lack the courage, if that's your meaning. I merely meant that it will cause delay.' She looked through the rain dripping off the brim of her hat. 'How do you know there is even a coach on the road? We could wait all day.'

'I heard the horn and saw them in the yard of the White Hart. You must learn to use your ears and eyes if you wish to live much longer.' He paused. 'You don't have to do the fleecing, if that's what bothers you. Just stand look out.' He leaned forward in his saddle. 'If you want to stay with me, you will do as I say.'

'That is not what bothers me,' Sovay replied, stung that he would think her squeamish in any way. 'I've done enough of that to hang twice over, as you say. I'm in a hurry to get to London, that is all. What if I choose to leave you here and go on my own?'

'Oh and what will you do there?' He gave a scornful laugh. 'In five minutes you would be relieved of that fine horse, at the very least. If you ever want to be Miss Sovay again in your fine house, if you ever want to *see* your fine house again, you need my services. So look sharp.' He consulted a handsome pocket watch. 'By now, they'll have finished their inedible mutton and will be on their way.'

Sovay did not like being ordered about by him, but she decided she would do as he said. She might need his help when she got to London. She hid in a brake of young trees and positioned herself where she could see the road and felt some of the old excitement returning. A coach was approaching, just as he had predicted. Sovay loosened her weapons, her heart beating harder, she felt the familiar prickle at the back of her neck as she eased her mask into place. She put two fingers to her mouth and prepared to whistle. Then she saw the horseman riding alongside. There was something familiar about him. She craned forward. There was something about the horse, his seat, the way he held the reins. Then she was sure. Her mouth dried and her whistle died. The black horse with a white blaze was her brother's, Starlight. The rider was Gabriel.

She broke cover just as the coach gained the top of the rise, galloping down the hill in front of it. The lead horses shied and the driver struggled to control them as the coach began to slide on the muddy slope. Gabriel rode fast to gain the front horse and grab his bridle to steady him down and bring the rig to a halt before the whole thing overturned. The guard reached for his gun, fearing an attack, and let off a shot after the retreating horseman.

'What are you doing?' Greenwood was furious. 'It was waddling down just right, like a fat goose to the slaughter!'

'I had to warn you. Stop you. I know the horseman.'

What was Gabriel doing here? She had no time to speculate. The guard had had time to reload and had noted the place where she had turned into the trees. A shot whined through the branches above their heads. Worse. The gunfire had alerted others. There were cries and shouts, the clatter of hooves on the road, more gunshots. A ball hit a tree, showering them both with leaves and splinters of wood.

'That was near.' Greenwood flicked a splinter from his sleeve. 'It's a horse patrol. We better make ourselves scarce. Follow me and keep your head down. I presume you can ride that fine horse of yours. This'll give him a chance to stretch his legs. Get rid of all this,' he drew his sword and cut the bundle tied to the back of her saddle. 'It'll slow you down. When we get to the edge of the trees, ride like the devil is behind you!'

Sovay's clothes spilled across the muddy ground, but she had no time to worry about that or what she would wear when she got to London. From down on the road and from the fields on both sides of them, men shouted and weapons discharged in white puffs of smoke. Sovay spurred Brady on, following the fleeing highwayman as he wove a way through the close-growing trees. She clung to her horse's neck, all the while trying to avoid the flying bullets and the low-growing branches which threatened to take off her head.

Gabriel glimpsed the fleeing horsemen stitching their way through the woods and breathed a sigh of relief as they broke across a patch of open ground to freedom. Their speed left the pursuing horse patrol scattered over the hillside with no likelihood of catching them. The guard on the coach let off another shot, but his line of fire was fouled by trees and by the time the horsemen broke cover, they were too far away for him to do any damage.

'Did you see who it was?' the driver asked.

'Jake Greenwood, like as not,' the guard replied. 'I recognise that plume in his hat. Showy bugger. T'other on the grey is new to me.' He scowled down at Gabriel. 'You had the scoundrel clear. You could have got 'im. Winged him at least.' He hawked and spat. 'You country lads ain't the shots you crack yourselves up to be, that's for certain.'

The passengers settled back now that the excitement was over and the driver cracked his whip for their onward journey into London.

Gabriel trotted along behind, lost in thought. He had recognised the horse at once and held his fire. He wouldn't mention it to Fitzwilliam – he didn't want to complicate matters – but this was a puzzle indeed. What was Miss Sovay doing in the company of a real highwayman?

CHAPTER 8

Gabriel went with Fitzwilliam to the set of rooms he kept in Hanover Square.

'It's a bit rough and ready but it suits an old bachelor like me.' He laughed and his pale hazel eyes flashed amusement. 'My man can do for both of us. 'Rufus!' he called as he mounted the stairs. 'Rufus!'

The room that they entered had high ceilings and was elegantly furnished with pale green moiré silk on the walls and a deep red Turkey carpet on the floor. Large windows looked down over the square. A leather-topped writing table stood in front of one of the windows with a mahogany bureau next to it. One wall was covered by tall, glass-fronted bookcases.

'This is the drawing room and library. I like having everything near.'

'Mr Fitzwillam, sir. We wasn't expecting you.' A narrow-faced youth with a spattering of dark freckles and close-cropped rusty red hair appeared at the door.

'Well,' Fitzwilliam removed his gloves, 'we are here now. I have a friend with me, Mr Gabriel Stanhope. Take our travelling clothes and bring us some wine, would you? And have our rooms made ready. Put Mr Stanhope in Henry's room. I would like a bath and I'm sure Mr Stanhope would, too. Then something to eat. Send round to the chophouse for steaks and grilled bones. Don't stand there gawping. Off you go!'

Rufus scurried off, repeating the orders to himself, just so he did not get them the wrong way round.

'He's young, but willing. He'll come. I don't have need of him in college and I fear he grows lazy here in town.' Fitzwilliam yawned and put his hands to the small of his back to ease the ache there. 'You were right to ride. Those coaches are devilish uncomfortable.'

Rufus returned with two glasses and a decanter of wine on a butler's tray. Fitzwilliam thanked him and, handing a glass to Gabriel, he raised his own in a toast.

'Here's to our enterprise. May we have success in the search. Do sit down. Make yourself at home.'

He indicated a pair of walnut armchairs, upholstered in grey silk, which stood on either side of the hearth. Gabriel perched nervously, fearing to test the thinness of the legs with his weight. Fitzwilliam drank his wine.

'We will make ourselves human again after that beastly journey, then we'll go to Soho. Visit the house, see if there is any news and call on Miss Sovay. She must be there by now.'

Gabriel inclined his head. He did not like to disagree with his host but somehow he doubted it.

◆►❂◄◆

Gabriel was wrong. Miss Sovay was in residence. She had not arrived dressed as a man but the clothes she had been wearing, although female, had Mrs Crombie's eyebrows shooting towards the ceiling. She had got past awkward questions about that by tales of having been waylaid and having to borrow clothes after an accident on the road. She ignored Mrs Crombie's curiosity about what kind of person might have lent her such outlandish attire.

Mrs Crombie had not seen the master for a week or more.

'He didn't stay over a day or two.'

'Did he say anything about where he was going?'

'Called away. "Urgent business" was all he said.'

'No more than that?'

'I'm not privy to his private plans, Miss Sovay,' Mrs Crombie answered, masking her concern with a certain asperity. 'He does not confide in me. I thought he had returned to Compton.' She relented a little. 'No sign of him, you say?'

Sovay shook her head.

'Then perhaps he's gone visiting.' Mrs Crombie brightened and folded her arms over her ample bosom. 'Yes, that'll be the way of it. The master is a great one for visiting. He has friends all over the place. He might have gone to see one of them.'

'Yes,' Sovay agreed. The sinking in her heart told her that it was unlikely, but there was no need to worry Mrs Crombie further. 'He might.'

'There we are, then! Now let's get you out of those dreadful clothes!'

Mrs Crombie was only ever seen in black, out of respect for her deceased husband, although he had passed on so long ago that Hugh doubted his very existence and declared that the housekeeper had come into the world a Mrs. That aside, she had a good eye for fashions and knew exactly what should be worn by whom and under what circumstances.

'I've never seen the like, not outside a theatre, not that I've ever been into one of those establishments. I don't know what kind of *lady* lent them, I'm sure,' she remarked, still piqued by Sovay's reticence and determined to have the last word on the matter. 'Now, up you go. It's a good thing Lydia has arrived with your proper things.' Mrs Crombie shooed Sovay towards the stairs. She had worked at Compton before moving to supervise the London residence and had a tendency to treat Sovay as though she was still the child she remembered from her time at the other house. As for that chit Lydia, when Mrs Crombie left Compton, she had been a cheeky little scullion, lax in her duties and inclined to be slovenly. How she had ever risen to the heights of lady's maid was beyond reckoning. 'She should have drawn your bath by now and tell her to do something about your hair!'

❖❖❖

By the time Gabriel and Fitzwilliam presented themselves, Sovay had bathed, changed, had her hair dressed by Lydia and was ready to receive visitors.

The two young men were shown into the drawing room. Gabriel had never visited the London house before, never having had the occasion to come here. The house was older than Fitzwilliam's residence, the rooms smaller and more crowded with furniture, but he did not feel so out of place here. He liked it better.

Sovay made every show of surprise at seeing him now, but did not have to feign her astonishment when she saw his companion.

'Mr Fitzwilliam. How nice to see you. To what do I owe this honour?'

'Miss Sovay.' He took her proffered hand, smiling up as he kissed it. He was adept at flirting. 'The honour is mine and I would like to say the pleasure is meeting you again, but I'm afraid we come on graver business.'

'Grave? How so?' Sovay withdrew her hand from his. 'What is the matter?' She turned to Gabriel. 'What has happened?'

Gabriel looked uncomfortable. Although Sovay appeared every inch a lady and harmless as a dove, he could not rid himself of the image of her spurring her horse on a violent course, while dressed as a highwayman. Sovay turned away from his troubled gaze. She always knew what he was thinking.

'It's Hugh,' Gabriel said eventually. 'I went to Oxford, to his college. He's been sent down.'

'Sent down?' Sovay frowned. 'What does that mean?'

'Asked to leave the University,' Fitzwilliam explained.

'For Heaven's sake, why?'

Fitzwilliam told her the reason. 'I thought he was safe at Compton,' he added. 'But Gabriel says not.'

'We've not seen him since Christmas. Father missing. Now Hugh . . .' Sovay shook her head.

'Sir John is not here?'

'No,' Sovay replied. 'He hasn't been seen for over a week. Where can they be?'

'That's the problem,' Gabriel said. 'It may be even worse . . .'

'Worse?' Sovay stared at him. 'How could it be worse?'

Gabriel's discomfort grew. He looked to Fitzwilliam for help.

'Hugh may have gone to France, to Paris, to join in the Revolution.'

'Are you sure?'

'Not certain.' Fitzwilliam shrugged. 'But he did mention his intention on more than one occasion.'

'Do you think Papa may have gone after him?' Sovay looked from Fitzwilliam to Gabriel.

'It's possible,' Gabriel replied, 'if he thought Hugh was in danger. He might have gone to fetch him back.'

'We don't know that,' Fitzwilliam interrupted. 'First we must seek for word of him in London. Among his contacts here, people he might have met.'

'But if he has gone to France . . .' Gabriel gave a despairing shake of the head. If Sir John had followed his son to Hades, the idea could hardly have been less shocking.

'If that is the case, then we will go there.' Sovay began to pace the room. 'Follow them.'

She would do it, too. Gabriel stared at her, despair giving way to resignation. He remembered how he'd seen her, not six hours earlier. Nothing she said or did now could surprise him.

'A brave sentiment, Miss Sovay.' Fitzwilliam gave a slight bow. 'I commend you for it, but such an action might not be possible. France is in a most dangerous condition. We would be arrested as soon as we landed and tried as spies.'

'If that is the case, what about Hugh? Or Papa?'

'If Hugh went at Christmas, conditions then were slightly less dangerous. Besides, his French is fluent. He could pass as a native. I doubt that the same could be said of us.'

'M Fernand was my tutor, too,' Sovay objected. 'I have some French.'

Her father had insisted on the two children being

taught together, but Sovay had been very much younger. She had mastered more than basic vocabulary and grammar but her conversational powers were rather limited.

'But you did not spend a year travelling with him in France,' Fitzwilliam smiled, taken by her spirit. 'Switzerland, Italy, other places. Fernand is, or was, a man of some influence within the Revolution. He might be in a position to protect Hugh, although such things change day by day.'

'But what about my father?'

'We do not know even that he is there.' Fitzwilliam moved to calm her. 'If he is, he may come under Fernand's protection.'

'In the past, he certainly had many correspondents in France. Mr Paine, others, too. Oh, but now I recollect, Mr Paine was arrested –' Sovay stopped her pacing, fully alert now to the dangers that might be threatening her father. 'What are we to do?'

'It's like Mr Fitzwilliam says.' Gabriel spoke, as much to reassure himself as Sovay. 'We don't even know if he is there. Would it not be best to make inquiries in London before we start jumping to conclusions?'

'Yes.' Sovay commenced pacing again. 'That would be sensible. The sensible thing to do.' She turned to the two of them. 'I trust that I can rely on your help in this?'

'Of course!' They both spoke at once.

'Good,' she said. 'For if you will not agree, I will do it myself.'

That bold statement seemed to bring the conversation to a close. Fitzwilliam began to make his farewells, but Gabriel interrupted.

'Before we go, could I have a word, Miss Sovay?' He glanced towards Fitzwilliam. 'On an estate matter.'

'Of course,' Fitzwilliam smiled and took the hint. 'Do carry on.' He glanced around. 'You have some fine paintings that I would like to examine more closely.'

He strolled off to look at a handsome Dutch interior as Sovay opened a connecting door into her father's study.

The room was a smaller version of Sir John's library at home, the walls lined with books and cabinets. A terrestrial globe and a spherical astrolabe flanked a desk scattered with slides and piled with books and papers. It was as though Sir John had just got up and left to look for a book in another room. A portable microscope stood next to the inkstand. It was typical of the man. Gabriel felt a deep pang of fear for his master and hoped that no harm had come to him.

Outside the room, Fitzwilliam ceased to be interested in the Dutch Master and drifted to the study door, which did not quite shut flush to the panelling. He listened out of pure curiosity at first, but what he heard pricked his interest.

'It won't happen again,' Sovay said.

'I hope not. It's madness, Sovay.'

'I was caught on the road –' Sovay broke off what she was about to say. 'I do not have to justify myself to you.'

'What were you doing with him? Who is he?'

'What does it matter?'

'I want to know. Since your father and brother are absent, I am here –' Gabriel began.

'To take over charge of me? I think not, Gabriel!'

'To protect you, I was going to say, but perhaps you prefer the protection of that scoundrel.'

'His name is Captain Greenwood.'

'Captain?' Gabriel snorted. 'Every villain of a highwayman calls himself Captain.'

'Plain Jake Greenwood, then, if it is at all relevant. And as I will never see him again, then I think it is not.'

'Let us not quarrel. You do need my help. You must admit that.'

'Yes,' Sovay sighed, some of the fight gone out of her. 'The wallet I took. I would like you to look over the contents with me. The papers there may hold clues as to where to find Papa.'

'If he has gone to France?'

'Like you said, we don't know that. There are names, contacts. People who *might* know. I want you to help me go through them. Come tomorrow, but don't tell Fitzwilliam –'

Just then came the sound of steps approaching. Fitzwilliam moved smartly away from the door. He did not want to be caught eavesdropping by a servant.

'Is there anything you require, sir?' Mrs Crombie asked.

'No, nothing. I was just admiring this fine collection of Sèvres porcelain. Mrs Crombie, isn't it?' Fitzwilliam smiled. He prided himself at remembering the names of servants.

'Yes, that's right, sir. Didn't I see you at Compton with Master Hugh?'

'You did, many years ago now.' Fitzwilliam's smile widened. 'Fancy you remembering!'

'Oh, I forget nothing, sir.'

Mrs Crombie's face closed like a shutter. She remembered him all right, and there was something about him that she didn't like. He'd been a knowing child, too ready with the charm, and there was something about those odd, light eyes. They saw too much, always darting about. He hadn't changed. She could have sworn he was listening at the door to a private conversation for all he said he was examining the contents of the china cabinet.

◆➤◆◆◆

On the way back to Hanover Square, Fitzwilliam asked when Gabriel might be visiting Miss Sovay again.

'She has asked me to call on her tomorrow morning. On estate business,' Gabriel added, mindful of her warning to come alone.

'Morning, you say? Rather you than me. After a night in town, I am not good in the morning. Estate business sounds desperately dull.' Fitzwilliam laughed. 'A pity to worry such a pretty head over such matters.'

'Miss Sovay is no fool,' Gabriel replied. 'She might be headstrong at times, stubborn, too, but she is no silly young thing. Rather the opposite. With her father absent, her brother too, responsibility rests with her and she has a good enough head on her shoulders.'

'Doesn't she have an aunt?' Fitzwilliam inquired. 'Surely she –'

'Lady Harriet is an invalid and rarely leaves her room,' Gabriel answered. 'Miss Sovay is quite capable, I assure you.'

'I meant nothing by it,' Fitzwilliam said mildly. 'It is

just that she is so young.' He patted Gabriel's arm. 'It is good that she has you to help her.'

The aunt drank. He remembered that from his visits to Compton. A perceptive boy, and older than Hugh, he had read the signs that the family had tried to hide. Anyway, he had aunts of his own who liked to nap in their room after a brandy or two laced with laudanum. He had found Hugh interesting, with his passions and his poetry. He was one of the only boys who *had* interested him in the slightest bit, even among his contemporaries. That he was younger had mattered not a jot. The rest had been so deadly dull, apart from one or two of the prettier ones, who had been diverting in their own way, but Hugh had looks *and* conversation. A captivating combination. In return, Hugh had worshipped his older friend and continued to do so until this day, which was pleasantly gratifying.

'The night is young,' Fitzwilliam said, when they came to his rooms. 'What say we go to my club? Seek some entertainment.'

Gabriel declined, pleading tiredness and that he did not have the right clothes.

'Nonsense!' Fitzwilliam ran an appraising eye over him. 'You are about the same size as my brother, Henry. He leaves a press of clothes here for when he is in town. I'll send Rufus to attend you. You are sure to find something to suit.'

Gabriel chose a set of clothes in the most sober colour that he could find: midnight blue with the minimum by way of decorative embroidery. Fitzwilliam's tastes were more extravagant. Perhaps he wished to show himself to be different from the young Oxford don, for he appeared in the height of fashion, his hair powdered, his dark green velvet coat lined with ivory silk, the facings embroidered with quantities of pastes and spangles which winked and glittered in the light. He wore his black velvet breeches tight and his low-heeled shoes were fastened with shining steel buckles. He looked down to make sure that there were no wrinkles in his white silk stockings and laughed to see Gabriel's reaction.

'The don transformed.' He poured a glass of brandy from the decanter that Rufus had left in the drawing room. 'I'm the third son,' he said. 'In my family, the third son is destined for the Church. I find University life more congenial than some country parish. College life is rather like a club. Fine cellar, reasonable company for the most part, only the food leaves a little to be desired.'

Upon leaving the house, he summoned a couple of chairs for St James's. Gabriel felt uncomfortable, he did not like to be carried and felt sorry for the poor fellows who would have to bear his weight, but Fitzwilliam had no such scruples.

'How else are we to get there?' he asked. 'The streets are a midden. The muck will be over our shoes before we've gained the corner of the square. Besides, the poor devils are glad enough of our money. Would you deprive them of a living?'

Fitzwilliam looked at Gabriel. He was a pleasant enough fellow, but there was a fresh-faced naivety about him, a lack of sophistication. He wondered if taking him to the club might turn out to be a mistake.

●━◆━●

Fitzwilliam went to play cards, leaving Gabriel to wander from room to room to observe the occupants eating and drinking, laughing, talking and gambling. So this was how rich men enjoyed themselves? He settled against a wall, sipped his glass of wine and smiled to himself. Not so different from the local inn, apart from the opulence and the lack of women. He supposed that they would be visiting the ladies later.

He was not aware of it as he surveyed the passing scene, but he in turn was being watched. Sir Robert Dysart's eyes scarcely flickered from his cards but he saw Fitzwilliam as soon as he entered the gaming room and noted his companion. He'd never seen Fitzwilliam's young friend before and saw immediately that he was not used to such surroundings, yet he did not seem ill at ease. He conducted himself with a natural grace and dignity. That in itself was enough to make him stand out in the present company. Sir Robert turned in his hand, much to the relief of those who remained in the game. Dysart had a reputation for always winning. The only men who would sit down with him were as skilful as he was, or rich fools who thought they could go up against him and win. There were plenty of those sitting around the table.

Dysart was above average height, although his narrow build and slightly stooping posture made him seem smaller. He wore an old-fashioned wig, curled at the sides and queued at the back. His face was thin, with a rather prominent, pointed nose above narrow lips and a sharp chin. His pale, watchful eyes seemed focused on nothing in particular, but Dysart saw everything: who was at play and who was not, who was winning, who was losing, who was betting, how much and on what. He gave up his place to another and went to prowl the room. Neat to the point of fastidiousness and always dressed in black, he stood out among so many men of fashion like a raven in a room full of peacocks.

The men gathered here were among the richest, most powerful in the country: politicians, members of the aristocracy. They greeted Dysart genially enough, but few stopped to exchange words with him or cared to meet his eye. Dysart passed with a nod here, a thin smile there. His smile never reached his eyes. He was not here to socialise. He had something of interest on almost every one of them and liked to remind them of his presence.

Certainly, he knew a great deal about Mr Fitzwilliam. The young man was heavily in debt. He had no head for cards but he liked to gamble. He was the kind who became more reckless with every poor hand, throwing good money into the same pit as the bad. A younger son, dependent on a rich but miserly father, he had expensive tastes and lived far beyond his allowance. He was perfect for Dysart's purposes. He was well connected. And desperate. He was handsome, personable, with an open face and charming manner, he moved with ease in many different circles. However vicious he might be underneath, people had a tendency to like Fitzwilliam, to trust him. The young Irish don was the very image of an aristocratic gentleman, yet all Dysart had to do was call in a tenth of the promissory notes in his possession and Mr Fitzwilliam would find himself in the debtors' ward in Newgate Prison.

Dysart positioned himself behind the young man in

question. Another poor hand. No high cards and no tricks. He was doing both Fitzwilliam and his partner a favour by taking him out of the game.

'Fitzwilliam. Losing, I see. Care for a turn round the room with me?'

'Ah.' Fitzwilliam turned at the touch on his shoulder. 'Dysart . . .'

'Tell me, who is that young man who accompanied you here tonight?'

'Oh, his name is Gabriel Stanhope. He's a friend of Hugh Middleton's.'

'His Steward's son, more like.' Dysart's dry, creaking laugh was without a shred of humour.

'How do you know?' Fitzwilliam turned to him, genuinely amazed.

'You are not the only spy I have in your ancient foundation. Would that be the same Hugh Middleton who was sent down from his college and is currently residing in Paris, a cowardly traitor to his country?'

'How do you know . . .' Fitzwilliam started, but what was the use of asking? Dysart knew everything.

'My understanding is that his father, Sir John Middleton, has lately joined him there, but that is of no interest to me. At the moment. I'm wondering if you might know something of Miss *Sovay* Middleton.'

'Why, I was just now at her house!' Fitzwilliam expressed surprise. 'That *is* a coincidence.'

'Perhaps, so.' Sir Robert gave a thin smile. 'If one believed in coincidence. I do not. So,' he went back, calibrating the conversation as finely as if he were operating some exact instrument of measurement, 'she is in town? When did she travel down?'

'She arrived today, I believe.'

'Did she?' Sir Robert nodded, although Fitzwilliam failed to see any particular significance. 'Their neighbour, Sir Royston Gilmore, has lately arrived from the country.'

'Another coincidence?' Fitzwilliam laughed at a higher pitch than he would have liked. Conversations with Dysart always made him nervous.

'I told you, I don't believe in them.'

'Is he in tonight?' Fitzwilliam looked about. Sir Royston was even worse at cards than he was and it would be a good excuse to get away from Dysart.

'Unfortunately not. He is feeling incommoded. He was set about by some ruffian on the road. Used most cruelly, poor fellow. He's of a mind that this rogue is the very same one who recently attacked his son and several other coaches. A highwayman, new to the trade, who goes by the name of Captain Blaze.'

'These highwaymen are everywhere. We had a narrow escape coming from Oxford. You should do something about it, Dysart.'

'Sir Royston's very words. Much obliged, Fitzwilliam,' he turned as if to leave him, 'unless you have anything else for me?'

Fitzwilliam thought hard. It would be good to give Dysart something, but it was like taking a turn round the room with the Grim Reaper; his disconcerting presence tended to put everything out of one's mind.

'Wait!' he said, just as Dysart was about to drift off. 'Stanhope and Miss Middleton had a bit of an argument, I couldn't help but overhear, you understand?' Dysart nodded impatiently for him to go on. 'Stanhope accused her of consorting with a highwayman – but his name wasn't Blaze, it was Greenwood.'

'Was it, indeed?' Dysart's death's-head grin showed that he was pleased.

'There's another thing.' Emboldened by this success, Fitzwilliam had thought of something else. 'Now I do recall . . .'

'What, man?'

Something in their conversation was making Dysart impatient. Fitzwilliam was tempted to spin it out, make him wait, but then a look from those cold eyes changed his mind.

'Their talk turned to a wallet and some papers. I don't know what was in them, but she was anxious to keep it secret, from me, at any rate.'

Dysart nodded, showing his satisfaction with another skull-like grin. 'Much obliged, Fitzwilliam.'

Fitzwilliam was just about to ask him, in a round-about way, whether this information might be worth something, but Dysart was already gliding away.

'Who was that man?' Gabriel asked when Fitzwilliam joined him.

'Sir Robert Dysart. The spy master. Some say he's the most powerful man in London. He is certainly the most dangerous.' Fitzwilliam laughed. 'They call him the Pox Doctor. To be avoided if one can possibly help it.'

◆━►◄━◆

If Dysart did not believe in coincidence, neither did he believe in mysteries. There was always a solution. It just required thought, reason – and information. Like any game of chance. Recently, he had been bending his considerable mind to discovering the identity of the mysterious Captain Blaze. This afternoon, Sir Royston Gilmore had dealt him the winning card.

'I'm loath to tell you, Dysart. Don't reflect well, if you get my meaning, but with things being as they are, with the state of the country, I can't let family pride stand in the way.' He'd sighed heavily and the spindly chaise longue groaned under his shifting bulk. 'It's my boy, James. He did well to expose the nest of treasonous vipers, can't fault him on that, but he let the little baggage best him.' He told Dysart the story of the robbery. 'Wouldn't tell me, too ashamed, I suppose, but then she held up the tipstaff and stole the warrant, well, he knows where his duty lies.'

'Indeed,' Dysart had replied. 'This Captain Blaze, then. You think it is Miss Sovay Middleton?'

'I know so,' Sir Royston said with a shake of his head. 'One can hardly believe it. Unnatural, that's what it is. Hyenas in petticoats, Walpole calls them. She's more like a wolf. As bad as the father, or the son. Worse, in my mind, than either one. She threatened violence on me and my officers when we were trying to carry out our lawful duties, then she attacks me and overturns my carriage.'

Sir Royston would have gone on for some time in this vein but Dysart interrupted him.

'And she is this Captain Blaze? You are sure?'

'Certain! That horse she rides, the grey. He's out of my own stables. A betrothal gift, would you believe?'

Dysart had left him, still fulminating. He had found out what he wanted. The mysterious Captain Blaze was really Miss Sovay Middleton. She had taken something of his, Fitzwilliam had confirmed it, and he wanted it back.

After he left the club, he directed his driver to the Old Bell, Holborn, where he hoped to find a Mr Slevin. Dysart had used him on many occasions. Apart from his other talents, he was the best cracksman in London and Dysart had a job for him in Soho, to be carried out tonight.

CHAPTER 9

Sovay woke from thrilling dreams: a plunging ride through wild country had taken her to a narrow warren of streets and a house where every room was a bedchamber and everyone was in a state of undress. It was all very odd because boys turned into girls and girls into boys in an endless confusing parade. An old woman in a bright russet wig counted coin and leered from behind a battered lacquer table, her face a ruin under thick layers of rouge and powder, her teeth brown, streaked stumps in a painted mouth. It was all set to a refrain that she woke up humming and could not get out of her head.

Sovay's mind had returned to the scenes of the day, but dreams are without compass and dreamers are free to go where they will without the constraints that waking life might put upon them. She had started from sleep in a state of heightened excitement, experiencing again the thrilling danger of that wild chase across the heath and the feeling that this was by far the most exhilarating day that she had so far spent in her life. She found it impossible to unravel what was real and what was not from among the images and sensations that crowded in upon her. Some of the images she had seen that day, the places she had been, seemed to belong more in the realm of dreams, although she knew them to be real.

Captain Greenwood had promised to find her female attire and he had taken her to a tall, crooked house in Covent Garden, full of the most bizarre people. The harridan with the vibrant hair and rotten teeth was called Mother Pierce. Her eyes were small and round, like beads on an abacus, and in her house everything was for sale, even if she had never encountered the request before. She had her hand out to the Captain as soon as they came through the door. Sovay had been conducted up the stairs by a pretty young woman in an abundant curling wig. Her heart-shaped face was rouged and painted, the brows above her pale blue eyes plucked to a thin line and she was wearing a low-cut gown. It was not until she spoke that Sovay realised that she was a boy. Such was the order of the day at Mother Pierce's. Sovay refused to think about the reason for this, or what went on there. The pictures on the walls were hint enough. She was nervous of meeting any customers, but it was still early, so business was slack just yet, the boy informed her. She was mighty relieved about that. The boy laughed and addressed her with easy confidence, as though she was familiar with the ways of such establishments. His name was Toby, he said with a toss of his curly wig, and he was doing this just until he could buy himself an apprenticeship. The Captain had snorted at this, pronouncing that all whores had some story about how they would climb to respectability, but Sovay liked the boy and hoped that he would escape from Mother Pierce's clutches. He had brought her clothes to wear, the soberest he could find. The gown was still rather gaudy even after Toby had removed most of the frills and flounces, and so low cut that it made Sovay blush.

'Clean, though,' Toby announced cheerfully. 'Just

come back from the laundry.'

Sovay reflected that there were some things to be grateful for at least. Downstairs, the Captain was waiting, striding about with impatience. He whistled when he saw her and his face broke into a grin.

'You were handsome dressed as a boy, but this suits you much better. Come.' He put his gloved hand out to conduct her. 'I will find a chair for you. You will be home in a trice. Miss Sovay again.'

'I'm not normally so attired,' she replied, looking down at the plunging décolletage.

'That's a pity.' His smile widened and his dark blue eyes gleamed with amusement.

Sovay was searching for some suitable retort when she realised that he was teasing her and it was probably best to keep silent.

Mother Pierce came out of the little booth that served as her office.

'You off now, Captain?' She turned to Sovay. 'I'll be expecting them back, young lady. I ain't made of money.'

'Now, Ma.' The Captain wagged his finger at her. 'I've paid for those rags twice over.'

'Rags, is it?' Mother Pierce's carmined cheeks reddened further. 'I'll have you know my girls wear the finest Mayfair can offer! No better quality anywhere in the Garden.'

'Oh, Ma,' the Captain caressed her cheek, 'your anger inflames me so.'

He seized Mother Pierce about the waist and whirled her round, much to the amusement of her 'girls' who stood round cheering and clapping. They made no move to help her. The Captain was the kind of man who could charm any woman; even Ma Pierce was not immune. It was clear that she was enjoying his attentions, despite her loud protests.

He sang as he danced her across the room and back again.

> 'Roses and lilies her cheeks disclose,
> But her ripe lips are more sweet than those.
> Press her,
> Caress her
> With blisses,
> Her kisses
> Dissolve us in pleasure, and sweet repose.'

It was an air Sovay recognised, from *The Beggar's Opera*, and she joined in the laughter to hear it sung to such a one and by a real highwayman.

'Desist, you rogue!' Ma Pierce cuffed him as she finally struggled out of his embrace, careful to adjust her wig. 'Be off and take your doxy with you.'

The Captain swept off his hat to her and bowed low before conducting Sovay out of the door. When they were outside, he put his arm round her, to protect her from the mill and press of people. Sovay was aware of his closeness, the faint scent about him of leather and horses. He turned to her, his face close, and began to sing again, quietly this time, more slowly, so the words gained significance.

> 'Roses and lilies her cheeks disclose,
> But her ripe lips are more sweet than those.'

As he sang, he drew one gloved finger down her cheek

and across her lips. Quickly, before she had time to think what he was doing, he kissed her hard on the mouth. Nobody looked or even noticed; on these streets embracing couples were a common sight. She knew that she ought to struggle, but did not. The kiss belonged to the Sovay who held up stagecoaches and did outrageous things. She would step out of her at the same time as she shed the whore's clothing and put on respectability with her own dress. Besides, the kiss thrilled her far more than any caress that she had ever received from Mr James Gilmore.

Greenwood let her go and smiled down at her, one eyebrow raised.

'You are better at that than I would have imagined. You are full of surprises, Miss Sovay.'

With that he hailed a chair and sent her off to Soho Square. The Captain had a good voice: a powerful tenor, sweet and pure. All the way back, as the chairmen wove their way through the crowded streets, she could hear his singing: *Press her, Caress her* . . . That was the tune she could not get out of her head.

❖

Her reverie was broken by a tiny sound followed by a slight draught of cold air. Sovay's heart beat hard and she opened her eyes to see a dark shape, a shadow within a shadow, detach itself from the heavy drapery of the curtain and glide with silent stealth across the room. Sovay was suddenly fully awake. As she did not believe in ghosts, this had to be a burglar set to steal from her. He was dressed entirely in black and could move with no noise at all. Only the gleam of his eyes showed as he moved to the bureau, easing open drawer after drawer.

He failed in his search and turned, looking around as though wondering where to search next. That is when he must have caught a movement from the bed. He came towards Sovay, hand outstretched, as if to stifle any noise she might make.

'I will not scream, or cry out,' she said in a low voice, 'but I have pistols under the covers and I will not hesitate to use them.'

'Don't shoot. I mean you no harm but don't make no noise, I beg of you.' The boy advanced cautiously. '*He's* downstairs and he won't hesitate to kill the both of us if you do.'

'Who's downstairs?' Sovay held the guns so he could see them.

'Ne'er you mind. Best you don't know, but he's a holy terror.' The boy broke off. 'Miss Sovay, isn't it?' He reached up and pulled off the knitted hat that he'd rolled down over his face. 'You was at Ma Pierce's with the Captain. It's Toby. Toby White. Although they don't call me that there. It was my dress you borrowed.'

He looked away from her and his pale face flushed, as if he was shamed to admit such a thing in the outside world.

'I remember,' Sovay replied. 'Although you look somewhat – different.'

She remembered his delicate face, the long dark lashes, the pale blue eyes. She really had thought that he was a girl.

'Out of me molly clothes, you mean?' He grinned, his white teeth bright in the darkness.

'What are you doing here?'

'When I ain't mollying, I'm a sneaker. A snakes-man.' He searched for a word she'd know. 'A burglar, but I come in through upstairs windows. I'm small, see? Good wi' locks, too. Get in and out of anywhere. Pride myself on it. Don't do no rough work, though. Leave that to the others.'

'Others?' Sovay looked slightly more wary. 'You mean there's a whole gang of you?'

Toby sat on the bed. 'On this occasion, no. Just me and one other. But he's enough.'

'What are you after? Jewellery? Silver? Plate?'

The boy shook his head. 'Nothing like that. He's after a wallet. Leather. Front latches. About that big.' He described the shape with his hands. 'He's doing the downstairs, I'm doing the up. Ssh!' He put his finger to his lips. 'He's coming! He's a big man. I heard a creak on the stairs. You pretend to be asleep. I'll say I ain't found nothing, but there's no telling if he'll believe me.' She thought he'd left but then his voice was there, little more than a breath in her ear. 'Get rid of the thing he's after, as soon as may be, or he'll come looking again and if he don't get it one way, he'll try another and some of his methods ain't what you'd call gentle.'

He stole away, as silently as he had come. Sovay did not pretend to be asleep. She sat bolt upright, pistol clutched to her chest. She would blast the first man through the door, even if it was that charming boy. She heard them move along the corridor to search her brother's room. Having found nothing there, they went on to her father's apartment on the next floor. From the time they took, they were thorough. At last she heard their tread on the stairs. The boy as quick as a cat with hardly a creak. The other one moving more slowly, with the caution of a heavy man trying to be silent.

When they left, they went empty-handed. She had the wallet safe under her pillow.

She would go to her father's lawyers first thing in the morning and deposit the wallet into their safe keeping. It was clear that she could not keep it here. Who had known that she had it in her possession? Who had betrayed her? What had Greenwood said? Trust no one. How right he had been.

CHAPTER 10

By the morning, her fear had turned to anger. Someone had betrayed her.

By the time Gabriel was announced, Sovay had decided that there were only two possibilities. Either Gabriel had gone against her instruction and confided in Fitzwilliam, or the culprit was Greenwood. Sovay did not like to think it of him, but the evidence was not in his favour. He knew about the wallet. He knew the whereabouts of her house in London. He consorted with rogues and thieves. He knew what they should look for, and it did not take a mind of great subtlety to determine where in the house the papers might be kept.

She conducted Gabriel into her father's study where he expressed horror at the danger that she had been in and denied most vehemently that it had anything to do with him. He had said nothing to Fitzwilliam, he swore, and was upset that Sovay could even think such a thing. Sovay apologised for ever doubting him. Which only left the highwayman. Greenwood must be the culprit.

'He'd likely sell his grandmother for a handful of silver,' Gabriel remarked. 'Let that be a lesson. Such men are like that.'

'The involvement I had with him was none of my choice!' Sovay flared back.

'I never suggested otherwise.' Gabriel put his hands up to ward off her anger. 'Let us not quarrel, Sovay.'

Sovay was slightly placated, but still thoroughly out of temper. She busied herself putting the papers out for Gabriel's inspection. She needed the opinion of another before she deposited the documents with young Mr Oldfield at her father's firm of solicitors, near to St Paul's.

Gabriel studied the documents on the worn green leather of the desk. He read them with distaste, hardly wanting to touch the sheets. Some of them were much folded and greasy to the touch, and some had an odd, sharp smell about them, reminiscent of rotten onion. To Gabriel, they all gave off the same dark reek of subterfuge and spies, as pungent and offensive to him as the unwholesome stink of the crowded city streets outside.

'What do you think they mean?' he asked her. 'Why were they being sent? For what purpose?'

'The warrants are obvious. As for the rest, the bulk of them are evidences against people, like those collected against my father, and they were being sent out to magistrates in different parts of the country with the runner acting as courier. Some others,' she shook her head, 'I can't be sure about. They appear to be of little consequence – innocent missives on un-related subjects, but if that is the case, why are they in the same wallet? I'm hoping that Mr Oldfield may be able to tell us more.' Sovay collected the papers together. 'I will give them over to him. Greenwood was right about one thing, they are too dangerous to have in one's own keeping.'

◆➤✕◄◆

The offices of Oldfield and Oldfield were off Ludgate

Hill where Carter's Lane met Shoemaker Row. Sovay hadn't visited the offices in years, not since she used to accompany her father as quite a little girl.

Young Mr Oldfield came out of his office to greet Sovay personally. He was always known as *young* Mr Oldfield, even though he was now approaching middle age. Under his crisp, white wig, he looked very much the same as she remembered him, with a rather stern look upon his face and his brow furrowed into a permanent frown. Sovay had been a bold child, but something about his austere demeanour had made her wary. She had sat in a corner of his office, keeping mouse quiet, aching to play with all the pens and inks, papers and ribbons but thinking it wise not to and trying to keep still. Now, she found him somewhat less off-putting. His mouth was firm but in no way mean or cruel; his grey eyes were sharp, but not unkind. It was the face of a man who could have been cold and ruthless but had chosen not to be.

'Miss Sovay,' his countenance relaxed into something that was almost a smile, 'you *have* changed. You quite light up our dull offices. Does she not, Skidmore?' He addressed his clerk who was staring at her in admiration. 'Would you like some tea? Skidmore, don't stand there gawking! Tea for Miss Sovay and be quick about it.' He ushered her into his office. 'Now, what can we do for you?'

The room was lined with bookcases full of legal volumes and all piled about with the ribbon-tied bundles of papers that she had found so enticing as a child. Wood panelling darkened the room and the small leaded windowpanes of green and grey glass were coated with yellowy London grime and let in little light. Lamps were lit, despite the early hour, and a fire burned bright in the grate. It might be summer outside but the law knows no seasons and in here it was always a winter's day.

'This is Mr Stanhope,' Sovay introduced Gabriel. 'He's the son of my father's Steward and my most trusted friend. I would like him to stay.'

'Of course.' Oldfield bowed slightly. 'Mr Stanhope. Pleased to make your acquaintance, sir.' He took his place behind a wide oak desk stacked with further bundles and strewn with documents. A newspaper lay cast aside, as if he had just been reading it. 'Now,' he repeated his question, 'what can we do for you?' He looked from one to the other. 'No trouble, I hope.'

Sovay and Gabriel took chairs opposite the desk.

'Firstly,' Sovay looked at Oldfield directly, 'I would like to know if you have seen my father recently.'

'Sir John has not visited Oldfield and Oldfield for some months. Skidmore would be able to tell you when it was exactly. That's if he ever arrives with that tea.' He sprang up and went to the door. 'Skidmore!'

His clerk was a tall youth of about nineteen or so, dressed in lawyer's black, his curly black hair neatly tied back. When he looked up, his startling green eyes were as sharp as his master's. He put down the tray he was carrying and commenced pouring tea.

'Sixteenth of February,' he said. 'That was the last time Sir John was in. I remember distinct.'

'Thank you, Skidmore. Off you go. Call you if I need you. Wonderful memory,' Oldfield commented as the young man left. 'Just like his father. Old Skidmore. Never forgot a thing. Married late. The lad a bit of an afterthought. Father's getting a bit long in the tooth now, like my old pa. Neither comes into the office much any more. Anyway, tea to your liking?' He suddenly looked at her, brows more deeply furrowed. 'Your father is missing. You are concerned.'

Sovay remembered his habit of talking inconsequentially, his mind busy all the while on some other thing.

'Well, yes.' Sovay nodded. 'And Hugh.'

'Hugh? He is missing, too?'

'He's been sent down from his college.'

'Oh, when was this?'

'Christmas, it seems.'

'Oh, that long ago. And for what reason?'

'He wrote a seditious pamphlet.' At the word, *seditious*, Oldfield's face grew graver still. 'He's not been home since the New Year,' Sovay went on quickly. 'We've had no word and don't know where he could be. Except . . .'

'Except?'

'Mr Fitzwilliam, his tutor, mentioned he wanted to go to Paris . . .'

'Hmm.' The lawyer looked at her over steepled fingers. 'Not a wise choice of destination, given the present political circumstances. Find one, however, and you'll find the other. Your father always gave the boy too much rein. Always getting him out of some scrape or another. Never could deny him anything after the death of your dear mother. Boy took it very hard, you see. You were too young to remember, but he was just the age . . . Now,' he collected his thoughts again, gripping the side of his chair, as though about to spring into action, 'what to do. Tricky.

Difficult.' He glanced at the newspaper. 'Things over there are worsening by the day.' He stood up and began to pace about. 'Needs thought. Indeed it does. Tricky one, like I said, but,' he suddenly smiled, 'I like puzzles.'

He went to the windows and commenced to stare out of the smeared grey and green panes.

'Now,' he turned back to her, 'what is the other thing that brought you here?'

'How did you know . . . ?'

'In my profession, it does to make as close a study of faces as any deed or document.' He switched his attention to Gabriel. 'All the while we've been talking, your young companion has been staring at that case he has with him. He has his hands gripped round it as if it has something live inside it, something that needs containing. Every now and then he looks at me, as if that something is matter he both does and does not want me to see.' He stood behind his desk again. 'Hand it over, young man. Let me relieve you of whatever it is that is so worrying you so.'

Gabriel opened the small portmanteau that he had been carrying and took out the wallet. Oldfield removed bundles from his desk and spread the documents that Sovay passed to him over the cleared surface. When they were set out to his satisfaction, he leaned over, his hands gripped on the opposite edges of the desk, studying each one in turn. He stood for a long while, his stern face brooding down at them. Then he looked up, his grey eyes clearing, like the sky after rain.

Sovay had determined not to say a word about how she came upon the documents. What could she say without giving her felony away? Oldfield was a lawyer above everything, a profession that took a dim view of lawbreaking, whatever the justification. She did not think he would turn her in to the nearest magistrate, but she did not relish being the object of his disapproval or his censure.

Oldfield welcomed her reticence, but could not help smiling to himself. As a lawyer, what he did not know, did not concern him. Hadn't anyone told her that?

'I won't ask where you came upon these, er, documents,' he said, his face as grave as ever. 'But you did right to bring these to me, Sovay. Yes, you did right.' He let go of the desk and began pacing, hands clasped behind him. 'These papers are of importance. National importance. They must be returned to the Government office which has,' he paused, as if to search for the correct euphemism, 'mislaid them. I'm sure they will be glad of their safe return.' Sovay started forward, alarmed by the very idea. He put his hand up with a smile, as if to anticipate her objection. 'I will not pass on how *I* came upon them; you may satisfy yourself on *that* score.'

'That is not my concern,' Sovay said quietly. 'I'm concerned for those mentioned here, they might lose their liberty.'

'I know. And I am concerned, too, perhaps for different reasons, but you are my client, and as such your safety is my *first* concern. If these documents are no longer in your possession, then no one will come looking for them.' He looked at Sovay sharply, then to Gabriel. 'Has someone come looking for them?' Sovay gave a slight shake of the head, but Gabriel nodded. Oldfield watched the exchange of looks between them. 'If that is the case, they must be returned without delay.'

Sovay gave her consent. She had brought them to him for safe keeping merely. She had not expected them to pass out of her possession, still less to be returned to the spy master himself, but she remembered Toby's whispered words and could see the logic behind Oldfield's decision. He had her best interests at heart.

'There is danger here, most certainly there is threat, but I will find a way to draw the venom,' Oldfield went on, sifting the letters with the point of his letter opener, as if they had poison upon them. 'To alert those concerned in a way that will not bring attention to me. Or to you. Do not mistake me, I am not of the same opinion as your father, or those named here. I am not of the same stripe, not of the same colour.'

He returned to the desk and picked up his copy of the *London Chronicle*.

'I deplore the Revolution in France, despair for that poor country, and dread the prospect of such a thing ever happening here. We live in a time of very great danger, Sovay, very great fear. Each day the news from France brings details of some fresh cruelty, each as unimaginable as the one that went before it. Fear breeds repression. We have only the law to protect us, but our laws on sedition, even treason, are vague and open to interpretation. The temptation is to introduce ill-considered legislation which will do more harm than good. Statutes to persecute rather than to protect. Unfortunately, that is already happening and what we have here is proof of it.' He pointed his letter opener at the papers. 'All sorts and kinds of people rounded up and arrested on little more than hearsay and gossip, much of it with malice behind it, or collected from spies who are paid to make up lies, but in these uncertain times that may be enough to get men arrested, even convicted. Men like your father. Once that happens, then the innocent are swept up with the guilty, if, indeed, such guilt exists. Association, open debate and discussion are stifled and pushed outside the law. When men are deprived of such freedoms as they *do* enjoy, then conditions are right for rebellion and the very thing that is most feared will be brought to pass.'

Having delivered his lecture, Mr Oldfield stared down, arms folded. He sniffed, his thin nostrils flaring, and then selected one letter after another.

'Hmm.' He held up each in turn to his long nose. 'What do we have here?'

He held one so close to the lamp that the light shone gold through the paper. Still not satisfied, he took the paper over to the fire. Sovay started from her seat, thinking he was going to fling it into the flames.

'Mr Oldfield! I do not think you should . . .' she began to say, but he was not listening. He squatted down, holding the paper up to the blaze.

'Come,' he said, 'come here and look at this.'

Sovay feared for the lawyer's hands as he held the paper taut and steady and as close as he could without it burning. The glow of the fire showed red, the thin paper rendered almost transparent by the light from behind it. Sovay leaned closer, ignoring the heat on her face. Tiny lines of writing began to appear, creeping across the warming paper as if by magic.

Gabriel joined them, brows drawn together. 'What is it?' he asked. 'What does it mean?'

'Invisible ink. Onion juice by the smell of it. Revealed only when heat is applied to it. As to what message is contained?' The lawyer brought the paper closer. 'It's in cipher.' He studied the page carefully. 'That is unexpected. The unexpected always makes me suspicious. I distrust things that are secret. I like things to be above board. I haven't seen this cipher for many years, but I have seen it before.' He took the paper away from the fire and the symbols disappeared. 'I'm curious to know what needs to be concealed in this way. I will give these pages some study before I pass them on to their rightful owners. Indeed, I will.'

He walked back to his desk, distracted. His mind on the cipher, he began to sort through the papers anew. Sovay deemed that it was time to leave.

'Well, thank you for your time, Mr Oldfield. Will you tell me if you make any discoveries?'

'Oh, you are leaving.' He looked up, his grey eyes barely seeing her. 'Skidmore will show you out. Skidmore!' The clerk appeared immediately. 'Show Miss Middleton and Mr Stanhope to the door.'

Oldfield closed his own door, his mind already on the mysterious document written in invisible ink. He had not seen this cipher since his youth. As a student, he had studied in Germany, at the University of Ingolstadt. While he was there, he had joined a secret society that had since gained considerable notoriety. His code name had been Lusus, companion to Bacchus. He sighed at the reminiscence, such a very great distance had grown between who he was now and the young man who had chosen such a sobriquet.

One of the tasks that they had been set as they progressed from one level to another in the Order was to master this cipher.

He sat down and began to transcribe. He called for a candlestick and candles. He would copy the document first, then he could decipher it at his leisure. When he looked up from his task, the candles were guttering stubs and the room had grown dark. He sighed and swivelled on his chair to stare at the dying embers of the fire. The young Mr Oldfield believed in the law above all other things. At first, he had not been averse to the happenings in France but, like many others, he had looked on askance at each new turn of events. He did not believe that any faction had the right to take over a nation, to make their own laws and then break them, which was what he believed to be happening now. To take a king out and try him and then execute him; to treat his queen in the same manner; to slaughter innocents indiscriminately with no hope or recourse to proper trial. Like Saturn, the Revolution had begun to eat its own children, so one of its leaders had said. That man was now dead. This was not the rule of law, in his opinion; it was a tyranny, brought about by the rule of the mob. He feared the mob above every other thing. He remembered the Gordon Riots. He'd been a young man then, a young lawyer, just beginning in practice with his father.

To have lived through it was never to forget it. Although the demonstrations had started peacefully enough, he had felt deep perturbation at the tens of thousands streaming through the streets towards the Houses of Parliament, all wearing blue cockades, waving banners and chanting 'No Popery' with Lord George Gordon at the head of them, carrying his petition. It had not taken long for it to turn ugly, once entry was denied them and the petition refused.

By nightfall, the city was given over to the rule of the mob: shops and commercial premises looted; churches and chapels broken open and sacked, furnishings, vestments, dragged out and made into great bonfires. The night sky had been blotched and badged with the red glow from burning buildings, while the mob, made filthy by their own destructions, had roamed with wild, restless fury, their faces blackened with soot, or made pale as ghosts by plaster dust, all quite mad with the sense of their own importance and power.

For over a week, the city had been entirely commanded by the rioters. Oldfield and his father had stayed, watching from behind the shutters, with anything valuable and important moved to the cellars, while the Bank of England was attacked, the bridges over the Thames seized. Finally, the infantry and cavalry had been called out and together they had succeeded in restoring order, firing on the crowd wherever they found it, charging them with sword and bayonet.

It was not the people he despised, he felt sorry for the poor devils, hundreds of their number dead in the streets, others ending up swinging at Tyburn. No one a jot the better off. No, he reserved his loathing for those who led them, men like Lord George Gordon who sought to use them as a blunt instrument to cudgel their way to power.

He turned back to documents that he had lately

translated. Terrible as those riots had been, they were nothing compared to what was planned here. Gordon and his petition had been like a torch thrown into a hayrick, causing it to flare up and burn with such a fierce heat that none could go near it, but the fire had died down just as quickly, once the fuel was spent. This was something entirely different and far more destructive, as in a fire carefully and artfully laid with each part of a building connected with fuses and mined with black powder. All that was needed was the initial spark.

Except this was not a building, it was a nation. If he understood this correctly, then all over the country, one armed faction would be set against another, until the streets of every town and every city ran with blood. National leaders would be picked off, one by one, leaving the way open for a mad king to be removed and a weak and dissolute regent swept away. At this point, others were primed to take over, to be initially welcomed by a terrified, exhausted population, grateful to anyone who could restore order, but ushering in a tyranny never witnessed in this country before. It was a cunning and evil conspiracy that made the blood run cold to even contemplate. Clever in the extreme and impossible to stop, once the fuse was lit. It would make the Gordon Riots appear as nothing. It would rival the Revolution in France for bloodshed and mayhem, but there could be no possible pretence that this was the will of the people. This was the will of one man and a fiendishly clever one. To oppose and defeat him would require equal cunning.

Oldfield spent a moment or two more pondering

what to do as he collected all the materials together and put them back into the wallet. Then he summoned Skidmore.

'Get me string and brown paper, will you?'

Oldfield parcelled the wallet himself, dripping melted wax down on to the knots and careful to use a plain seal. Then he addressed it to *Sir Robert Dysart, Care of the Home Office*, *Whitehall*, before giving it to Skidmore to take to the Post Office in Lombard Street.

'Too late for tonight's post,' he said and then looked at the address. 'His offices ain't there, anyway. They're in Leggatt's Court. I can take it over there, if you like.'

Oldfield looked at his clerk, surprised yet again by the things that the boy knew. 'Thank you for your offer, Skidmore, but just this once, do what I ask of you! Now go.'

When Skidmore left, Oldfield's thoughts turned to Sovay. He hoped that his actions would act like a lightning attractor and take the danger away from her. She really had no idea of the true significance of her chance discovery. Her concern had been for her father only, and those like him. The arrest warrants, the evidences, were incidental, ultimately unimportant except for the way that they fitted into the whole. She could have no inkling of what was contained within the innocuous-looking letters. He hoped that Dysart would think so, too, and that returning the wallet would take his attention away from her, but Oldfield did not want it redirected onto himself. Oldfield was not afraid of putting himself in danger, but they must tread carefully and avoid alerting Dysart in any way. The coded missives were addressed to third-party intermediaries, to be passed on to yet others, so no one would know who their co-conspirators were. They could not be identified in any way, but one strand linked them. They were all Illuminati.

CHAPTER II

Sovay left Oldfield's office much relieved to be free of the wallet. The great bell of St Paul's chimed the hour as she made her way with Gabriel through the great press of people on Ludgate Hill: lawyers' clerks with briefs under their arms, barristers in wig and gown, merchants, men of business, porters and servants all came towards them, unwilling to give right of way even to a lady, each one preoccupied by his own affairs. There was precious little room on the pavement and the road was crowded with chairs, carts and carriages. Sovay was glad of Gabriel's strong, guiding hand on her arm. They went over the crossing at Fleet Market and Bridge Street, a boy sweeping a way for them, and came to Fleet Street which was no less busy. The way was so crowded towards Temple Bar, and Sovay was so busy looking out for Turnbull's Bank, her next place of call, that she almost walked headlong into a stranger and Gabriel had to steady her.

'Oh, I'm sorry. I . . .' she began to apologise but was immediately interrupted.

'On the contrary, it is I . . .' The man was removing his hat to bow to her, when he suddenly smiled in recognition. 'Why, Miss Middleton. I did not know you were in London.'

'Mr Barrett, isn't it?' She was looking into the mild blue-grey eyes of the American who had called on her father.

'It is! I am very pleased to meet you again, even if the circumstances are accidental. In fact, I have news . . .' he began to say, but checked himself, aware of her companion.

'Oh, let me introduce Mr Gabriel Stanhope. A trusted friend of our family.'

'Pleased to meet you, sir. Perhaps I might accompany you on your way?'

'I would very much like you to,' Sovay replied. 'What is your news?'

Despite the anonymous indifference of the crowd, Virgil Barrett looked round. He took her other arm and fell in beside her.

'After I left you, I went north to Manchester, to warn the societies in those parts and to Liverpool. From there I went to Dublin and that is where I picked up news of your father.'

'Dublin!' Sovay exclaimed.

'Shh, have care. It is hard to know who's about! Yes, your father had been there, seeking news of Hugh.'

'Is he still there?'

'No, he left for France accompanied by Sir Henry Fitzwilliam, a leader of the United Irishmen. It was them I had gone to see. As a matter of fact.'

'Fitzwilliam?' Gabriel asked. 'Is he a relation of Gerald Fitzwilliam?'

'His older brother. Do you know him?'

'He is Hugh's tutor at Oxford,' Sovay replied.

'Is he?' The American frowned. 'Have a care of him. He's of a different political persuasion to his brother, if he believes in anything beyond himself, that is. Whatever the way of it, he's not to be trusted. He's in thrall to some dangerous men.'

'You are right,' Sovay agreed. 'This is not a conversation for the street.' They were hard by Turnbull's now. 'This is where we must part, I'm afraid. Perhaps you would call on me? This afternoon, about four o'clock?'

'I would be delighted.' He turned to Gabriel. 'Do you accompany Miss Sovay into the banking house, or might I offer you some refreshment? Brown's coffee house is hard by.'

'I'd be delighted to accompany you, sir,' Gabriel replied.

Virgil Barrett smiled. 'Good man. Until later, then, Miss Sovay.' He raised his hat to her. 'I will bid you good day.'

◆➤◼◆

Turnbull's Bank was in no way grand and, except for the bars upon the windows and the liveried porter, it was little different from the other establishments along the street. Sovay's family had banked here ever since the original Mr Turnbull, a goldsmith, had opened his establishment in 1625 at the sign of the Golden Bottle, Cheapside. The present Fleet Street premises were always referred to by the bank's employees as the 'new shop' even though the old one had disappeared well over a century ago, destroyed in the Great Fire. The bank's considerable assets had been kept safe from that terrible conflagration, secure in vaults deep underground. Bankers rarely took chances.

A clerk looked up from his ledger as Sovay approached his high desk. He peered through a brace of pewter candlesticks and a pen pot containing turkey-feather quills to enquire as to her business.

'I am here to see Mr Turnbull.'

The clerk beckoned to a bank messenger.

'And who may I say is calling?'

Sovay gave her card to the messenger and the clerk went back to his ledger. The only sounds were the tick-tock of a tall case clock and the scratch of the clerk's pen. The small portmanteau that Gabriel had been carrying for her was heavy. Sovay rested it on a table as she examined a display of plate contained within a glass cabinet and tried not to count the seconds passing by. The silence began to unnerve her. Various doors led off the vestibule. Every so often, one would open, and a man would walk through and enter another. Some were clerks and plainly dressed, others were gentlemen with much gold hanging from their waistcoats. They all ignored her as the doors whispered shut on their hidden world of vaults and ledgers, locks, secrets and the turning of keys.

Eventually, the messenger returned and took her through one of the sighing doors to the office of Mr Adam Turnbull, the fourth generation of Turnbulls to head the bank. A marble fireplace held busts of his predecessors and the walls were adorned by portraits of chairmen and partners going back to the founder.

Mr Turnbull rose from his seat to conduct her to a chair. He was so grand that Sovay almost felt inclined to curtsy. He was above middle height, soberly but exquisitely dressed in dark grey velvet and silk. His perfectly fitted flaxen wig curled crisply above his ears and his skin shone with good health and good fortune.

'What can I do for you, Miss Sovay?' he asked as he

resumed his seat behind his wide mahogany desk. He looked at her over clasped hands and the skin round his brown eyes crinkled, as if he was prepared to be amused.

'I would like you to look after this for me.' Sovay opened the small portmanteau, swung up the leather bag containing the guineas and heaved it onto the desk. She loosened the ties round the neck. Some of the coins spilled onto the desk.

'Good Heavens!' Adam Turnbull sprang up, as if the clink of coin was the last thing that he had been expecting. 'I hope you did not come here unescorted with such a quantity of gold upon you. The London streets can be most dangerous. *Most* dangerous.'

'No, Mr Turnbull, do not trouble yourself. I was accompanied to your door.'

'That is a relief.' He took out the paper money, examining the denominations, and tipped the rest of the coin onto the table. He began counting the guineas and arranging them into piles, as if he had never forgotten the skills that he had learned as a young counter clerk.

'A tidy sum, Miss Sovay,' he said when he had finished. 'A tidy sum, indeed. Now what would you have me do?'

'I would like you to look after it for me.'

'Your father's account?'

Sovay shook her head. As the money was of doubtful provenance and obtained by means scarcely less dubious, she'd decided that it should be kept in a separate account.

'On your own account? Unusual, in one so young, but it can be done. Of course,' he leaned back in his chair, 'to open an account in your name, we would need your father's written permission.'

Sovay bit her lip. 'That might be difficult. I don't know where he is, you see . . .'

The banker looked up in alarm. Sir John wasn't the kind of man to go missing.

'I came to London,' Sovay continued, 'hoping to find word of him here, but he is not at the house and hasn't been seen for some while . . .'

'I will certainly make enquiries. Your brother, Mr Hugh . . .'

'He is missing, too.' Sovay looked at him. 'He is not at his Oxford college. I have received information that he might be in Paris. I think it possible that my father might have followed him there.'

Sovay sat back, surprised. She had not intended to tell him any of this when she came through his door.

'Paris, eh?' Mr Turnbull leaned back in his chair. The look he gave her was full of meaning. He was not a man to state the obvious and never pried into a client's business but his clients often confided in him nevertheless. 'Our French House is closed,' he went on, 'due to, ahem, local difficulties.' Most of their customers had fled the country, but he saw no point in telling her that. 'But we still have agents there looking after our interests. I will enquire among them. We will find them, young lady, never fear, and safe from harm, I trust. Meanwhile, unorthodox it may be, but I will make sure that these funds remain at your disposal. There are procedures, for orphans, and so on. Unusual times require unusual remedies.'

'Thank you, Mr Turnbull,' she said. 'And thank you for your discretion,' she added, aware that at no time had he asked how she had come by such a large sum.

'Bankers are known for it, young lady.' He rose to escort her to the door. 'How could we operate else? Now, do not hesitate to call on me if I can be of any further assistance.'

Sovay left Turnbull's office, the portmanteau she carried now empty and light. Gabriel was waiting outside, but without the American.

'He sends his compliments and will call on you later, although he can tell you little more, at present, as to where Sir John might be.' Gabriel looked around, his eyes searching the moving crowd. 'He also said that he thought that we might be followed. It would be best to behave like innocent visitors to the city and to talk of inconsequential things until we reach the house.'

To this end, they walked along the Strand, looking into the windows of the shops, and returned home by way of Covent Garden Market. As they approached, the streets looked disturbingly familiar, as in a place remembered from a dream. Sovay looked around, certain that she had been here before. They took a narrow street from the Strand and, although it looked different in daylight, one of the tall, crooked houses crowding in on them was the very place that she had been taken to by the Captain, she was sure. It was early, but there were already streetwalkers standing on corners, wearing too much face paint and too few clothes. They cast a bold eye over the men strolling by and Gabriel cursed the fellow who had given them directions. What could the man be thinking of, he wondered, to send a lady this way? Sovay kept silent. She certainly was not going to tell Gabriel that she had been here recently and in the company of Captain Greenwood.

Eventually, the narrow streets opened out on to an elegant arcaded square and a broad piazza full of people. The air was sweet with the scent of flowers and the pavements spread with great, heaped baskets of fruit and vegetables. Shoppers wandered past, smiling at invitations to taste and buy, going on to inspect the market stalls, stopping to look at this and that, to pick up a notion, examine a novelty, stroke the softness of a scarf. Street sellers weaved through and around them crying their wares, while hawkers shouted from booths or a little patch of paving, and a quack doctor offered a cure for every ill known to man or woman, a bottle in each hand. A crowd roared encouragement to a pair of prizefighters, one black, and one white, both bloodied and glistening with sweat. A man dressed as a jester capered past, beating a little drum, accompanied by a little white dog with a ruff round his neck. He was surrounded by a yelling mob of children, all shouting, 'Mr Punch! Mr Punch!'

The children sat down in front of a tall stall and Sovay followed, pulling Gabriel along with her, curious to know what lay behind the red curtains of the striped booth. The crowd settled in expectation as the curtains jerked back to reveal a very peculiar-looking fellow dressed in a red coat and a pointed hat, with scarlet cheeks and a hooked nose. He spoke in a strange squawking way that had the crowd laughing and he brandished a stick and laid about him in a furious manner that had them laughing harder. Gabriel guffawed, declaring that he looked like the church warden, Mr Pollock, and Punch's wife, Joan, bore more than a passing resemblance to Pollock's wife, Betty. Sovay was soon wiping tears away as Punch's wife gave him a good drubbing for dropping the baby and all sorts of mayhem ensued in the two-foot-wide booth. The crowd hooted and roared as sausages whirled about along with the baby and Mr Punch took on all comers, including ghosts and crocodiles. All this was accompanied by a great deal of squawking talk.

'How does he make that sound?' Sovay asked no one in particular.

'Thing he talks with is called a swatchel,' an amiable voice answered from beside her. 'Him inside's called the professor. He's an Italian. Always around the Garden. Amiable cove. Fond of the bottle. Near as red in the face as Mr Punch.'

It took Sovay a minute to recognise that the boy standing next to her was Toby.

'Watch.' He smiled up at her. 'We're coming up to the best part.'

Sovay laughed along with the crowd as an officer with a warrant and a constable came to take Mr Punch to prison. There was an edge to the cheering as Mr Punch set about the constables with his stick. The crowd quietened as Jack Ketch joined them, rope in hand, and the gallows jerked into view. Mr Punch, still defiant, was about to be hanged. There was a ripple of amusement as Mr Punch pretended not to understand what to do. The ripple turned to a rumble of anticipation as Jack Ketch, with much exasperation and contemptuous squawking about Punch's stupidity, demonstrated by putting the rope round his own neck.

The hush of anticipation turned to an appreciative roar and deafening cheering as Punch hanged the hangman. The play was not ended yet. A painted devil popped into view, intent on carrying Punch down to hell. The crowd howled their delight as a triumphant Mr Punch squawked, 'Huzzah, huzzah, I killed the devil!' and did for him, too.

'I love that part.' Toby rubbed his face with his sleeve. 'Gets me going every time. Captain sends his compliments, by the way.' He winked at Sovay and tipped his hat. 'I bid you good day.'

'Who was that?' Gabriel asked, noticing Sovay blush as the boy turned away. 'Did he insult you?'

'No, of course not,' Sovay answered as she dropped a few coins in the hat being passed around. 'He was just a boy who explained to me how it is done.'

They walked back to Soho Square as the city quietened and dusk fell. They talked about the puppet play and laughed all the way, the worries of the day put aside, at least for the moment. They were so deep in conversation that neither thought very much about the American's warning, although they were, indeed, being watched and followed every step of the way.

❖

When they returned to Soho Square, there was a note waiting for Sovay. It was from Virgil Barrett, a few lines explaining that business had detained him and he would not be able to call on her until the next day. Sovay felt a brief flicker of disappointment. She found she liked the American and, although there was little more that he could tell her about the whereabouts of her father, she found his solid presence, his air of capability, comforting amidst all this uncertainty and would like to have talked more with him.

Sovay read the note quickly, her eyes already on the card beneath it. She picked it up from the silver tray. The name was enclosed inside a heavy black border, as if the sender was in mourning.

Sir Robert Dysart, Bart.

'When did this arrive?' she asked sharply. Lydia was slow to answer, too busy hovering about, snatching looks at Gabriel from under her lashes, simpering nervously while inquiring about his health and welfare and generally behaving most uncharacteristically. That she had a yen for him, and was determined to set her cap at him, was no secret, and Sovay would normally have teased her about it, but at the moment, the girl's behaviour merely irritated her.

'I said, when did this arrive?'

'Oh, not long since, neither of them. Just before you came in. Boy brought the note, t'other was delivered in person. 'Tis a wonder you didn't see him. Tall, thin streak of misery, dressed all in black.'

'That's enough, Lydia,' Mrs Crombie said sharply. She was annoyed with the girl for making eyes at Gabriel and it was not for the likes of her to comment on visitors. 'If Miss Sovay doesn't need your services, you can come and help me sort the laundry.'

Lydia's appealing look fell on stony ground. She followed the housekeeper meekly enough, but it was one of the jobs she liked least in the house (the other one being laying the fires) and she was dying to know all about London, having hardly put her nose outside.

Gabriel left almost immediately, going to collect his things from Fitzwilliam's house. Sovay went to the sitting room, brushing the card against her chin. She set it on the mantelpiece and stared at it. What could he want from her? Under the ripple of anticipation ran a thin current of fear. She turned away, dismissing it. He very likely knew nothing, and even if he did, what could he do?

Sovay suppressed any apprehension about a visit from Dysart, determined to put it out of her mind. Instead, she concentrated on household duties and getting rooms ready for Gabriel. Lydia immediately volunteered to take that responsibility on herself.

'You do like him, then?' Sovay asked, head on one side. 'By the way you behaved when you saw him just now, I thought you might.'

'It was just sport, Miss,' Lydia said, as she collected sheets from the linen press. 'I meant nothing by it.'

'I know.' Sovay put her hand on Lydia's arm. 'I didn't mean to snap at you.'

Sovay smiled and Lydia grinned back, glad they were friends again.

'I do,' she said, blushing despite herself. 'I can't help it. He's that handsome and well set up. I like a well-made man, but he's different from the other boys back home.'

Sovay was curious. 'How so?'

'Well, he's more refined, in his manners, and the way he speaks. Never swears in women's hearing and he always has a book in his pocket. He don't say so much, but he's a deep thinker. I can't abide a blatherer, or a bellwether. He don't put on airs, but he behaves like a gentleman.' Lydia laughed. 'Far more of a gentleman than some I could mention, that's for certain. I don't have any chance with him.' Her face fell into lines of resignation. 'But,' she set off up the stairs, 'I can still have a go.'

'What do you mean, you don't have a chance with him?' Sovay asked as she brought flowers up for Gabriel's room. 'I'd say you stood every chance. You're pretty and clever, warm-hearted and generous. You'd make an excellent wife and mother and companion, besides. He would be lucky to have you.'

'No,' Lydia shook her head. 'He only has eyes for one person. Believe me, many have tried.'

'Oh, and who might that be?' Sovay asked, arranging the roses just so.

'You, Miss,' Lydia smiled, and their eyes met in the mirror. 'Didn't you know?'

CHAPTER 12

A note arrived from Sir Robert, saying that he would call at ten o'clock the following morning. Sovay intended to rise early, in order to give her time to prepare for their meeting.

She had Lydia dress her hair carefully, brushing it to bring up a fine, smooth, bird's wing gloss, before turning the natural curl into ringlets. Sovay wanted her hair as natural as possible, caught up in a ribbon, and curling and falling down to her shoulders. She decided on a simple day dress of Indian cotton. Whatever Dysart knew, whatever he wanted, it would be wise to act the artless ingénue. Timidity was not in her nature, but she did not want any part of her manner or appearance to suggest the kind of boldness which might allow her to act the highwayman and go about the country holding up coaches and making off with other people's property. To begin with, at least.

When Sir Robert Dysart was announced, prompt at ten, she was ready.

He was shown into the drawing room, where Sovay had arranged to have tea served.

'Sir Robert,' she rose to greet him. 'I do not think we have met before.'

'No,' he bowed as he took her hand, 'I believe not, Miss Middleton. It is a pleasure to make your acquaintance.'

Sovay remembered Lydia's description. He was tall, and dressed all in black. It was difficult to tell his real age, the old-fashioned, white curled wig he wore made him look older than his years. He might once have been handsome, but his face had the greyish pallor of someone rarely out of doors. His cheeks were sunken, the skin stretched tight over his bony forehead, high cheek bones and prominent nose as though he was being consumed from within. He reminded her of someone, something. Then she had it. He looked like one of the puppets that she had seen yesterday in Covent Garden. Jack Ketch, the hangman, could have been modelled on him. His eyes were an odd colour, clouded and opaque, yellowish grey, like flint. His touch was cold, his long, thin fingers dry and hard. Coarse black hairs sprouted above his bony knuckles and carpeted the backs of his hands and his long nails were stained with ink at the cuticle. Sovay withdrew her hand from his as quickly as politeness would allow.

Dysart watched as she busied herself with kettle, caddy and teapot. She was artless in an artful way, striving to give an impression of prettiness that did not suit the strength of her features, or her dark colouring. He studied her profile as she turned to pour the tea. She was a fine-looking young woman, he would say that, with large eyes, strong curving brows and a straight, Grecian nose. Too handsome for prettiness, but only time would tell if she would grow to be a real beauty.

'I was hoping to see your father.' Sir Robert looked around as if surprised at not finding him here.

'He is from home, at the moment. How do you take your tea, sir?'

'Without milk and without sugar.' He looked at the

blue cup and saucer that she handed to him. 'The work of Mr Wedgwood, if I'm not mistaken?'

'Yes,' Sovay smiled. A tea set of this pattern had been a present from Mr Wedgwood on his last visit to Compton. Her father had ordered another for the London house. 'From his Etruria Works. My father is a great admirer of his.'

'And a personal friend?' Dysart sipped the hot liquid and raised a dark eyebrow. Josiah Wedgwood was known for his radical views.

'I believe they are acquainted,' Sovay replied.

More than acquainted, Dysart thought, although he said nothing. Thick as thieves more like, along with the traitorous Joseph Priestley and the other self-styled Lunar Men.

'I'm sorry to miss your father. When is he expected to return?'

'I really cannot say . . .' Sovay let the sentence lapse into vagueness.

'And yet, chance finds you here.' Dysart put down his cup. 'Why *are* you here, Miss Middleton?'

'I came to meet my father. He means to introduce me into society. Papa has promised me a whole new wardrobe, but when I arrived, I found him away from home.'

She was acting the spoilt daughter of an indulgent father. Everyone knew that Middleton was besotted. Look at that ridiculous portrait he'd commissioned from that idiotic painter who had managed to uncover nothing of any interest. It was a plausible story, but it did not suit her to play empty-headed. Dysart turned his cold eyes on her. She did not flinch, but returned his stony gaze with one so void of expression that it mirrored his own.

She was good. He would concede that to her. Every inch the clever young miss. Remarkable, given her youth, and in a woman? He had never seen it before. She had nerve. He would give that to her also, but surely she did not think that she could best him? She was just a girl. His hand shook very slightly as he replaced the cup on its saucer. He would uproot her. He would shake her to the very foundations of her being, then he would shake her some more.

'And your brother?' Dysart's tone remained light, as if he were genuinely inquiring after family members. 'How does he do at Oxford?'

'Well, I think,' Sovay answered. 'He does not confide in me.'

'Something of a poet, so I hear. He is gaining quite a reputation, even here in London.'

'Is that so?' Sovay shrugged. 'Hugh is too modest to brag of his talent and we hear nothing of such things stuck away in the country.'

'He has gone up for the Trinity term?'

Sovay paused before answering. His eyes gave nothing away, but Sovay remembered something Hugh had told her when they were children, do not lie unless absolutely necessary.

'I *believed* he had done so, but . . .'

'But?'

'But his tutor, Mr Fitzwilliam, called on me just the other evening and said he hadn't seen Hugh for some time.'

'Really?' Dysart nodded as though taking in the information. 'I wonder where he can be?'

Sovay allowed concern to cloud her face for a

moment, then smiled. 'Perhaps Hugh is visiting. He has friends in many places.'

'And you have heard nothing from him? I find that hard to believe.'

'We've had letters, certainly. But not many of late.'

'From Oxford?'

'I did not study the post office marks, Sir Robert.'

'From Paris?'

Sovay looked shocked. 'Certainly not. I would have remembered that.'

Sir Robert's features remained a mask. 'Because Fitzwilliam tells me he could be there.'

'Really!' Sovay started forward, nearly spilling her cup and saucer. 'He did not tell me that!'

'Perhaps he wanted to save you the worry of knowing,' Sir Robert answered smoothly. 'Paris being so dangerous.'

'Yes, indeed.' Sovay stood and began to pace the room. 'That is most concerning, especially with Papa away from home.'

'Ah, yes. Your father.' Dysart shifted in his seat. 'Perhaps he has followed him there?'

'Oh, I hope not!' Sovay bit her lip hard, bringing tears to her eyes. 'I truly hope that is not so!'

'So do I,' Sir Robert agreed. 'That would be a most unwelcome turn of affairs, especially as Sir John does not enjoy the best of health. Let us hope that he does not find himself somewhere that will affect his constitution.'

'Indeed!' Sovay swayed and gripped the back of the chair, hoping she was not laying this on too thickly. 'Please, Sir Robert, do not alarm me further.' She turned to him, eyes big with tears. 'I hear you are a man of some power and influence. Please, please do all you can to find out where they might be!'

'I will certainly do that, Miss Middleton,' he smiled, an expression more like a grimace on his cadaverous face. 'You may depend on me. You travelled up to town recently?' he asked, tipping the conversation, setting it to run in another direction, observing her all the while.

'Yes,' Sovay answered. 'The day before yesterday.'

She resumed her seat, watching him closely. He was as slippery as mercury on a board.

'I was talking to a neighbour of yours, Sir Royston Gilmore. He must have travelled on the same day. You are affianced to his son, I believe.'

'Not . . . not any more.' Despite her intention to hide all real emotion from him, Sovay felt herself blush.

'I'm sorry to hear that!' Sir Robert looked up with an apparent show of sympathy. 'But I'm sure you do not lack for suitors. Sir Royston told me that he was attacked by a highwayman. Only just escaped with his life. You encountered no trouble of that nature. A young woman, on her own. You *were* on your own . . .'

'I was with my maid, Lydia.' She looked him in the eye, defying contradiction. 'We encountered no trouble of that kind. Sir Royston has my sympathy. That is truly shocking.'

'Shocking, indeed. I would see every last one of them brought to justice and hanged.' He was watching her now as a huntsman might observe a hind. 'There are a sight too many of them operating. The scoundrel who attacked Sir Royston is new to us but it seems he joined forces with one who calls himself Captain Greenwood. He *is* known to us and his days of freedom are numbered, you have my word on that! Now,' he made to stand up, 'I must go. My department is responsible for order and security, and we have agents both here and abroad, including Paris.' He looked at her, his hooded eyes heavy with words unspoken. 'Little escapes us. You can be sure that I will do my best to locate your father and brother. Paris is a dangerous place for any Englishman to be.'

He rose to leave. His warning delivered. He clearly knew exactly where they were and was informing her that they were in his power.

'Thank you, Sir Robert.' Sovay stood to accompany him to the door. 'I am comforted to know that you will do everything you can. But surely, you do not have to go so soon?'

'I'm afraid so. I fear I have taken up too much of your time already. In truth, I only came to deliver this.' He handed her an invitation card. 'I am hosting a small gathering, at my house, Thursley Abbey. I was hoping that your father might join me. I would be delighted if you would accompany him. If he has not yet returned, I would be honoured if you would come in his stead.'

'That is very kind of you, Sir Robert. I thank you on our behalf. I have heard about Thursley, and would very much like to see it,' she said, and then she frowned. 'But I see that it is in but a few days. If my father has not returned, I fear I will not be able to take up your invitation. It would hardly be seemly for me to come alone.'

'Do not worry, young lady,' his mouth stretched in a smile, 'Lady Bingham will also be my guest. I'm sure you know her. She is a confidante of your aunt and was a close companion of your dear mother, I believe. A family friend. Who could be more suitable? She will act as your chaperone. I will arrange for her to call on you.'

He had it all worked out. He would have her there willing or no.

'In that case, I will be delighted to accept,' Sovay replied with a smile as genuine as his own.

'Until then.' He bowed and kissed the hand she held out to him.

'Indeed.' She clenched her other hand to control her impulse to snatch her fingers from his grip. 'Until then.'

She rubbed the back of her hand on her dress as she showed him to the door. It was like being caressed by a pair of those thin, grey slugs that infested the kitchen garden. She studied the embossed invitation card as she returned to the drawing room. Sir Robert clearly wanted her there. Why? He knew where her father was, Hugh, too. That much was clear from their duel of a conversation. If going there would take her nearer to finding them, then that is what she would do. She would deal with Lady Bingham when the occasion arose. Sovay had met her several times. She knew that her father thought her to be a poisonous troublemaker: a bad influence who was at least partially responsible for Aunt Harriet's nervous condition. Sovay remembered her as sallow-faced, hiding her own thin, tow-coloured hair under elaborate wigs. She was always dressed in the height of fashion, although the clothes hung on her spare body like so much cloth on a tenting frame.

Lady Bingham was a tireless society hostess and

partygoer. She invited confidences and accumulated gossip and snippets of information as a sharper collects gold. She used her store to good effect. What she knew made her welcome everywhere. No door was shut to her. No salon closed. Her unpleasant nature did not affect her social acceptability. Rather the contrary. It was the reason for it. Sovay was not surprised that she was a friend of Dysart. She wondered if the two were lovers. They would make a handsome pair. The very idea made her laugh out loud.

◆►◄◆

Sir Robert Dysart left a note for Lady Bingham at her town house in Cavendish Square and went back to his offices in Leggatt's Court, a dark, sunless yard at the centre of a warren of streets that ran behind Fleet Street. He ran his office from there, at some distance from the imposing splendour of Whitehall, and used the rooms above as his private apartments when he was in town. His department reported directly to the newly formed Committee of Secrecy. The nature of the work carried on meant that its existence went unacknowledged and, although Sir Robert was one of the most powerful men in the country, he had no official position. This location suited the work. The kind of people who visited Dysart, or most often his clerk, Gribbon, would have felt out of place in the great Offices of State.

The building was old. He liked that about it. Part of a narrow crowded row that made up one side of the dank courtyard, the steeply pitched roofs showing against the sky like a row of uneven teeth. Cracked and crooked wooden beams showed between small bricks which were blackened by smoke and scorch marks. Somehow, these buildings had survived the Great Fire while all around others had been rendered to ashes.

Gribbon sat in the outer office, his tall, thin frame hunched over his desk. He wore black, like his master, but there was a rusted quality to his clothing and his head craned forward on his scrawny neck. He reminded Dysart of a heron, as though the words on the pages in front of him were fish that he was about to spear.

'I trust your visit was satisfactory, sir.'

'I believe so, Gribbon. I believe so.'

'Is there anything you want doing, sir?'

'I don't think so. Not at the moment. Oh.' Dysart stopped, recollecting something that he had thought of on his way back to his office. 'Recall Digby Clayton. I may have need of his special talents.'

Gribbon nodded. Clayton was the best peepsman they had in their employ. He reached for a file that would inform him as to his whereabouts.

Dysart left the outer office and went into his room. The only natural light came in through a narrow window that gave onto a small yard which was surrounded on all sides by buildings, the dark paving clotted with moss and dusted with green mould. Dysart liked its air of desolate neglect: the way weeds and straggling trees grew up and died back again, struggling towards light that they could never attain.

He removed his wig and put it on its stand. He did not like to wear it when he was alone. He brushed a hand over his own cropped iron-grey hair and stared at the chart pinned to the panelling. His campaign map. Small symbols were scattered across it: from East to West, North to South. The largest number was clustered around the capital, but there were strong concentrations around other centres of population: Birmingham, Sheffield and Manchester as well as Norwich, Nottingham and the county towns. The map was marked up in a complicated system devised by Gribbon and showed different kinds of agents, as well as the groups and individuals who were being watched. Gribbon was a genius at this kind of thing. Gribbon was meticulous in his deviousness; a genius at every underhand thing. He'd introduced the pigeon post. Dysart was sceptical at first, but he had to admit that the system had much to recommend it, being both speedy and secret. There was not much Dysart kept from him. When the time came, he would receive the prominence he deserved. The time was not yet, but it was near.

Gribbon had added more symbols to the map, Girl, Hayseed, Lawyer, Highwayman. In time, there would be a spider's web of lines tracking their movements. He had thought for a while that the highwayman might be useful to him, having no personal loyalty to the others, as far a Dysart could see. Unfortunately, he knew from experience that highwaymen were a difficult group to penetrate. They could not be relied upon in any significant way. They *were* open to bribery. Everyone had their price and release from Newgate and the threat of the hangman's noose was a considerable incentive, but to hold them to the bargain was another matter. They operated alone, were loyal to no one and believed in nothing but themselves. The rogue in question, this *Captain* Jake Greenwood, seemed more capricious than most, but living outside the law made him the most vulnerable of those whom Dysart now saw as conspirators.

The theft of the wallet could not be allowed to disrupt Dysart's plans. The wallet had been returned, but that act in itself was suspicious. It had the whiff of conspiracy about it and Dysart did not like conspiracies, unless they were initiated by himself. This girl, this Sovay Middleton, had taken to the road disguised as a highwayman, behaviour that brought her under suspicion. Their recent meeting had only served to make her more suspect. She was not what she appeared to be and was obviously a skilled dissembler, but above that, she was a rogue card and he did not like rogue cards. If he was to succeed in this enterprise, nothing could be left to chance. Everyone involved in the theft of the wallet, everyone who knew anything about it, would be brought to Thursley for him to deal with at his leisure. To pick them off beforehand would attract attention. And afterwards? He would be in a position to do as he liked.

Thursley was his own domain. The vast building was situated a little way out of London and had been built on the site of an ancient abbey destroyed at the Reformation. He had incorporated the ruined remains into one of the wings. The rest had been built to reproduce the original, or rather, Sir Robert's idea of what that original should have been, complete with flying buttresses, tall arched windows filled with stained glass and tracery, and soaring towers bristling with pinnacles and gargoyles. The River Thames marked the southern boundary and a stone wall, nine foot high and six miles long, surrounded the rest of the estate.

An army could be secreted in the numerous wings and towers and the extensive undercroft provided secure accommodation for unwilling guests. The crypt was especially equipped for Sir Robert's purposes with ancient instruments of torture which he had collected from all over Europe. It was truly a joy to see those old pieces put to work again. Such fine workmanship. Some of them were centuries old, but so well built that they could be new. Seeing them in operation was like seeing times long past come back to life. A fascinating and most illuminating process.

Recently, he'd introduced something new to his collection: a guillotine, a scale model of the one used in Paris. He'd had a special well put in under the central stairs to obtain a sufficient drop so that the blade would efficiently sever the head from the neck. Sir Robert now used this to dispatch the bloody, broken bodies of his victims: informants who thought to double cross him, agents who fell down on the job or who were not up to the mark. That fat runner had already paid the price for his stupidity. The thickness of his neck had necessitated two drops of the blade. It was all scientific, he had explained to Gribbon. All to do with height, weight and momentum. Sir Robert had conducted his own experiments, if the height was not sufficient, if the blade was too light, then it was impossible to obtain clean severance.

The French had introduced Dr Guillotin's invention for reasons of equality, the blade having been for so long the preserve of the aristocracy, although they seemed to be the ones beneath it now, more often than not. Equality in death, as in everything else. Whatever their reason, it was an excellent form of execution, especially when large numbers were involved. Far preferable to hanging. He had recently had a quick-lime pit constructed deep in Thursley's well-wooded grounds to dispose of the headless corpses.

Reluctantly, he recollected himself from his pleasant reverie and looked at the chart before him: Girl, Hayseed, Lawyer, Highwayman, all under suspicion. And one other. He was interested to note that Gribbon had recently added a miniature Stars and Stripes.

CHAPTER 13

Sir Robert was true to his word. The next day found Lady Bingham settling her silks upon the sofa and patting Sovay's hand.

First, she enquired after 'poor, dear Harriet'. Then, before Sovay could answer, she went on to exclaim it all to be '*Such* a shame! With my darling Harriet so incommoded and your poor, poor mama . . .' She let the sentence trail into sadness, but almost immediately rallied. 'You lack a woman's guidance.' She cast a large, pale blue eye over Sovay. 'That is sure. How old are you, my dear?'

'Seventeen,' Sovay replied.

'Seventeen! Why! These days, that is practically an old maid! What is your father thinking? Keeping you buried down there in the country?' She eyed the book Sovay had been holding. 'You need to be taken out into society, and I believe I am the very woman to do it. Now, my dear, I have a list here . . .'

She went on to rattle through a litany of appropriate engagements that would keep Sovay busy from now until midsummer. Dinner parties, supper parties, soirées and tea parties at addresses in every fashionable part of London to be held by a dizzying array of society hostesses, all Lady Bingham's 'dear, dear friends'.

Sovay kept her eyes downcast and considered. She had been expecting a visit, certainly, but she had not expected to have her life taken over.

'Lady Bingham,' she began. 'You are very kind . . .'

'That's settled then!' Her visitor beamed. 'Now,' she regarded Sovay with a freshly critical eye, 'what about your clothes?'

'I have gowns enough,' Sovay countered.

'They will be last *season*,' she explained as if talking to a halfwit. 'And this is London! Provincial dress-makers –' She closed her eyes and shook her head, as if the idea was too terrible to contemplate. 'I will send my dressmaker round tomorrow. She's a French seamstress, absolutely marvellous. She's served all the leading French families, including the Queen herself. Now, let me see. What would you need?' She began counting items of dress off on the fingers of her hand. 'Day dresses, certainly. Evening attire suitable for several different occasions. It doesn't do to be seen wearing the same thing. Then hats, gloves . . . but that will take weeks!' Lady Bingham exclaimed. 'What am I thinking? Stand up, child,' she ordered. 'Let me look at you. You could be quite a beauty, given the right attention. No point in hiding it.' She turned Sovay this way and that. 'You are similar in height to my Charlotte. And she is slender. As like as two peas, I shouldn't wonder, and she has more dresses than she could wear in a year.'

'Oh, no!' Sovay's provincial wardrobe might be wanting, but this was too much. 'I couldn't wear another's cast-offs. Papa wouldn't like it.'

'Then he should equip his daughter better,' Lady Bingham said crisply. 'That is settled. Don't you worry.' The grip on Sovay's arm tightened. 'Madame Chantal can do wonders! And, of course,' Lady Bingham added, 'there is your visit to Thursley. Apart from your other engagements, you will want to look well for that, won't you?'

She had saved the real reason for her visit until the last.

'Of course, Lady Bingham,' Sovay replied. 'I'm very much looking forward to it. I wouldn't miss it for the world.'

'That's just as well, my dear. It is an occasion that cannot be missed.'

Her visitor's perpetual smile never slipped, but for a moment it seemed to set into something like gloating cruelty and the blue eyes were as cold and hard as chips of glass in that long, sallow face.

◆➤✦◀◆

Sovay scarcely had time to gather her wits when Lydia came in to announce the arrival of Virgil Barrett.

'It's one after another!' she exclaimed, her green eyes sparking with excitement. 'Not like Compton. Hardly time to catch your breath!'

Gabriel was with the American, which went some way to account for the light in Lydia's eye.

Once Lydia had gone, Sovay did not waste time on pleasantries. She was only too aware of their interrupted conversation of the day before and wanted to be told exactly what Mr Barrett knew about her father, but he could add little more to what he had told her already.

'So my father will be safe with Henry Fitzwilliam?'

'Well, not safe exactly,' Virgil Barrett replied, trying to choose his words. He did not want to alarm her but he was well aware that she was a young woman with unusual qualities, not least of which was honesty. She deserved no less from other people. 'Up until now, Fitzwilliam would have been a guarantee of safety. The French are interested in fermenting rebellion in Ireland, and he has been happy to help them, but just lately events in France have taken a considerable turn for the worse and it appears that no one is safe there. Arrests and executions increase day by day,' he paused, and took a moment to collect himself. 'Excuse me,' he cleared his throat. 'I did not mean to allow emotion to get the better of me. It's just that so many of us had such very high hopes. Now it appears that liberty is dead and the Revolution is turning to a tyranny of the few over the many.' He turned to Sovay, his light, grey-blue eyes magnified by sudden tears. 'I cannot give you comfort, or tell you not to worry, but I will do all I can to find out what has happened to your father, and to Hugh, you have my word upon it.'

'Thank you, Mr Barrett.' Sovay looked up at him, moved by the intensity of his feeling. 'I will take what consolation I can from that. I'm glad you are here. You, too, Gabriel.' She took Dysart's invitation from the mantelpiece. 'I have had a visitor and would welcome your advice on what I should do about this. I have been invited to Thursley Abbey.'

She gave them the card to examine.

'Well,' the American turned the invitation over and back again, 'I call this strange.'

'It is addressed to Sir John,' Gabriel observed.

'But he knows your father is in Paris.'

'Can you be certain?' Gabriel asked the American.

'He must do,' Virgil replied. 'He knows everything.'

'He does,' Sovay confirmed, 'or, at least, he implied

as much to me in the course of our conversation.'

'If he knows that, why did he invite Sovay?' Gabriel looked at the American, his face full of worry.

'I have no idea,' Virgil shrugged, 'but it won't be good.' He turned to Sovay. 'You disrupted his plans and he won't take kindly to that. Moreover, you might have forced him to move before he is ready. This meeting was planned for midsummer and it is well short of that.'

Sovay frowned. 'How do you know that?'

Barrett smiled and suddenly he looked like a mischievous boy. 'Because I'm a spy, Miss Sovay. Didn't you guess?' The levity left his face and he began to pace before the fire. 'It would be good to know what he plans, what he intends to do next . . .'

'Are you suggesting that I should go to Thursley?'

'Forgive me, no!' Barrett returned to her side. 'Nothing could be further from my mind. It would be *far* too dangerous.'

Sovay looked over to Gabriel. 'What would Father do? Or Hugh?'

'They would go, but . . .'

'They are men.' Sovay finished his sentence. 'If they would see it as their duty, then I see it as mine. Besides, I've already accepted.'

'Let's not decide hastily,' Virgil said to her. 'Things in London are moving quickly. Arrests here are accelerating, suspects being taken for questioning. Habeas corpus has been suspended. There is to be a meeting of protest at the Golden Globe in Cheapside, tomorrow at seven o'clock. We will see what happens there.' He took out his watch, the same one she had returned to him at Compton. 'I am meeting some of the organising committee and fear I'm late. I must leave, I'm afraid. Good afternoon, Miss Sovay.'

With that, he left. It was clear from further conversation with Gabriel that he was going to attend the meeting.

'In that case,' Sovay said. 'I will go with you.'

'You cannot,' Gabriel began, but Sovay stopped him.

'I can,' Sovay said quietly, 'and I will. Hugh would go in the blink of an eye, so would my father. At this very moment, they are braving who knows what horrors for what they believe. Do you think that it is just men who love liberty? Whatever they are prepared to do, so am I.'

CHAPTER 14

The next morning, Wallace, the butler, announced that there was a French person to see her. Madame Chantal appeared with a train of bearers behind her carrying armfuls of gowns. Sovay had almost forgotten that she was coming and was of a mind to send her away again. She didn't feel that she had time for such frivolity, but Lydia, whose eyes had widened to take in so much finery, persuaded her to let the woman stay.

'What harm is there in seeing what she has to show you?' Lydia was at her most wheedling. 'Who knows? It might take you out of yourself.'

Sovay relented. Perhaps it would be a diversion. After further cajoling, she even allowed Lydia to stay and help with the fitting, just as long as she held off exclaiming over every frill and trimming.

Madame was a small, busy little woman, dark-skinned and dark-eyed, with a brisk, forthright manner. She wore a dress of yellow-and-blue striped silk. Her hair was carefully coiffured, rising up in a high roll from a row of crisp curls which were arranged with careful precision across her smooth, white forehead. She was either wearing a wig, Sovay decided, or was using some kind of dye. No person's hair could be that shiny, or that black. Her face was expertly rouged and powdered, with two dark lines arching above eyes as bright as twin jet beads. Her English was good, if heavily accented, and she spent much time lamenting the terrible events that had forced her to flee her own country, follow her clientele to England and set up her shop: *Madame Chantal of Mayfair, Magazin des Modes* (formerly Mrs Hooper's), *modiste and milliner* (muff and tippet adopted by the princesses), in New Bond Street, Mayfair.

'It is terrible, mademoiselle. Very terrible. What is happening in my poor country,' she said. 'Le Roi. Tué. La Reigne. Tuée! Et tous les autres? Ils sont des monstres! Monstres vraiment.' She reverted to French as though her English could not support such outrage. 'In the old days, the Queen, the Court, her ladies. Such coiffures! Such headdresses! And at court! Les panniers.' She described a wide circle around herself. 'Comme ça! Et les robes! So rich, so magnificent. La belle mode. Now – all gone.' Madame brushed her cheek as if to wipe away a tear, whether for France, or the fashions, her customers, the old regime, or Queen Marie Antoinette herself, was not clear. Maybe all of them. 'No more beauty. No more elegance. Glass replace diamonds and every person look like every other person or . . .' She made an ominous gesture at the back of her neck that Sovay took to mean the guillotine. 'The women, they wear sacks, and the men with their hair chopped short.' She shuddered. 'And those terrible pantaloons!'

She liked it in London little better. The weather did not suit her. So cold, so damp. It affected her in the hands and business was bad.

'The English watch every *denier*. They do not like to spend money on how they look.'

'What about your French émigrés?' Sovay asked. 'Surely they are good customers?'

'Poof!' Madame Chantal made a dismissive gesture. 'They are here, but they have no money. I cut and recut but there is only so much you can do. There is nothing new! Before the Revolution, every year was different, every season! Here?' She gave a gesture of disgust, as though the right words had deserted her. 'The English have no idea of fashion.'

'But these dresses,' Sovay touched the fabric. 'They are very fine.'

For indeed they were. The dresses that hung in her dressing room waiting to be fitted were all of the latest fashion. Sovay could not help but admire the beauty of the decoration, the silver lace robings, the brocading on the polonaises, the delicate patterns woven into the silk.

'French weavers in Spitalfields!' Madame was triumphant. 'Do you think the English could produce something like that?'

The gowns were exquisite, but being fitted for dresses was something Sovay heartily hated. She loathed being measured and pinned, turned this way and that, prodded and poked about. It was one reason that she preferred to dress simply. Her indifference cracked, however, as she ran her hand over a gown of lustrous cotton, striped cream and madder, beautifully decorated with raised roses that combined both colours.

'Oh, miss!' Lydia exclaimed. 'That's lovely! It would suit you so.'

'C'est jolie, n'est pas?' Madame's eyes gleamed as she saw the girl seduced by the beauty of the fabric. 'And with your colouring!' She gestured perfection. 'We will start there, shall we?'

The fitting began in earnest and Madame's chatter was stopped by a mouthful of pins. This took longer than expected even with the help of a willing Lydia. Despite Lady Bingham's assertions, her Charlotte was somewhat shorter in the leg than Sovay and considerably broader. When Madame had finished, she stood back to survey her handiwork with a certain amount of cheek-blowing and huffing and puffing. The gowns would need *much* alteration. Madame sighed and threw up her busy little hands. Then she paced round Sovay, surveying her from every angle, as if she were a statue.

'Chère mademoiselle,' she said at last, 'with your colouring, you can wear anything, but I think plain colours suit you best. Madame Bingham's daughter, she loves the more elaborate styles which I think are not to your taste.' Sovay surveyed the ornate, embroidered brocades and nodded her agreement. 'So!' Madame clapped her little hands and her eyes sparkled like black sequins. 'Here is what I propose. I have some very fine silks of pure colour, scarlatine, turquoise, rose, jaune de primevère, vert d'émeraude, so beautiful, like les ailes d'ange woven from jewels. I have them from la couturière de Marie Antoinette herself. I would like to make a dress for you. Simple, mais élégante. Have I your permission?'

Sovay hesitated. Charlotte's wardrobe was not to her taste, Madame was right, apart from the possible exceptions of one or two items, and she found the thought of wearing another's cast-offs somewhat distasteful. She *would* like a dress made for her in the fabrics Madame described . . .

'If money is a concern . . .' Madame murmured

tactfully.

'Oh no,' Sovay shook her head. 'It is not that. I just wonder if there is time.' She explained about the visit to Thursley. 'I would need it quickly.'

Madame's face cleared; a big smile threatened to crack her carefully applied powder.

'Do not worry, chère mademoiselle. You will be la plus belle, vraiment. Trust in Madame Chantal.'

◆►◄◆

All the measuring and pinning put Sovay in mind of another project that she'd had in mind ever since she reached the London house. She sent Lydia off with Perkins, the butler's boy, to guide her. They were to go to her brother's tailors with instructions for him to prepare two suits of clothes, as well as shirts and boots and what have you; they were for a Mr James Middleton, cousin to Hugh. She sent measurements with her, for the young man was shorter than Hugh, with a slender build. The young man had been set upon on the road, all his luggage taken from him, and was badly in need of a new set of clothes. As an afterthought, just in case the house was being watched, she sent Lydia off dressed in her clothes.

It was quite a different Sovay who left the house at six o'clock that evening. She had raided her brother's wardrobe once again, picking out the plainest attire that she could find there, selecting brown jockey boots, fawn twill breeches, a brown broadcloth coat, and a plain waistcoat over a white linen shirt with a high collar and matching neck stock. She had plaited her hair back in a neat club secured by a black ribbon and had chosen a narrow-brimmed hat which she wore cocked over one eye. She liked the feeling of freedom Hugh's clothes gave her. She could go where she liked, do what she would and no one would know her. She smiled to herself as she left the house. Soon she would have clothes of her own.

Gabriel was waiting for her under a plane tree in the square. She tipped her hat to him and wished him 'Good evening'. It took him a second glance to recognise her.

He whistled to a waiting driver who trotted his horses forward. Sovay had to remember not to wait to be handed up into the carriage. She took hold of the sides and pulled herself in with Gabriel following.

'Golden Globe, Cheapside,' he shouted up to the driver, and they were away.

Neither of them noticed a small, dark man loitering nearby. If Sovay had thought to fool Digby Clayton, she was sadly mistaken. He'd seen the servant girl dressed in her mistress's finery and dismissed her; it took more than silks and fancy bonnets to fool old Digby. A young man comes out, when none had gone in, and a young man with something familiar about him. Never forgot a face, didn't Digby, but it wasn't just that. It was in the stance, the walk, lots of little details gave the cull away. Young lady of the house disguised as a man. That was a turn up, to be sure. He had heard the instruction to the driver and set off to follow. No need to go to the expense of a carriage, with the city streets so congested with people and traffic, he would probably arrive at the Golden Globe before they did.

CHAPTER 15

They arrived to scenes of confusion. A crowd of men and a few women were milling about on the narrow pavement outside the inn and spilling onto the road.

'What is the trouble?' Gabriel asked someone standing near.

'It's the innkeeper,' the bystander said. 'Stopped us from using the upstairs rooms for the meeting. Says it's illegal and he don't want his boozing ken shut down.'

'What shall we do?' Sovay asked. There was no sign of Virgil.

'Wait and see, like everyone else,' the man answered, thinking the question directed at him. 'Tom Hardy and Mr Adams have been arrested. No one seems to know what to do.'

'Mr Stanhope, ain't it?' A young man came up behind Gabriel, tapping him on the shoulder.

'And you are?' Gabriel turned.

'Algernon Skidmore at your service. My friends call me Algie. French it is. From me gran on me ma's side.' The young man was wearing a cutaway tailored coat in moss green over a matching waistcoat and dark breeches. He grinned at Gabriel's continued inability to place him. 'You was in with my governor, yesterday, along with Miss Middleton. Bit of all right, *she* is, if you get my meaning,' he added with a wink and a tap on the side of his nose.

'Oh, yes, of course. You're Mr Oldfield's clerk.' Gabriel hardly recognised the fashionable young fellow standing before him. He turned quickly to Sovay. 'May I introduce Mr James Middleton, the young lady's cousin.'

'Pleased to make your acquaintance, sir. What I said,' he added, slightly subdued, 'I meant nothing by it. No offence meant.'

'And none taken.' Sovay spoke as gruffly as she could.

'She's a handsome gal, that's all.'

'Indeed. Much admired.' Sovay looked away, willing herself not to blush.

'I'm sure she is. I was telling my friend Morris who works in an adjacent office . . .'

'What brings you here, Mr Skidmore?' Gabriel interjected, hoping to divert the direction of the conversation.

'I attend regular.' Skidmore nodded towards the milling crowd. 'Just to listen. I didn't have much by way of education and there's learned men here, reading and talking and entering into disputation. I like to hear them and what they say makes sense to me. Mr Oldfield don't know that I come to meetings,' he went on. 'And I'd be grateful if you didn't tell him. We don't see eye to eye on matters of a political nature.' He laughed. 'That we don't. I'm strongly of Mr Paine's persuasion, and he leans to Mr Burke. Not that he'd stop anyone from having his opinion and speaking about it. He wouldn't hold with this here commotion.'

'Why?' Sovay asked. 'Do you think the meeting has been deliberately disrupted?'

'No doubt about that! They've been trying to stop us for months. No, Mr Oldfield wouldn't hold with that. What we're doing ain't illegal, not yet anyways, and the law's all he cares about. He's a straight up and down sort of cove in that way and as good a lawyer as they come. The law's his religion, you might say. He don't hold with no one breaking it, whatever their stripe, or their position. No one's above it and no one's below it, that's what he says. The law's there to protect us from ourselves and it's there for everyone. Some things don't sit right with him. Like yesterday. You know them documents you and Miss Middleton brought round for his safekeeping?'

Gabriel nodded.

'Well, something about them got him all riled up. Not angry, you understand. That's not his way. But he weren't happy, he weren't happy at all. I know him, see? Working with him every day. He put all his other matters aside and we got plenty on at the moment. He shut himself in his room. Not to be disturbed. I could hear him pacing, a sure sign that things ain't right with him. Sent me off to the post and when I come in the next morning, he's there before me, the grate full of candles burnt down to stubs. I reckon he'd been there best part of the night. That's if he'd been home at all.'

Before Sovay had time to ask, or even wonder, what had disturbed Mr Oldfield so greatly, the crowd was on the move.

'Good evening.'

Gabriel bowed to the newcomer.

'Ah, Mr Barrett. May I introduce Mr Skidmore,' he said. 'Clerk to Mr Oldfield of Oldfield and Oldfield in the City of London. And this,' he turned to Sovay, 'is

Mr James Middleton.'

'Mr Middleton.' Virgil smiled and put out his hand. He gave no outward sign of knowing her true identity, although there was a hint of a smile in his blue-grey eyes. 'I don't believe I have had the pleasure. Virgil Barrett, at your service. We are about to move off.' He looked around at the crowd. 'They're going to hold the meeting in the open air at Fender's Field.'

'I have a message for Miss Middleton,' he said as they walked along. 'I have had word from France concerning her father and brother.'

'Are they safe?' Sovay asked in her normal voice, anxiety making her quite forget her male identity.

'I wish I could answer that.' He looked around. 'All I can say is that they are alive. Tell her to be patient. I will know more in a few days.'

His words thoroughly alarmed her, but the noise and press of the crowd about them in the narrow streets made further talk impossible as they followed the crowd towards Fender's Field. There were men and women of all classes and persuasion but most were of a middling sort: tradesmen, shopkeepers, printers, apothecaries, porters and warehousemen. The penniless, the starving, the beggars, scavengers and crossing sweepers had more to concern them than the reform of Parliament and universal suffrage. As the crowd surged through the streets, more joined them, some sporting the tricolour cockade of liberty. There was an air of excitement and expectation, a feeling of celebration, of jubilee. Well-wishers, sympathisers and the merely curious left their houses, some to stare, some to cheer, others to swell their number. They poured into Fender's Field from all directions to hear the opening address.

'Brothers and sisters,' the speaker began. 'Comrades and citizens . . .'

'That's John Baxter, the silversmith,' Skidmore whispered. 'He's chairman of the Corresponding Society. They ain't served a warrant on him yet.'

Sovay craned to get a better look. The man was hardly visible above the mass of people but immediately he spoke, the crowd around him grew quiet. The words he spoke were familiar: liberty, equality, brotherhood, the right of all, men and women alike, to a roof over their heads, food in their bellies, bread on the table. The crowd listened with rapt attention. He had a way of making each word, each idea, seem fresh minted, as though he were showering the crowd with immense wealth and riches to be spent in the new dawn of the coming day.

He reminded Sovay of her father. She wished he were present to hear this with her, with so many others, all of like mind. Tears sprang to her eyes as she imagined him nodding and smiling at each point the speaker was making. She could hear his voice whispering, 'Have I not said that very thing, my dear?'

'Ain't no shame in it, young sir.' Skidmore handed Sovay a handkerchief. 'First time I heard it, I bawled like a little child. Takes a lot of people that way.'

Sovay had been so transported by the orator's words that she had forgotten who was with her. Gabriel was still there, tall and solid by her side, although she had no idea of Virgil's whereabouts. The American had disappeared as quickly as he had arrived. She turned her attention back to the speaker.

The centre of the crowd and those at the front were

still listening with undivided attention, but unrest had begun to nibble at the margins. It ran through the crowd like fire through a dry cornfield, causing the speaker's voice to falter then stop. In the momentary silence, everyone heard it: the scrape and crash of boots on cobbles, the *chink*, *chink* of equipment, as armed men came at a run up the side streets that gave onto the open space.

The cry went up: 'Soldiers, soldiers!' and the conflagration broke out in earnest. Fury rippled through the crowd and men turned to fight the hated enemies of liberty who had dared to show their faces. The speaker bid the crowd be calm, stating that soldiers were brothers, but these were irregulars with no fraternal feeling.

A phalanx of runners and Government officers led the way, truncheons raised, beating a path through the crowd to arrest the leaders. Virgil saw them coming and slipped away. He looked for Sovay and Gabriel, but it was impossible to find anyone in the melee. Shots added further to the panic and obscured the scene in clouds of smoke.

Screams rang out above the echoing shouts and cries of the panicked crowd and all was chaos, all was confusion. The vast throng sought escape by any means, thrashing towards the streets that fed into the square, only to be forced back again. The front rank retreated, knocking into those pressing behind them. One person fell, then another, and soon people were tumbling over each other. Screams of panic turned to shrieks of agony until the weight of bodies silenced those crushed underneath.

Sovay was snatched from Gabriel's firm grip and

fought hard to keep her feet as she was borne along by the seething torrent of people swirling this way and that. Eventually, bruised and winded, she fetched up like flotsam in a doorway on the far side of the square. She clung onto the frame and shrank back against the wooden panels for fear of being swept off again. A man reeled past, hand clamped to his head, blood pouring from between his fingers. Faces blurred by, heedless and indifferent, each one intent on his or her own survival. She knew none of them. Gabriel, Skidmore and Virgil had all disappeared. Sovay was alone. She dare not venture out in search of them. Volunteers roamed about, using their rifle butts on the fleeing crowd. They cornered someone, brave or foolish enough to be wearing the *bonnet rouge*, the red cap of liberty, worn in France by supporters of the Revolution. Sovay turned her face away as he was thrown to the ground, surrounded by militia and beaten where he lay.

❧❦❧

Hobb's Alley ran down the side of Leggatt's Court and was decidedly busy with messengers coming and going. Some of them handed written notes to Mr Gribbon, others passed on verbal messages. He assessed each for its worth and paid, or not, according to his judgement. Rarely did he have to refer to Dysart to make this decision, although each report was conveyed to him almost as soon as it arrived.

Dysart sat in his offices, making notes in a ledger, as the slips of paper mounted. He allowed himself an icy smile. He was well pleased with the reports coming in from Fender's Field. The Committee of Secrecy would be perfectly satisfied with the action that he had taken to break up a dangerous assembly. He would have used grapeshot, like the Revolutionaries in Lyon, but unfortunately the nation was not quite ready for that. The Volunteers would have cowed them for the moment. Those who had seen fit to assemble were ordinary men for the most part, in meagre employment or a small way of business, with little between their present condition and want. The plague from France had spread among them. They had developed ideas above their station. That politics should be open to all. That every man should have a voice, a part to play in the destiny of the nation, the *right* to decide who ruled and who didn't, that all should be allowed to vote on this. He would teach them. He would disrupt their meetings, smash their premises, terminate their employment, destroy their few belongings, and hound them from one rented hovel to another, right down to the gutter and that would just be the beginning. He would have the leaders arrested. Habeas corpus had been suspended, so their stay in Newgate would be indefinite. While the husbands languished, what would happen to the wives, the children? Poverty and starvation. They deserved nothing less. It would teach them a necessary lesson. Only men of property could afford politics. So it had always been. So it would always be.

There was a knock on the door and Gribbon entered.

'Note, sir.'

Dysart barely looked up.

'Put it with the others.'

'From Digby Clayton. Sent a boy with it.'

Dysart's long arm shot out. He held his hand, palm up. 'Let me see.'

Gribbon handed him the small folded slip of paper.

Subject of interest. Will follow unless otherwise instructed.

Terse. As most of his notes were.

'Where did he post this from?'

Gribbon retired. There was a squeal as he twisted a child's ear.

'Fender's Field.'

Dysart folded the paper and put it with the others. Clayton had been set to watch the Middleton house. Specifically Miss Middleton. Dysart allowed himself a rare moment of excitement. What was she doing at Fender's Field?

❧

When Sovay looked out again, there was no sign of the man whom she'd seen being beaten so viciously. The crowd had taken their injured and wounded with them. Within minutes, the field was an empty expanse of trampled mud, flattened grass and dark-stained cobbles. Scattered about here and there lay remnants of the battle: a child's shoe, a man's scarf, a woman's kerchief, a rag of red which might have been what was left of the *bonnet rouge*.

Sovay set off with no sense of panic. The Volunteers had dispersed with the crowd. She was dressed as a young man, so would not attract that kind of unwanted attention and, although poor, the streets around appeared respectable enough. She did not know London well, nor was she sure exactly where she was in the city, but her sense of direction had not deserted her. She knew that she was north of the river, for the simple reason that at no point had they crossed that expanse of water. She also knew they had travelled east, which meant that she must go west into the setting sun.

The street she took away from the square was deserted: shops boarded, windows shuttered, doors locked and bolted against the recent disturbances. The evening sun slanting through the crooked roof tops cast long shadows and threw an odd amber glow over everything. Suspended motes of dust floated in the fingers of light and seemed to be the very embodiment of the heavy hanging silence. It was as if the sudden outburst of violence had exhausted the air, allowing no movement there.

Digby Clayton allowed his subject a bit of a head start before setting off in pursuit. He had taken up a position on the margins, so he could keep an eye on the crowd and pick out chosen targets. He had assigned different men with a nod of the head to Stanhope and the American. This one was his, and his alone. After so many years, he rarely felt even a hint of excitement, but this one was different. His interest had been pricked right from the first sighting on the steps of the house in Soho.

❧

It took Sovay some time to realise that she was being followed, but she had good hearing and picked up the faint sound of footsteps behind her as she walked down the deserted streets. When she looked round, she saw no one, but as soon as she started off again, the footsteps fell in with her. At first, she thought that her mind had become overwrought by the scenes that she had just witnessed and that the footsteps were a figment of her imagination but no, when she increased her pace, the footsteps followed, when she slowed, so did they. The life in the streets increased as she moved away from Fender's Field, but still she sensed the presence of someone behind her. She was used to being in field and wood, picking up and interpreting every small noise when out hunting with Gabriel or Hugh. The sounds here were different: a voice raised in anger, the crying of a baby, the wailing of a child, the crack of a whip, the whinny of a horse, the creak of a passing cart, but the situation was not so very dissimilar. The difference lay in the fact that she was not stalking deer, or hare, or pheasant. This time she was the quarry.

<hr>

Digby Clayton paused, looking up and down the street. Target had given him the slip. Must have dodged up an alley just at a bend in the street. Digby was not far behind, but the narrow entrance was out of his line of vision. By the time he'd got there, the subject had disappeared. He cursed himself for not seeing it coming, not anticipating. He looked about him. This was not the best of neighbourhoods. The alley fed into a warren of dingy passageways and stinking courts. A remnant of the old city. A tongue of poverty that extended between the neat squares, wide streets and shops and houses for the wealthy. Clayton peered down the noisome alley piled with unnamed filth and rubbish. He pushed himself off the wall. Better get after the party, and quick, before all the light was gone. It would be dark as a cave soon in between those rookeries and a young 'gent' was a prime cull to be knocked over and end up in the gutter with a slit throat.

❖➤◄❖

Sovay realised her mistake almost immediately, but could not retrace her footsteps for fear of encountering her pursuer. She was forced to go on, picking her way through the piles of ordure. The decaying tenements were close together and little of the already fading light penetrated here. The buildings were in poor repair, the brickwork crumbled in bright red gashes against a dark patina of soot. Some were patched with planks nailed over jagged cracks and props set at angles to stave off imminent collapse. The wooden panels of the doors had rotted into jagged holes and the windows were empty of glass, covered in tar paper or open to the elements. From darkened doorways, huddled children watched her passing. Barefoot and ragged, they stared, huge eyes in filthy faces. Some held shapeless bundles that might have been babies. Some held the infant out to her, but most were too listless even to beg.

Sovay turned a corner and a young woman approached and asked through a gust of gin fumes if the young gentleman would like company. It was the coquetry of desperation. She seemed little older than the children in the doorways, her dress a ragged cobweb with hardly enough substance to hide her nakedness.

Sovay dug in her waistcoat for a coin and hurried on, hoping to escape, but others were appearing like phantoms, all with the same desperate pleading behind the casual question, all with the same grey, pinched faces, like aged fairies. Sovay felt tears springing to see that some had added the odd, brave, wisp of colour, a red scarf, a yellow ribbon, to the uniform drabness of the rags that they wore. She remembered the milkmaid she'd encountered on her way to London and wondered how many of these had come fresh-faced from the country, looking to make their way. How many had arrived ruined already? Forced to make a living in the only way left to them, seduced and deserted by someone like James Gilmore.

She took a turn to the left, hoping to avoid further advances, to find streets that she knew, or gain some sort of safety in wider, more populated thoroughfares. She had dressed as plainly as her brother's wardrobe allowed, but she was as conspicuous on these streets as if she were wearing court dress and decked out in silk and velvet. The little light that remained was fast disappearing and predatory eyes seemed to be watching from every doorway, every corner. She had no weapons about her and knew that she was unlikely to fare well in any attack upon her person.

They caught her just as Sovay thought she was safe. Down a side street, she glimpsed a wide thoroughfare, where well-dressed people walked and there was the noise of traffic and carriages. With a sigh of relief, Sovay turned and hurried towards what she thought was sanctuary. Alerted by some deep warning instinct, she was just quick enough to dodge the blow that would certainly have crushed her skull. The cudgel struck her just behind her right ear, sheering through the scalp and glancing off the bone.

She fell, insensible. The robber caught her, dragged her into the alley where he had been lurking and began searching through her clothing with quick, expert fingers.

'Well, I'll be,' a grin spread across his broad coarse features and he passed his hands over her body a second time, just to make sure.

'What you found?' His mate who was acting as lookout twisted round to stare at the sprawled body. 'Anything interesting?'

'You might say so, Coddy, my lad. You might say so.'

'Valuable, like.'

'Could be. To the right person.' Her attacker hauled Sovay up by her arms as though she had no more weight than a child and threw her over his brawny shoulder, balancing there like a bundle of kindling. 'Could well be.'

◆━✕━◆

Digby Clayton watched them disappear down the alley, all the while making notes in his head for the report he would write for Dysart as soon as he returned to his lodgings in Whitefriars. It wasn't his place to interfere. His job was to observe and report, nothing more. The fate of the party did not concern him. Maybe the two were resurrection men. In that case the unfortunate young 'gentleman' was destined for nearby St Bart's, where the doctors would appreciate a fresh, warm corpse, no questions asked. He turned and walked away, shoulders hunched, hands buried in his pockets, already thinking of the pie he would purchase for his supper, along with the pint of porter that was waiting for him at the Black Lion.

CHAPTER 16

Sovay was not destined for the anatomist's table. She was delivered, still insensible, to Mother Pierce's establishment in Chandois Street, Covent Garden.

'I don't know, Mr Slevin.' Mother Pierce scratched under her violent red wig and crushed whatever she found there under her fingernail. 'Ain't exactly in my line of business, if you take my meaning.'

'Must be worth summat, Mrs P!' Slevin's broad bull-dog brow furrowed further. 'She's uncommon good-looking.' He moved her head to show the less bloody side of her face. 'Look at that. Skin like a peach. And most likely a virgin. You can charge top bit for that.'

Mrs Pierce sighed. 'In the ordinary way of things, that would be true, Mr Slevin, but my clients are gentlemen of a certain bent, or ain't you noticed?'

'Mollies, I know that, but this one ain't yer regular Judy. Don't you ever get no women? I know there are such . . .'

'I don't like that term being used about my clientele, Mr Slevin.' Mother Pierce pursed her withered lips. 'And no. No women. Leastways, I ain't seen 'em. This 'ere is an exclusively male establishment.'

'Whichever road,' Slevin conceded. 'There's got to be push in it somewhere, like I said.'

Mother Pierce held Sovay's face by the chin. 'A looker, that I'll grant you, once we clean off the blood and such. Tell you what I'll do, Mr Slevin. On account of me being a fair woman. I'll get in touch with my sister establishment, Mother Marples' in Maiden Lane. She's in a more regular way of business and, as you say, may well pay top coin for one such as this 'ere.' Mother Pierce considered. The girl might, indeed, be worth a pretty penny. Her looks and breeding could be enough to make her the toast of the sporting young gents. At the very least, Mother Marples would be able to sell her over and over again, as a fresh young thing, until, of course, her freshness was spoilt. 'If Ma Marples agrees, I'll split with you.'

'Half?'

Mother Pierce shook her head. 'A third and that's my last offer. Look at the trouble I'll be taking, got to get her cleaned up and dressed right. You could take her yerself,' she added, 'but with her in this state, I doubt you'd get the price.'

Slevin considered. 'You're a hard woman, Mrs P.'

Mother Pierce laughed, releasing a gust of foul breath and showing her uneven stubs of teeth. 'Known for it. Proud of it. How else can a lady like myself make her way in this wicked world?'

Slevin shook her hand and left, still grumbling, although he knew he'd made a good bargain. If anyone could get top tin, it would be Mrs P.

'Now, now,' Mother Pierce clapped her hands at the boys who had gathered around, 'show's over. Back to your places.'

The boys drifted off. It was still early, before the theatres emptied; business was slack, but it did not do to cross old Ma Pierce.

One of them remained behind.

'You still 'ere?' Mother Pierce scowled at him. 'Out

of my sight or I'll get a switch to you.'

'I know her, Ma,' he said. 'The Captain brung her in, t'other day, don't you remember? We give her some clothes.'

'I do recall . . .' Mrs Pierce rubbed her chin and gave the matter some thought. Gin had a habit of making things a bit hazy, and she'd had a good drop lately, but now it was coming back. 'And here she is again, similarly attired. Well, well. Never thought to see her again, never mind hauled in by Mr Slevin like a sack of coal. There's a queerness, here, no doubt. And I'm still owed for them clothes.'

'She's a friend of the Captain's,' Toby went on, hoping to save Sovay from whatever fate Ma Pierce had lined up for her. 'He wouldn't like it if anything were to happen to her.'

'What's that to me?' Mother Pierce eyed him suspiciously.

'I mean, maybe you hadn't ought to sell her on, like.'

Her scowl did not bode well. 'I'll thank you not to listen in on private conversations. And what I do, or don't do by way of business ain't got nothing to do with him, or you, Master Toby White.'

'I know, I know.' Toby thought fast. Time to try a different line of attack. 'But the Captain brings in top-notch swag. If he finds out, he might go elsewhere with the make.'

Mother Pierce was a fence as well as a brothel keeper. She considered this for a moment, before rejecting it for the money the girl would bring.

'He's welcome to try it. I'm the best and he knows it.'

'She's from a good family!' Toby was getting desperate. 'Likely, she'll be missed.'

'So what? Got knocked over and disappeared. Won't be the first, will she? Won't be the last. Didn't want it to happen, she should've stayed at home respectable, not gone wandering the streets dressed as a toff! And who's going to miss her? Sneaked out for a bit of adventure, that's my thinking. I'll wager her family don't even know she's gone. No, Toby, my lad, plead all you like, I've made my decision. She's destined for Rosie Marples'. If you're so interested,' she clipped him across the ear, 'you get her cleaned up.'

She waddled off to the little room she called her *boudoir* for much needed refreshment. She pulled the stopper out of the gin bottle and closed the door.

Toby looked around for help.

'Give us a hand, Georgie,' he called to a boy who had just come in still dressed in his street clothes.

They took her between them, supporting her up the stairs.

'Do us a favour,' he whispered as they helped her into a room and dropped her onto a bed. 'Find the Captain. He'll likely be at the Cross, opposite St Martin's. There's coin in it if you find him.'

'What about Ma?'

'She's in her room with Mother Gin for company.' Toby winced in sympathy as he turned Sovay's head gently to look at the wound behind her ear. 'Ask Jack to come here while you're at it. Tell him to bring a needle and thread.'

When Georgie had gone, Toby fetched a clean towel, poured water from the pitcher and began to wash away the sticky streaks of black blood that had dried onto her face. He then turned her head, parted her hair gently and began to bathe the wound. He worked slowly and carefully, not wanting her to wake up just yet. There was a nasty gash, long and jagged and still seeping blood. It would need stitching. Jack had been 'prenticed to a surgeon apothecary before he came here. He was a far better doctor than the ancient brandy-soaked quack Ma Pierce employed to check over her charges. Toby had never seen that one sober and his hand shook so hard he couldn't even thread a needle. Jack would know what to do.

Sovay woke thinking that she was still dreaming. Specifically, the nightmare that she'd experienced a few nights ago. The surroundings were the same, as were the faces looking down at her, but when she turned her head, surely the pain was sharp enough to wake her? The realisation came more slowly than physical sensation. She was not dreaming. Somehow, she was back in this place again. Alarmed, Sovay tried to sit up but immediately felt weak, sick and light-headed. She fell back onto the rough linen towel that covered the pillow. Her stomach heaved and her head ached abominably. She tentatively put a hand up to her ear. Her hair was wet, the skin behind her ear felt strangely rucked and pleated. When she took her fingers away they bore faint traces of blood.

One of the faces she recognised as Toby, the other was a stranger. A dark boy with flawless skin, his face freckled as a speckled hen's egg, his high cheek bones accentuated by sweeping lines of rouge; long thick lashes fringing undeniably beautiful violet-blue eyes outlined with kohl. They both wore female attire of flimsy, shiny material, low cut and deeply cinched at the waist.

'Steady,' the dark boy laughed down at her. His accent sounded Irish. 'You've had a bit of a clout. Likely, you'll be feeling a bit muddle-headed. Nasty gash there, but I sewed it up, clean as a whistle. It'll scar, no doubt, but ye've got enough hair t'cover it. Ye'll have a bump the size of a duck's egg, but that'll soon go down.'

Sovay tried to rise again, but the boy pushed her gently back onto the bed.

'Rest now,' he said. 'Recover your strength.'

'I'll square it with Ma Pierce,' Toby leaned over her, his face full of concern. 'I've sent for the Captain at his usual place, the Golden Cross. He should be here soon. It's only a step away at Charing Cross. He'll help get you out of here.'

'Greenwood? No!' The stitches tugged as she shook her head. 'I don't trust him. He has betrayed me already. To . . . to an enemy.'

'Oh, no!' Toby was shocked that she would think such a thing. 'He wouldn't do that. Not the Captain. He wouldn't peach on anyone. He's a gentleman. I mean a real one. He was a captain in the army. Cashiered, he was, for something he didn't do.'

'That's what he told you.'

'And I believe him. I met a few liars in my time, Miss Sovay, more than a few, and he ain't one of them.' There were voices, noise from downstairs. 'It's getting busier. I better go, or Ma Pierce'll be livid. You stay here and rest a while. I'll make sure no one disturbs you and I'll look in when I can.'

When Sovay woke the second time, it was dark in the room. For a second or two, she didn't know where she was. The door was open a crack, letting in enough light for her to see the gaudy drapes, the peeling mirrors, the screen in the corner hiding the washstand and chamber pot. She turned her eyes away from the indecent images on the wall and tried to block her nostrils to the pervading reek of male sweat and cheap perfume. She had to get out of here. She sat up slowly, feeling a little less faint this time. She swung her legs over the side of the bed, and waited a few more moments before attempting to stand. Using the bedpost as a prop, she hauled herself upright and took a few steps before her knees buckled under her.

She was caught by strong arms and a voice she knew said, 'Steady now!'

She held onto him for a moment longer and Captain Greenwood smiled as he helped her back to the bed.

'I have to get out of here!'

'All in good time. How do you come to *be* here, I'm intrigued to know.'

'I – I can't quite remember. I was at a meeting that broke up in fighting. I became separated from my friends. I must have been trying to get home when I was set upon.'

'You were at Fender's Field? I heard there had been trouble.'

'Yes, and I must get home.'

'You would do well to wait until you are recovered a little.'

'I cannot stay a moment longer in this dreadful place!'

'In time, as I say!' He sat down and grinned at her. 'You should be grateful. If it wasn't for Mother Pierce, you would be locked up in some trull's parlour, waiting for the highest bidder. And it's cost me a pretty penny, I can tell you.'

'So I must be grateful to you, too?'

'Now, Sovay. I thought we were friends.'

'How can I be friends with one such as you?'

'If not friends, then at least compadres. Fellow gentlemen of the road.'

Sovay scowled and winced; scowling hurt her head. 'If you *were* any kind of gentleman, you would get me out of this place. Immediately.'

'All in good time, like I say. We will wait until you are feeling a little stronger and the coast is clear.' He leaned forward, his handsome face sincere. 'Why this hostility? Pray tell me.'

'You betrayed me to Dysart.'

'I did no such thing!' The Captain was indignant. 'I would never betray a friend. Never! And after what we went through together, I did consider us to be friends.' He attempted a look of grave sincerity, but his teasing nature got the better of him. 'I am most disappointed that you should not feel the same way. As I recall, our parting was most cordial.'

Sovay blushed to be reminded. 'Well, someone did,' she said to change the subject. On balance, she considered his protests to be genuine. Toby had said that he would not betray her and there was something about the boy's artlessness that she trusted. But who could it have been if not Greenwood?

'How do you know that someone betrayed you?' he asked.

'My house was burgled. They were searching for the wallet.'

'Well, it wasn't me. You will have to look for

someone else. You were not exactly discreet, were you? Half the county knew you were riding about dressed as a highwayman.'

'That is not true,' Sovay objected. 'Anyway, hardly anyone knew about the wallet.'

There was a knock and Toby came in.

'Getting busy,' he said. 'Ma P will be wanting the room. You'll have to leave soon.'

There were shadows outside. A voice, high-pitched and rather slurred, enquired, 'What about in there?' Another answered, 'That one's taken.'

'I know that voice,' Sovay said.

'It's Jack,' Toby replied, 'the lad who stitched your head.'

'Not him, the other.'

Toby put his eye to a crack in the door.

'That's Mr Fitzwilliam. He's a regular. He's a . . .' he caught a warning look from Greenwood, 'but you don't want to know that. How do you know him?'

'He's a friend of my brother's. And,' they both looked at her, expectant, 'he was there when I was showing Gabriel the papers. Not in the room, but he could have overheard us.'

'There's your peacher,' Greenwood said, trying not to sound too vindicated. 'He's thick with Dysart.'

'How do you know?'

'I've seen them together. Here – and other places.'

'Dysart comes here?'

'Not in that way, no,' he grinned. 'The good lady is one of his sources. Ask Toby.'

'Tall cove,' Toby described him. 'Dressed always in black. Quiet voice. Looks like he'd have you hanged for breathing the same air as he does? Yes, he has a look round, seeing who's in, then disappears with Ma to her boudoir.'

'It's a useful arrangement, advantageous to both parties. She keeps him supplied with information. In return,' Greenwood rubbed his fingers together, 'he keeps her supplied with money. We better get on our way.' He turned to Toby. 'Have a scout, there's a good fellow, and get some proper togs on while you're about it. You're coming with us.'

'What about Ma?'

'Tell her I'm hiring your services for the evening.' The highwayman dug into his pocket. 'Give her this and tell her it's private business. I would take it ill, if it is disclosed.'

When the boy had gone, he turned to Sovay. 'Now how are you feeling?'

'A little better.'

'Have a swig of this.'

'What is it?'

'Brandy. Cognac. Smuggled from France. Very best quality. From the cellar of some sacked chateau, I have no doubt.'

Sovay shook her head but the Captain ignored her. He removed the cork with his teeth and handed her the bottle.

'Sorry I haven't got a glass, m'lady. Now, drink!'

Sovay was too weak to argue. She did as he instructed and felt the silk smooth liquor spread through her, raising her spirit and bringing strength back to her limbs.

'That's enough!' The Captain reclaimed the bottle from her. 'This is strong stuff.' He took a nip himself, then stowed the bottle in his pocket.

'Why do we need Toby?'

'Because he's the best cracksman in the business. His father was a locksmith, did you know that? He can break into anywhere, or out. Do you have a key?'

She shook her head.

'Thought not. How else are we going to get you into your house? Now, hold on to me.'

He reached down to help her to stand.

'I can manage, thank you,' she said, and immediately fell back, dizzy. He put his arm round her and pulled her to her feet.

'That's it. Steady! Are you sure you are all right?'

'Never better.' She managed a weak smile.

'More lilies than roses this time,' his fingers stroked her cheek. 'You are as white as linen.'

His touch threatened to take what strength she had left from her. She held onto the back of a chair.

'I can walk without help once the dizziness goes.'

'I'm sure you can,' Greenwood said, surprised at her abrupt rebuff. 'But the stairs are steep and you might break your neck trying. Is my touch really so loathsome?'

'I did not mean that . . .' She took a step to the door and her knees buckled. 'Perhaps I do need your help.'

He put his arms around her and supported her down the stairs. Anyone seeing them would assume that she'd had too much to drink. It happened here, as everywhere, and would provoke no comment. Toby met them in the street, perfectly respectably dressed now in his ordinary clothes.

The Captain hailed a chair, paid the men and instructed them to go to Soho Square.

'Toby will come with you,' he said. 'And see you

safe into the house. Go well, Sovay.'

With that, he was gone. The chair moved off with a strange, lurching motion which made Sovay feel sick. To take her mind off it, she asked Toby about his father.

'He was a locksmith. He tried to stay honest, but it ain't so easy in that line of business,' he told her. 'Draws cracksmen like a magnet draws filed iron. Anyways, he was caught and transported. My ma ended up in the Fleet and us kids on the street. I look after 'em. Still do. I'm the oldest, see? I was small and quick and I'd learnt a thing or two in the shop, so Mr Slevin found me useful.' He paused, wondering whether to confide in her. In his short life, he'd learnt to trust very few. 'When I've got enough to go 'prentice, I'll learn the trade proper.' He paused, wondering whether to confide. 'I like making things, seeing how they work.'

'But how will you resist falling into crime, like your father?'

'I'm intending to take a boat to America, when I've finished my time,' the boy answered. 'I'm thinking there's more chance to be an honest man there.'

'What about your brothers and sisters?'

'I'll take 'em with me. That way we all get a fresh start,' he said with a smile, but the bleak look in his blue eyes suggested that he knew it to be a dream, an impossibility.

Sovay wished him luck and hoped that his ambition was beyond just fantasy. Anything to get him out of Mother Pierce's clutches and her den of vileness. She thought of Dysart's money in Turnbull's vaults and an idea came to her that eased her heart and even served to soothe the ache in her head. But that would have to wait for tomorrow. Now, all she wanted was to find her own bed. The pain in her head was getting worse with every step the chairmen took. She could hardly see for it. Her arms and legs felt as though they were made of cotton. The events of the day were fast overtaking her, threatening to engulf her in a big black shadow. She must have drowsed for the next thing she knew, Toby's hand was touching her shoulder.

'Are you all right, miss? Only we're nearly there.'

Sovay swallowed and nodded, really fearful now that she would vomit. Luckily, at that moment, the chairmen set her down.

'You stay here,' Toby said, leaning her against the railings by the front door of her house. 'I won't be a minute.'

He untied a cloth roll containing a set of twirls, his name for skeleton keys, and other types of tools, selected a pair of long, needle-nosed pliers and disappeared down the stairs to the basement. In what seemed like seconds he was opening the door to her.

'Tell whoever it is that locks up to throw the bolts on the area door and take the key out of the lock.'

Sovay thanked him and asked him to come and see her tomorrow.

'Where? At this house?' Toby was hard put to hide his surprise.

'Of course, at the house.' Sovay gave him a tired smile. 'Where else?'

The boy agreed, then melted into the night. Sovay was left in the black and silver silence of the moonlit square, staring into the dappled shadows under the great plane trees. It was as if she'd been dumped on her own doorstep by the fairy folk. It could have been a dream. Only the clothes she was wearing and the throbbing of her head served as reminders that the night's events had really happened.

She closed the door carefully, locked it, removed the key and eased the bolts across. She was careful to make no noise, although the servants would have all gone to bed. She had told Lydia not to wait up, Wallace had the night off and was visiting his brother and Mrs Crombie slept like the dead. It was a good thing Sovay did not require a full staff. When her father was at home, there was a hall footman in attendance at all times.

In the safety of her room, she stripped off her brother's clothes. Besmirched as they were with blood and mud, she could hardly put them back into his wardrobe. She would bundle them up and have them given to one of the beggars who were ever at the back door in search of scraps and cast-offs. In the future, if there were to be any more of these excursions, she would be wearing her own set of clothes. She put on her nightdress and climbed into bed. She badly wanted a bath and to wash the matted blood from her hair, but did not want to wake the house. It would have to wait until morning.

◆➤◀◆

Mother Pierce sat in her private parlour counting her gold, all the while scheming. His Nabs had expressed an interest in the good Captain, and she would be sure that he got his information. Threaten her indeed! Who did he think he was? Try and buy her off? It would take more gold than *he* could offer. Getting too big for his boots, that one. Ideas above his station. She'd taken his money and she'd have him took and get more for her trouble. High tobies were as common as crows on the heaths they infested. She had no patience with their pretensions. She'd bring him down, that she would. By the time he found out who'd peached on him, he'd be swinging at Newgate.

CHAPTER 17

Sovay hardly had time to bathe and dress before there was a violent hammering on the door.

'There's a boy downstairs,' Mrs Crombie announced, much put out. 'I told him you weren't in a state to receive visitors, but he said he had to see you urgently.'

Sovay hurried downstairs, thinking to see Toby, but it was Skidmore she found when she came down, wearing out the carpet with his pacing. His dark curls stood out about his head and his appearance was considerably dishevelled. He was nothing like the dapper young fellow that she had seen the day before. His stockings were muddied and wrinkled, his coat was torn with buttons missing and what looked like dried blood stained the front of his shirt. There was a cut on his cheek and his hands were swollen, the knuckles bruised and bleeding. No wonder he had alarmed Mrs Crombie.

'Skidmore?' Sovay called from the stairs. 'What ever is the matter?'

He turned and the look in his eyes alarmed her further. There was wildness there and a deep, burning anger. His colour was high, his dark skin flushed as if he was gripped by a fever.

'It's Gabriel,' he said. 'He's been hurt bad. You better come, Miss Sovay.'

'Where is he?' she asked. 'What's happened?'

'He was in a fight. In Clerkenwell. Where I live. We

went there after we left Fender's Field.'

Skidmore was about to say more, but Sovay interrupted him. It was impossible to know who was listening.

'You can tell me about it presently. I'll order the carriage.'

'Gabriel told me who you were, miss,' Skidmore said when they were settled inside. 'He had to, he was that alarmed when we lost sight of you in the chaos and confusion. We searched and searched, but when we could find no sign, he came back with me to my lodgings in Clerkenwell. I have a room there in Dick Chapman's house, he's a printer and engraver. We arrived to find the place in turmoil. Dick's wife and children crying in the street. Ruffians were smashing up his print shop. Others of 'em were up and down the street, busting up houses, throwing people out on the road. Women and children. It was a cowardly stroke. They knew most of the men would be at Fender's Field.' He gave a mirthless laugh. 'Didn't reckon on us coming back so quick. We saw the fellows off, or so we thought, but a whole mob of them came back in the middle of the night. Bent on destruction, they were. And thorough. They smashed up the workshops and houses, dragged stock, machinery, furniture, everything into the street, making bonfires of what they couldn't carry off. They didn't care, threw an old lady down the stairs. Tipped a pregnant woman out of bed. There was a big fight but this time we got the worst of it. Gabriel got badly beaten, kicked insensible. He hadn't come out of it when I left this morning.

'As if that weren't enough, this morning a couple of

runners appeared, sharp at nine o'clock, and pounced on Mr Chapman. They accused him of printing seditious material and helping to publicise an unlawful assembly. Marched him off to the magistrate. They had pamphlets stolen from his workshop the night before as evidence. Mr Oldfield's down there now, trying to get him out.'

Sovay listened gravely to Skidmore's headlong account. What had happened had affected him deeply, and when they entered Vine Street, with its small brick-built houses, she saw for herself the source of his distress. The bonfires were still smouldering. Charred chairs and tables, beds and bedding, had been raked out but much of it looked beyond saving. Women clustered in doorways, wiping their eyes on their aprons, silent children clinging to them, while the men stood about, as rigid and wooden-faced as puppets, all their livelihoods gone up in smoke. Some did not even have a place to live any more; their dwellings were burnt-out shells.

Yet these people had cared for Gabriel, even paid for a doctor to attend him. It was not smoke from the fires that made Sovay's eyes sting as she entered the house where he lay. Mrs Chapman, a tall, slender dark-haired woman with a delicate face, took her to him. She was followed closely by a couple of pretty flaxen-haired children who looked up at Sovay with huge blue eyes and would not leave their mother's side.

'He's come round a bit, miss,' Mrs Chapman said, 'and he's taken some water.'

Gabriel's head was bandaged, his left eye swollen shut. Sovay ordered the coachman to put him in the carriage.

'We will not trespass on your hospitality any longer,' she told Mrs Chapman. 'You have enough troubles. Is there any news of your husband? Mr Skidmore told me that he had been arrested.'

Mrs Chapman shook her head. 'Not yet, although we are hopeful. Algie has great faith in his Mr Oldfield.'

Sovay nodded. 'He is a good man.'

Mrs Chapman would not accept any payment, even for the doctor's fee.

'All I can do is thank you, then, for your care of Gabriel.' Sovay held out her hand. 'Mr Skidmore knows where to find me if there is anything that I can do.'

Back at Soho Square, Sovay had Gabriel carried up to his room and sent for the doctor to attend him. The doctor gave him a careful examination but declared his colleague had done a good job and there was little more that he could do.

'He's a strong young man,' he pronounced. 'And there is nothing broken. Rest is the best cure for him. Leave him to sleep and when he wakes, give him strong beef tea. I'll leave drops for any pain he may have.'

Gabriel didn't wake until late afternoon. Sovay checked on him every half-hour until told not to do so by Mrs Crombie.

'He'll wake in his good time,' she said. 'You heard what the doctor said. He doesn't need you fidgeting in and out disturbing his rest. Lydia has volunteered to stay with him,' Mrs Crombie sniffed, not quite approving, although the girl's concern was genuine enough. 'She can sit here with some sewing. She'll let you know if there is any change.'

Sovay came back later to find him sitting up in bed sipping beef tea, the cup tiny in his big hands.

'Gabriel! Are you all right?' Sovay went over to the bedside. 'You gave us quite a fright.'

'I might have been hurt in my body, Sovay,' he smiled at her, 'but I've been salved in mind and spirit. I've been talking with Skidmore and Chapman and their circle of friends. I've never heard men talk more sense. They spoke of nothing new. I've heard the same ideas and views expressed at Compton. Hugh has talked to me for hours and I've always admired his strength of belief, his passion, but listening to these men was different. They spoke to the very heart of me, Sovay.' He put his cup down and clasped his hands in front of him. 'They are ordinary men. Like me.' He paused. 'I am not of your class, and never will be, do not aspire to be. I just want to live in equality. Your family can vote, can stand for Parliament if they want to, because they own land and property. Why can it not be the same for me?'

I cannot vote, Sovay thought to point out, although she didn't want to tax his strength further by debating with him now. Women were little short of slaves, no matter how privileged. If she married, all her wealth, all her property, everything she had would belong to her husband, down to her very person. Votes or no, Gabriel was still a man.

'Such basic liberties are denied to me as well, and all of my gender, no matter how rich and landed,' she said quietly. 'We have that much in common.'

'That is true,' Gabriel conceded. 'There is much that

is wrong with the world and it will be a great struggle to redress it.' He looked at Sovay. 'I have not the words to explain well, but it is as though I have been walking blindfolded, never noticing anything but where my feet were planted. Now, the bandage has been taken from my eyes. For the first time, I can see clear.

'I know that some would think me well placed. Your father is a kind master and a fair one. I have an education thanks to him, and I am grateful, but I've always felt betwixt and between. I count you and Hugh as my friends . . .'

'I hope you do!' Sovay reached for his hand on the covers, wanting him to know that it would always be so.

'But we can never be equals, not as things stand at the moment. A steward is in a strange position, above the servants and the labourers, but not of the house. We own no land and have no prospect of ever owning any. We always have to work for others. I'm determined to make my own way. Be my own man. I will not be going back when this is over. My father is still relatively young. He can manage very well without me. So can Compton.'

He sat back, exhausted, his piece said. Lydia, who had been listening with quiet attention, looked stricken, and for once, Sovay could think of nothing to say. His words had shocked her, shaken a complacency that she had not even realised existed within her. She had never heard him speak at such length before, or with such passion. Indeed, she experienced a stab of envy for the fire that had ignited within him and burned with such a pure flame.

She would miss him cruelly, so would everyone at Compton, including her father and brother, but to object, to seek to dissuade him would sound childish, petulant, or worse, would sound as though they had some kind of claim upon him and that he had a duty to remain. It would not do to act the chatelaine.

'What will you do?' she asked.

'I don't know yet. I want to travel about the country. Spread the message of liberty. I can turn my hand to many things, blacksmithing and wheel-wrighting, working with animals, working on the land. All I know is, I cannot go on as before, watching from the side, blocking my ears and eyes, stopping the channels to my heart at what is going on around me, at what is happening to my fellow man. But,' he smiled, 'that is for the future. For now, I intend to stay here to see this thing out.'

'I'd never stop you from leaving us, Gabriel, or try to dissuade you from doing other than your heart dictates, but I have to say,' she smiled back at him, 'I'm mighty relieved that you do not intend to go on the tramp quite yet.'

From her place by the window, Lydia nodded her agreement with vigour. She did not want him to leave either. Her dreams for the future did not include traipsing about the country like a tinker's drab.

◆➤✖◆

That evening Mrs Crombie announced the arrival of Mr Oldfield and his clerk. The lawyer came in, Skidmore behind him carrying files. Sovay showed them into her father's study. They had come straight from the magistrate's court in Bow Street. Oldfield's first words were to enquire after Gabriel, but he hardly listened to the answer. He seemed distracted, his mouth set grim in his pale face, his eyes ringed with tension and fatigue.

Sovay sent Wallace upstairs to tell Gabriel that the lawyer and his clerk were here. Wallace returned to say that Mr Stanhope insisted on coming down to meet them. He wanted to know what had happened to his friends. Much against Mrs Crombie's advice, he was helped down the stairs by Wallace and Perkins with Lydia bringing up the rear with a pillow and blanket. He was settled on the chaise longue with a cover about him, his face quiet and composed, his cheeks as pale as the bandages binding the wounds to his head.

'These were not isolated acts.' Oldfield tapped the files. 'These are not isolated cases. They were coordinated from a central point. The attack on the meeting, the rampage of the Volunteers, the arrests. None of this was coincidence. The list of those taken by the runners, Skidmore!' His clerk handed him a document from the bundle he carried. 'Those named are moderate men, reasonable voices. The hotheads were left alone. It is all part of a scheme.' He turned to his clerk. 'If one removes the damper from a fire, Skidmore, what will happen?'

'The fire will flare up, sir,' the boy replied. 'It will rage out of control.'

'Exactly!' Oldfield said and smiled at his clerk. He turned to Gabriel.

'Your friend, Chapman, is safe for the moment. I had him released on a detail. The runners sent to arrest him seized the wrong matter. Instead of pamphlets full of incendiary material written to incite the nation to revolution, they took away self-improvement tracts and advice on home economy. He might not be so lucky a second time. The officers will be better prepared the next time they come knocking at his door. Others were not so fortunate. The case against them will likely not stand up at trial, but the way things are, they may be imprisoned for months, even years, before they see the inside of a court.'

'I thought there were laws against people being held without trial?' Gabriel interjected.

'Indeed there are. Or were. The writ of habeas corpus has been suspended. A new law enacted. Prisoners can be held without trial for an indefinite period. I detect a plan in this, a pattern.' He used the furniture on the desk to demonstrate, moving them like men on a chessboard. 'If the moderate leaders are removed,' he took away the pen holders and laid out a row of steel nibs on the blotter, 'then their more revolutionary brethren will come to the fore and take to the streets, demanding the release of their comrades and threatening general insurrection. Against them, loyalists will be set.' He took more steel pens and arranged them in opposition. 'The same pattern will happen all over the country, one group set against another. If both groups are armed, paid for by Dysart, then . . .'

He toppled a bottle of carmine ink, drenching his improvised armies. The stain spread out across the blotting paper, surrounding them in a great ragged circle of red.

'Dysart is funding *both* sides?' Sovay asked.

'Oh, yes. I divined that from the contents of the wallet that,' he hesitated, 'came into your possession. That is why he was so anxious to get it back. I thought at first that it was because his agents might become known, but no. His concern is that this greater plot might be exposed.'

'Surely he cannot think that this plot will work?' Sovay shook her head, unable to believe such madness.

'Oh, he does. And it is clever, fiendishly so. He is not to be underestimated. He has crafted something that works with a devilish logic, and once it is put into operation, it will be very difficult to stop. The ensuing violence will eventually be quelled by troops loyal to Dysart and his party. Dysart is not acting alone. He heads a group, a cabal of already powerful men, all hungry for even more power. They will stage a coup d'état and rule the country much as Robespierre and his Committee of Public Safety are doing in France. They will be able to do as they wish, curing the nation's ills with copious bloodletting, I've no doubt. A White Terror will be upon us.'

'What about His Majesty?' Skidmore asked.

'What about him? Who knows when his madness will return? He will be confined, whatever his state of mind. His son will be declared Regent with Dysart pulling the strings. If he proves unsatisfactory to his purpose, then Dysart will get rid of him. There is a precedent. France is not the first nation to kill its king.' He turned to Sovay. 'Tell me, Miss Middleton, has Dysart been in contact with you?'

'Why, yes. He called to give me this.' She showed him her invitation to Thursley. 'He said it was for my father, but insisted that I should come in lieu of him.'

'Did he, indeed?' Oldfield studied the black-rimmed invitation, with its heavy, gothic lettering. He walked about, brushing the edge against his chin, as he put his thoughts in order. Then he turned to Sovay. 'The time has come for us to act. Dysart and I are old acquaintances; we were students together at Ingolstadt. I have also received an invitation. The date is nearly upon us.' He looked from Sovay to Skidmore and Gabriel. 'If we are to save our friends and prevent the entire nation descending into bloody revolution and savage suppression, I feel that we must go to Thursley.'

Before Oldfield left, Sovay asked if she could see him on a matter of private business.

'Certainly,' he nodded to Skidmore to wait for him in the hall.

When they were alone, he turned to Sovay. 'It is only fair to warn you, if you go to Thursley you may be in very great danger. You are perfectly at liberty to refuse the invitation. Dysart does not welcome interference and will certainly strike at any who he perceives to be his enemy. His chosen method is to destroy all who might have any knowledge, however peripheral.' He described concentric circles on the desk. 'And you are at the centre of the web.'

'I understand that,' Sovay replied to him. 'I am not stupid. But if Dysart succeeds, who will protect Gabriel's friends? Who will defend their liberty?' Sovay straightened her shoulders. 'I will meet such danger when I come to it.'

'I do not doubt it,' the lawyer smiled at her. 'Skidmore has told me a little of your exploits of last night.' He waved a hand to quell her protest and dispel any anger she might feel towards his clerk. 'Do not be angry with him. He did not mean to betray you, he was mortified to think that he had, but I know how to unearth secrets. I would not be worth my salt as a lawyer if I did not. He admires you greatly, Miss Sovay.' His smile grew broader. 'It is a wonder your ears were not burning. Now what is this business?'

The business Sovay wished to discuss with him was regarding the money that she'd found in the wallet. The money belonged to Dysart, but she was determined that it should not be returned to him. Ever. Nevertheless, the money had been stolen. Moral scruple prevented her from spending it on herself, but she saw no reason why she could not spend it on others.

'I have a sum of money,' she began to explain. 'Deposited at Turnbull's Bank, in my name. I want you to arrange to put it to particular purposes.'

She sat down at the desk, removed the ruined blotter, took a fresh sheet of paper from her father's drawer, dipped his pen in the inkwell and began to write.

To Master Toby White, to be found at Mistress Pierce's establishment in Chandois Street, Covent Garden, the sum of £100, to pay for his apprenticeship to a reputable locksmith and to pay also for his passage to America.

To Mr Algernon Skidmore of Vine Street, Clerkenwell, the sum of £100 to pay for his articles to the firm of Oldfield & Oldfield, and to meet any other expenses he might incur.

The residue to be given to Mr Gabriel Stanhope to disperse as he sees fit.

She blotted the ink and handed the paper to Oldfield who studied it carefully.

'Generous.' He nodded. 'Very generous. Money well spent on Skidmore, he will make a fine solicitor. Now, this other, Mr White . . . This establishment, ah, if I'm not mistaken, it's a –'

'I know very well what it is, Mr Oldfield.' Sovay looked up at him, her steel-blue eyes clouding to thunder grey. 'Do not seek to interfere. I want to save the boy from a life of criminality and vice, because I think he is worth saving.'

'Certainly, of course.' Oldfield was at his most conciliatory. He had not seen her angry before. 'I will make the arrangements immediately, rest assured. I will . . .'

As Oldfield talked on about escrow and fiduciary duty, Sovay sat back in her father's chair and stared at Dysart's invitation lying on the desk before her. She ran her fingers over the embossed script and tried to dismiss the uncomfortable feeling creeping through her that she was putting her affairs in order, as people do when they think that they are going to die.

'A lad came for you, while you were with Mr Oldfield,' Mrs Crombie said after seeing the lawyer out. 'He's downstairs in the kitchen. Said he weren't hungry, but he looked half-starved to me. I told Lydia to give him a few slices of beef and a mug of ale.'

Toby stood up when Sovay came in, wiping his

mouth with the back of his hand.

'Toby!' After the events of the day, she had quite forgotten that she had asked him to call on her. 'I'm glad to see Lydia has taken care of you. If you have finished, perhaps you would like to accompany me to my father's study. We can talk there.'

'Very well, miss. That were very nice, miss, missus,' he smiled and bobbed his head to Lydia and Mrs Crombie. 'My thanks to you.'

Sovay led the way to the study and closed the door, eager to tell him about her plans for him. To get his agreement.

'I want you to find a good master,' she told him. 'A locksmith, an honest one, and have yourself apprenticed.'

'But I ain't got near enough money for that!'

'I will give you the money,' Sovay said, 'but you have to promise me something.'

'Oh, what's that?'

'That you won't go back to Ma Pierce.'

'I got to, miss. What will I do for tin?'

'I'll give you money, I just told you. I have made arrangements to that effect with my lawyer, Mr Oldfield. All you have to do is present yourself at his offices in Carter Lane. Do you know where that is?'

'Yes, miss. Off Ludgate Hill, just down from St Paul's.'

'Very well. If you go there, he will make the necessary arrangements and release a sum of money to you, for expenses and so on. When you need more, you just apply to him and he will give it to you.'

Sovay sat back, thinking that she had explained it very well. Toby looked at her. He could not help but be sceptical. He had never trusted anyone in his life and was not about to start now. It wasn't Sovay, as such. She was well-meaning and good-hearted, he didn't doubt that, but like as not she'd get bored with all this nannicking, or she'd take fright and go back to country life and old Tobe would be left with nothing. He didn't see anyone handing the darby over on his say so, especially not a lawyer. He'd promise, of course he would, but he had no intention of leaving Ma just yet.

'Have you had any word of Captain Greenwood?' Sovay asked, as she rose to show Toby out.

The question was casual, but Toby wondered if she was sweet on him. She wouldn't be the only one. Devil for the ladies was the Captain. He was counted a special friend by every innkeeper's daughter from here to Bristol.

'Not since he left us. Probably out on the pad,' he replied. 'He better watch hisself when he comes back.'

'Oh, why's that?'

'Ma's got it in for him. She's a terrible one for a grudge is Ma, or sometimes it's just pure spite.' In fact, Ma had taken against Sovay as well, but Toby judged it best not to tell her that. Sovay was beyond Ma's power and couldn't be harmed by her, but the Captain was a different matter. 'You know that tall, thin cove, dresses in black, you and the Captain was talking about?'

'Sir Robert Dysart?'

'That's him. There's something funny going on between him and Ma. He was in earlier and when he left, Ma was mighty pleased with herself. She asked after the health of my *friend*, as she put it, meaning the Captain. "Tolerable well when I last I saw him" is what I said. To which she replied, "Well, he ain't goin' to be for long." She had a nasty little gleam in her eye and went off cackling. She intends to peach on him just as soon as he's back in town.'

What could Dysart want with the Captain? Sovay thought as Mrs Crombie showed Toby out. Would they all be caught in a web of Dysart's weaving as Oldfield implied? Was there no escaping, for anyone?

CHAPTER 18

The next morning, as Sovay was at her dressing table, Lydia came in to announce that a quantity of boxes had been delivered.

'From Madame Chantal. Oh, Miss, I can't wait to see what's inside!'

Sovay smiled. 'I think that is what I'm supposed to say.'

'Shall I tell Mr Wallace and the boy to bring them up?'

Lydia ran off down the stairs, without waiting for an answer. Wallace and Perkins duly arrived, the boy hardly visible behind an assortment of pale green boxes, all of different sizes, edged with gold and inscribed in elegant black lettering:

Madame Chantal of Mayfair
Magazin des Modes

They laid the boxes on the bed, Lydia desperate to view the contents that were so carefully wrapped in fine tissue paper.

Sovay allowed her to open the boxes and throw back the filmy wrappings. Madame had certainly been busy. There were day dresses, evening dresses, robes à la française and robes à l'anglaise, jackets and caracao, shirts and petticoats, clothes for every occasion. Indeed, a whole wardrobe. Sovay refused

Lydia's entreaties to try things on. Instead each item was to be unpacked and hung in the clothes press. The last box was empty, Lydia stepped back.

'Oh,' she exclaimed. 'Why should that be? There's just this.'

She handed a note to Sovay.

Dear Mademoiselle,

I have not forgotten. Your special gown will be ready. Never fear!
Your friend,

Hortense Chantal

'Special gown?' Lydia frowned. 'What's that, Miss Sovay?'

'What it says. Something Madame is making especially. For a weekend party I am attending.' Sovay kept her tone vague and distant. She did not really want to talk to Lydia about it. The invitation made her feel odd. Excited, but at the same time apprehensive. Slightly queasy in the stomach. She thought that this must be what a soldier felt going off to war, or a sailor to sea. 'Now, fetch the clothes I'm to wear today.'

Lydia did not move. 'You said nothing about this party. Does Mrs Crombie know?'

'I haven't told her, no.'

'You'll need a maid if it's a grand affair.'

'Not necessarily. I'm accompanying Lady Bingham. If I need someone, I'll use whoever she brings with her. Now get my clothes, there's a good girl.'

Lydia stared at her mistress, her green eyes shiny with hurt and an anger she had to suppress. 'You're

201

ashamed, that's it, isn't it?' She looked away, finally. 'Ashamed to have a maid who is just a country girl.'

'Nothing could be further from my mind! Why on earth would I think that?' Sovay smiled and put her hand out to Lydia. 'I'm a country girl myself.' She had not asked Lydia to accompany her, in case something happened to put her in danger, but she did not like to see her upset like this, or to be misunderstood by her. When the time came, she would find a way of putting her off. 'If it means that much to you, of course you can come with me. I will welcome the company.'

Somewhat mollified, Lydia brought Sovay her day gown and began hanging the new clothes.

The bell downstairs sounded. As if summoned by some black art, Lady Bingham's servant had come by to leave her card. Wallace reappeared. Sovay took the card from him. Lady Bingham would be calling on her at three o'clock that afternoon.

❧

Lady Bingham was determined to introduce Sovay into London Society, beginning with a visit to Lady Kilderry and then an evening party at Lady Sarah Jersey's residence at 38 Berkeley Square.

The former was not so onerous. Once the ladies had patted her hand, grown momentarily tearful at the memory of her mother and enquired after the health of 'poor, dear Harriet', they more or less ignored her and carried on with their own concerns, gossiping about people Sovay neither knew, nor cared about. Often their voices fell to murmured exchanges, whispered confidences and delighted exclamations that excluded her entirely. All Sovay had to do was remember to nod and smile when called upon to do so. The other young women present offered nothing and seemed entirely uninteresting, sitting with eyes downcast, paying close attention to their mamas, so they would know how to behave when they were married ladies. Her mind roamed away from the inconsequential chit-chat around her and she wondered what she was doing here.

There was still no news of her father and brother. She had not seen Virgil Barrett since Fender's Field and he had sent no word despite his promise. And then there was the Captain. She knew that she should not be experiencing any concern about him. If anyone here even suspected an acquaintance, she would find herself outside the door of polite society. But who knew what would have happened to her without his help? She was beholden to him, and did not like to think of him getting into difficulties on account of her. The life he led was dangerous enough. He could look after himself, she was sure of that, but she would have liked some news of him. She could not go herself to find news of him, but perhaps she could send Gabriel. She dismissed the idea. He was much recovered, more or less his old self, but he would ask too many questions and she did not want him to know about her escapades in Covent Garden. Besides, she could not imagine him at Ma Pierce's. She smiled to think of it. There was always Oldfield. If Toby had been in touch . . .

'I'm glad you find our gathering amusing.' Suddenly Lady Bingham was beside her, making her start. 'Lady Kilderry thinks you most charming, if a little shy. She would like you to come to her again next Thursday, so put it in your diary. Now, we must be going if we are to be ready for this evening.'

Between tea party and soirée, Sovay found time to write a note to Mr Oldfield to ask if Toby had been to see him. After she had folded, addressed, sealed the letter and sent Wallace's boy to the nearest receiving house, she felt very much better.

Her lift of mood did not last. The evening party was somewhat more of an ordeal than her visit to Lady Kilderry. Since Lady Bingham had discovered that Sovay had no current attachment, she was introduced to a succession of young men, fops and fools to a man. They paid her extravagant attention, indulging in frivolous banter and elaborate flirtation until Sovay's face ached from the constant smiling and her brain sickened from so much confection. No one seemed capable of serious conversation. Such a thing would probably be frowned upon anyway, as exceeding the bounds of etiquette.

This did not mean that the underlying purpose of these occasions was not serious. Far from it. Every look, every word and gesture was regarded. Everybody was watching everybody else. Lady Bingham glided through it all, like a pike through the reeds. Sovay was not the only young lady in whom her mentor took an interest. She began to wonder if the lady took a commission. What difference was there between her and Mother Pierce? It was all about money, just like the street and the brothel. Girls on the look out for rich husbands, wealthy older women on the look out for attractive young lovers. Men keen to oblige for the promise of a fortune, through marriage or patronage. Later in the evening, the disappointed among the gentlemen, or those not concerned with the marriage market, would begin to make their excuses and slip away. Sovay knew where they were going. This was the time when business picked up at Mother Pierce's and Rosie Marples', on the streets of Covent Garden. It was the whores who got the blame, who faced prison or transportation, but who was really to answer for it? Where would the whores be without their clients?

'Why the sour expression?' a voice said close to her. 'Anyone would think that you were not enjoying yourself.'

Sovay looked up to find Virgil Barrett smiling down at her. She strove hard to hide her surprise. For some reason, she hadn't expected to see him at one of these gatherings. He looked so fine that she hardly recognised him with his powdered hair and beautiful burgundy brocade jacket. His velvet breeches were a matching colour and his pale green silk waistcoat was embellished with tiny flower motifs, the front edges very prettily done with gold purl embroidery, gleaming sequins and floral ribbon.

'I can play the man of fashion as well as any here.' He smiled at her scrutiny. 'Or perhaps you are surprised to see that I move in such circles?' He looked around at the assembled company. 'They regard me as something of an oddity. An American cousin. Many here believe that our independence is just a passing phase.' His mouth twisted in irony. 'That we will soon see the error of our ways and return to the bosom of the mother country and our father, the King. A belief that I encourage. There are many here who interest me.'

Sovay followed his gaze. Marriage broking was not the only business being carried on here. Around the margins of the room little knots of men stood in quiet conversation, a word here, a word there and patronage was withheld or granted, fortunes made or lost.

It was a game of high stakes and Virgil pointed out the major players. Members of Parliament, members of the Government.

'Your friend Dysart is talking to Mr Burke. Mr Pitt himself is expected later, so I believe. There is much to concern them at the moment.'

'I was expecting word from you,' Sovay's look was accusing. 'After Fender's Field. Where did you go?'

'I was called away on urgent business. Let us take a turn around the room, shall we?'

'You are quite a man of mystery,' Sovay smiled, 'with your sudden comings and goings.'

'That is because of my occupation.' He smiled at her. 'Now I see you don't know whether to believe or trust me.'

'Why should I?' Sovay shrugged. 'Whenever people might have need of you, that's when you choose to disappear.'

'I'm stung by that, Miss Sovay,' Barrett strove to look hurt. 'Perhaps you will be less angry if I tell you that my business was in Dover.' He continued in a light tone, as if they were exchanging nothing more than banter or gossip. 'No need to say anything. Dysart is watching us. It would not be good for him to know that we are anything more than casually acquainted. Concern for your father and brother was one of my reasons for going. Whatever you may think,

I have been working hard on your behalf.' Sovay's spirits lightened at the prospect of real news after so long and she wanted to question him further, but he gave her a look of warning. 'You will know more, very shortly. I may have a surprise for you, but you must have patience. It is too dangerous to speak here.'

Just then, they were called into supper. They were seated at opposite ends of the table, so there was no further opportunity to speak with him. At the end of the meal, Sovay retired with the ladies and by the time the gentlemen joined them, Virgil had disappeared again.

'We seem to have lost your admirer.'

Sovay willed herself not to start at Dysart's voice in her ear.

'Admirer?' She turned to face him.

'The American. Barrett.'

'I'd hardly call him an admirer,' Sovay answered.

'He is one of many.'

'How gallant of you to say so, Sir Robert, but as it is our first acquaintance, I fear that it is too early to include him in their company.'

'Indeed,' Dysart smiled, but the look he gave her said, *I know better!*

He looked away from her, his opaque eyes resting on this or that person in the company. When he looked back, he was laughing as if at some inner jest that only he could hear. *There can be no escape from me*, he seemed to be saying, *I know everything about everybody here.*

'If you will excuse me.' Sovay moved away from him. With all she now knew, she found his presence disturbing. She did not want to give herself away to him and was beset with the uncomfortable feeling that he could look into people's minds. 'Lady Bingham beckons. She does not like to stay too late.'

'A moment more.' He nodded towards the lady who immediately turned away. 'She will not mind waiting. You see? She has already found someone else. I'm so glad you have made her acquaintance. She has grown very fond of you in this short time. There can be no excuse for you not to come to Thursley now. Indeed, I would be *very* disappointed if you do not. I am very particular about who I invite to Thursley. Let us walk, shall we? Do you know the Secretary at War?' A gentleman bowed to her, she bowed back. 'The war goes well – for us,' Dysart said as they moved on. 'But in consequence Paris grows ever more dangerous for any Englishmen mad enough to be caught there.' She looked at him, gauging his reasons for telling her this. 'The French grow every day more ruthless. They send friend and foe alike to Mme Guillotine, no matter how aged or infirm.' He shook his head. 'They are inhuman in their fixity of purpose. Even their erstwhile friends, the Americans, are suspect now. Tell me, Miss Middleton, what do you think?'

He looked at her, inviting a response and any trace of pleasantry in his flinty grey eyes had been replaced by thoroughgoing menace. The hint was oblique, he had not spoken it straight out, but there was a warning in the positioning of one subject against another. *Come to Thursley*, he seemed to be saying, *or it will be worse for your father and brother and do not look for help from Virgil Barrett.*

'About what?'

'About the war with France. That is what we were discussing, is it not?'

'Politics do not interest me and my knowledge is slight, so I have no opinion upon it, Sir Robert.' She looked back at him. He knew she was lying but she did not care. She was tired of being played upon and jerked about like a puppet. She would have liked to tell him that there was no need to threaten her. She would be at Thursley, and not because she was afraid of what he would do to her, or her family. 'I'm very much looking forward to my visit,' she said, changing the conversation back to the original topic. 'Your house sounds most impressive. I will be there.' She met his gaze, unflinching. 'Never fear.'

'There is none to equal it in England.' Lady Bingham had come to join them and had overheard Sovay's last remarks 'Is that not so, Sir Robert? You will see a wonder, my dear.'

'Modesty prevents me from agreeing, my dear lady.' He bowed to the newcomer. 'Miss Middleton must judge for herself. Now if you will excuse me,' he added and with one last bow he was gone from them.

On the carriage ride home, Lady Bingham talked of little else except Thursley. Everything was to be marvelled at, from the height of the tower (three hundred feet) to the amount it had cost (four hundred thousand pounds and still not finished). Sovay wearied of hearing about the exact dimensions of the place: the entrance door that was thirty feet tall, the length from north to south equalled Westminster Abbey.

'It has an oratory, galleries, libraries, cloisters and cabinets,' Lady Bingham counted rooms off on her fingers. 'I don't think I've explored it all, and every room crammed with the most fabulous riches from all over the world.'

Lady Bingham looked expectantly at Sovay, waiting for her comment.

'I've never desired to live in a cathedral, or anywhere so grand or large,' Sovay said at last. 'I'm sure it is full of wonders, but Thursley does not sound such a comfortable place to me.'

They continued the rest of the journey in silence, each looking out of their separate window. Lady Bingham noted the crowds had thinned with the approach of evening. The town looked so much better with fewer people about, she thought, and was just going to remark as much to Sovay, but the girl had that sullen look about her. Sulky little thing, not much of a companion, that was certain. Lady Bingham wouldn't be sorry when this was over and the girl was delivered to Thursley. What happened after that was none of her concern.

CHAPTER 19

By the time they arrived back at Sovay's door, any pretence of cordiality between them had nearly broken. Sovay did not mean to be discourteous but she found Lady Bingham's company exhausting. On the surface, everything was relentlessly trivial but beneath Sovay sensed deep waters. Even ordinary conversation felt as though they were engaged in an elaborate cotillion to which she had to guess the steps and putting a foot wrong would spell disaster.

Sovay stripped off her gloves and removed her wisp of a headdress, ready to hand them to Mrs Crombie, her mind still on Lady Bingham.

'Oh, Miss Sovay!'

The housekeeper stayed by her, gloves and headdress crushed in her hand. She was hovering somewhere between tears and mirth, excess emotion fairly vibrating through her. It was so unlike her that Sovay felt immediate alarm.

'Mrs Crombie, what is it? Whatever is the matter?'

'In your father's study. He arrived not an hour since. So thin . . . Like a skeleton . . .'

Sovay failed to hear the rest of her words. She ran down the hallway, threw open the doors of her father's study and hurled herself into the arms of her brother.

He seemed all bone and skin, she could feel his ribs through his coat, but he was strong enough to lift her off her feet and whirl her round as he always did when he was back from school. When he finally released her, they looked at each other both too filled with emotion to speak. Sovay was so glad to see him that she could not find words for it. Anyway, she could not think of what to say. His appearance surprised her greatly. He was rake thin, his clothes were hanging off him, but what he was wearing was even more shocking. He wore the dress of a French patriot: a long riding coat over a plain white shirt open at the collar. He wore the *pantaleons* of the *sans-culottes* and black boots turned down. His hair was cropped short into a gold cap of curls, like those of a young Greek god, or Roman hero.

'At least I left off my *tricolour* and *bonnet rouge*,' he said, smiling at her reaction.

'Good that you did.' Sovay shuddered at what could have happened, recalling the man she'd seen beaten in the street.

'You must forgive me appearing as a *citoyen*. I did not think it would trouble you so. I left Paris in a hurry in what I stood up in.'

'Why did you go there? I've been so worried . . .' Sovay felt tears threatening again.

'Shush.' Hugh took her in his arms again, much as he used to comfort his little sister when she had fallen over and grazed her knee. Finally, he held her away from him and looked at her. 'I'm here now, aren't I?'

'Yes, you are here now. But why on earth did you not tell anyone?'

She looked at him, her large eyes magnified by tears. Hugh could never decide between blue or grey. Storm clouds or summer's day?

'I went because I wanted to be part of the greatest event to happen in our time, perhaps any time,' he answered. 'I had to be there. I had to see for myself. I acted partly on impulse. I could not tell father, he would have tried to dissuade me and I did not want to quarrel with him. I never dreamt that he would come after me.' He sighed. 'That is my only regret.'

'Do you know where he is?'

'He is in hiding. In a village outside Paris. He is safe there.'

'For how long?' Sovay remembered Dysart's veiled warning. She could hardly contain her agitation or her anger with Hugh. He was standing there, safe and sound, while who knew what was happening to her father. Her relief at seeing him was over. She turned on her brother, accusing. 'How could you have left him there?'

'It is difficult for him to travel,' Hugh's shoulders slumped, and Sovay was immediately sorry for her anger. 'The English are *interdit* and liable to immediate arrest as spies or enemies of the Republic. I have papers, thanks to M Fernand, and can pass as a *citoyen* but Father might as well have the Union flag emblazoned on his forehead. He got to Paris with Henry Fitzwilliam, who is a familiar presence there. The French want to ferment rebellion in Ireland, so he should have been safe with him, but the situation grows ever more volatile. Circumstances change day by day, sometimes hour by hour. What is safe one day will get you guillotined the next. We thought it better for him to be out of Paris. We were set to leave together, across country to a port in Normandy, from there by a smuggler's vessel to the south coast. But . . .'

He hesitated, aware of the effect his words might have on his sister. 'He is not well, Sovay.'

'What is the matter?'

'Congestion round the heart is what the doctor we found for him diagnosed. He ordered absolute rest as the only cure and I fear that difficult travel, beset about by constant danger, then a long sea journey might have been too much for him.'

'How could you leave him like that?' Sovay shook her head. 'I still don't understand.'

'He begged me to go. He is safe enough where he is. Some areas, even close to the capital, remain almost untouched by the work of the Revolutionary Committees and the Tribunal who orchestrate *la Terreur*.'

'That still does not answer my question. How could you have left him and saved yourself?' Sovay turned away. Her anger surged back and threatened to overwhelm her.

'Do not be angry with him.' A quiet voice came from the shadows at the side of the room. 'He came at my request. He didn't want to leave your father. I had to persuade him.'

Sovay recognised the soft tones and measured cadence of the American, Virgil Barrett. She had been so transported by seeing Hugh again, that she had not stopped to think that another might be there.

'You said you had a surprise for me.' Sovay turned away, embarrassed at his presence.

'Virgil told us about Dysart's plans, about this gathering at Thursley,' Hugh said. 'That he has invited you to be there. Sovay, you do not realise the danger that puts you in –'

'That is no reason for you to leave Father!' This

time her anger included them both. 'I do not need you to come and rescue me like a distressed damsel in a fable.'

'That may or may not be so.' Hugh took her hand. 'But saving you from your impetuous nature is only part of the reason. As soon as Father heard of this, he insisted I come back and go with you. He would not hear of you facing such danger alone. I came with his full sanction. Dysart plans to plunge the country into a chaos at least as bloody as anything that is happening in France. Father wants us to stop him.' He picked up the invitation. 'This will be no ordinary house party. It will mark the beginning of a coup d'état, unless we can stop it. This is an invitation to our family. Fortunately, you are no longer the sole representative. I have the right to attend on another count. As I understand it, Thursley will be hosting a meeting of the Illuminati.'

Sovay had never heard of them. 'Who, or what, are they?'

'It's a secret society. It was started in Ingolstadt in Bavaria and has since spread all over Europe. I am initiate, through Fitzwilliam in Oxford, and I've attended a brother group, Les Cordeliers, in France where M Fernand was a founder.'

'I am also a member,' Virgil spoke. 'I belong to a lodge in Portsmouth, Virginia, which numbers Thomas Jefferson among its members.'

'You belong to the same society as Dysart!' Sovay looked from one to the other in horror, not knowing whether she could trust her own brother any more.

'It is not how it seems!' Virgil put his hands up to placate her. 'Most lodges are harmless, like the Masons.

They are simply places where like-minded men can meet together and share in the pursuit of knowledge and enlightenment through reading and discussion. Some lodges, however, have become corrupted, little more than dens of depraved libertines. Others have used their secrecy to cloak their sinister intentions and the ruthless pursuit of power. I fear that Dysart's Lodge may combine both evil aspects.'

'Why he wants your presence,' Hugh took both her hands, 'I can only guess at, but it is why I've returned. I cannot see you put in danger's way.'

'I can take care of myself,' she said.

Brother and sister stared at each other. To Sovay, he seemed to have changed completely. He looked very much older than the picture of him that she carried in her memory. There was little trace left in his face of the dreamy poet, the passionate freethinker who delighted in ideas and flitted like a butterfly from one novel concept to another. Veins showed blue under the translucent skin of his temples and high forehead; his thinness had pared away at the rounded cheeks, draining the high colour, reshaping the boyish face to reveal the pale, aesthetic handsomeness of a young Renaissance saint or scholar. Passion still showed in his large eyes, but there was the blue glint of steel there now. A tightness in the jaw and tension lines around the mouth indicated a new strength brought about by tempering experience.

He, in turn, noted changes in her. She had come in wearing evening dress. The gown was a simple design, but bare at the neck and shoulders, which made her look much older. Her face, too, was changing. There had been a subtle shifting of proportions: eyes that had appeared too large, nose too straight, brows too marked, lips too full for a young girl's face had, by some alchemy, undergone a dramatic change. As she grew towards womanhood, she was beginning to fulfil the promise of great beauty that had long been predicted for her. That she, as yet, seemed unaware of this transformation, lent it even more power and aroused within him a strong feeling of brotherly protectiveness. In her younger self, her expression had often been marred by a sullen, resentful air of abstraction. This had been replaced by an active animation, which suited her much better, and there was a new softening, a kindness and concern in her intelligent gaze, that he did not remember seeing there before.

'Hugh!' Gabriel burst into the room. 'Mrs Crombie told me you were here! I can't tell you how glad I am to see you!'

'Or I you!' Hugh went over to meet him. 'Old friend! I had not thought to see *you* here!'

Gabriel took his friend in his strong embrace and Sovay wondered if Lydia was right in her judgement of exactly who was the object of Gabriel's affection.

'I've just come from Oldfield's office.' Gabriel turned to Sovay. 'He's taken on the cases of those arrested after Fender's Field. The hearings have been put back as he predicted. Skidmore has come across something interesting.' He looked to Hugh and Virgil. 'He's Oldfield's clerk. Enterprising young fellow. He's taken up spying,' he laughed. 'On the spy master at that! He has a friend who works in Leggatt's Court, where Dysart's offices are. He's taken to loitering there, seeing what he can find out.'

'And has he?' Sovay asked. 'Found out anything, I mean.'

'Plenty. He's got his friend to log comings and goings. This evening, Gribbon, that's the name of Dysart's clerk, left the office in a hurry. Skidmore contrived to bump into him. The letters he was carrying went flying and Skidmore, polite young man that he is, helped the old man pick them up.'

'Did he notice the addresses?'

'Naturally he did. Dover, apparently. Gribbon was taking them to the Post Office for the night coach.'

'Those letters will be bound for France,' Virgil Barrett said. 'To be delivered by some smuggler's boat running the blockade.'

'That's what Oldfield thought.' Gabriel looked at Hugh. 'He will be glad to know that you are here. And safe. But what of the master?'

'Is Oldfield still at his offices?' Hugh asked.

'I think so,' Gabriel answered. 'He seems to fairly live there at the moment.'

'There are things I want to discuss with him,' Hugh went to the door. 'I will tell you about my father on the way.'

Virgil elected to join them and the three men left Sovay in her father's study. It did not occur to them to ask her to go with them and they barely had time to say farewell. They left engrossed in conversation and had dismissed her from their minds by the time they reached the front door.

'Is there anything more, miss?' Mrs Crombie came into the room, rousing Sovay from her thoughts.

'No, nothing more. I am rather fatigued. I think I will retire.'

'I'll call Lydia.'

'No need to, Mrs Crombie. I can manage very well. I will need nothing more tonight.'

Sovay went up the stairs, her thoughts on the letters destined for Dover. They would be taken on the night mail coach. She paused on the first landing and listened. The house was quiet. The servants had retired to their quarters in the basement.

Sovay went to her room. Earlier in the day, Lydia had taken another delivery, very different from the clothes from Madame Chantal's establishment. These were from Hazell and Smith on Old Bond Street. They had done well, even with Sovay's approximate instructions. The suit fitted far better than her brother's. She put on the cloak and hat and admired the effect in the mirror. Captain Blaze would ride again.

CHAPTER 20

She went to the livery stables to find Brady. He was standing, patient in his stall. He whinnied when he saw her and tossed his head in greeting, as if to say, I knew you would come for me sooner or later. She put her arms round his pale neck, nearly as glad to see him as she had been to see Hugh. He nudged her, whickering into her shoulder. He had been well looked after and his coat gleamed with grooming. She gave the boy a couple of coins for his care and rode out of the stables. She made her way down Oxford Street and Crown Street, glad to be on horseback and above the dirt and press of the streets.

She was going towards the river and the Golden Cross Inn at Charing Cross. She was praying that she would find the Captain there, remembering what Toby had said about it being his usual place at this time of night. When she reached the inn, she dismounted and sent a servant in to find him, saying a friend would like an urgent word out in the yard.

There was a few minutes' delay before he came out, but it seemed to Sovay like a very long time. He smiled as he came towards her.

'Do I have the pleasure of addressing Mr Middleton?' He put his hand on Brady's neck. 'Or is it Captain Blaze? I think by the cloak and spurs that it might be the latter.' He stroked Brady's neck gently, running his fingers through the silky mane. This time the horse did not bridle, instead he nuzzled into the man's chest. 'What can I do for you?'

'I need your help,' Sovay answered, her voice muffled by her scarf. 'I have to stop the Dover coach.'

'Do you now?' Greenwood grinned down at her. 'And may I ask why?'

'There's something on it I want.'

'Is there? And what would that be? Person, letter or package?'

'Letter.'

'I see.' Greenwood looked round. 'I'm afraid you've missed it.' He consulted his watch. 'It went this hour since. Eight o'clock sharp.'

'I know. I thought we might be able to stop it. Somewhere on the road.'

'Did you now?' He pulled Brady to him, so the horse's head and neck hid them from view. He drew near her, his voice a dramatic whisper. 'Are you suggesting highway robbery? But that would be against the law!'

Sovay stepped away from him, his proximity made her most uncomfortable. 'I wish you would stop teasing! Will you help me or no?'

'Mount up,' he said, throwing the reins to her. 'They've a start on us, but we should be able to catch them at Shooter's Hill.'

❖❖❖

Shooter's Hill on the Dover Road was a notorious haunt of highwaymen. The hill was a wild, lonely spot, rising up from the desolate waste of Blackheath and flanked on both sides by dense woods. It was so steep and frequently muddy that the passengers had to get out and walk, and mailbags and luggage had to be carried.

Drivers often stopped at one of the coaching inns along the way to fortify themselves before taking the hill. This is what Greenwood was hoping. It was the only way that they could get to the hill before the coach did.

The coach was in the yard of the Catherine Wheel Inn. They rode past and went on towards the hill. The day had been wet and overcast. The rain had stopped, but the night was cool and damp with mist creeping out of the hollows on the heath. Gorse grew on either side of the road and Sovay bent to pick a sprig. Greenwood grinned as she fixed it to the brim of her hat.

'Captain Blaze! It is good to be riding with you again!' He stopped at the bottom of the hill. The mist was thick here; the road churned by cartwheels and muddy. 'They will likely make the passengers get out. The ground is soft and if the wheels slip, they could lose the whole rig.'

He set off at a quiet and careful trot, looking about him all the while.

'We seem to be the only ones out,' he said as they approached the top of the hill. 'Which is good. Shooter's Hill is popular with those on the pad and this is a perfect night for it. We don't want to have to give way, or fight off another crew before we can be about our business. We will wait here for the coach's approach and we will take care. As I said, this is a popular spot so they will be well armed and on the look out. I will take care of the driver and the guard. You keep an eye on the passengers.'

Sovay nodded that she understood and they withdrew under the trees. The mist was thinner here, drifting in wisps across the road and hanging between the branches like gauze. Water dripped from twig and branch, covering them in glistening drops. It was very quiet, except for the occasional stamp and snort from their horses. Greenwood was listening intently for the clamour of the horn, the beat of hooves, the rhythmic turn of wheels on the road. Sovay strained her ears but could hear nothing except a curious creaking.

'What's that strange noise?' she asked Greenwood. 'Listen. There it is again.'

Greenwood cocked his head. 'It's a gibbet,' he said. 'There's a spot very near called Gallow's Field. It likely comes from there, although I can't tell from this distance if it is occupied, or the state of decay of the unfortunate suspended there. Like as not, he'll be one of our kind. So, it's best not to get caught. Robbing His Majesty of his mail is a hanging offence. Best to remember that, Miss Sovay.' Just then, the shrill call of a distant horn sounded through the soft, cool air. The Captain exhaled with a puff of breath. 'That's them, if I'm not mistaken. Now remember –' He repeated his instructions. 'Do not move until my signal. Not one muscle.'

They withdrew further under the trees. Sovay's nervousness had been growing through the waiting time, just as it had done before, but as soon as the labouring horses came into view and she heard the driver's shouts and the crack of his whip, as soon as she felt Greenwood's touch on her arm, all her fear left her. She adjusted her scarf, drew her pistol, and spurred Brady out in one convulsive movement, making him rear and plunge in order to terrify the passengers who were trudging beside the coach. She succeeded. They cowered back against the coach's painted sides, fearing for their lives as well as their property. She kept her pistol trained upon them, watching for any small move, while Greenwood demanded the mailbags be thrown down to him. She had insisted that nothing else was taken, so within minutes the robbery had been completed and they were galloping down the hill, disappearing into the mist. A couple of shots followed but fell hopelessly wide of their targets.

As they rode back towards London, the mist thickened to a fog.

'You can hardly see your hand,' Greenwood indicated to turn in at an inn. 'We will spend the night here.'

Sovay had not anticipated this, and had thought to get back to the city as soon as possible, but Greenwood shook his head.

'The horses are tired. They need resting. I know this place. The innkeeper is a friend.' He grinned. 'We will go on first thing in the morning. I will get you back before the milk seller comes calling. Have no fear.'

Greenwood ordered food to be sent to them. 'We will have to share a room, I'm afraid. The inn is full because of the fog.'

He took the heavy mailbags up the stairs. He suggested that they threw them in the Thames when they had finished, but Sovay only wanted Dysart's letters and did not think it right to destroy the rest of His Majesty's mail.

Sovay went through the letters and packets while Greenwood ate. It was easier than she thought it would be to find Dysart's correspondence. She read the letters carefully, then screwed them into a ball and threw them on to the fire.

Among other matters, he had betrayed both her father and her brother to the Committee of Public Safety and had helpfully included instructions as to where he thought they might be found. She returned the rest of the mail to the bags.

'We can leave them here with the landlord. He can give them to the next mail coach.'

'How very thoughtful. Not to say responsible.' Greenwood shook his head. 'You have a taste for the life, it is true, quite a talent for it, there's a lot I could teach you, but I fear your scruples would always get the better of you. I fear we will never make a true highwayman of you, Sovay. Tell me, what have you done with the money you stole from Dysart? There was money, I take it?' Sovay nodded. 'I knew it! You don't plan to give it back to him, surely?'

'No, of course not.' Sovay told him about the various uses she had made of it, the provisions for Toby and Skidmore and Gabriel.

Greenwood listened without comment. 'Again, very commendable,' he grunted. 'Now, let's get some sleep. I'll take the chair. You take the bed.'

She woke with no idea where she was and a man's shape loomed over her. She cried out in alarm as Greenwood shook her by the shoulder.

'Shh, shh, it's only me.' Greenwood sat on the side of the bed. 'You were shouting in your sleep. You must have had a dream.'

Sovay nodded. She had dreamt that it had all been for nothing. That all she could do was watch, helpless, as her brother and father, in white shirts with their hands bound behind them, rode in a lurching cart towards the looming shadow of the guillotine. They did not even look at her, or see her standing there. Their eyes were already on the fate that was about to befall them and she was left, bereft, in the middle of a howling mob, filled with the bleak feeling that it had all been her fault.

'I'm cold,' she said. Her teeth were chattering. The covers were thin. She pulled them to her. It was as though the chill from the fog outside had penetrated right in here.

Greenwood took off his coat and arranged it about her shoulders. 'Is that better?'

The coat was still warm. She held the collar closed round her throat and turned her face into his shoulder, the despair and horror of the dream still upon her.

He held her until she stopped shivering. 'I'm going back to my chair now,' he said gently, stroking her hair away from her face. 'You should sleep.' He moved to disentangle himself from her. 'We will have to be away in a few hours' time.'

'Do you not like me?' she said very quietly. 'Do – do you not want me?'

After the desolate horror of her dream, she longed for some human warmth, some show of affection. The darkness in the room gave her the courage to ask him for it.

'Now, what would make you think that?' He turned back with a laugh, as though he was teasing her, but his jesting was laced with bitterness. 'You are young, you are rich, you are beautiful, but these are the least, the very least, of my reasons. I've wanted you ever since the first moment I saw you asleep in that chair by the fire.'

'So . . .'

'Oh, no!' He shook his head as if ridding himself of a siren's song. 'Do not look at me like that! Your eyes are like storm clouds just before lightning strikes,' he smiled. 'I like lightning. I like to ride when a storm is threatening. I would love to spark the fire that lies within you, but I *am* a gentleman, Miss Sovay, whatever you may think. I would not take advantage.' He sighed. 'That pleasure will not be for me. Save your love for him, whoever he may be. You will meet him by and by.' He gave a low, throaty laugh. 'I'll be devilish jealous, so make sure he's good enough for you.' He turned her face to his and stroked her cheek. 'At one time, perhaps, it might have been me. I could have gone to your father and asked for your hand. I was not always the reprobate you see now. But it is far too late for that. What would I say to him? I earn my living by highway robbery, my prospects are the gallows?' He turned away. 'Do not grow fond of me. I am warning you. I do not know how much time there is left to me. There is no romance in the life, Sovay. Leave that to the songs and plays.'

'You could give it up! You could –'

'Do what? It is all I know now. Do not mistake me. I live like this because I choose to do so. I would not have it other. A short life and a merry one, is that not what the pirates used to say?'

'But if they catch you, they will hang you! You said it yourself!'

'That is so. It is only a matter of time. Life on the road is short and I've lived out my span many times over. They will catch me and hang me, as you say. When they do, I hope you will shed a tear for me.'

'I don't want to. I want to –'

'Save me? Like Toby? And t'other one, Skidmore? And Gabriel and his friends in Clerkenwell? And how many more? You cannot save them all, Sovay. Not with all your money. Not with all the money in the world.'

'So you do not believe that we should help people? Or try to change things if we can?' Sovay pulled away from him, her pent-up passion spilling into anger. 'That we should not want things to be better?'

'That is not what I said, nor is it what I believe, but it is harder than you think to change one person, let alone the whole world. Take Toby . . .'

He broke off, reluctant to say more, angry with himself for saying anything at all but she had a way of provoking him. The kindness she showed, her generous heart, these were things that he admired. She seemed to care little for birth or station. What was she doing here else? And she did not judge others by those measures. He did not want to attack her for the ideals that she held. It was not her fault that she was young, had never known hunger or want, or been shown anything but loving kindness. He could not criticise her for that, but if she was going to stray from her world into his, she should see that world for what it was; to do otherwise was to invite disaster.

'Toby? What about him?'

'Nothing,' he said and stood up.

'Tell me!'

'Very well, since you insist.' He looked down at her. 'Mother Pierce's place has been raided. Everyone in there arrested, apart from her. By the time the runners arrived, she'd made herself scarce.'

'I told him to stay away from her.'

'I fear he did not heed your advice. You can't keep those lads out of the Garden. It's the nearest thing to a home they've ever known. I heard he was taken along with his friends.'

'Taken? You mean, to prison?'

'That's what I'd think in the ordinary run of things, but the rumour in the street is that Dysart is involved. Ma Pierce has traded her precious charges and Toby has been taken with the rest of them to a place called Thursley.'

'Thursley?' Sovay frowned. 'How strange. I'm going there myself this very weekend.'

'You are going to Thursley?' Greenwood could not have looked more surprised if lightning had, indeed, struck him.

'Yes, Dysart is holding a party and has invited me.' Sovay was puzzled. 'But it is all perfectly respectable, as far as I know. What would he want with Toby and those others? I don't understand.'

'As far as you know! You know nothing! As for understanding . . .' He made a gesture of despair. 'What a sheltered life you have led. What do you think he would want with them? Use your head.'

'Oh,' Sovay coloured. 'Surely not!'

'Oh, yes. I'm afraid so. Worse, in fact.'

'What could be worse?'

'Dysart and his kind. They are evil people. More evil than you could possibly imagine. You think that they are opposed to liberty. Not at all. You misunderstand them. They are liber*tines*. They believe they have the right to do anything they like, with anyone they like, to anyone they like. They believe there should be no limits set upon an individual's freedom, but only for them, for their small circle. Not for anybody else. Others have been taken there, for these *parties* of his, and they have not come back.'

'You mean he *kills* them?'

Greenwood looked down at her, his face brooding and solemn. 'I do not like to talk to you about these things, but since you force me. From what I've heard, death comes as a mercy.' He paused, considering, choosing his words carefully. 'I do not think you will be in danger of this kind of corruption. He likes to keep these dealings secret, known only to a few. They see street boys and girls as there to be used and discarded; they would not prey upon someone of their own class. Even so,' he shook his head, 'for you to even consider going there seems like madness to me.'

'I will not be alone. Hugh will be with me and Gabriel will be our driver. There will be others, too. Anyway, now I have to find Toby. Whatever you say, I feel responsible for him. It is another reason for me to go.'

'I have never known anyone so stubborn or foolhardy.' He leaned over and kissed her forehead. 'It is almost morning. Get what sleep you can.'

Greenwood returned to his chair, but he did not sleep. If he could not stop her from going there, then so be it. He would let Dysart find him. He would contrive to be there, too.

CHAPTER 21

The light was fading as Gabriel whipped up the horses, urging them on to Thursley. The way they took was lonely. On the map, Thursley seemed little distance from London, but its setting was wild and isolated. There were few settlements near it and they were crossing bleak heathland broken by frowning coppices. The coach rocked and rattled from their violent pace and outside the wind was rising, tearing at the summer leaves of oak and beech.

Sovay rode inside the coach with Hugh. When Lady Bingham arrived to collect her, she would be gone. Hugh touched her arm, pointing to a great arched gateway. High walls extended to the left and right as far as the eye could see. They were entering Thursley.

The gravelled road took a winding course between rolling grounds and dense, dark woods. Far below, lay the fat curve of the Thames in milky brown swollen flood. They rounded a bend and Sovay felt Hugh's hand on her arm again.

'There it is.' He pointed in a kind of excited wonder and ordered Gabriel to stop the coach.

Thursley Abbey lay in front of them at the end of a great avenue of trees. Sovay stared, as amazed as Hugh. She had never seen a private dwelling of such size. Compton could have been tucked behind just one wing and completely hidden from view. This was not a house; it was on the scale of a duke's castle or a royal palace. Different-sized turrets and towers serrated the sky, sprouting square, round and pointed, from an extraordinary complexity of buildings that spread out in four arms around a great central tower which showed like a thick finger of darkness, against the dull red glare of the western sky. Black birds, crows perhaps, or rooks, cawed and whirled like flecks of ash around its castellated and pinnacled summit. Tall lancet windows pierced the walls at different levels. The building seemed archaic in the extreme, a vision of some time long distant and altogether forgotten.

It was a strange place. The proportions were all wrong, as though it had been made from parts of other buildings that did not quite fit together. It lay sprawled in the landscape like some monstrous creature, some brooding, heraldic beast, all crests and spikes, with the head of one thing and the tail of another. Whatever its aesthetic oddities, it undoubtedly had power. It was the kind of place that, once seen, was never forgotten. Sovay knew, almost by premonition, that she would revisit it in her dreams.

'You shivered.' Hugh looked at her with concern. 'Are you cold?'

'No,' Sovay shook her head. 'It's just . . .'

'I know what you mean,' Hugh agreed. 'It *is* enough to give one the shivers. One man's vision,' he gave a nervous laugh, 'is another's phantasmagoria.'

Sovay nodded. She felt a powerful jolt of homesickness for Compton, its plain, four-square elegance, the warm tones of its dark, honey-coloured stone. She longed to tell Gabriel to turn the carriage around and take them all back there but knew that was impossible. Compton was no longer a place of peace and safety and never would be again if Dysart had his way.

Gabriel cracked the reins and the horses trotted on down the Great Avenue which ran between straight rows of tall beeches to the entrance of the house.

As they got closer, the scale of the place became clearer. Sovay looked out of the window and pulled her travelling cloak round her as the coach entered the long finger of shadow cast by the central tower.

Hugh handed Sovay out of the carriage and Gabriel passed down the luggage. He would not be waiting around; he had other business. He whipped the horses up and wheeled away. Hugh and Sovay were left standing in front of doors that seemed out of any human scale. Impossibly tall, they were suspended from eight massive, ornate hinges and were made from oak beams the length of forest trees. The surrounding stone architrave was ornately carved and soared upwards, curving steeply to a point. The shield at the apex was so high above them that it was impossible to make out the coat of arms blazoned there.

Hugh pulled on a twisted wrought-iron handle and a bell tolled, doleful and deeply sonorous, sounding funereal and ominous. While they waited for someone to come, Hugh ran his hand over the grey stonework on either side of the entrance.

'It is not made of real stone,' he said.

Sovay leaned forward to look more closely. 'It looks like stone to me.'

'Well, it isn't. I've seen real gothic buildings on my tours with Fernand. This is most probably a timber frame, covered in some concretion, rendered and marked to look like true masonry. That is how he has been able to build so quickly and so massively. Nothing is as it seems here.' He stepped back and looked upwards, his brow clouded. 'How can such materials support this massive tower?'

Just then, there was the sound of some kind of mechanism and the doors slowly yawned open. For a moment, Sovay could see no one. Then she looked down. The man who had opened the impossibly tall door for them was himself very small. No taller than a child of six or seven. He was in immaculate livery and, despite his diminutive size, he had strong arms and powerful shoulders. His face was broad, with wide cheeks and a spade-shaped nose. The empty cruelty of his dark, tilted eyes smothered any possible amusement at his size.

'Can I help you?'

'We are here at Sir Robert Dysart's invitation,' Hugh announced. 'Mr Hugh Middleton and Miss Sovay Middleton. If you would kindly announce us.'

He said nothing to this, merely nodded to two equally diminutive footmen who stepped out smartly to collect the luggage. The butler ushered them into a vast entrance hall. It was like stepping into a cathedral. The wooden roof soared to at least seventy or eighty feet; the embossed shields on the great cross beams made as small as studs by their distance from the ground. The tall, pointed stained-glass windows set into walls must have been splendid with daylight falling through them, but had grown opaque and dull with the setting of the sun. Fat candles set into brackets and huge candelabras suspended from the ceiling provided wavering pools of yellow light.

Darkness crept in from the sides and the great

expanse of stone made the room discomforting, cold and drear. Sovay was not normally superstitious, but the hollow boom of the great wooden door shutting behind them sounded like an ominous warning that they would never get out of here. She had to will herself to keep walking across the vast stone-flagged floor that seemed wider than the courtyard at Compton. She would happily face any physical danger, but this place unnerved her. A great flight of steps led up towards a narrow archway which exactly mirrored the entrance.

The arch led through to an octagonal area which lay under the Great Tower. The butler indicated that this was where they should wait. Sovay looked up at the soaring pillars, the tall arches and pointed windows. Crimson curtains, at least fifty feet long, hung down from the upper galleries. They rippled a little, disturbed by a breeze or some movement, the material lifting for a second to show dark spaces, adding an air of mystery, a sense of areas hidden from view. A great eight-sided brass lantern spun very slowly, swinging and twisting in the passage of air. The light gleamed through painted glass panels and intricate filigree to produce richly coloured, undulating patterns of light. The effect was faintly oriental and oddly disconcerting. This was by far the strangest place that she had visited in her life.

It was designed to overmaster the visitor, to make one feel like Jack in the giant's castle. Hugh reached for her hand and held it tightly.

'It is like an ogre's fortress,' he said, echoing her thought. 'And we are like two children who have wandered in from the woods. Look there.' He pointed upwards. 'Do you see them? He's even got bats.' Sovay had not noticed them before. The creatures swooped near and sheered away from the great lantern, flitting and fluttering above them like little flaps of silk. 'At first I was reminded of a cathedral but I have a feeling that there is nothing that is holy here.'

'What do you think will happen?' she asked.

Hugh shrugged. 'I have no idea. Best not to anticipate. We will take obstacles as they come and deal with each one.'

They were whispering more from the lingering feeling of being in a church than from any fear of being overheard, but high above them Dysart leaned on the balcony smiling to himself. The acoustics were such that anyone in the Listening Gallery could hear every word spoken in the Octagon. He often made visitors wait there. He liked to hear their first impressions, the whispered mixture of awe and fear that the building had the power to instil. He had no intention of going down to greet his guests. He didn't even want them to know he was here. He nodded to Meldron, his diminutive butler, who returned down the spiral staircase.

The servant returned to Sovay and Hugh and indicated that they should follow him. They went under an arch surmounted by a music loft and into a vestibule that led to a long gallery. After the cold emptiness of the Entrance Hall and Octagon, the prospect made Sovay stumble and catch her breath. The room disappeared into the distance, door after door opening onto magnificent opulence. The ceiling was covered with rich and elaborate fanwork that sprang like slender branches from exquisitely worked corbels, each carved with the face of an angel. The floor was carpeted in richly patterned blue and red; the walls were covered in pale crimson damask. The room was lit by hanging lamps and candles set in silver sconces. Their soft light gleamed on mahogany bookcases filled from floor to ceiling with rare volumes. Renaissance paintings glowed with jewel-like colours: young men in caps of emerald velvet and ruby red tunics; magi in pearly capes knelt to Madonnas cloaked in costly ultramarine. Stands made of exotic materials were spaced at intervals. They bore rare objects: an oval cup carved from rock crystal, a golden box covered with birds, a great nautilus shell, beautifully engraved and mounted on silver, a cup carved from topaz with a ruby-eyed dragon handle of pale yellow gold.

The effect on the eye was dazzling, an excess of riches which made it difficult to know what to look at. Each thing spoke of beauty, rarity, incredible wealth.

At length, the butler turned right and pushed back a pair of lofty folding doors. They entered a room, no less fine, but smaller, more intimate in size. A circular table in the centre gleamed with glass and silver.

The butler ushered them forward and then looked up to address them. 'My master regrets that he cannot meet you at present. He has many things that claim his attention. Meanwhile, he hopes that you will be comfortable.'

He eased a chair back for Sovay and then for Hugh. He poured wine for them both and then he disappeared.

The table was sumptuously set. A plate of sorrel soup with eggs steamed before them and there was a chicken set in aspic, trout and salmon, celery with cream and stuffed artichokes. On a sideboard stood a pyramid of fruits and sweetmeats: a pineapple crowned layers made up of fresh grapes, dates, figs and oranges, candied apricots, mandarins and ginger, marrons glacés, marchpane leaves, comfits and sugar almonds coated in gold and silver leaf.

'It is strange,' Sovay said as she dipped her spoon into the soup. 'The food is ready and warm, as though we were expected, and in quantities enough for a whole party, yet the table is set for two.' She put her spoon down and shivered. 'I still feel as if I'm in a story.'

Hugh dipped his own spoon and tasted. 'Well, this is real food and I am hungry.' He broke a small white roll and took a bite. 'Come. Eat. We are not in the realms of fairy, Sovay, whatever the evidence to the contrary.'

The butler reappeared the instant that they had finished.

'Perhaps you would follow me,' he said, opening the doors for them.

'Are we to meet Sir Robert?' Hugh asked.

'Alas, not today,' the butler informed them as they followed him out. 'Urgent business detains him. He sends his apologies. He will see you tomorrow. He hopes that you find Thursley to your liking and everything satisfactory.'

With that, he conducted them back down the long gallery. Just before they reached the Octagon, he took them up a flight of stairs.

He stopped at the first landing.

'These are your rooms, Miss Middleton.'

He showed her into a spacious apartment. Her trunk had been brought here, her clothes unpacked and her night attire set out on the bed ready.

'Mr Middleton, if you would follow me?'

With that, they departed and Sovay was left alone in the quiet vastness of the huge house.

CHAPTER 22

Sovay wandered from one room to the other. Fires burned in the grates of the sitting room and bedroom and both were well lit with lamps. The furnishings were in the baronial manner, with dark oak wainscoting and heavy furniture. A large ebony armoire stood in one corner of the bedroom and the washstand was inlaid with onyx and carved from marble. Sovay had not seen a maid or servant, but the water in the ewer was warm.

The bed was hung with pale green silk, the valance and counterpane embroidered with little knots of flowers. The bed was made up with the finest linen and the goose-down mattress looked extremely comfortable, but Sovay was not feeling in the least bit tired. She prowled from room to room, unable to settle. She wondered where Hugh was, and at the absence of their host, or of any other guests.

However much she fought against it, a sense of menace, vague, but all-pervading, began to seep into her soul. Despite the lamps and the blaze in the hearth, shadows seemed to gather around her. She eyed the tall armoire. She had read enough novels to know that if something, or someone, was lurking, they would be in there. Then she saw a glimmer of white in the corner. Fear caught at her throat and then she laughed in a strangled gasp. She must not let nursery terrors get the better of her. The 'ghost' was merely her own reflection in the cheval glass.

She used the armoire for its proper purpose and put her clothes away, then sat in an ornately carved chair by the fire. Still she could not settle. It would be better to do something than stay here with her imaginings. She decided to go and find Hugh.

She opened the door a crack and peered out. The stairway outside was well lit with lanterns set into the wall. She proceeded cautiously up to the next landing. There was a door there, just like hers. There was no answer when she knocked and whispered Hugh's name and when she tried the handle the door was locked. She went on up the stairs, thinking that he might be on the next landing.

Here, she was faced with a choice to go left or right. To the left, behind a heavy curtain, lay the entrance to another long gallery, disappearing towards some dark, distant turret and not worth her exploration. To the right stood a tall oak door. To her surprise, this one was not locked. She lifted the latch and slipped into a large room, the length and width of the Octagon that lay beneath it. Sovay recognised immediately that she was in a laboratory, much bigger and grander than her father's at Compton. The room was hot, heated by a brick-built furnace; its surround held a large crucible and a copper still. The oppressive atmosphere was permeated by a sharply pungent, chemical smell, underlain by something sweetish and unpleasant.

The room was illuminated by moonlight streaming through a high plate-glass window which spanned one wall. A huge magnifying instrument stood ready to catch the rays of the sun. An array of microscopes and other instruments stood on a wide, handsome desk, their brass gleaming in the light from outside. Various other larger pieces of equipment were scattered about, one of which Sovay took to be a friction machine, but again much larger than any one that she had ever seen.

Shelves set into the walls held ranks of coloured glass bottles which contained liquids and chemicals. A zinc-topped table was set out for experiments with apparatus for distillation, glass jars and spherical containers all very much larger than any her father used. A wooden bench stood parallel with drains down each side and stout leather straps and buckles dangling from it. There was a shape underneath the discoloured covering sheet. Sovay approached reluctantly, the unpleasant smell growing stronger as she lifted a corner of the coarse, grey linen. The table held a partially dissected cadaver. She dropped the cover quickly after catching a glimpse of grey and yellow flesh laced with blue and red veins and arteries. The thin, sweetish smell of the pickling alcohol did little to disguise the overwhelming stench of decay. A buckled strap snagged in her skirt as she stepped away and she wondered, briefly, as to their purpose. Then the realisation came upon her. Only the living required restraint.

Sovay was not tempted to investigate what other hideous secrets the laboratory might contain, but her retreat towards the door was halted by the sound of voices and footsteps on the stairs. It was too late to escape. She looked for somewhere to hide and prayed that there was space enough for her behind a curtained-off alcove at the side of the room. More guests had arrived, or perhaps they had been here all the time. Thursley was large enough for platoons to be billeted and kept secret, one from the other. She hid herself just in time. The door opened and the thick, aromatic scent of cigar smoke added itself to the general pungency of the room.

'Gentlemen, welcome to my laboratory.' Dysart's voice was close. 'I would be grateful if you did not touch anything,' he added, as murmurs of wonder and words of appreciation added themselves to the sound of movement about the room. 'For your own safety. Many of the chemicals are dangerous, poisonous and highly corrosive. Some of the instruments are delicate and many are irreplaceable.'

As they moved away from her hiding place, Sovay risked a peek through a crack in the curtains. Six or seven men, some of them in uniform, stood grouped around the bench.

'I have replicated the experiments of the radical Joseph Priestley and the distinguished French scientist, Lavoisier, who recently perished at the guillotine,' Dysart addressed them. 'I have proved to my satisfaction that the element, oxygen, is necessary to life. Further, I have proved that we are no different to the animals in this.' He rested his hands on one of the giant bell jars, easily big enough to contain a human child. 'Thus life is sustained, but how is it generated? This is the question, sirs, to which I now address myself. We live in an age when Reason reigns supreme. It is time to discard ancient superstitions, blind belief in some mysterious divinity whose existence cannot be proven. I have dissected many a corpse, gentlemen, some still warm, and have never found the seat of the soul. No, I have come to believe the secret lies elsewhere. Watch and I will demonstrate.'

Dysart moved towards a complicated array of delicate devices and began to turn a wheel, slowly at first then faster and faster. As the rotations increased, the mechanisms began to whirr and whirl. The room was filled with a low humming, then there was a sharp crack. Some of the audience uttered audible cries of alarm and stepped back as a crooked violet flash, like miniature lightning, leapt across the space between one machine and another.

'Electricity, sirs, electricity! It is the very spark and force of life!' The sparking began to die as he let the turning wheel wind down. 'Could one garner enough of it, it might even be possible to *re*animate that which is no longer living. To that end, I have connected this mechanism to the top of the tower so that I may use the power of lightning to prove my theory. But I have not brought you here to merely witness demonstrations, or to talk of science. I show you this in illustration only. I have brought you to Thursley so that we might act together to reanimate the moribund body politic which, I'm sure you'll agree, is as dead and stinking as the corpse beneath this sheet. We must act as that bolt of lightning: to bring new life, to create a new creature, one never seen before, and one entirely within our power. We must act to disperse those who stand guard over that which is dead; then we must drive away the carrion dogs of revolution that even now sniff after the carcass. What better way could there be than to turn each upon the other?'

He gave a conspiratorial grin. When he laughed, the others joined in.

'The fuses are set, gentlemen. After tomorrow you will return to your places, within the country, within government, ready to take over after the conflagration.'

He held out his hand to the globe before him and they watched entranced as the room was filled with violet and blue light. Threads of lightning extended from his fingers and played within the sphere.

Excited conversation broke out among the group as they left to make their way down the stairs. Sovay stayed in her hiding place until all sound had died away except for the occasional fizzing splutter and spark from the infernal machine. So their host *was* in residence, but only to his friends, it seemed. Their conspiracy was every bit as dastardly as Oldfield had predicted. She should find Hugh and tell him, but he could be anywhere within this vast building. That would have to wait until morning. It would be better not to wander the abbey in darkness. Who knew what other horrors it might contain?

CHAPTER 23

Sovay stole back to the sanctuary of her room. Once there, she shut the door behind her and prepared for bed. She changed into her nightdress quickly and blew out all the lamps. That done, she climbed under the covers and pulled them over her head.

She woke from oppressive dreams, fighting for breath. Something was squatting on her chest, crushing the life out of her . . . She was all in a sweat, lying with the covers wound tightly about her, half in and out of the bed. She rose and lit the lamp, determined not to close her eyes again.

She must have slept, despite her intention, for when she next opened her eyes it was morning. A girl had drawn her curtains and was pouring water into the basin.

She turned as she heard Sovay stirring. It was Lydia. Sovay struggled to sit up, amazed to see her here. She had never intended to bring the girl with her, but had forgotten how determined Lydia could be.

'How did you get here?'

'Lady B came to call you early this morning. I told her you'd already gone, but had left me behind by some oversight.'

Lydia's smirk of triumph faded as Sovay leapt out of bed and seized her by the arms.

'You cannot stay here, Lydia.'

'But who will attend you? Lady B's brought your

dress and everything. Don't you want to see it. It's –'

'No. I do not want to see it. I want you to go. Immediately.'

Lydia's face threatened tears. 'If you'd rather Lady Bingham's maid –'

'It's not that. If you stay, you could be in very great danger.'

'What danger?'

'I cannot say, but I believe it is so.'

'All right.' Lydia dabbed at her nose. 'I'll get your things ready, and I'll go. Mr Hugh called when you were sleeping. Says to meet him in the Blue Room when you're ready. Says you'll know where it is.'

Sovay washed and dressed quickly and descended the stairs to the Octagon. Daylight revealed the full majesty of the place. The sun streamed through the tall, stained-glass windows setting the dull stone slabs at the centre of the Octagon to shine like a great, jewelled shield. She walked along the same gallery as last night. The light warmed the pale stone of the vaulted ceiling to apricot and emphasised the delicate carving and interlocking patterns. To the left of her, ran a cloister, with a fountain at the centre. A big black bird flew down, perched on the edge of the carved basin and dipped to sip water with its long curved beak. As if aware of her presence, it looked up suddenly, head on one side, and regarded her with a beady, dark eye.

She found Hugh waiting for her. He had already breakfasted.

Sovay spooned some oatmeal into a dish and poured herself a cup of coffee.

'Did you sleep well?' he asked.

'Tolerably,' she replied, 'considering what I had seen.'

She told him about Dysart's laboratory and the men who had been with him.

'There were military men there, you say?' Hugh poured himself more coffee from the silver coffee pot.

Sovay nodded.

'They probably have command of their own regiments. We are at war with France. Troops have been dispatched to Holland and Belgium. The Fleet is busy in the Caribbean and the Mediterranean.' He paused, his face grave. 'Dysart only has to have the backing of a couple of regiments on his side for this coup d'état to work. Even if their efforts fail, think about how much blood will be shed in the attempt.' Hugh put his cup down. 'We must stop it. Tonight. It is our only chance.' Hugh took Sovay's hands in his and looked into her eyes. 'Whatever happens, we must be equal to it. You did good work last night. Now, I am going to find out who these conspirators are, and I must speak to Oldfield as soon as he gets here, and Virgil. But remember,' his grip tightened, 'we trust no one. Only each other.'

'What shall I do?' Sovay asked.

'Play the innocent lady guest. Go for a stroll in the grounds. Seek out that spiderous woman, Lady Bingham. Above all, use those sharp eyes and keep your ears open.'

❖❖❖

Sovay let herself out by a little postern door and followed a gravel path through a rustic archway that led to a flight of steps and down on to a broad sweep of lawn.

She set off across the expanse, holding up her skirts a little to avoid the dampness of the grass. The lawn suddenly ended in a precipitous drop. Far below lay a large pool. Sedge and reed grew round the borders, but the dark stillness of the water indicated great depth. She startled a little at the sudden loud call of a moorhen. Its cry was answered by another, although no living creature disturbed the black, mirror surface of the lake. Wooded ground rose away from the water on three sides with trees overhanging the banks. Although the lake was only perhaps a hundred yards from the house, it seemed remote and mysterious, as though she had come across some bottomless tarn deep in the wooded isolation of the hills.

Through a grove of tall pines, she could see the domed roof of a round building. The hidden aspect and odd shape gave it an air of strangeness. Sovay set off, determined to discover what it might be. She found a walkway, flanked by high hedges of dusty yew. She followed the twists and turns, rather in the manner of a maze, and found herself standing in front of a temple.

The squat, circular building of straw-coloured stone stood on a stepped platform and was surrounded by a covered colonnade of Doric columns. It was set into a steep hillside, as artificial and foreign to the landscape as the building itself. The rocky slope rose steep, punctuated by tall, dark cypress and slender poplar. Sovay guessed it was meant to emulate some Arcadian scene, or a Tuscan hillside of the kind glimpsed over the shoulder of one of Dysart's Renaissance Madonnas.

It was hard to tell if the building had been constructed to gratify some extravagant fancy or whether it served a real purpose. Impressive double doors sheathed in bronze, each side embossed with a head of Medusa, marked the entrance. Sovay turned the twisted circular handles but the doors were locked. She stepped back and looked up at the decorative frieze which ran along the space between the roof and the top of the colonnade. The carving appeared weather worn, as though stolen from some actual pagan temple, the stone deprived of detail, sucked by the elements until it was almost impossible to tell exactly what was represented. As Sovay studied the forms, decayed faces seemed to leer down and she saw figures, half human, half animal, writhing together, centaurs and satyrs, engaged in some profane dance. Their eroded quality contrasted strongly with the carving set above the entrance; here the large curving horns of the great god Pan had a sharp-edged clarity, as if hewn recently. The curls hanging from his bearded chin were crisply sculpted. The narrow, slanted eyes, glaring down from either side of his broad nose, appeared disconcertingly lifelike above his jeering, goat-like grin.

The day was bright but it was cold in the shadow of the building. Sovay shivered as though some dark bird of ill omen had flown over her grave. As if summoned by her thought, two of the great birds that seemed to haunt the place alighted in the tops of the tall pine trees with a loud cawing and flapping of wings. One solitary black feather floated down to her. Sovay picked it up and turned back to the abbey. She had done enough exploring for one day.

The path she took led her back to a walled garden in the north-east quadrant of the building. Sovay stepped between the carefully tended beds towards the long northern wing. Suddenly, a flash of colour in an upper storey caught her eye. A woman wearing a vibrant orange wig was hurrying along a vaulted corridor above the long gallery. Sovay doubted there could be two hairpieces the same violent shade in all of London, or the surrounding counties. It had to be Mother Pierce. What was she doing here? Sovay quickened her own step, determined to find out.

CHAPTER 24

Sovay reached the upper gallery just in time to see Mother Pierce disappear through a door into the squat tower which stood with its twin at the end of the northern wing. She followed swiftly and got there just in time to see skirts disappearing upwards round a twist in the stairs. She mounted the steps cautiously after her quarry, taking care not to be seen.

The other woman stopped at the first landing. Sovay halted at the sound of voices and listened, hidden by a turn in the staircase.

'How are my little chicks today?' she heard Ma Pierce say. 'No more trouble, I trust?'

'Quiet as mice they've been, ma'am,' she heard a male voice reply. 'Quiet as mice.'

'That's what I like to hear,' the woman replied. 'Now, let me in, there's a good fellow.' There was the clink of bottles. 'Don't want 'em pie-eyed, but a little tipple won't hurt. Can't deprive the dears of their mother's milk.'

'That gin you got there?' one of the men asked. 'Can't spare us a bottle? Man gets a thirst on him sitting here all day.'

'Here, only the one, mind. Got to keep 'em happy.'

Sovay heard the scrape and turn of a key in a lock. This must be where Toby and Jack and the others taken from the streets were being kept. For what purpose Sovay only had the haziest idea but it made her shake with disgust and rage. Some of them in there would be little more than children, to be bought and sold for the profit of Mrs Pierce and to gratify these gentlemen's lust and pleasure. Sovay would prevent it if she possibly could.

Mother Pierce did not stay long. The door was locked behind her and after some more banter with the guards she came back down the stairs and hurried off down the vaulted corridor. When the door closed at the other end, Sovay emerged from her hiding place. She went back to her room and was glad to find no sign of Lydia. She changed into her plainest dress and found her grey woollen shawl. She rang for a servant and ordered a bottle of wine.

At the bottom of the tower stairs, she pulled the shawl up over her hair. She stooped her shoulders and stared down at the ground as she approached the men on either side of the door.

'Mother Pierce sent me,' she muttered to the larger man's boots. She showed him the neck of the bottle.

'Did she now?' the big man said.

'Yes,' Sovay replied. 'Told me to bring up another bottle.'

'Where's she been keeping you, then?' he asked, making no move to unlock the door. 'Keeping the prettiest somewhere else, eh? Sly old mare.'

He stood up and came towards her. Sovay tightened her grip on the bottle. She had to get to Toby and the others and she must not be discovered, but she did not know what she would do if this loathsome creature started pawing her.

'Now, now, Billy boy.' The other guard laughed and took hold of his arm. 'No sampling the goods.'

'I suppose.' The fat guard reluctantly fished up a

bunch of keys hanging from a chain at his belt.

Sovay dodged his groping hand and stood as far away as she could as he opened the door.

'Hard to get, eh?' The guard held the door. He came close enough for her to smell the sweet stench of gin on his breath. His body pushed against her as she squeezed past him.

Finally, he let her into the room. Sovay set down the bottle, her eyes wide. She had discovered another of Thursley's surprises. Along with the architecture, fine rooms and furniture, Thursley boasted its own bordello and although her experience of such things was rather limited, she judged it to be a very fine one. Themed like every other room, this seemed to be in the style of a Turkish harem, or how Sovay imagined one to be: furnished with low couches and sofas covered in the most luxurious materials, the floor strewn with cushions, the ceilings hung with silk curtains and brocade awnings, drifting loose or held back by tasselled swags. A group of boys were sitting on the floor playing cards. One of them was Jack, the Irish boy from Ma Pierce's, Toby's friend. He looked up as she came into the room, as surprised to see her as she was to be here herself.

'Miss Sovay,' he said coming towards her. 'What are you doing here?'

'I saw Mrs Pierce and wondered what she was up to so I followed her. Where's Toby?'

'I don't know,' Jack shrugged. 'He tried to escape and they took him away. That's why those two clowns are out there now.'

'Not here?' Sovay was stricken. How was she supposed to find him now? 'What happened?'

'Got caught and brought back here, so Ma Pierce could teach us all a lesson. Then they took him off somewhere.'

'Took him where?'

Jack shook his head. 'I dunno. I heard Ma say summat about "down below". That's all I know.'

'This place . . .'

'Ain't it something? There's more rooms through there. Upstairs, too. A regular warren. Thought of everything. There's even opium.' He nodded to a silver-inlaid rosewood cabinet, various elaborate smoking devices and a rack of long pipes. 'We ain't allowed to touch that, though. That's there for the nobs.' He dropped his voice and looked round warily. 'Most of the others are as happy as pigs in you know what. They believe whatever fairytale Ma's spinning 'em, but I don't like it. Nor did Toby. That's why he decided to go look see.' He shook his head. 'It's too good to be true. All my life, no one showed me no kindness, nor never give me nothing, especially not her, and suddenly it's all little white loaves and delicacies.' He indicated crumbs left on a brass plate on the floor. 'It's like in one of them stories, like we're being fattened up before the kill.'

'I'll get you out of here, I promise,' Sovay said, although she had no idea how she would do it. 'But first I have to find Toby.'

'We'll be ready. It ain't just Tobe and me, some of the others don't like the smell of it, neither. When you find old Tobe, give him these.' Jack held out a bunch of thin keys, ranging in size from very small to very large. 'Them's his picklocks and he might be needing them. He managed to slip 'em into the guard's pocket while he was being searched. I filched them out again, sweet as you like.' He grinned at her. 'The old one-two. Then they dragged him off.'

A girl reeled in from an adjoining chamber. 'Old bitch brought the gin yet?' She looked around and her uncertain focus centred on Sovay. 'Who's yer new friend, Jacky boy?' She came weaving towards them. 'What's your name, then? Ain't seen you before. Ain't you going to say hello? Or you too good for us? Is that it? What you looking at?' She lurched towards Sovay, fists curling. 'Give over eyeing me like that, you stuck up bitch!'

'Now, now, Rosie.' Jack moved to intercept her. 'It's just the gin talking. No need to get riled. I reckon you'd best go,' he whispered to Sovay. 'Good luck, miss.'

'Thanks, Jack.' Sovay was already moving towards the door. 'Good luck to you, too.'

❧❧❧

Down below, that was the only clue Sovay had as to where Toby might be. There were many stairways in the abbey, and the cellars were no doubt extensive, running under each part of the building. She paused when she reached the level of the upper gallery. The stairs carried on downward. They were unlikely to drag Toby kicking and struggling to some other part of the building. She could do no worse than start here.

She took one flight and then another, determined not to stop until the stairs gave out. The cold smell of earth and stone told her that she was underground, but still the steps led down. Sovay had to feel her way as the light from above began to recede. She cursed herself for not thinking to bring a candle and was about to turn back when she saw a faint glimmer coming up from below. Finally, the stairway finished under a brick archway. Sovay looked out cautiously into a wide stone passage lit by torches held in stanchions on the walls. Rooms gave off to left and right, the wide entrances curved, like the mouths of caves. The stone was worked in massive blocks, the marks of the masons' tools clear upon them, and it was grey, like the remnants of the ruin left above ground. If the abbey had all but disappeared up there, it still existed below the ground.

Sovay stepped out, ducking her head under the low ceiling, and took a torch down to light her way. Her heart sank inside her. The rooms to left and right appeared to be wine cellars full of racks of dusty bottles, the entrances barred and locked. These could go on for miles. What if the cellars were only used for their most obvious purpose, that of storage? Toby could be anywhere and she might never find him. She carried on until the passage branched. As she stood, trying to decide which way to take, she heard rough voices and raucous laughter coming from the right. Sovay moved with great care, extinguishing the torch she held and edging along the wall. She had no desire to be discovered down here by men like the two that she had encountered upstairs.

About halfway along the passage a door stood open. Sovay hesitated, listening to the deep rumble of male voices and wondering how to get past without being seen. She need not have worried. The four men inside were intent on the cards in front of them. A bottle stood at each elbow. They drank from small pewter cups and coins chinked and rolled into the pile at the centre of the table. The cards slapped down. One man laughed as he claimed his winnings and another objected. She waited for the shouting and laughter to build to a crescendo and flitted past.

There were no wine cellars along this passage. The wide-mouthed entrances were bricked up and small doorways of stout wood were set into the middle of each one. Along with every other convenience, Dysart had his own prison. Sovay peered through the small, barred grating at the top of each door and her heart beat faster. If Toby was anywhere, he was likely to be here.

Sovay came to the end of the row, hardly able to contain her disappointment. The cells were empty, apart from a few rats and mice running about in the dirty straw, and showed no signs of recent occupation. If he wasn't here, where could he be?

She went on round the next corner, wondering if there were more cells and, if they were empty, what other thing they could have done with Toby. The passage widened out into a square inner court. Sovay stopped short, unable to take in what she was seeing. She shrank back against the wall, her fingers gripping into the soft, decaying stone.

At the centre of the underground yard stood a machine. She instantly recognised the tall, oblong frame and huge slanted blade. Although she had never seen one in her life, it was as familiar by now as the gallows. A guillotine. A wide gutter led from a point underneath the circular collar to a square drain sunk into the floor. Dysart's voice, talking of corpses still warm on the dissecting table, came back to her. She swallowed, nausea threatening to overwhelm her. Was there no limit to this man's wickedness? Then she made herself step forward. Was there fresh blood on the blade? She had to see.

Something hit her on the arm and she almost screamed. She looked down and a stone plinked to the floor by her feet.

'Over here! Sovay! Don't scream whatever you do!'

She had been so transfixed by Dysart's personal instrument of death that she had completely failed to notice the cell that had been constructed opposite to it. The condemned cell was made differently from the others with open bars from floor to ceiling, so nothing could come between the prisoner caged within and contemplation of the fate that awaited him. A man was sitting on a chair bolted to the ground, his wrists circled with manacles, his legs in irons, chained to rings set into the floor. His shirt was torn, one eye was closed and his face was bruised and crusted with dried blood. Captain Greenwood might have lost some of his dash and élan, but the look in his eyes suggested that his spirit remained undaunted.

'Why, Miss Middleton! We do meet in the most unexpected places!' He managed a lop-sided smile. 'Forgive me for not rising.' He held up his chains. 'How did you find me? How did you even know I was here?'

'I didn't. I was looking for Toby.'

'They took him down there.' Greenwood pointed to a dark, brick-floored passageway.

'How did you get here? What happened to you?'

'I allowed Dysart to take me,' he looked down at the chains binding him, 'but I must confess my ruse did not quite go according to plan. He seems to think I'm part of some kind of conspiracy against him.' He touched his split cheek and bruised jaw. 'I can't tell him what I don't know, but he doesn't believe me. That's why Madame Guillotine and I are as yet unacquainted. Sovay? Where are you going?' Greenwood made to stand up but the chains pulled him down again. 'Don't leave me! I expected just a little sympathy!'

'I must find Toby,' Sovay said over her shoulder. 'He might be able to get you out of here. Better than I can, anyway.'

'I don't see how.' The highwayman grasped his chains and shook them.

'You'll just have to trust me.'

Sovay took a torch from the wall, ducking her head as she went down a dark, low passage, little higher than a tunnel. She peered through the grilles of cells left and right, calling Toby's name in a low voice. There was no response, and she was about to turn back, when she heard a hoarse whisper.

'Over here.'

The whisper came from a cell at the very end of the passage where fingers of green slime plaited the walls and moisture seeped from the brickwork to form stagnant pools on the uneven floor.

Toby's cell was narrow, dank and dismal, with a low stone platform to sleep on and a bucket in the far corner. He had clearly been hurt in some way and found it hard to rise from the sleeping shelf and drag himself to the door. Like the Captain's, his face was bruised and bleeding and he cradled his right arm close to his body in the way an animal might protect a wounded paw.

'What have they done to you?' Sovay put her fingers through the close knit of the bars as if this would bring her nearer to him.

Toby winced as he tried to smile and brought his hand to his face. 'Old Ma didn't take too well to me trying to run away.'

'What did they do to your hand?' His fist was blackened, oozing and swollen. The fingers curled under, twisted and bent. She fumbled in her pocket and held up the bunch of keys where he could see them. 'Jack gave me these but I fear you will have no use for them.'

She bit her lip, near to tears with anger at the way they had used him and frustration that everything she did seemed to come to nothing.

'Oh, I don't know. I can try.'

'How? Your hand is crippled.'

'Me right is, but I'm mauldy-handed.' He held up his left, uninjured. 'Didn't know that, did they? Give 'em to me.'

Hope flared within her, only to be dashed. The bunch of keys was too big to pass through the mesh of the grille.

'They won't go through!'

'I only need one, don't I? Hold 'em up so I can see. That long thin 'un will do. Take it off the ring and feed it through. Leave the rest outside, I'll pick 'em up after.'

The key went in after some manoeuvring and clinked on the stone floor inside.

Then, from down the corridor, came the sound of a man singing:

'*Fill every glass, for wine inspires us,*
And fires us
With courage, love and joy.'
The singing became more sonorous, the words fairly bellowed:
'*Women and wine should life employ.*
Is there aught else on earth desirous?'
The chorus followed, louder yet and more frantic:
'*Fill every glass . . .*'
'It's the Captain! He's giving us a warning,' Toby whispered. 'The guards are on their rounds.'
'Shut that caterwauling,' a rough voice roared. 'Or I'll shut it for you!'
Iron bars clanged down the passageway and the song faded to one or two words drowned out by angry swearing, and replaced by grunts and yelps of pain.
Sovay doused her torch and tried to quell a mounting sense of panic. They could come at any moment and there was no way out of the passage. She was in a dead end.

CHAPTER 25

She dodged into an empty cell and flattened herself against the slimy wall, trying to control her breathing, praying that they would not hear her or sense her presence; but after they had checked on Toby, the sound of their voices receded and she judged it safe to come out.

'They'll go back to their drinking,' Toby hissed through the grille of his cell. 'You should be able to get away. Good luck, Miss Sovay.'

'Good luck to you, too, Toby.'

She crossed the passage and touched fingers with him through the bars before creeping cautiously along to the Captain.

'Toby has his keys.'

'Then we are as good as free.' Fresh blood oozed from his mouth as he gave her a crooked smile. 'Go carefully, Sovay,' he added, his voice suddenly serious.

'Don't worry about me,' she said. 'I'll be quite safe. Look to help Toby and his friends. Gabriel will be back later with the coach and –'

Before she could tell him more, there was a shout from the guardroom.

'I'll find him. Now go, before they catch you.' He raised his manacled hand in farewell. 'Until we meet again.'

When the guards were again intent on their cards, Sovay sneaked past. By the time she reached the upper levels, it was well past noon. She met no one and regained the sanctuary of her room without having to use the story about getting lost in the grounds and grappling with thickets to explain her absence and dishevelled state.

She scarcely had time to change her clothes and make herself respectable when there was a knock on her door.

'Sovay! Where have you been? I've been looking for you everywhere.' Lady Bingham entered without a by-your-leave and looked around with some interest. Sovay was glad that she had secreted her soiled dress in the closet and had thought to rumple the bedclothes.

'I fell asleep.' She indicated the creased coverlet. 'I was rather fatigued after a walk in the grounds.'

'They are *wonderful*, aren't they?' Lady Bingham was easily diverted into praising their host's feats of horticulture, rather than wondering further about what else Sovay might have been doing. 'He has spared no expense there, as everywhere. Not to be equalled the length and breadth of England, I truly do believe. The rhododendrons and azaleas are over their best, I fear, but the roses are coming into their own. Did you see the Orangery?'

'No.' Sovay shook her head. 'But what I did see was magnificent. I have already gained many ideas for Compton.'

'You must get him to show you the Orangery. Superb collection: lilies and camellias, figs, peaches, pineapples, and I don't know what. It is quite a wonder, my dear. Quite a wonder.'

'And to what do I owe the pleasure of this visit?' Sovay asked her, sure she had not come to discuss exotic fruit.

'I am here to welcome you to Thursley. Since Sir Robert is not married, it falls upon me to act as his hostess. But I understand you and Hugh arrived yesterday evening? Sir Robert sends his apologies. He was called away suddenly and could not welcome you in person. I hope all was satisfactory.'

'Yes, thank you, Lady Bingham. Everything was perfect.'

'I have another purpose.' Lady Bingham's large blue eyes took on a conspiratorial gleam. 'Surely you have not forgotten?'

Sovay frowned. 'Forgotten what?'

'Oh, come now.' Lady Bingham's tone became uncomfortably intimate and cajoling. 'It would be uppermost in the minds of most young ladies.'

Sovay shook her head. 'I'm sorry Lady Bingham; you have me at a loss.'

Lady Bingham sighed, and spoke slowly, as though talking to an idiot. 'Yesterday, I paid a visit to a certain dressmaker of Mayfair, a Madame Chantal. She was most anxious that I see a certain dress that she had been making. Since you were not at home to take delivery, she asked me to bring it to you. Your girl has it.'

'Lydia? I thought she'd –'

'She's downstairs with my maid, Emily. I'll send her to you. Wait until you see it! Madame has excelled herself. It makes all other gowns seem positively dowdy. It is a work of art, Sovay. A work of art!'

'Well, I thank you for bringing it to me, Lady Bingham.'

'The reception is in the Mirror Drawing Room at

six-thirty this evening. Make sure you are ready by then. Have you seen the Mirror Room?'

Sovay shook her head again. She had not.

'Truly astonishing. It is said that he copied the Glass Drawing Room at Northumberland House. I've seen both and, to my mind, Sir Robert's room is the more magnificent. Plate glass from France, painters brought from Italy . . .'

'Thursley must have been so very costly.' Sovay shook her head in wonder. 'How can any man afford it?'

'Sir Robert is very, very wealthy.' Lady Bingham's voice took on the note of deep seriousness she reserved for matters pertaining to land or money. 'One of the wealthiest men in England. He could spend his days in idle self-indulgence, yet he is tireless in the service of the King.'

'Tell me, Lady Bingham, I have often wondered, what does Sir Robert *do*, exactly?' Sovay asked, as artless as before.

'There are many ways in which a gentleman can be useful to his country,' Lady Bingham replied, telling her nothing. 'Sir Robert gives vital service, you may rest assured. It is such a shame that he has no one to whom he can leave all this.'

'He has never married?'

'No, my dear, and he is the most eligible bachelor in England, outside the royal family. I had hopes for Charlotte but it was not to be.' Her face brightened. 'There is always Isabel. It's said he favours youthfulness.'

Lady Bingham's younger daughter was a sallow-faced child of eleven or twelve. What could the woman be thinking? Sovay looked away appalled.

'Don't be cast down!' Lady Bingham misinterpreted Sovay's expression and patted her hand in sympathy. 'Not *everyone* can be as blessed as my two darling girls. You'll find someone eventually, I'm sure.'

Sovay swallowed back the biting remarks that ached to be said and managed to smile as sweetly as she could. She was relieved to hear a knock at her door.

'Sovay? Are you in there?'

'Hugh!' Sovay went to let him in. 'I have a visitor,' she added before he could say anything more. 'Lady Bingham has been kind enough to call.'

'Lady Bingham.' Hugh strode forward and bowed. 'What an unexpected pleasure.'

'Mr Middleton.' Lady Bingham returned his bow. 'It is good to see you safely returned from Paris.' He had exchanged his pantaloons for breeches but she surveyed his cropped hair with barely disguised distaste. 'Is that the latest fashion there? How very unusual.'

'It is,' Hugh replied, his eyes sparking with humour, and he touched the knot of tricolour ribbon in his buttonhole. 'And it is my greatest hope that it will soon be the fashion everywhere.' He ran a hand over his shorn locks. 'So much more manly and hygienic, don't you think?'

'Perhaps you are right, although I don't find it very becoming. Well, I must go. There is much to do before tonight. I'll see you both later.' She turned to Sovay. 'I'll send Lydia up with your dress, my dear.'

'What dress?' Hugh asked when they were alone.

'One she ordered from a Mayfair dressmaker,'

Sovay replied. 'It is of no importance. I have things to tell you.'

She quickly went through what had happened, what she had discovered in the tower and the dungeons beneath it. Hugh listened without interruption.

'I did not realise that you cared so much for this highwayman,' he said with a smile.

'I do not!' Sovay objected, a little too vehemently. 'It is Toby and – and his friends.'

'If it is any comfort, Dysart will hold off doing anything to him until after tonight's proceedings. Why waste such a spectacular entertainment? He will reserve that spectacle for his very special guests.'

'What about Gabriel? Will he be back in time?'

'Of course he will! I trust him like my own brother.' Hugh stood up and went to the window. 'He is more to me than a brother. I would trust him with my life.'

CHAPTER 26

Sovay looked into the cheval glass with an intense dissatisfaction that brought her near to tears.

'What's wrong, miss?' Lydia could not understand why she should be so discontented. 'You look lovely.'

'That's a matter of opinion,' Sovay said, staring at her reflection in the mirror. 'But thank you for helping me, Lydia. You've done all you can. Now you must go.'

Lydia sat down on the bed. She didn't want to desert Sovay but neither did she want to cross her, not in this kind of a mood. And she was slightly awed by her mistress. In that dress, she looked like a different person, older and, well, even more beautiful.

'I can't say I'll be sorry,' she said. 'Summat queer's going on, that's for certain. All the servants are leaving. They are all terrified, won't say a word. None of them live here, 'cept for that creepy little butler and a couple of footmen and the men they call guards. What does he need with guards? And who's that woman in the frightful wig?'

'Never mind about her.' Sovay turned to face Lydia. 'If the servants are leaving, that's good. You can go with them and not attract attention. When you get to the gate, wait there for Gabriel and stay with him, no matter what happens. You must stay with him. D'you understand?' Lydia nodded and began collecting her things together. 'Good girl.' Sovay gave Lydia a quick kiss on the cheek. 'Now off you go.'

When Sovay was alone, she turned back to the mirror, perhaps expecting to see something different, but the reflection was the same. Not exactly displeasing, but not a self that she recognised. Her hair was piled high, caught up in a black bandeau set with pearls. Lydia had worked with painstaking care, winding and teasing the long, dark ringlets until they fell in perfect curling tendrils down to Sovay's neck and shoulders. Sovay had never worn anything as low cut, anything that exposed so much flesh before. And never anything this colour. Light hues suited her best, because of her dark colouring, and she had assumed that Madame Chantal would make something in primrose perhaps, or pale green, or blue, but this? This was scarlet. The colour became her, certainly, the effect augmented by Lydia's discreet application of rouge and the blush that was presently washing Sovay's cheeks. The gown was high-waisted and she could wear little by way of stays and petticoats underneath it, just an inner linen bodice. When she moved, the thin silk clung to her almost as if she was walking naked. Sovay's blush deepened. What with that and the colour and the fabric, how could she possibly wear it?

She had been bested, she had to admit it. In this little contest between them, Lady Bingham had won; there could be no doubt.

Her anguished scrutiny was interrupted by a knock at the door.

'Are you decent?'

'It depends what you mean by decent.'

'Oh, I say!' Hugh exclaimed as he came into the

room.

'There!' His reaction drove Sovay back to near despair. 'I can't possibly wear it. It's scarlet! I look like a whore!"

'Oh, I don't know . . .' Hugh adopted an expression of judicious scrutiny. 'More crimson, I'd say.' He laughed. 'As for the other, you'd have to be a very high-class one to wear such a gown. Steady on, now.' He dodged the hairbrush that came flying towards him. 'Don't lose your temper. I was only teasing.'

'You know I don't like to be teased.' Sovay sat down, her anger dissipating. 'What am I going to do? It has shocked even you.'

'I'm not *shocked* as such. Just surprised. I've never seen you looking like this before.'

'But what shall I *do*? I have nothing else suitable.'

'Wear it, of course. You'll be a sensation. Dressed in the height of fashion.'

'I don't *want* to be a sensation and I've never even *seen* a dress like this, so how can that be?'

'Not *here*. Not in London. I meant in Paris.'

'The dressmaker's French.'

'There you have it. She must still maintain her contacts there. That dress is very *à la mode*, believe me.'

'I should not have put my faith in Madame Chantal. Lady Bingham knew I'd have to wear it, that I'd have nothing else remotely suitable. She's beaten me.'

'Sovay!' Hugh turned her from the horrified contemplation of her own reflection. 'Look at me. You are not beaten unless you let yourself be. She *wants* you to be miserable, she *wants* you to feel uncomfortable. Don't hang back, embarrassed. Show her that she hasn't won, that you have not been defeated. That's a beautiful dress; you are a beautiful girl. Wear it as Madame Chantal meant it to be worn. Now, if you can bear to think of someone else for a moment, what about me? Will I do?'

Sovay tore her attention away from herself to look at her brother. He turned around to show off his coat of pale turquoise, leopardskin-spotted velvet, throwing back the facing to show the ivory embroidered waistcoat and dove-grey breeches.

'You look very fine,' she said, although his formal attire was rather at odds with his short blond hair. The curls along his forehead and the clusters at his temples made him look very boyish.

'Very well then, if I pass muster, Miss Sovay, may I have the pleasure of escorting you to this evening's reception?'

He bowed and held her wrap. His large blue eyes under quirking brows seemed incapable of gravitas and when he smiled at her, she found that, despite her misgivings about the dress, she had to smile back. He took her arm, proud but at the same time somewhat apprehensive. She seemed entirely unaware of how very beautiful she was.

❦

A pair of footmen opened the doors and the butler marched forward into the room, announcing their arrival in a loud sonorous voice entirely at odds with his diminutive size. Heads turned and conversations faltered. Sir Robert Dysart detached himself from one of the casually formed groups and came to welcome them. He was dressed in glossy black silk, with mere wisps of white lace at his neck and cuffs. His coat was faced with beads of jet, which glittered in the light from the candelabra. The effect was imposing and somewhat sinister; he more than ever resembled the glossy black birds that perched on his battlements and roosted in his tower.

He was at his most charming and most apologetic that other business had kept him away from the house and their company until now. He was lying to them, but if he realised that they knew it, he didn't show it, or perhaps he didn't care. Lady Bingham accompanied him. She clapped her hands in triumph when she saw Sovay, claiming for herself the girl's beauty and elegance. Hugh went off for an urgent word with someone before she could claim him, too. Just as Lady Bingham was about to put a hand on her protégée's arm and steer her away with a proprietorial air, Sir Robert Dysart stepped in between them.

'A word before you do, Lady Bingham. A word before you do.' He took Sovay's arm himself and led her away from the older woman. 'I'd like to show our guest something of the splendours of my Glass Drawing Room. Some call it the Mirror Room and I think you can see why.'

He conducted her through the knots of men scattered through the enormous room. Sovay was surprised at how few people there were. Thirteen in all, she counted, not including herself and Lady Bingham. They were the only women. Sir Robert took a glass of champagne for her from a servant who stood so still that he might have been carved from ebony, all the while talking of plate glass from France, cut glass from Ireland, marble from Italy. The walls, made entirely of glass, glittered and dazzled with the light reflected from branched candles held in silver sconces and the magnificent candelabra that hung from the ceiling. At intervals along the room huge mirrors, had been placed in opposition one to another and gave a disquieting illusion of the room reflected to infinity.

'I got the idea from the interiors of the villas of Nero and Caligula that I saw as a young man in Italy. There, of course, the walls were of porphyry, but the coloured glass does very well . . .' He indicated to the fluted pilasters, each one aglitter with gilt and copper, and the red glass panels that ran from floor to ceiling between the mirrors. 'The tiny flecks of foil held within catch the light and make them glisten. A remarkable effect, do you not think?'

Sovay nodded her agreement, although they looked to her like freshly spilt blood.

'I'm so pleased to be able to welcome you to Thursley. Hugh as well. I'm so sorry your father could not come, too. He has many friends here. We would like to welcome him to our circle. This is very much a meeting of minds. His contribution will be missed. I have read his writings on many subjects, most particularly science, with very great interest. I have ambitions in that direction myself. He is still in Paris? I am surprised that Hugh left him there.'

'My father was unwell . . .' Sovay faltered. Dysart already knew that.

'I wish him a speedy recovery and that he can get away soon. You must be worried. I know how difficult it is to send or receive word now. The road to

Dover is so plagued by highwaymen. I will do what I can. I have sent an agent. He waits at Dover. My instruction will be relayed to him by messenger. So much safer than relying on the mail.' There was a warning in his words; he looked sideways to see if Sovay had heard it. 'I don't know what you have been told about this evening?'

'Very little,' she replied.

'After this reception, we will have supper, and then there will be a short ceremony.'

'What kind of ceremony?'

'Harmless, really. Think of it as acting in a charade. It is a way for us to demonstrate our belief in enlighten-ment, reason, man's perfectibility. Women's, too. You believe in those things, don't you, Sovay?'

Sovay inclined her head. They were hard to deny.

'Good, good.' He patted her arm. 'You hardly have to do anything, anything at all. When it is over, we can think about getting your father back to you.'

'And if I refuse?'

'Why would you refuse?' Dysart feigned astonish-ment. 'I told you, it is nothing. To refuse such a small request would not be seen as a friendly act.' He drew closer and his voice dropped the pretence of carrying anything but menace. 'I think we spoke of this before. A pity you do not seem able to heed my warnings. Let me speak more plainly. If you are not our friend, then you are our enemy, and for any Englishman, let alone a sick one, France is a very dangerous place to be.'

Sovay looked past him to the mirror on the opposite wall and saw their images reflected there. The scarlet and the black, locked together, stretching off to infinity.

As soon as he left her side, she was uncomfortably aware of the attention she was attracting. The dress was exactly the same shade as the panels on the wall. She was sure she'd heard the words *silk* and *scarlet* and *whore*, but she did not care what they were thinking, after the first shock she rather liked it. She braved the hostile, appraising glances, searching the faces turned away too quickly, looking for someone she knew. In a distant corner, she saw Virgil Barrett talking to Mr Oldfield. The American was looking over the other man's shoulder, staring right at her, but with a strange expression on his face, as if he had never seen her before. Sovay started across the room towards him, only to find Lady Bingham bearing down on her.

'Supper is just about to be announced,' she said, taking Sovay by the arm and guiding her in the opposite direction.

The guests moved into a room hardly less magnificent than the drawing room to find a series of sumptuous dishes laid out along a lengthy sideboard. They grazed up and down, helping themselves, and Lady Bingham was soon intent on filling her plate before the choicest morsels disappeared. Sovay took advantage of the freedom thus afforded to go off in search of Virgil or Hugh.

'Mr Barrett,' she said as she accosted him. 'Have you seen my brother?'

'I believe he has stepped outside.' The American smiled. 'The view from the battlements is very fine, so they say.'

'Is it indeed?' Sovay raised an eyebrow. She wanted to know what Hugh might be doing up there, but knew enough not to inquire. 'Am I to think that you have been avoiding me?' she asked, steering them back to safe ground.

'Certainly not,' he replied. 'On my life!'

'It seems so to me.'

'How am I to get near to you when you are as closely chaperoned as a girl at her first ball?'

'There is no one with me now.'

'No.' Virgil looked around. 'No, indeed.'

'Yet you still look askance.'

'I do not mean to,' he answered. 'It's just that you are . . .' He stopped. 'You look . . .' He could not meet her eye and glanced about him, thoroughly discomforted. 'Damn me if I can find the words for it.'

'You think I look like a whore,' Sovay supplied, her ire rising. 'Don't you?'

'No, never!' he exclaimed with some indignation, his fresh complexion colouring. He dropped his voice, aware that he had raised it. 'Nothing was further from my mind, I do assure you!'

'What is it then?'

'It's just, it's just that –' He shook his head. She certainly looked nothing like the vision of Flora that he had first seen coming in from the garden at Compton. 'It does not signify what I think. There is something else of much greater importance.' His voice took on an increased urgency. 'Despite what you say, I have been trying to get near you all evening. There's something you must know –'

Sovay never found out what Virgil had to tell her, or what he thought of her appearance, or why it had so disturbed him, for just then Lady Bingham reappeared at her elbow, prompted by a nod from Sir Robert. It would soon be time for them to move on to the next stage of the night's business and she had been given special charge of Sovay. From this point on, no one was to come near the girl.

❖❖❖

Captain Greenwood stood with Toby, gazing out from the battlements. It was a clear night. The stars glittered in great profusion, stretching from horizon to horizon, their light dimmed by the brightness of the moon. A full moon. A hunter's moon. Much favoured by the fraternity. The heaths would be thick with them tonight. Somewhere near a dog fox barked. The sound sudden and sharp in the clear air. Next to him, Toby started. These city boys knew nothing. Everything out here was strange to him, but he had sharp eyes. He'd found a lantern, the wax still tacky. Someone had been signalling from up here.

'Easy, lad!' The highwayman put a hand out to steady him. 'It's just a fox.'

Toby had done very well so far. Greenwood rubbed his wrists where the manacles had chafed the skin, but now was not the time for the boy to lose his nerve. It had been simplicity itself to subdue the guards, already befuddled by gin, and leave them, bound and gagged, in their own dungeons.

'What are we looking for?' Toby asked. His voice was brave enough, but nerves or the night air were making him shiver.

'Hush!' Greenwood answered in a whisper, his finger on his own lips. 'Sound carries out here. We're looking for a sign.'

'A sign of what?'

The highwayman shook his head. He wasn't sure, but he knew from his military days that it didn't do to move too soon. They had no idea of the size of the force pitted against them. There were servants, certainly, and the men who had acted as their gaolers. Greenwood guessed they were recruited from the prisons and the scum of the regiments, but they were hard men just the same. How many more of them? This place was big enough to contain an army. As for his own forces? A wounded boy and a bunch of whores, who might fight like demons, or might cower in corners. They might run amok and start up who knew what alarms before making off and getting lost in the surrounding darkness. There was no telling how they would behave. It would be like herding cats. Although their presence here was none of his doing, he felt responsible for them. Probably better to leave them where they were, for the moment anyway. He paced, angry and frustrated. He wanted to help Sovay. All his instincts told him she was in danger, but on his own, with only Toby to help him, there was precious little he could do.

The highwayman was so lost in his brooding thoughts that Toby was the first to see anything.

'There, out there, Captain!' The boy tugged at his sleeve.

'What?' Greenwood scanned the area around, out to the horizon. 'What do you see?'

'A light. Then another.' Toby looked out anxiously, pointing. 'There in them trees.'

Greenwood stared into the dark parkland but could see nothing.

'Are you sure?'

'Yes. And there's something else.' The boy was tugging at his sleeve again, shifting his focus. 'A coach with its lights out, just come over the rise.'

Greenwood felt a surge of excitement. The boy's sharp sight had served them well a second time. There it was! A faint grey presence etched on to the blackness, as faint as the phantom coach of legend. It showed, just for a second, before slipping under the covering canopy provided by the great avenue of trees.

They both listened intently, but could not hear the crunch of the wheels on gravel. Either the coach had stopped or the driver had muffled the wheels. Greenwood gripped the parapet until his knuckles whitened. It had to be Gabriel. Who else would come with such stealth? He hoped he'd brought some sort of force with him. What difference would one man make?

There was a smell, acrid and pungent. The Captain turned his head, following the scent like a dog. Smoke, coming up from below, drifting on the night air.

'Over here, Captain!' Toby was tugging at his sleeve again, dragging him to the other side of the tower. 'Look down there!'

They both ducked down instinctively to avoid any possibility of being seen from the ground. Greenwood crawled along, spying through the deeply cut crenulations until he found a position where he could remain hidden but could see what was going on below.

'What are they doing?' Toby whispered.

Greenwood shook his head. 'I do not know.'

A line of people were walking in procession, flanked by servants bearing torches. Dysart led the column. In the torchlight, the black silk of his coat shimmered greenish-black, like a blowfly's back. Six pairs of men followed behind him at a careful, measured pace, gaudy in their evening attire, but subdued and quiet, as solemn as monks.

Sovay was at the back of the procession, accompanied by Lady Bingham who walked close to her, as if she held the girl by the arm. They were taking a path between high yew hedges that wound in the way of a maze towards a circular building. The rounded roof, just visible through the dark, spreading branches of tall pines, gleamed in the moonlight. Why were they going there? For what purpose? Sovay did not seem to be a prisoner, and was going willingly, but there was something he did not like about this little procession, something sinister that smacked of ritual. The Captain watched until the height of the hedges and the density of the surrounding grove took them out of his sight.

Once they had disappeared, he judged it safe to move.

'What about Jack and the others?' Toby said as they took the stairs.

'Leave them where they are for the moment,' Greenwood replied. 'They are in no danger that I can judge. We'll come back for them. I don't want them running around, drawing attention.'

They were outside now, edging along the side of the building. Greenwood was without a pistol, but he had helped himself to rather a fine sword that he'd found in one of the galleries.

'Where are we going?' Toby asked.

'To the stables to borrow a horse. From the turret, it

looks to be in the north-western quadrant.'

'Where's that?'

'Over there. Quiet now.'

There was activity in the kitchens, servants talking, but the stable block was in darkness. Any footmen or drivers who had come with their masters would be away eating and drinking, knowing they would not be needed, and grooms likewise.

The stable was dark except for the moonlight slanting through the windows, and quiet with just occasional snorting and pawing from the horses in their stalls. The Captain left Toby on lookout, found a saddle in the tack room and went in search of a horse. He was good with horses and the animals liked him. He went along the stalls speaking softly to them, finally settling on a docile-looking chestnut. He didn't want anything too mettlesome prancing and dancing about. He led her out of her stall, talking all the time as he put the saddle on her. He rode out quietly and reached down for Toby.

'Up behind me, Toby lad. We'll be off into the park to meet the phantom coachman.'

CHAPTER 27

The entrance to the temple was flanked by two guards dressed in some kind of oriental armour. In the torchlight, rows of overlapping metal plates glimmered across their leather tunics and quilted skirts. Their gauntleted hands clutched tall halberds, equipped with long, curved blades. They held these crossed, barring the entrance. As Dysart approached, they withdrew their weapons. The great bronze doors yawned open with an exactly synchronised, smooth motion as if they were part of the same linked mechanism. Only the gleam of sweat on the guards' bronze faces and the glitter of dark eyes under the edge of the flaring wide-brimmed helmets betrayed that these were men and not mechanical exhibits from Dysart's collection.

When everyone had entered, the doors swung shut on oiled hinges. They closed with a hollow boom and the halberds clicked back into place. The sudden draught of air agitated the flickering torchlight and sent strange, fantastic shadows dancing around the semicircular entrance hall. Around the yellow stone walls, a line of black robes hung, bunched and drooping from their hooks like crows on a gamekeeper's gibbet.

Each man went to his allotted peg, marked with roman numerals in gold, to collect his robe: plain black gowns, with full sleeves and cowled hoods, like monks' habits. As soon as they were robed, their individual natures disappeared. Except for Dysart, who wore a gold insignia denoting some kind of office, it was impossible to tell one from another. They had become the Order of the Illuminati.

Two further bronze doors opened and the robed men processed into a shadowy chamber. Virgil, Hugh and Mr Oldfield went with them. Sovay began to fear that she had made a disastrous misjudgement. Perhaps loyalty to this society was greater than any obligations of friendship or family.

'Calm yourself, my dear.' Lady Bingham patted her arm, her blue eyes mild. 'It is but play-acting, that is all. You know how men like to dress up.'

Sovay took no comfort from Lady Bingham. She walked away from her captor towards the massive bronze inner doors. Embossed faces of hideous monsters and leering satyrs grinned and grimaced at her and she shivered. The room was chill inside its stone walls and her cloak had been taken from her, but whatever fate awaited her in the room beyond, she was determined to show no fear.

◆➤⊹◆

The doors opened and two cowled figures escorted her into the inner chamber. Sovay turned, expecting Lady Bingham to accompany her, but the older woman made no move to join her.

It was play-acting merely, Lady Bingham told herself. Many women had gone through the ritual before to become associate Illuminati: sisters, daughters of members, why she herself had, many years ago, when she was a young girl. Surely, Sovay had been warned in some way, schooled as to the part she had to play? Perhaps it was that look behind, or the thought that she should have been the one to warn Sovay, but at the very last moment, Lady Bingham's blue eyes softened and her expressionless face creased with concern. Seized by a powerful sense of misgiving, she stepped forward, but the doors were already closing. It was too late. Sovay was imprisoned with her fate.

The semicircle of robed figures stood, heads bowed, facing the Grand Master. Sir Robert Dysart stood on a raised plinth in front of a plain stone altar, set into a recess that had been carved from the living rock. Above it, a beam of red light shone out through the centre of a great lens shape carved into the wall. The All-Seeing Eye of the Illuminati.

Dysart raised the sword that he held in his hands, the tip pointing out at those assembled before him.

'Shouldst thou become a traitor or perjurer,' he began, 'let this sword remind thee of each and all the members in arms against thee. Do not hope to find safety, whithersoever thou mayest fly, shame and remorse as well as the vengeance of thine unknown brothers will torture and pursue thee.'

The cowled heads bowed in deep obeisance. The hoods shadowed their faces so Sovay had no way of knowing one from another: who was her friend and who was her foe.

'Doest thou swear eternal silence and everlasting obedience to all superiors and regulations of the Order? Doest thou renounce all personal views and opinions, consider the wellbeing of the Order as thine own and swear to serve it, as long as breath remains in you?'

'We so swear,' a rumble of male voices intoned the response.

'I don't like it.' Hugh used the cover of the ritual responses to mutter to Virgil who stood next to him. 'What if he really means to go through with it? I'm going to stop this!'

'We cannot act yet!' Virgil put a hand on his arm. 'We have to wait until he swears the oath.'

'And doest thou further swear,' Dysart continued, 'to break the bonds that bind you to father, mother, brother, sister, wife, family, friends, King, and church, and any and all to whom thou may have promised faith, obedience and allegiance?'

'We so swear.'

'Then from this moment forth, you are free from the so-called oath to country and from the laws and tyranny of kings and governments.' Dysart raised the sword above his head in a gesture of benediction. '*Homo est Deus*. Live in the name of the Generating Fire and the Illuminating Light!'

That was it. The oath was sworn. It put allegiance to the Illuminati above everything, above King, country, and it was treasonous as the law stood now.

Dysart turned away to face the glare of the All-Seeing Eye. Hugh and Virgil began to move forward but found their way blocked by a tight phalanx of cowled figures. Two attendants seized Sovay by the arms and took her towards the altar: a slab of marble, the colour of ancient, dripped candle wax. The slab was chipped at the edges, the surface marked with scratches ingrained with dirt, as though it had spent much time under the ground and had been recently disinterred from some antique pagan temple. Here and there the stone was washed with red, either the result of natural pigmentation, or the porous stone's tendency to take on the colour of sacrifice.

Sovay's eyes widened. She struggled against the men who held her, but their arms were strong. They backed her onto the altar and the hard stone caught her behind the knees, threatening to throw her off balance and onto its stained surface. Sir Robert advanced towards her. Only she could see the greedy gleam in his eyes, the flare of his narrow nostrils, the rictus grin of anticipated pleasure as he held the sword ready, poised above the altar. It was as if he could already see the billowing flow of scarlet onto scarlet, as if he could smell and taste the hot, coppery gush of her deep heart's blood. Where were Hugh and Virgil? Where was Mr Oldfield? Would nobody step forward to save her? Was loyalty to the brotherhood so much greater than the love of family and friend?

This was a ritual enactment. A token sacrifice. Often, the woman in question, taken by excitement and euphoria, joined in the pleasurable activities which inevitably followed one of Dysart's 'ceremonies'. Indeed, many here were hoping that this beautiful young girl in that dress that revealed her magnificent figure would be willing to do so. Then there was a rustling, shuffling from those assembled, a restless movement of expectation, almost precognition, as Dysart raised his sword. The disturbance at the side of the chamber was hardly noticed as a wave of excitement rippled through their ranks. All eyes were on Dysart. Surely, he did not really mean to carry out this thing?

'Enough!' A voice rang out from the gathered

congregation. The two men holding her stopped in their motion. Their grip tightened as the voice went on, 'I declare this gathering to be a seditious assembly and furthermore declare that any and all present here are guilty of treason, having openly and publicly denied allegiance to the King and to the laws and rightful Government of this country.'

Dysart whirled round, the sword now no more than a theatrical prop in his hands.

'Oldfield! And what are you going to do about it?'

Virgil and Hugh had fought their way to the front of the assembly. They threw back their hoods and stepped up to confront him.

'I declare you to be apostate!' Dysart roared, holding them at bay with his sword. 'Your lives are forfeit!'

'That might be so,' Oldfield shouted back as Hugh and Virgil continued to circle him. 'But you will find that, even now, magistrates are approaching Thursley with the appropriate warrants.' He looked around at his cowled brethren. 'They are accompanied by sufficient forces to ensure that the warrants will be served upon everyone present. They might even be here.'

At the mention of magistrates and warrants, confusion spread among those assembled. The confusion turned to panic at the sound of gunshots from outside, followed by repeated blows on the great bronze outer doors and shouts demanding admittance. The Illuminati threw back their hoods to reveal their startled and frightened faces. They became ordinary men again; the sinister ceremony diminished to a foolish charade. They began to run in every direction, desperate to escape, but knowing they were trapped.

Some tore off their robes, frantic to divest themselves of their regalia and there was a rush to prise open the door of the ante-room, to get out of the incriminating chamber.

Hugh went to Sovay, put his robe around her shoulders and held her to him. Sovay was trembling. She might have appeared calm and dry-eyed, but all the while fear had been dissolving her like an acid from the inside. It had not been fear of Dysart and what he might do that had most worked on her; it had been the fear of betrayal, that the oath to the Illuminati was real, that Hugh, Virgil, men she trusted above all others, might turn their backs upon her. That had nearly unstrung her. An echo of that feeling swept through her as she clung to Hugh, but it soon receded to leave her stronger than before, determined to play her part in Dysart's downfall.

'Are you all right?' Hugh asked as he held her.

She nodded, hiding her face in his shoulder.

'Really?' Hugh looked down at her, tipping her chin up to see her more closely.

'Of course. It was only a little play-acting, after all,' she said as she smiled up at him, but he saw that her eyes were brimming with tears.

'Where's Dysart?' Virgil interrupted them.

In all the confusion, the spy master had vanished.

CHAPTER 28

He was nowhere to be found in the chamber or the milling confusion in the room beyond. The battering at the outer door was intensifying. The forces outside would be in soon enough. Oldfield was trying to instil some sort of order. The game was up.

'He must not get away!' Hugh shouted, casting round for Dysart's means of escape.

He seemed to have vanished into the air, as if he really did have supernatural powers, but then Virgil noticed some of the stones behind the altar appeared to have become dislodged. They formed a doorway which was worked by some hidden mechanism that had failed to fully close. By heaving together, Virgil and Hugh managed to force a wide enough aperture to allow them entrance.

Virgil took a torch from the wall and squeezed through.

'It is the entrance to a tunnel. He must have escaped through here.'

Hugh went after him, but when Sovay made to follow, he stopped her.

'No, Sovay. Stay with Oldfield. This may be dangerous.'

'And coming near to being sacrificed was not?' Sovay gave a mirthless laugh. 'No, Hugh, I'm coming with you.'

She remembered the look in Dysart's eyes as she

was being dragged backwards onto that loathsome altar. He had made her feel somehow defiled. Her cheeks burned with the shame of it, even now. She could not stay behind and just wait for others to catch him. She had a personal score to settle. She had to be there when he was caught.

'Let her come, Hugh,' Virgil called back. 'We don't have time to argue. She has shown more courage than most men I know and he gets further away with every minute we waste.'

Virgil swept his light around, illuminating the chamber in which they were standing. They had entered a series of tunnels carved into the soft rock. Strange shapes and grotesque faces loomed out of the chalky stone, whether carved by pagan peoples, or there as part of Dysart's bizarre rituals, it was hard to tell. Just above the entrance, a red light hung in a deep niche, positioned to shine through the pupil of the carved eye. From this side of the wall, the All-Seeing Eye was diminished to a tawdry illusion, like the face carved on a country child's turnip lantern.

The outer chamber gave onto a tunnel which became progressively lower and narrower, leading off into darkness. Far ahead, the tiny spark of Dysart's torch got smaller by the second.

'We've got to keep him in sight,' Virgil said. 'He knows these tunnels better than we do. There's no telling how much of a warren they are, or which way he'll go.'

Dysart knew his advantage. He increased his pace and for a time it seemed that they might have lost him. Virgil led them on into the darkness, taking one tunnel after another, ruled by instinct, and finally they were rewarded by a distant red flicker. The air was becoming fouler, ever more stale. Sovay noticed that their own torches were beginning to burn dim, ready to fail. They would be left in utter blackness, with no way back and no way forward. They could be down here forever with Dysart getting clean away.

Hugh reached back for her.

'Hold my hand. We must stay close together. I've been counting paces, working out the distance,' he whispered. 'If Dysart is making for the main part of the abbey, it can't be far now.'

'What if he isn't?' she whispered back. 'What if he's seeking to escape through some distant part of the grounds?'

'Then he is going in the wrong direction.' Hugh squeezed her hand harder. 'My mental compass works even underground.'

Sovay smiled in the darkness. If Hugh was right, they still had a chance of catching up with Dysart, and Hugh never got lost. When they were children, playing in the woods, he always knew exactly where they were, no matter how far had they wandered, and which was the quickest way home.

'Why would he go back?' she whispered. 'Why not try to escape?'

'Who knows?' Hugh shrugged. 'Who can read the mind of a madman?'

The end of the tunnel was marked by a small iron door. It had been left slightly ajar, as if whoever had left by it had not had time to lock it. The doorway opened onto a flight of steps leading up to a narrow spiral staircase, which appeared to be above ground. Lancet windows pierced the walls, admitting a faint silver wash of moonlight. Although Dysart had long disappeared beyond the first tight twists of the stairs, they could hear the swift patter and scrape of his fleeing footsteps. They started after him. Here and there, curtained doorways offered access to the abbey proper, but still the footsteps fled away from them, mounting ever higher. Why Dysart would try so hard to get away, only to climb the tower, was another mystery.

Suddenly, the footsteps stopped. Virgil put his arm out and indicated that they should proceed quietly, with all caution. They were approaching the laboratory. Sovay recognised the peculiarly pungent mixture of chemicals and organic decay.

Dysart was busy at the brick-built furnace, shovelling paper and documents into the fiery aperture, destroying the results of the vile experiments that he had conducted here. He resembled some demented alchemist with flames leaping and licking about him, surrounded by arcane instruments and pot-bellied copper stills.

He was so absorbed in his work that he did not notice them until they were fully in the room. He whirled round like some guilty thing, surprised. They stepped back in horror. For one terrible moment it appeared as though he really had undergone some dreadful, demonic transformation. His chest and abdomen were cased in an oval jointed carapace. His grey mask of a face glowed dull red in the glare from the fire and huge, round, protruding eyes glittered greenish and flickered with twin images of leaping flames. He hissed when he saw them, sucking breath through a series of holes and serrations.

He was wearing special clothing designed to protect him during experiments. On the bench, yet more papers were dissolving in a bubbling, choking bath of acid. He picked up a bundle of papers from the bench, clutching them to his chest.

'No one will steal my work from me. No one.' His voice came thick and muffled from behind the grille that covered his mouth. 'My rule would have ushered in a golden age of science, unfettered by matters of conscience and paltry consideration of ethics. Human life is nothing! Knowledge is everything! What are the rights you bleat about, when set against the shining advance of scientific discovery? Human beings are dust, mere grist to be crushed and ground between the great millstones of knowledge. You know nothing. You stand there staring, as ignorant as children, as stupid and unthinking as barbarians before the greatness of Rome.'

He threw the papers he clutched into the air to drift down and scatter over the floor, then he paced to the end of the bench. He took a large flask from a stand and held it in his hand, shaking it, admiring the viscous movement around the bottom of the round glass, the yellowish, greenish hue of the contents.

'Do you see this? An interesting substance. A discovery of mine which was later stolen by the German, Scheele. He called it dephlogisticated acid of salt. The theory of phlogiston has, of course, been discredited, but, unfortunately, we don't have time for that debate.' As he talked, Virgil and Hugh had been moving, making ready to close in on him, to cut off any avenue of escape. His grip on the flask tightened. 'Stay where you are, gentlemen! My lecture has not finished! As I was saying, an interesting substance. As Scheele's nomenclature suggests, it forms part of the make up of common salt. A harmless element, necessary to all life, I'm sure you'll agree. We can tell by taste that it is in your sweat, gentlemen, and your tears, my dear. It is in our blood. This.' He shook the flask, agitating the contents, causing the greenish-yellow fumes to swirl. 'This is *very* different. It leaches the colour from flowers and is highly toxic to man and beast alike. I know, from experimentation, *scientific* experimentation, that it burns the skin, irritates the eyes to blindness, dissolves the tissue of the lungs so that you drown in your own blood!'

With that he dropped the flask. Hugh and Virgil leapt backwards. A pale green miasma curled up from the spreading liquid, giving off the sweetish, sharp smell of pineapples, laced with the sting of pepper.

'Cover your mouth!' Virgil shouted. 'Cover your nose!'

Dysart raced for the main door, knocking over a lamp to cover his retreat.

They heard a key turning, as spilt oil soaked the scattered papers and snaked towards the blazing furnace. In moments a spurt of flames, a chance spark, would turn it into a spreading river of fire.

'Back! Back towards the staircase,' Virgil shouted through green, drifting fumes that tasted of metal and attacked the nose, throat and chest, making it hard to breathe. 'No! Don't go down! See how the gas clings to the ground? It will pour downwards. The stairs are narrow. We will have no chance. Up! We must go up!'

◆━◆━◆

It was a long climb to the top of the tower. Sovay could hardly see where to put her feet, her eyes were watering so profusely and her chest felt as if she was caught in the closing fist of a giant. Her throat was raw and each breath was a labour, wheezing and ragged. Hugh had to stop frequently, racked with coughing. He had always suffered from a weakness of the chest. Virgil came behind, urging them upwards.

'Keep on. Keep on,' he shouted, his own voice hoarse and roughened from the gas. 'It can't be far now.'

Just when Sovay thought she could not go any further for the burning in her legs and in her chest, the stairs took one more turn and she was under the open sky. She steadied herself against the parapet, taking great gulps of sweet air. Virgil came after her, bent over and retching. Then Hugh emerged. He collapsed to the ground and Sovay went to help him. His breath came in heaving ragged gasps, as if he could not get enough air into his chest.

'Help me to get him up,' she shouted to Virgil, but the American was distracted, staring upwards.

Sovay had been so glad to reach the open air and so preoccupied with Hugh that she had failed to see the huge structure that loomed over them. She stared, astonished. A balloon reared up into the night sky. A great globular bag encased in a mesh of strong netting, looking much like the ones that she had seen in illustrations with the panels painted a bright cerulean blue and lavishly decorated with billowing clouds. Apollo's golden chariot rode across the heavens, accompanied by frolicking spirits of the air. She and Hugh had made small versions when they were children, setting haystacks afire and getting into a deal of trouble. They had watched the frail, glowing paper globes floating off across the evening sky and had dreamed of making an ascent of their own. She had never seen a real one at such close quarters. It was huge. Cords, taut with strain, tethered the enormous floating structure to hoops driven into the stone floor of the tower. Some of Papa's friends had taken flights, but he considered it far too dangerous. He would never countenance anything so reckless.

Virgil came over to Sovay. Together, they helped Hugh to his feet.

'I'm sorry,' Hugh managed to whisper. He could hardly speak.

'Not at all.' Virgil steadied him against the parapet. 'You must have taken in more of that infernal gas. Stay here until your strength returns. Sovay, you must help me.' He sniffed the air. Sovay, too, could smell burning. 'I fear we do not have much time.'

Beneath the great balloon was a wicker gondola, a boat-shaped basket filled with bags of sand, blankets and items of clothing. There was even a hamper, with champagne and various delicacies.

'Dysart thinks of everything. If we meet him again, we must thank him.' Virgil gave a grim little smile.

Sovay looked up at the balloon. 'What on earth is it doing here?'

'My guess is it is here to provide yet another of Dysart's little surprises. A dawn flight after a night of debauchery. Something else to cause his guests to marvel. He cannot resist showing off. Then it became his way out of here. He's a quick thinker. I will grant him that. Now, we have to couple the gondola to the balloon. See the cords that are dangling from the balloon? They attach here, here, and here.'

'You don't mean for us to go up in it?'

'Of course! How else are we to escape?'

Sovay fell silent and did as she was told. All the while, the smell of burning was stronger. Smoke curled from the entrance to the narrow circular staircase. It was acting as a chimney. Dysart's laboratory must be well and truly ablaze.

When all was ready, Virgil helped Hugh into the gondola. His breathing still troubled him but he managed a weak smile.

'Remember when we were children?' he whispered and Sovay nodded. He turned to Virgil. 'This was always a dream of ours.'

They climbed in after him and Virgil began to saw through the cords that tethered the balloon to the ground. Sovay took Hugh's knife and helped him. She was careful to match him; the cords had to be severed in a certain order or the gondola would tip.

'Quick! Together!'

They were still attached by two cords when great tongues of flame spurted from the windows of Dysart's laboratory. Sovay felt the heat from them licking her face.

'Fast now! The bag is filled with hydrogen,' Virgil called. 'If we cannot free ourselves, it will go up like a fire balloon.'

The last cord gave and the balloon lurched, bumping across the floor of the tower. It began to ascend, but the blast of hot air rising up the spiral staircase caused it to veer sharply and the base of the gondola became caught on one of the pinnacles at the corner of the parapet.

Virgil grabbed a pole and pushed frantically but the gondola would not budge.

'There's no help for it.' He threw the pole from him. 'I'll have to climb out.'

'No!' Sovay shouted in horror, but the American was already over the side of the gondola and standing on the narrow crenulations of the battlements, some three hundred feet above the ground. A series of deep detonations caused the fabric of the tower to shudder beneath his feet. He hung onto the cords trailing from the sides of the gondola and swung himself inside the parapet. The cradle around the wickerwork base of the gondola had snagged on the decorative flourish that capped the pinnacle.

'Sovay! Give me that pole!'

Sovay hung over the side to hand it to him.

'A couple of knocks should do it. Move the sandbags over to the other side of the basket and then you and Hugh get over there when I shout. Be ready.'

Virgil secured the rope round his waist. He used the pole to push at the base of the gondola and work it free from the obstruction. Sparks flew about like fireflies, flakes of burning paper danced in the air, brought up on the fierce updraught from below. At any moment, one of them could alight on the balloon's panels. It would take seconds for an ember to eat through the thin layer of rubberised silk and ignite the gas beneath. He tried to put such thoughts out of his head. He worked methodically, patiently levering the thickly plaited band of wicker away from the stone hook of the pinnacle. Any element of panic would render his actions futile, making it impossible to free the balloon and save its passengers.

The balloon wasn't budging. The gondola was firmly hooked and the wind was holding it against the pinnacle. Time to try a different tack. He looked for a joint and dealt the thin spire one mighty crack and then another. One more blow and the pinnacle began to topple. He braced himself. He had to be ready. If he wasn't ready, they were all doomed. He was the only one who knew how to fly the thing.

'Now!'

Virgil's voice came from below. Sovay rolled over to the opposite side from him, dragging Hugh with her. She'd already moved most of the sandbags. Indeed, so much weight had been shifted that the gondola yawed alarmingly and for a heart-stopping second Sovay thought that they might be tipped out. Then Virgil's counterweight began to bite.

Sovay looked over to the opposite side of the gondola, expecting to see the American, but he wasn't there. She scanned the wicker edge of the basket, thinking to see his hands there pulling himself back over to them, but there was no sign of that either. His weight was there, preventing the gondola from tipping, which must mean . . . Sovay's eyes widened and her hand went to her mouth, stifling a gasp. Virgil must be hanging, helpless, unable to regain the safety of the gondola. They were floating free now, the tower somewhere below and to the side of them. How long would it be before he would be forced by weakness and exhaustion to let go and tumble to certain death many hundreds of feet below? She made ready to dash over, to see where he was, to offer assistance, when Hugh grabbed her arm.

'If you do that, you'll tip the basket and we'll all

tumble.'

'I will be careful, Hugh, but I have to go.'

Sovay shook herself free and began edging slowly over to the other side of the gondola, ignoring her brother's protests.

She leaned over the side of the gondola. Virgil was pulling himself, hand over hand, up the rope that he had secured round his waist. She reached down, ready to help pull him in to safety. Virgil took her hand and swung up to grab onto the side of the gondola. He hauled himself over, falling into her arms.

All about was the rush of black wings as the birds that haunted the tower rose in a dense cloud around them. The air was loud with their harsh cries as they ascended in a great beating of powerful wings. Their feathers flashed silver in the moonlight as they flew higher, wheeling above the tower. The birds, alerted by some ancient instinct, sensed that some dreadful disaster was about to occur.

'Look!' Virgil drew her to the side of the car. 'Look down there.'

They were gaining height with every second and the abbey seemed to be plunging away from them, its elegant cruciform shape laid out like an architect's drawing. Sovay could clearly see the cloisters and long galleries, the steeply pitched roof of the Great Entrance Hall, the rounded towers and square turrets, spiked with spires.

The impossibly tall tower stood proud, as slim as a pencil against the night sky. Suddenly, from deep within its narrow compass came a series of loud detonations. The whole length of it seemed to vibrate like a needle, as if shaken by an earthquake. Showers of sparks shot from the sides: white, blue, green, red and purple like a huge firework display. Saltpetre, black powder, phosphorus and sodium. Who knew what devil's brew of chemicals he kept in his laboratory?

The fireworks were followed by great gouts of flame and further explosions. Sovay leaned out of the basket to see more, and then froze in an attitude of horror. With a great groan and a rending of timber and cement, the tower began to fall.

Far, far below figures, tiny as insects, had stood transfixed, as fascinated as they had been by the fireworks and flames and even more astonished to see a balloon sailing up into the night sky. Now they were scattering in every direction, running for their lives.

Hugh leaned over the other side of the gondola and they all stared down, trying to make out if any they knew were among the rushing figures scurrying on the ground. Their feelings of anxiety grew to a terrible sense of helplessness. The toppling tower would fall on friend and foe alike, and all the while they rose higher and higher, the wind bearing them away to the south.

CHAPTER 29

They floated, suspended between earth and heaven, heading for who knew where. The wind took them steadily southward over a landscape illuminated by the brightness of the moon. Sovay stared down, fascinated. This was the world as few had ever seen it. Shadowy patterns of fields lay scrolled out beneath them, defined by dark, knotted lines of hedges and black smudges of woodland. The moonlight turned lakes into mirrors and the Thames ran like a wide silver ribbon, winding towards the slumbering city. Here and there lay single homesteads, the buildings as tiny as a child's farm. Hamlets and villages huddled in clusters or lay strung out along the winding white threads of the roads. All full of sleeping people, quite unaware that they were being overlooked. Sometimes, the balloon swooped low enough to see the dark shapes of animals, horses and cows, standing in fields like slate statues, or sheep spread out over a hillside like scattered silk cocoons. Then, Virgil ordered sand to be emptied over the side and they would rise away again, up into the sky.

'Where are we going?' Hugh asked.

'Where the wind takes us,' Virgil replied. 'Let us hope it holds in this southerly direction. We will land before daybreak. Then we will make for the coast and from there to France.'

'Look! Look there!'

Sovay pointed backwards in the direction that they

had come. A horseman was galloping below them, apparently following their progress across the countryside.

'I see him!' Hugh yelled, leaning out as far as he dared. 'It must be Greenwood.'

He waved his kerchief and the horseman waved his hat.

'It is!' Sovay joined him. 'I'm sure of it!'

She held onto the side of the basket, willing it to be him. Perhaps all had not perished in the terrible collapse of that monstrous tower. If he was alive, so might the others be: Lydia, Gabriel, Oldfield, Toby and his friends. Innocents caught in the machinery of Dysart's evil intent. She had been weighed down by the thought that so many might have been killed. Now her spirit soared as the fear spilled from her like so much sand.

'Dawn is coming.' Virgil pointed to a smear of saffron just tingeing the eastern horizon. 'I'll look for a good place to land. We don't want to be up in this thing when day comes. It would draw too much attention. I'll try to come down in plain sight of him.'

Virgil released the valve which allowed the gas to escape and the ground rushed up towards them as cows scattered in every direction. The landing was smoother than Sovay expected. A gentle bumping of the basket spilled them out over the short grass of the low hillside.

Greenwood arrived soon after, leading his exhausted horse behind him.

'You led me a merry dance.' He threw himself on to the grass beside them. 'It's a good thing Toby has sharp eyes.'

The boy slid from the horse, staggering slightly as he reached the ground. Sovay asked after Gabriel and Lydia, praying that he would say that they were safe and well.

'They were, when last I seen 'em. And together.' His frown made furrows in the pale particles that still covered his face. 'It were like the world was ending. Great chunks of stone tumbling through the air, dust everywhere. I was lucky the Captain had his wits about him or I'd have been caught up in it, like the others. Jack's safe – he were wi' me. Captain saved the both of us. Ma Pierce weren't so lucky. All that was left was her wig sitting atop a pile of rubble. Must have been dead underneath, that's my belief. Never seen alive without it, that's a certainty.'

Toby gave a bleak little laugh. He owed her nothing. She'd brought misery and degradation into his short life and he was not inclined to show false sentiment. The world was better off without her, as far as he was concerned.

'And Mr Oldfield?' Sovay asked.

'He's safe,' Greenwood nodded. 'Busy rounding up the conspirators when I last saw him.'

There had been no sign of Dysart. Greenwood and Toby were jubilant. They both assumed that he had perished in the explosion. No one could have survived if they had been in the tower.

'We have no proof of it,' Hugh said. 'The place was a warren of secret passages. He could have left before the tower caught fire.'

'Even if he did survive,' Greenwood argued, 'he will be thoroughly discredited!'

'Let us hope that is so,' Virgil frowned. 'But it would

not do to dismiss him too soon and too lightly. Meanwhile, do you have any idea where we might be?'

'In Kent,' Greenwood replied. 'I know the country pretty well. One of the reasons I've been able to follow you. There's a town not too distant. I'll ride to get horses. I know an inn there and the landlord owes me a favour.' He rose and stretched. 'Then I'll be off back to London. See how things are with Mr Oldfield. I don't know how he regards men of my profession,' he gave a wry smile, 'but I am prepared to offer him my services. Are you coming with me, young Toby?'

Toby had never been outside the city before. This was his first country excursion. The great expanse of green was making him nervous. The cows had gone back to their grazing, but they kept looking in his direction.

'Reckon I will,' he nodded. 'If you don't mind, miss.'

'I don't mind in the least.' Sovay smiled. 'You look after things for me there.'

◆➤✦◄◆

Greenwood returned with horses and money to buy what they needed, for they had left Thursley with nothing. He would not accept refusal and would take no thanks.

'It is only what you would do for me, if our places were reversed. Besides, what is money?' he said with a smile. 'I can get more easily enough. Where will you go now? What will you do?'

'We will go to France,' Virgil said. 'But first I must go to Dover, to arrange for the necessary papers and a passage.'

'Will you sail from there?'

'No.' The American shook his head. 'Too many eyes, too many spies. I will find a small town on the coast somewhere, and we will go from there.'

'Very well.' Greenwood mounted his horse. 'May good fortune attend you. Go well,' he said to Sovay as he held her stirrup. 'I would counsel you not to go, to return to London with me, but I know that you would not listen and I do not like to waste my breath. I've never known a girl so wedded to risk and adventure, but be careful. Life is precious. You don't want to learn that lesson too late.'

He smiled and winked at her and, before she could think of a suitable riposte, he was up on his own horse, with Toby behind him, and away.

He was not the only one to try to persuade her to go back to London. When they reached the next town, both Hugh and Virgil insisted that she took the next coach for the city. Both of them failed. Sovay refused to listen. If they were prepared to go to France, then so was she.

'All foreigners are suspect now, including Americans,' Virgil told her. 'I cannot guarantee your safety. I may be able to trade on my special status, but I do not know how long that will hold.'

Sovay would not be swayed. 'I don't care. I'm prepared to take the risk. I will not sit at home being eaten away by doubts and fears while the two people who I hold most dear are in the severest jeopardy. I would rather share the danger. Hugh and Father are the world to me. What would life be without them?'

Virgil turned to her brother.

'Don't look at me!' Hugh laughed. '*I've* never been able to make her do anything. I say let her come, if she has a mind to.' He took Sovay's hand. 'At least we will be together.'

Virgil shrugged. Brother and sister were clearly as mad and wilful as each other. He had tried his best to dissuade both, being no means as certain as Hugh seemed to be about his status and safety. Hugh had his own papers. He was the Genovese nephew of his old tutor, now Citizen Fernand, member of the National Assembly. Fernand was a man of power and influence; he had been in a position to protect his young 'relative' before, but circumstances might have changed.

'Very well,' he acceded. 'I'll do what I can to get us over to Le Havre and into the country. After that, I can make no promises.'

They bought what they needed and journeyed on to the coast and the ancient port of Rye. Virgil announced it to be ideal, being much neglected but well known to smugglers, with a perfectly usable harbour as long as the vessel was not too large.

He left them at the Ship Inn and promised to be back just as soon their passage could be arranged. Two days, three at the most, he said.

❦

It was nearer a week before Virgil returned.

'I have a ketch waiting in the harbour,' he said as he joined them in their room at the Ship Inn. 'We sail on the morning tide.' He sat down and poured himself some wine. 'I had to go to London to arrange for papers to be made for Sovay.' He took a wallet from his pocket. 'You will be travelling as Miss Sophie

Weston, an American citizen, and –' He paused and cleared his throat, as though there was a sudden frog caught in it. 'And my fiancée. I know it is a shock,' he saw the look on her face, 'and not the most romantic of proposals, but I hope it is clear,' he looked from Sovay to Hugh, 'that I take no liberties here. It was the only way I could think of to keep her safe.'

Sovay did not know quite what to say, but Hugh grinned and clapped the American on the back.

'Congratulations, my dear Barrett. You are a vast improvement on her last choice, I must say. I wish you both every happiness.' He raised his glass, laughing at their discomfort. 'To the affianced couple!'

Neither Sovay nor Barrett joined him in the toast.

'I have other news,' Barrett said, his tone serious. 'I had to go to London to arrange the papers, and while I was there, I called on Oldfield. He gave me this.' He handed over a letter. 'Not good news, I'm afraid to say.'

Hugh opened it, placing the paper on the table for Sovay to see it. As he read, all the mirth drained from his face.

Oldfield & Oldfield,
Pilgrim Court
Off Carter Lane
London

6th June, 1794

My Dear Mr Hugh and Miss Sovay Middleton,

I thought it best to inform you of developments here without delay. Things have not gone quite according to plan.

I have been busy preparing the defence for Skidmore's friends, some of whom face charges of sedition, others the much more serious charge of treason. I wish I were confident that no court will convict them, but this is by no means certain. I am sorry to say that your friend, Gabriel, has also been arrested and charged for his part in what is being termed the battle of Vine Street. He has also been implicated in a further conspiracy, partly on the evidence of Fitzwilliam.

The bulk of the charges, however, have been laid against you. In short, you are accused of being French spies, stealing government papers, causing explosions, destruction of property, attempting to assassinate various government personages, and I don't know what else. Everything that has happened since the fateful interception of Dysart's correspondence has been twisted and used against you.

Dysart, meanwhile, far from being discredited as we hoped, goes from strength to strength. All that happened at Thursley has been subverted and turned into a dastardly plot, by you and other persons, to begin a revolution on British soil.

He is clever, far cleverer than we credited, and he is exploiting the very real fear that the French Terror is engendering in the Government and in the people at large. I will continue to collect what evidence I can in the hope that my clients will be vindicated and that Dysart's real intentions will be unmasked. If you are set on going to France, I encourage you to gather what evidence you can against him there, too. I suspect there will be much to find. I cannot prove it yet, but I suspect that he has been in touch all along with the Revolutionary forces through a web of double agents, but we must have proof of this to present as evidence. It is our only way to defeat him.

Your servant,

Graham Oldfield

Treason. Sovay and Hugh looked at each other. There could be no turning back now. A woman's punishment for treason was to be burnt at the stake.

◆➤◆

Sovay watched the coast grow smaller and then fade altogether as the half-light brightened to morning. She did not know what fate awaited her, or when, if ever, she would see her native land again. She was condemned to perpetual exile, unless she could clear her name.

The day was fair. The ketch Virgil Barrett had found for them was disguised as a fishing boat to fool the Naval patrols. It was fast and light in the water and they soon lost sight of land altogether. Out in the Channel the waves were edged with white, as if they brought with them the memory of distant storms. Hugh soon retired below, feeling unwell, but Sovay stayed on deck, undeterred by the occasional shower of drenching spray. Virgil was sailing the vessel himself, with the help of the men who had accompanied him from Dover and two local men from Rye who were smugglers by trade and were well used to the local channels and tides and had experience of running the Naval blockade.

Virgil came to join her once they were well out to sea. Sovay expressed her admiration for his skill with jib and sail.

'I learnt as a boy. My uncle was a commander in the United States Navy. I saw action with him in the War of Independence.' He gave an ironic grin. 'Of course, to your Navy, we were all buccaneers.'

'I did not know that you had been a buccaneer! You are full of surprises, Mr Barrett.' Sovay smiled. 'You don't look the least like one.'

'Good,' Virgil smiled. 'The key to safety is authentic disguise. Let us hope the principle applies here and the Navy take us as a fishing vessel.'

'What are you really carrying?' Sovay asked.

'Weapons. Guns and shot for the people's army. And food. Wheat, flour, butter, cheeses. The Republic is in dire need of these things. A few luxuries: soap, candles, cocoa, sugar and coffee . . .'

'Sugar and coffee?' Sovay was surprised that he would take such risks for what sounded like Mrs Crombie's shopping list.

'Oh, I have a very special customer,' he smiled. 'Someone I must keep sweet.'

Suddenly, Virgil was called by the lookout.

'There's a Naval vessel, on the horizon,' he said when he came back. 'Looks like a sixth-rate frigate. Small by their standards, but far overmatching us. We'll have to make a run for the French coast. You better go below.'

Hugh was beyond caring what was happening, or what it could mean for him. Sovay lay in the bunk opposite and clung on to the rope above her head as she was flung about by the violent movement of the ship. Through the rush of water and groan of wood came the muffled boom of cannon fire. Sovay listened intently, trying to work out the distance. Each crash and splash seemed nearer. The hull shook with the vibration and water cascaded down through the hatch. Finally, Sovay closed her eyes, convinced that, at any second, she would be blown to pieces, or thrown violently into the water as the ship disintegrated about her.

At last the vessel slowed and righted itself. Sovay opened her eyes to find Virgil smiling down at her, his fair hair wet and tangled, his face flushed, his blue-grey eyes still alight with the excitement of the chase.

'It was a bit of a close-run thing, but we lost them eventually. Come!' He held out his hands to help her from the bunk. 'Come up on deck.'

Sovay followed him for her first view of France. The coast sliding by them was not markedly different from the one that they had left behind them: the rise and fall of the low cliffs, fringed by pale beaches, broken by inlets; the green fields rolling away inland. But this was another country, with another language and a unique place in history.

The France that she could see was a republic, at war with half the nations of Europe, including her own. Sovay would be an alien, an enemy, but she had no choice. She had to go on. However hostile the country, her father was there, ill and perhaps in danger. She felt a hand over hers. Hugh was standing at her side, his pale face as set and determined as her own.

'We will find him, Sovay,' he said. 'We will find him and take him home. Dysart will not hound us from our own country. We will find the evidence against him and defeat him once and for all.'

CHAPTER 30

They sailed into the great port of Le Havre. The effects of the British Naval blockade were clear, with docks empty and ships lying idle, but where they tied up seemed busy enough with men moving barrels and sacks through the open doors of a large warehouse. They were not allowed to disembark but were met by a contingent of customs men, dressed in blue uniforms, who made a great show of examining everything and seemed increasingly suspicious, particularly about the passengers. Sovay had considerable misgivings that their adventure in France might be over before it had even started, particularly when a troop of National Guardsmen arrived in blue and white uniforms wearing red, white and blue sashes, the colours of the Republic. The soldiers took up position on the dock, while their Captain strode up the gangplank and swung himself on-board.

He was taller than Virgil, his long legs and wide shoulders accentuated by his uniform. He was a big man but he moved with easy grace. Sovay would not put him much above three and twenty, but his uniform was mended and faded, as though he had seen much action in it, and was decorated with marks of rank. Despite his youth, he was not a man to be taken lightly. He looked from one to another, his thick brows a straight bar over large intelligent eyes that were of a most unusual colour, somewhere between dark green and brown.

'What have we here?' he demanded.

The chief customs officer stepped forward to explain, but he was brushed aside.

'I'll deal with this, Citizen,' he announced with a natural air of command. 'I'm sure you have many other pressing duties to perform in the name of the Revolution. I would not want to detain you here.'

The man began to protest that customs were his jurisdiction, but faltered under the guardsman's menacing stare. The customs officers looked at each other. None seemed inclined to argue further with the big guardsman and his armed soldiers and they left the boat without more ado.

'Let's go below, shall we?' The guardsman looked from one to the other. 'You can give me an account of yourselves there.'

As soon as they were in the cabin, Virgil and the guardsman clasped each other like brothers.

'Citizen Barrett,' the soldier exclaimed, his fierce face lightening. 'Virgil! It is good to see you safely returned.' Then he looked towards Hugh and Sovay, his frown returning. 'And who do you bring with you?'

'Hugo Valette,' Virgil replied. 'Nephew to Citizen Fernand who is a member of the Convention. And this is my cousin, Sophie Weston,' he added smoothly. 'My, ah, fiancée.'

The guardsman looked Sovay up and down and whistled through the slight gap in his front teeth.

'*Veinard*!' he said.

'What does that mean?' Sovay whispered to Hugh.

'Roughly translated?' Hugh whispered back. 'Lucky dog!'

Sovay felt herself blush. The Frenchman had a scar on his upper lip, and his heavy features could not be ranked as handsome in the strictest sense, but there was something compelling about his countenance that disturbed her deeply. She wanted to look away from him immediately, but his dark green eyes held her. She could not help but stare at him, and his strong, frank gaze, just this side of insolence, disturbed her even more.

He broke the look first, removing his wide, plumed hat.

'Citizen. Citizeness.' He bowed slightly to each of them, although any displays of deference were now frowned upon as belonging to the old regime. 'Captain Théodore Léon, at your service. I am here to escort you to Paris.' He looked at Sovay again as though he found her presence troubling. Then he turned to the American. 'Virgil. A word with you.'

They drew away and Hugh and Sovay stood in awkward silence as a fierce argument ensued. The two men spoke in French, but Sovay had enough of the language to know that they were speaking about her.

'Are you mad? To bring her here? The way things are? You must be ruled by your –' then came a word that Sovay did not catch and Hugh showed no willingness to translate.

'No, you don't understand.' Virgil dragged him further away.

'Even more madness!' Léon came striding back. 'Do you realise what you do? Her presence here is a clear danger. I should report it. She is enough to get us all arrested and condemned.'

Sovay drew herself up to her full height. She was tired, worried, and not a little apprehensive, but she would not be spoken of in that way, by this man, or any other.

'I am not a fool, Captain,' she said in careful French. 'I'm not here to seek adventure. I have no choice in this matter, but others do. Including you. I do not ask for your protection. I only ask that you let us get on our way.'

Her response was clearly not what he expected. He regarded her for a moment or two, rubbing at the dark stubble that peppered his chin.

'I regret, that is not possible, mademoiselle,' he replied with elaborate courtesy. 'I am required to escort you to prevent any interference with the supplies Citizen Barrett brings with him. Some of the countryside grows lawless and we do not want any local officials thinking they can commandeer goods destined for the Republican Army and the people of Paris. My mission is to see that you arrive safely. Do not jeopardise it. Before you leave the ship, make sure you are wearing these.' He gave them each a tricolour rosette. 'From now on, you must never be seen in public without it.'

◆➤◆◄◆

They were only able to go as fast as the baggage train, so progress was slow. The villages they passed through were shuttered against them and each showed signs of poverty, or worse. The land was rich and fertile, but the fields lay uncultivated and the few animals grazing looked diseased and neglected. The only people they saw were haggard women, hollow-eyed children and

318

decrepit old men. They all looked close to starvation.

Occasionally, through the trees, they saw chateaux, great houses, shuttered and boarded, some in ruins, burnt-out shells, deserted by their owners who had fled the country as émigrés. They passed through villages where the churches also lay empty, the fronts defaced, angels and patriarchs mutilated and smashed to rubble, the plate taken for the Republic's treasury, the bells carted off to foundries to make cannon. In some places the cracked and broken remnants of wooden and plaster saints stood blackened on bonfires like so many Joans of Arc. Church doors hung off their hinges and scrawny animals wandered in and out as if these former places of worship were being used as barns or sties. In some places, the cemeteries had been similarly desecrated, the graves stripped of their crosses, the gates daubed with slogans: *Death is but an eternal sleep*.

'The people have paid a high price,' Léon said when Virgil remarked that conditions seemed worse than he'd ever seen them. The National Guardsman seemed devoid of sentiment. All his opinions were shot through with a soldier's pragmatism. 'The men are serving in the Revolutionary Army, the *levée en masse* has taken them from their fields and farms, but how else are we to prevent invasion with every nation in Europe ranged against us? The Duke of Brunswick has promised to raze Paris to the ground and kill everyone there – men, women and children. In the face of that, what are we to do? And soldiers must be fed. The people's army have been out, gathering supplies for them and for Paris, but there is never enough and the city is close to starvation. The farmers here have little left for themselves, but they cannot refuse to contribute. The price of hoarding is death.'

They encountered little trouble. The troop of National Guardsmen in their distinctive blue and white uniforms, hardened soldiers, carrying arms, proved a suitable deterrent. In a few places they were challenged by groups of men with pikes, brave and defiant in their red bonnets, but many of them were old and half-starving.

'I do not like to fight my own countrymen,' Léon said, halting the train with a wave of his hand and ordering a sack or two of grain or flour to be distributed to ease their passage.

He ignored Sovay, for the most part, preferring to talk to Hugh or Virgil. When she expressed shock at what she was seeing, he seemed surprised that she should hold any opinion at all.

'The people know what you do not,' he said in a tone that implied that she would not understand. 'Freedom comes at a cost. They are prepared to make the sacrifice. We are forced to fight for our very survival as a nation and few would want to go back to the old regime, even if such a thing were possible. We have come so very far. These people have lived under such oppression for so long, from the landowners, from the church. Each year, they had to pay taxes out of the little they had, to the King, to the Seigneur, to pay dues and banalities, while the King and the nobles grew fat and paid nothing. Is it not understandable that they would take revenge? That they would want to take a little back after being robbed for so many centuries?'

Sovay found it hard to understand Léon's

passionate and immovable support of the Republic, especially when she learnt that his full title had been Théodore de Léon, Écuyer, Marquis de Verand, but he had given up his noble rank to become part of the Revolution. He had been among the first to join the Third Estate and had taken part in the storming of the Bastille. Now, anyone of noble birth, or who had any aristocratic connection, was automatically suspect and subject to arrest. So far, his bravery in the field of battle and his Revolutionary credentials had kept him safe. For how long? The question remained unspoken, but Sovay was aware of increasing tension as they travelled nearer to the capital. Danger awaited them all.

❥

The first real trouble came on the afternoon of the third day. They were rumbling across a bleak stretch of land when their way was blocked by an improvised barrier. It was manned by a group of men in the striped trousers and rough jackets of the *sans-culottes*. They all sported red liberty caps over their shaggy locks, and were heavily bewhiskered, with quantities of facial hair and long moustaches. They were well fed and well armed, not at all like the scarecrow bands that they had met before.

Léon called a halt.

'*Armée révolutionnaire. Les Bons Patriotes*,' he said, looking up ahead. 'They could be trouble. They live off the people hereabouts. Scavengers and parasites. I thought that they had all been recalled to Paris.'

He ordered the passengers down from the carts and onto horseback. He put his own men up with the drivers, guns at the ready.

'Whatever happens, the supplies must get through. I will go and see what they want.' He looked over to Virgil. 'Any trouble and drive your wagon straight through them. Look to your weapons, gentlemen.'

'I don't have a weapon,' Sovay protested.

'Why would you need one?'

'To defend myself.'

He looked at her sceptically. 'Can you shoot?'

'Of course!'

'Here.' He gave her one of his own pistols. 'It is loaded, so be careful.'

As Léon rode towards them, a man in a different uniform strutted out from the rest of the mob. He was dressed in dark blue, his high-collared coat swathed in a tricolour sash and he wore a matching plumed cockade in his tall hat.

'Halt!' he shouted. 'State your business.'

'I escort supplies for Paris.'

'Passengers?'

'Yes.'

'Bring them to me, with their papers. Tell your men to stay back.'

Léon returned.

'I know him. Gernaud. He's *représentant-en-mission*, a Deputy sent out from the National Convention to meddle in the provinces,' he explained to Hugh and Sovay. 'He is a *terroriste*, also a prick. Come with me. But stay back and let me do the talking. Any trouble . . .' He inclined his head to Virgil who gripped the reins in his hands and nodded back.

'Citizen Léon.' The official held out a gloved hand for the papers.

'Gernaud.'

'*Deputy* Gernaud, *if* you don't mind.'

'*Deputy* . . .' Léon handed over the papers with exaggerated courtesy.

Gernaud spent a long time examining them, and then squinted up at Léon.

'I declare you spies and enemies of the Republic. Consider yourself under arrest and your shipment impounded.'

Léon laughed down at him. It was what Gernaud had been after all along. God only knew what he would get for such a cargo. A fortune at a time of such scarcity. Sovay kept her eyes on the men as Léon turned in his saddle, his arm raised in signal to Virgil. Gernaud's eyes flicked sideways. The man next to him eased back the hammer on his rifle and raised the weapon, ready to shoot from the hip. There was no time to warn Léon. At such close quarters, the shot would surely kill him. Sovay cocked the pistol she was holding down by her side, aimed and fired.

The man uttered a yelp as the bullet took him in the shoulder, the impact spinning him round before he fell to the ground. Léon's horse reared and he drew his own pistol and called his soldiers forward. Gernaud's men retreated behind their barricade, pulling their wounded comrade with them. Gernaud himself stood his ground, as if his authority alone could stop Virgil's horses thundering towards him. He leapt aside just in time and the others threw themselves into the ditches as the heavy wagon smashed through the flimsy barrier, breaking the long poles into kindling. The other wagons followed, their horses whipped to a gallop, as formidable as a battery of artillery. Sovay and Hugh spurred after them, Léon and his men covering their retreat.

❧

'I underestimated you,' he said to Sovay when they stopped for the night. 'I was wrong.'

This was as near as he would come to an apology. Sovay accepted his gruff statement with a gracious nod of the head to hide her slight smile. She sensed that apologies did not come easily to this big, rumbustious Frenchman, who seemed a stranger to both doubt and physical fear. She had never met any man like him.

'To fortune and *bonne chance*.' Léon raised his glass. 'We all live with our dangers. By rights I should be dead many times over. Let us have more wine. I still don't understand,' he said when their glasses had been replenished. 'You are a girl of considerable spirit, I can see your concern for your father, but why come here anyway, put your life in jeopardy?'

'We are both wanted for treason,' Sovay answered. 'We have no choice but to come to France.'

Hugh explained about Dysart and the accusations against them. Léon listened with careful attention.

'I have heard the name before, I'm sure,' he said when Hugh had finished. 'In the Ministry of War when Roland was there. Find this man.' He scribbled the name on a piece of paper. 'He collected the evidence against Fabre and Danton. He might be able to help. He's old-fashioned. Only works for money. Gold. Not assignats. Now, it is time to retire.'

He drained his glass and they all rose.

'We will reach Paris tomorrow,' he said to Virgil as

they climbed the stairs.'I will see you through the gates and then I have to report to my headquarters. She's a very pretty girl,' he added as they reached their rooms. 'Such a noble gesture on your part, Barrett, to make her your fiancée.'

'You misunderstand me,' Virgil said, quick to deny any underhand motive. 'It is for convenience only. I fear she has no feelings for me, in that way.'

Léon smiled. 'Does she have feelings for anyone, *in that way*?'

Virgil shook his head. 'Not that I know of.'

'What a waste!' The Frenchman laughed. 'If I was you, my friend, I'd marry her anyway. Before someone else does.'

CHAPTER 31

The elegant, imposing custom house that marked the entrance to Paris had been partially demolished, its function replaced by a rough wooden barrier hauled across the roadway. Everyone wishing to enter the city was stopped by a set of fierce-looking men, bristling with arms. They looked like Gernaud's men, dressed in striped trousers and short jackets with faded tricolour rosettes on their tattered and grimy red bonnets.

'What have you got there, Citizen?'

Their leader leaned on the side of the cart, looking up at Virgil in a belligerent, challenging manner, his scowling face made more ferocious by his long, trailing mustachios.

Léon stood back and let the man and his fellows go about their business. These were men of the Paris Commune, puffed up by the authority invested in them. Any interference could spark a major incident.

They insisted on everyone getting down and examined the papers Virgil gave to them with great care, although it was doubtful whether any of them could read. They were dangerous and volatile but also open to bribery. Léon waited until they'd had time to scrutinise the various documents and then he ordered sacks of flour to be taken off the wagon, along with boxes of soap and candles.

'For the people of your *Section*, Citizens,' he announced. 'With our compliments.'

Eventually, they were allowed to pass. Sovay had thought that Léon would stay with them and was surprised when he said that he must leave them.

'I have other duties to attend to, I'm afraid, and you might be better without me,' he said as he bade them farewell. 'There is no love lost between us and some of the committees that control different areas of the city. Our presence might impede your progress, or stop it altogether. Until we meet again!'

He gave no indication of when that might be. Sovay found that she was unwilling to see him go, and her reluctance was not altogether to do with fear for her safety.

Their wagon made slow progress. Each area of the city had its own committees and every one had to be bribed, convinced and placated. Everywhere they went, there was evidence of poverty and want, far more so than in London. There was an air of exhaustion about the hot, dusty streets; most doors and windows were closed and shuttered, just like in the villages.

Their route took them past the Place de la Révolution. The guillotine had been removed and the vast space seemed empty and desolate, ominous despite its openness. In the hot sun, the blood-drenched stones stank like a charnel house.

As the wagons trundled on, Hugh pointed out the landmarks: the garden of the Tuileries, full of trees, with people taking shade under their drooping leaves and walking down paths formerly reserved for the King and his court; the huge, sprawling palace, empty now of its royal occupants; the arches of the Palais-

Royal; the café where Camille Desmoulins leapt upon a table and incited the Paris mob to storm the Bastille. Every building, every name, it seemed, carried significance. It was as if they journeyed through the landscape of the Revolution and therefore history, and yet people sat in cafés, gossiped on corners, formed queues outside shops. Life went on, Revolution or not.

They were heading for the Rue Duval on the edge of the Marais district. Their way took them past the most famous monument of all, but there was nothing left to see of the Bastille. The huge prison had been reduced to so much rubble. The citizens had torn it down, stone by stone. Nothing that Sovay had so far heard or seen better attested to the power of the many than the complete and systematic destruction of that symbol of oppression, or was better testimony to the people's determination that they would never be so oppressed again.

The people had imposed their will in small ways as well as large. Statues had been toppled or defaced. Streets renamed, churches turned into stables and storehouses. *There is no going back*, these acts declared, *the only way is forward, whatever the consequences*.

Eventually, the wagons turned into a narrow street between tall walls of peeling yellow stucco. They stopped in front of the closed gates of a hôtel, the grand town house of some long-departed noble family, with a crumbling coat of arms on the arch above the entrance. Virgil got down from the wagon and rapped on the door. A grate slid open and shut again and the gates swung wide. The wagons were driven into a wide, cobbled courtyard and the gates clanged shut behind them. Sovay felt safe at last.

❖◗❖◗❖

The Hôtel Fonteneau had once been a very grand house, but the marble floors in the hallway were chipped and dulled with dust and grime. Struts were missing from the balustrade of the wide staircase, the pale green silk wallpaper was marked with water stains and smeared with dirty handprints.

The state rooms were bare, the furnishings looted or removed. Little remained below the decorated ceilings to bear witness to the building's former status, except cracked mirrors and painting-shaped spaces on the walls. They passed from apartment to apartment, their footfalls echoing over lengths of smeared and scuffed wooden floors which must once have been polished as bright as mirrors. Since the armies of servants had been dispersed, there was no one left to polish and sweep, clean and tend.

At the far end of the last room, a man sat in shirtsleeves, working at a desk piled high with papers that at any moment threatened to spill onto the floor. He stood up as they approached. His face was pale and tired, the skin drawn and greyish. He was wearing spectacles and his hair was sparse, receding from his forehead, the few fair strands streaked with grey. As he came towards them, Sovay realised with a shock that it was M Fernand, Hugh's old tutor. She could not recall ever having seen him without his crisp, flaxen wig before and could hardly find the handsome young man she remembered in that prematurely aged and careworn face.

'My dear, dear friends! Welcome! I thought that I would not see you again!' His voice shook with emotion as he clasped Virgil warmly by the hand and embraced Hugh as if he was his own son. He smiled when he came to Sovay, his eyes wide with surprise. 'And this must be Sovay! You look so different. So changed!' He took her hand and kissed it. 'Quite the young lady now!' He put his arms round brother and sister. 'We must talk, but first you must eat. You have had a long journey. You must be hungry.'

He took them down to the kitchen where they made a supper of bread, cheese and *saucisson*.

'Peasant food, I'm afraid, but it is all we can get. There are such shortages. We have wine, though.' He filled their glasses. 'Now. To business.' His face grew grave. 'Things have got worse, much worse since you left. Robespierre and the Committee of Public Safety have taken leave of their senses. Truly. They see conspiracy everywhere. Now, to merely be *suspected* of anything counter to the Revolution, no matter how innocent-seeming or trivial, is enough to get one brought before the Revolutionary Tribunal.' He removed his spectacles and pinched the bridge of his nose. 'To be tried by them bears no relation to trials as you know them. In Britain, even the lowliest, most vicious prisoner is allowed a lawyer and a defence; witnesses are called, for and against, before the jury decides. Here things are different. Once the accusation is made, the Tribunal decides. They are fanatical in their prosecution of the Revolution.' He closed his eyes, the lids papery in the lamplight. 'Since there is no defence, no lawyers are involved, no witnesses called. The alternatives are stark. It is acquittal or death.

They rarely acquit and the death sentence is carried out within twenty-four hours.'

'Since when is this?' Virgil asked.

'Since 22 Prairial by the Revolutionary Calendar – 10th of June by the old reckoning.' He glanced up at Sovay, in case she was unfamiliar with this new way of dividing the year. 'Life grows everyday more perilous. For all of us. No one is safe.' He shook his head in despair. 'No one.'

'And my father?'

Hugh leaned forward, searching his old tutor's face. The man paused before answering, as if gathering the last of his strength. Then he reached over to Hugh and Sovay, taking their hands in his long, thin, scholar's fingers.

'Bad news, I'm afraid. He has been arrested and brought to Paris.'

Fernand's words echoed round the empty room like a death knell. Hugh went white, his lips trembled and his eyes filled with sudden tears.

'Where is he?'

'In the Luxembourg, where he lies gravely ill. There is hope in that.' Fernand gave a bitter, ghost of a smile. 'They do not like to try those who cannot understand their sentence. Such strange days we live in.' He gave a despairing lift of the shoulders. 'That it should all end like this.'

'We must go to him!' Hugh was on his feet.

'You cannot go now. You have had a long and trying journey and, besides, they would not admit you.'

'Surely, M Fernand,' Sovay felt as though her heart was being wrenched from her, 'there must be something we can do?'

'Perhaps,' Fernand relented. He did not want to give out false hope but hated to see his young friends so distressed. 'There are many more awaiting trials than can be accommodated. Some wait for months. Let us hope your father is one of those. And with his illness . . . Until the blade falls there is always hope. Tomorrow, we will see what can be done. Meanwhile, Hugh, perhaps you would show Sovay to her accommodation? You will find rooms on the second floor.'

'No need to worry them further,' Fernand said to Virgil after they had left. 'But they are unlikely to see their father. The prisons no longer allow visitors. No one is admitted except to a cell.'

'Is that so?' The American stretched out his long legs, his grey-blue eyes distant as he turned over the problem. There would be a way. There was always a way. 'I have another matter,' he said eventually. 'Do you know this man?'

He pushed over the slip of paper that Léon had given him.

'Yes.' Fernand studied it. 'He's a journalist. Used to work for Marat's scandal sheet. Specialises in lies and slander. If he can't find anything, he makes it up. Or forges it.'

'That's what I'm hoping. Where can I find him?'

'He lives above a printer's on the Left Bank somewhere, but you'll likely find him in the wine shops of St Germain. What do you want with him?'

Virgil shrugged. 'He might be able to help with something.' He leaned forward. 'Those two are in more trouble than you know.' He told Fernand about

Dysart. 'He has spies everywhere. It's only a matter of time before he finds out that they are here. Sovay is travelling as my fiancée.' He waved away Fernand's congratulations. 'A matter of convenience only, unfortunately.' He laughed. 'I doubt the lady has feelings for me and I'm promised elsewhere, more's the pity. I'll own that I've grown fond of her. I fear being affianced to me will afford but flimsy protection. I would like to find a better way of keeping her from harm.'

◆➤◼◀◆

Sovay was shown to a cavernous chamber which must once have been a grand bedroom, but all the original furnishings had been removed, apart from a great armoire that was probably too heavy to shift, although the doors had been taken, for some inexplicable reason. Other than that, there was a battered washstand holding a chipped basin, and a rickety table and chair. Her bed was small, most likely brought down from the servants' quarters upstairs. She was so tired that she lay down upon it fully clothed and slept almost immediately.

She was torn from sleep by a sudden scream and woke thinking that she was back in her room at Compton, and had heard the cry of a vixen in the park, but the bed was too narrow, the huge room too empty. The shriek she had heard had been human and had come from the street outside.

CHAPTER 32

The next day, there was blood splashed on the wall and across the pavement outside.

'It is dangerous to be on the streets at night,' Virgil said with a grimace. 'Here you see the evidence.'

They were on their way to the Luxembourg. It had been a grand palace, built for Catherine de Medici, but like all the royal palaces, it had been confiscated for the use of the people. While Robespierre and the Committee of Public Safety held their meetings in the Tuileries, the King's old residence, the Luxembourg had been made into a prison. Until recently, conditions in there had been relaxed, even pleasant compared with other prisons. It was said to be the best brothel in Paris, Virgil told them, and anyone with money could be assured of a decent apartment and have food sent in from the local restaurants, but recently such laxity had been considerably tightened.

'We are unlikely to gain admittance,' he warned. 'It is difficult now even to get messages in or out, but we will see what can be done.'

Despite what Virgil told them, Sovay had been buoyed up by the expectation that they *would* obtain word about their father, might even be able to see him and be reunited, if only for a moment, but they were summarily turned away from the Luxembourg's grand, imposing facade, their hopes dashed. No one was allowed in or out. No letters could be taken, no messages conveyed to those held inside. Pleading was pointless. The guards were stern and steadfast in their purpose and implied that further protestation would result in their own imprisonment.

In the end, Sovay had to drag Hugh away. He was dangerously close to losing his temper at the guards' surly obduracy and was very likely to end up joining their father inside. Perhaps it was the stricken look on her face, or her beauty, or her dignified demeanour, but one of them softened and called her back.

'Go into the gardens,' he said, with a jerk of his head. 'From there you might get a glimpse of him, or him of you. That's what others do and it's as near as you are going to get, Citizeness.'

Sovay thanked him and led Hugh away. Sure enough, the park was filled with people of all estates, men and women, old and young. Some walked up and down in a constant parade, others stood with the stillness of statues, all had their faces turned upwards, their eyes fixed on the high windows opposite. Some spoke, in a conversational tone, as if to an invisible companion, others yelled and bellowed, their voices echoing back upon themselves. An old man stared in silence. A young woman held up her infant as if to be blessed.

People crowded the windows of the upper storeys of the Luxembourg. Sovay could see mouths opening and closing, but glass and distance rendered the speakers dumb and their features indistinct, their faces as undifferentiated as a row of pegs.

'This is hopeless!' Hugh declared. 'Hopeless!'

Nevertheless, he continued to stare upwards. Sovay joined him, caught up by the same despairing expectation as all the rest.

Meanwhile, Virgil was watching the traffic to and from the palace. Although no visitors were admitted, tradesmen brought food and goods, newspaper vendors delivered papers. In among the comings and goings, one young woman caught his eye. She was a pretty girl and very young, her smooth, brown hair caught up under a white cap. Her sober clothes were worn and faded, but she did not look like a servant or a shop girl. She carried a basket and approached the gates with confidence. The guards seemed to know her. They did not turn her away, rather they seemed well disposed to her, smiling and even holding the door for her as she slipped into the building. Virgil set himself to wait for her to re-emerge. Sure enough, after a little over a quarter of an hour, she returned, her basket now empty.

She stepped out quickly, eyes cast down. Then she unfolded a piece of paper and began to study it.

Virgil found Sovay and took her by the arm.

'Come with me.'

'Where are we going?'

'No time for explanations. Quick, or she will get away.'

They left Hugh to his vigil and followed the girl. She was moving briskly, already melting through the restless crowd. They followed her down Rue Garancière and around the imposing bulk of St Sulpice. From here, she took the Rue des Canettes towards St Germain. Virgil walked faster, fearing that if she disappeared into the tangle of streets they would lose her altogether. She turned one corner, then another into Rue Jacob. Finally she slowed her pace and stopped outside an apothecary shop, its windows filled with decorated jars and bottles. She unfolded the note she was carrying, as if to check again what was on it.

'Citizeness!' Virgil called to her. 'A word if I may.'

She started round, her large brown eyes full of apprehension. If Sovay had not been with him, she would have bolted into the shop, but the sight of another woman relaxed her a little.

'Forgive me for approaching you,' Virgil went on quickly. 'But were you lately at the Luxembourg?'

She nodded, her eyes widening, her wariness returning. 'You *followed* me?'

'With no ill intent, I do assure you, but I could not help but notice that you were one of the few to gain admittance.'

'Yes, my father is a doctor. Every day he sends out for medicines. I take the list to the apothecary here and carry the medicines back to the prison.'

'This young lady's father,' Virgil indicated Sovay, 'is in the Luxembourg.'

'I'd like to help you,' the girl looked from Virgil to Sovay, 'but there are so many . . .' She frowned, as if she could see them all before her.

'He is sick,' Virgil went on. 'Gravely so. And we are desperate for news of him. As a doctor, perhaps your father will know of him and could tell us how he does.'

'He might.' The girl's apprehension was creeping back, as though she feared a trap. 'We are not allowed to carry messages. Such things are forbidden by the authorities.'

'Oh, no.' Virgil shook his head. 'We ask nothing of the kind. We –'

'We just want word that he is alive,' Sovay

interrupted. 'Please.'

The girl considered this appeal from one daughter to another and her face cleared.

'I will see what I can do. What is his name?'

'Middleton. John Middleton.'

'*Milord Anglais?* Your father?' The girl looked shocked. 'It is not safe for you! Meet me here tomorrow. At the same time. I should have news by then.'

She turned to go into the shop, but Virgil detained her.

'One thing further. Do you live around here?'

'Not far. I have rooms on Rue Monsieur Le Prince. It is cheap there and near Father.'

'Do you know this man?' Virgil showed her the name Léon had given him.

She nodded. 'He lives above the printer's down by the Cordeliers.'

'Thank you. Much obliged.' Virgil gave a slight bow.

'Who is this man?' Sovay asked as they left the girl.

'I have a plan – to incriminate Dysart. If we can find evidence to show his connection to the Revolution, then we can still discredit him.'

The place wasn't hard to find, but the printer warned them that they would not find him at home.

'Wine shop next door.' He hardly looked up from his press. The place filled with the sharp, pungency of fresh ink as he began turning the machine.

The man, Lefere, was short in stature but solidly built with fleshy features and lank, greying hair swept back from his high forehead. His black suit was crumpled and greasy, his shirt stained with wine and his neckcloth none too clean.

'Citizen? A word, if I may. In private.'

They went back to Lefere's rooms, following him up steep, narrow stairs. The building was much older than it looked from the outside, the ceilings and walls hatched with thick, black crooked beams.

'Now,' the man turned, wheezing as they reached his attic rooms at the top of the stairs, 'what's this all about?'

'I've heard that you find information.'

'I have been known to,' the man cackled. 'I am a journalist.'

'I've heard that you collected information concerning Fabre and Danton and their connection with the British Government.'

'I follow the example set by Citizen Marat, before his sad martyrdom.' The man's expression became pious. 'I am pleased to do my part to expose any enemy of the Revolution.'

'I'm sure you are.' Virgil sighed at his hypocrisy. 'In that investigation, did you come across correspondence from Robert Dysart?'

'The English spy master? *Bien sûr.*'

Virgil took a purse from his pocket.

'Good. I need a sample of his hand. I've also heard that you have a happy knack of uncovering vital evidence, even if the necessary documents are missing, or cannot be found.'

'I hope you are not suggesting I would forge something!' Lefere did his best to look indignant at the very thought.

'For the right fee, of course.'

Lefere's protests subsided at the chink of coin and his small blue eyes grew narrow at the sight of gold spilling onto the table.

'This is what I will need from you . . .'

As the man listened to what Virgil had to say, he began to sweat. His eyes flickered with fear, but could not help but stare at the coins piling up before him.

'I don't know . . .' he said, licking his lips. 'It will take time to get what you describe. Besides that, I will need official paper, stamps.'

'I will take care of that.' Virgil neatened the gleaming column, as careful as a banker. 'You have a week.' He pushed the pile of coins towards the journalist. 'Get what I need and this will be doubled.'

'I'll see what I can do.' Lefere's hand shot out, his stubby fingers closing round the gold as if it might disappear by magic.

❖❖❖❖

'If it works, we will catch Dysart at his own game.' Virgil smiled at Sovay as they walked down to the Seine.

'*If* it works.' Sovay was not so convinced. 'Dysart is a spy master, after all. Evidence to show that he has been in touch with the Revolutionary powers here will merely show that he was doing his job.'

'Depends on what that evidence is, doesn't it?' Virgil took her arm. 'I will see you home, then I must make my deliveries. The coffee and sugar especially. They are destined for Citizen Robespierre. They call him the *Incorruptible*, but he has a weakness for coffee. It would be well to feed his craving. It might be the one thing that keeps us safe.'

CHAPTER 33

'I don't know where they are. How many times do I have to tell you?' Gabriel answered with quiet patience. 'I don't know anything about any conspiracy. I am a steward. Why would Sir John, or his family, confide in me?'

'You are here, Stanhope. They are not. They saved themselves and left you to suffer the blame. Is it not always the way of their class? They do not care about you. Why should they? You are merely a servant. Why should you care about them? Why do you protect them?'

Gabriel refused to rise to this, or to say anything, so Dysart tried a different tack.

'What about your other friends? The residents of Vine Street. Your co-conspirators in the London Corresponding Society?'

Gabriel shrugged, his strong shoulders pulled down by the heavy chains he wore on his wrists. 'I hardly know them. I met them once only. I'm a countryman. I know nothing about what goes on in London.' He spread his hands on the table. 'I cannot tell you what I do not know.'

Robert Dysart stared down at the prisoner chained before him. This could go on all day, as it had on previous days. He was careful not to let his frustration show, but so far the man had given him nothing. He had a feeling that this Gabriel Stanhope would turn out to be far more dangerous than all the rest of them put together.

He had a big man's capacity for physical endurance. His robust constitution had not proved in any way susceptible to the foul conditions of Newgate, despite Dysart's instructions to keep him in the darkest, dankest, filthiest part of this disease-ridden prison. Others were already succumbing to the vile contagions so rife here, but Stanhope always appeared fresh and ruddy faced, in the rudest health. He stayed calm, mild-tempered, however harsh or long the questioning. He seemed able to retreat to some place inside himself; a place that Dysart could not reach. Despite his mild manner, however, Dysart sensed a profound belief, a zeal for his cause that sustained and fed him. It showed sometimes, deep in his blue eyes, like a spark from a damped down fire.

He would love to be able to break him, to use methods that would shatter that strong body, stretch and rack it, separate each vertebra, pull each bone from its socket, turn those powerful hands to bloody paws, nails torn out, fingers smashed. But thanks to Oldfield, that could not be. Dysart silently cursed the lawyer. Cursed all lawyers. The way they stuck together. Even the judges. Oldfield had managed to wriggle out of all attempts to implicate him in the conspiracy that Dysart had spun for Hugh and Sovay. Now he had engaged Thomas Erskine, as defence counsel in this and his other cases. Erskine had made a career out of defending these radical swine and any hint of torture would be pounced upon and made much of in court, for Stanhope and the rest were to be tried by judge and jury. How Dysart wished he could sweep all that away as they had done in France. How he longed for the clear, shining simplicity of the Revolutionary Tribunal. No troublesome lawyers, no endless parade of pointless witnesses, no stupid jury, just the rightful judgement of true believers. Death or acquittal. If Dysart had his way, it would be death in every case. And he would have his way. It was only a matter of time and he would be First Minister in the Departement of the Thames. He had the highest assurance of that.

Perhaps it was time to move things on. Conditions were ripe. Despite the draconian action that had been taken against Stanhope and his kind, unrest was spreading. Ireland was in ferment; Ireland might be the key to this. He would send a representative. Someone whom he could trust, someone with the right connections, of high enough rank to be believed. A man of no scruples at all, who was heavily in debt and who would be more than happy to be relieved of such obligations. Dysart smiled to himself. He knew just the man. If he was successful, he might even receive a large and lucrative estate in Warwickshire for his pains.

◆➤◓◄◆

'What did he want?' Lydia asked as she came into the cell.

'Oh, the usual.' Gabriel gave a weary smile. He put a brave face on with Dysart, but these sessions tired him beyond measure.

'Shrivel-hearted crow,' Lydia grimaced. 'Don't let him get you down, Gabriel. Cook's sent a squab pie to keep your strength up. She knows it's your favourite, and Mrs Crombie's put in some warm vests she's been knitting you to keep off the chill.'

As Lydia kept up a light chatter about the goings-on at Soho Square, Gabriel's eyes filled with tears. They could have no idea how these simple acts of kindness sustained him through the endless hours of interrogation. They helped to keep his resolve to the forefront of his mind and cut out Dysart's voice and his insidious accusations. Gabriel would fight all his life long for the rights of ordinary people, people like them.

Lydia came almost every day to bring food for him and clean linen. As often as not she was accompanied by Skidmore, Oldfield's clerk, who brought news on how the case was progressing and how the others were faring. Gabriel was kept in solitary confinement, but he was not deprived of visitors, Oldfield made sure of that.

'The thing is, Gabriel, the fact of the matter is . . .' Gabriel looked up at Lydia's seriousness of tone, her uncharacteristic hesitation. 'With me being distant from my own people, and the mistress away, I wanted your opinion.'

'About what?' Gabriel asked, intrigued.

'Well, it's this. Mr Skidmore, Algie,' the words came in a sudden rush, 'has asked me to walk out with him. I've asked Mrs Crombie, and she thinks it would be acceptable.'

'I'm sure the good lady is right, in this as in most matters.' Gabriel went to rise, to embrace her, but was pulled back by his encumbering chains. 'You don't need anyone's permission, Lydia, if it is what you want.'

'Oh, it is, Mr Gabriel. I love him with all my heart.'

'There you are then!'

Gabriel smiled. He was happy for her; Algernon Skidmore was a fine young fellow with good prospects, thanks to Sovay, and would make an excellent husband. He'd thought, at one time, that Lydia might have had feelings for him. He had not wanted to tell her that there could be no place in the life he planned for a wife and perhaps children. It would not be fair on them. How could he devote himself to the many, if he was distracted and occupied by the happiness of the few?

That's if he ever got out of this place. There was no trial date as yet. It would be October at the earliest, according to Oldfield, and much could happen between now and then.

CHAPTER 34

It was hard to keep track of time. France was no longer ruled by the same calendar as everywhere else. All the months had been renamed after the weather, or crops. They were presently in Messidor, which meant *harvest*, or perhaps they were in Thermidor, which meant *hot*. Sovay could not be sure. She didn't even know what day of the week it was, since the normal seven had been increased to ten. The weather was certainly living up to the new naming. Even with the windows open, there was hardly a breath of air. They were living in Year 2. The new calendar was calculated from the day the Republic had been declared, and there hadn't really been a Year 1, because no one had thought of it then. It was as if time had been broken. As if the past had never existed and the future was there to be invented along with everything else. Who knew what to believe? Or how to behave? The rules were made up and changed from day to day. The arrogance bordered on madness. It is what sent the tumbrels rolling to the guillotine day after day.

Sovay had not seen any of the gruesome executions, and she didn't want to, dreading to see her father riding among the condemned. Amélie Thery, the doctor's daughter, reported that Sir John was gravely ill but his condition was far from hopeless. Either Hugh or Sovay went every day to get news of him, torn between hoping that he was better and knowing that any recovery speeded him towards the Tribunal and the guillotine. Hugh had taken quite a fancy to Mademoiselle Thery and often elected to go on his own to the Luxembourg, in the hope of accompanying her on her shopping rounds and then back to her home on Rue de Monsieur Le Prince. Sovay was often left alone in the Hôtel Fonteneau where she sat in her shift because of the heat and wrote letters that it was impossible to send.

In the evenings, she went out with Hugh and Virgil, among the expatriots who remained in the city. They met in clubs, private *salons* and hotels. Subdued parties of Americans mainly, and some Irishmen. Among them was Lord Henry Fitzwilliam, now plain Henry since he had given up his title, celebrated United Irishman, brother to Gerald, Hugh's Oxford friend and tutor. He was very different from his kinsman, being very much taller and bigger altogether, with thick, curling auburn hair and large, expressive brown eyes. He had a deep voice and a rich laugh and, considering the state the country was in, he laughed a lot.

'Always entertainment to be found,' he declared. 'Champagne and oysters to be had. I don't see it very different, as long as one avoids the tumbrels, except the theatres are full of those confoundedly boring patriotic plays.'

The only time he was ever serious was when the talk turned to Irish politics. Then his handsome face grew sombre and he burned with a quiet anger at the fate of his fellow countrymen.

'Revolution is our only hope,' he declared, 'if we are to free ourselves of the English yoke and become independent.'

He was here to solicit French support for an Irish rebellion. Virgil didn't hold out much hope for his ambitions. The French were fighting on all sides. With every country in Europe against them, they had neither men nor money to squander on such an expedition, but Henry would have none of such talk.

'On the contrary, my dear Barrett, it is very much on the cards. I am in negotiation with those in the very highest authority. They see it as a means to deflect English attention away from war with France.'

Sovay enjoyed the diversion such evenings afforded her. Henry Fitzwilliam and his friends were charming company and the women she met were interesting, being of an adventurous and independent frame of mind. But there was something brittle in the laughter, as though danger gave a frantic edge to the frivolity. Fear was always there, real but never spoken. They could all be arrested at any time. There was often a space at the table where someone had been taken, or else had left for Switzerland or some other place of safety. If a person was absent, their presence was missed, but never spoken of or questioned. One learnt not to ask.

Despite Henry Fitzwilliam's brave words, it *was* different. Very different. Society of any kind was dwindling, even among the French. A year ago, she was told, the *salons* had been filled with politicians, journalists, men of learning and letters, soldiers on leave from the wars. Now they were in the grip of *La Grande Terreur*, many such men had fled, or had been arrested and sent to the guillotine. There was a distinct lack of stimulating male company. One young captain was very much missed since his duties had taken him from Paris. His absence was especially regretted, particularly by the ladies. Sovay was oddly galled to find out that Léon was so popular and felt an unwelcome stab of jealousy to hear him spoken of in that way.

Although Sovay liked going out in society, the relentless pleasure-seeking left her giddy, and the single-minded focus on the trivial in the face of daily enormity was difficult to reconcile. She was glad when Virgil told her that he had arranged a meeting with Lefere. Going with him would give her something to do that had a real purpose.

'It took longer than I thought, but he has uncovered a letter from Dysart. I've taken him the blank forms stamped with the seal of the Committee of Public Safety that Fernand procured,' he told her. 'He's not happy about it, but will do anything for money. We have to collect them tomorrow night.'

It was a hot night and the attic above the printer's shop was stifling, the atmosphere stale and thick with the onion stench of sweat and the sweetish reek of unwashed clothes.

Lefere was clearly having second thoughts. Sovay positioned herself behind him. At a nod from Virgil, she eased a small pistol from her pocket. Lefere turned at the click behind his ear, the beads rolling off his oily forehead and onto the paper on the table before him.

'Careful!' Virgil threw him a kerchief. 'Mop your brow. We don't want to soil the evidence. Now, I find a gun to the head a great persuader, so let's get on with it shall we? And I want a fair copy, so keep your hand steady or that paper will be stained with more than sweat.'

His hand ceased to shake as soon as he applied pen to paper and he wrote to Virgil's dictation with a forger's careful precision. Finally, he copied the signatures, each one an exact imitation of the members of the Committee of Public Safety.

'Good!' Virgil looked down at his work. 'Very good. Now for the annotations.' Virgil picked up the letter that Lefere had procured which was written in Dysart's hand. 'I want you to add, here, here, and here.' Virgil completed his dictation. 'Let me see.'

Lefere shook sand over his work, blew away the residue and handed the paper to Virgil.

'This will do very well.' He passed it to Sovay. 'What do you think?'

She read it through quickly. It was perfectly executed and worded in such a way as to implicate Dysart in a plot against his own Government. She smiled at the cleverness of it. There would be no gainsaying it. Given in evidence, it would be enough to get him hanged, or worse.

'Thank you, Citizen Lefere.' Virgil scooped up the other papers and put them in his pocket. 'We should have plenty here. Your money.' He took out a purse. Gold spilled across the table. 'I'm sure you've betrayed people of much greater worth for far less than that. You can consider yourself well rewarded.'

With that, they left him, making their way quickly down the narrow turns of the crooked stairs. As soon as they were out in the street, the casement above them flew open.

'Spies! English spies!' Lefere bawled out. 'Ring the

tocsin. Rouse the *Section*! Spies in our midst!'

Faces appeared in doorways and at open windows. Men spilled onto the street.

'Where?' They looked up to Lefere for direction. 'Where?'

'There!' He pointed at Sovay and Virgil. 'Don't let them get away!'

There was nowhere to hide. People were appearing on every side, armed with anything that they could find, and the street was well lit, with lanterns swinging from chains strung from one side to the other.

Virgil grabbed Sovay's hand, making for the end of the street. Two men wearing liberty caps shouted a challenge and attempted to block their way with improvised pikes. Virgil dodged sideways, pushing one man into the other, their unwieldy weapons tangling together. One of the long poles skittled out of the man's hand and bounced into the path of another band of pursuers, causing the front rank to trip and fall. Those following behind fell over their fellows in a confusion of arms and legs. Virgil and Sovay sped on, but all the while more people were pouring down side streets to join in the hue and cry.

It seemed that they would be caught in a matter of moments.

'Amélie Thery lives up here.'

Sovay pulled Virgil after her, praying that the gate to her courtyard would be unlocked. It was their only hope. Up ahead, the narrow street curved away, sheer as a canyon. The house was first on the right. She pushed and the gate creaked open on to a little garden crowded with trees and shrubs. Virgil and Sovay hid among the foliage, trying to control their ragged breathing as many feet clattered past in the street outside.

'Which door is hers?' Virgil whispered.

'The one at the end.' Sovay crept forward and rapped lightly on the door. 'Amélie. It's me,' she called quietly. 'Sovay.'

The girl's big brown eyes grew wide when she saw who was standing outside. 'I heard the shouting,' she said, pulling her shawl round her shoulders. 'But did not want to go out. Too dangerous. I'm on my own here at the moment. My neighbours have all fled or moved out. Come this way. Quick! They may be back!'

She led them through to the back of her house. She put her ear to the panels of the door, then looked out cautiously.

'There's nobody about. Good luck.'

She gathered her shawl tight around her and prepared to answer the distant hammering that had started up on her front door.

The street Sovay and Virgil entered was quiet. The disturbance started by Lefere seemed local to the area around his house.

'It is odd how one place can be in ferment,' Virgil said, 'and right next door there is no sign of anything.' He looked around, relieved. 'We should be able to proceed unmolested.'

They made their way through the streets of St Germain until they reached the river and then they crossed over the Pont Neuf to the relative safety of the other bank.

'I dropped into White's on my way to see Lefere,' Virgil said as they walked up towards the Marais. 'I met Henry Fitzwilliam there. Who do you think he's expecting?'

Sovay had no idea.

'His brother, Gerald Fitzwilliam.'

'Hugh's tutor?'

'Due to arrive tomorrow.'

'Why is he coming here?'

'To see his brother. Undergone a late conversion to the cause, apparently, and become a United Irishman. Henry is overjoyed, of course, but I call it mighty strange.'

'You suspect him?'

'Don't you? He will be up to no good, we can be sure of that. I suggest we pay him a visit tomorrow evening. Welcome him to Paris.'

CHAPTER 35

The house where Henry Fitzwilliam now resided had been divided into apartments. The concierge took his time answering the bell and when he did appear he was surly to the point of rudeness. He opened the door a crack and scowled out, his face folded in lines of ill temper and dissatisfaction. Virgil barely had time to state his business before he grunted, 'Not in,' and went to shut the door on them.

'We'll wait.' Virgil put his foot inside the threshold.

'Please yourself.' The man let the door go and wandered off.

Henry's rooms were at the top of the stairs. Virgil knocked, expecting to be answered by Henry's manservant. Instead, he was confronted by a rusty-haired boy who spoke in English.

'Sir Henry ain't here.'

'It's not him we've come to see.' Virgil walked past him into the apartment. 'It's his brother. And less of the "Sirs" if you value your life, or your master's. I'm Virgil Barrett. This is Sophie Weston.'

'Pleased to make your acquaintance. I'm Rufus Brook. I work for Mr Gerald. He's gone out for the evening with his brother, *Mr* Henry,' the boy added with a wide grin.

'In that case, we'll wait for them.' Virgil sat down.

'No guaranteeing when they will return. Knowing my master, it may be late.'

'Even so,' Virgil smiled. 'Perhaps you could offer us some refreshment?'

'I would, sir. Certainly I would, but the decanter up here is empty, and blowed if I know where to find any more, or any vittles.' His freckled forehead wrinkled in frustration. 'We only just got here. His manservant's ran off to join the army. I'm doing for both of 'em and I can't speak the lingo.'

'Henry probably sends out for food and wine. Did they not tell you that?' Virgil rose. 'Why don't I come with you? I'm sure we'll find something, somewhere.'

He shepherded the grateful boy out of the room, giving Sovay her cue to get to work.

She slipped out of the main salon and into the corridor, checking each room as she passed, and identifying Gerald's by a number of open trunks. They had evidently disturbed Rufus at his unpacking. She looked around. Where to start? What would Toby do? Look in the most obvious places first.

The trunks were empty, their contents transferred to drawer and press, and contained no secret compartments, as far as Sovay could see. The chest of drawers held nothing but shirts, linen and stockings. The suits hanging up had empty pockets. She moved to the desk. The drawers were empty. The writing case on top contained nothing but blank sheets of paper, writing implements and a letter Gerald had started to his mother. The drawers in the bedside tables were empty. She looked around, sighing her frustration. An occasional table by the window held several bundles of books secured from slewing about by leather straps. Latin, Greek, desperately dull. She turned the next stack to her. Rousseau, Voltaire and Thomas Paine.

Rights of Man: being an Answer to Mr. Burke's attack on the French Revolution. She undid the straps and opened the calf-bound book: printed for J.S. Jordan, No. 166, Fleet-Street. She turned the pages. The centre of the book had been neatly hollowed out to provide a secret compartment. Inside lay a wad of letters. All in the same neat, small, spiky hand that she had seen being forged just the day before. Three letters. Each addressed to Citizen Robespierre. Her heart beat hard as the paper crackled under her fingers.

'Rufus! Where are you?' A voice called out in the hall. 'Where the devil is that boy?'

Sovay looked round. There was nowhere to hide.

'Rufus . . .' His voice tailed off in surprise. 'What the blazes? What are you doing here?'

'I was looking for some reading matter,' Sovay showed him the book in her hand. 'And I found it.'

'Now, look here,' Gerald Fitzwilliam came towards her. A vein beat in his temple and his face, already flushed from the wine that she could smell on his breath, reddened further. 'You can't –'

'I just have.' Sovay didn't feel like bandying words with him, especially as she had her pistol about her. 'The letters concealed in here prove you to be an enemy to me, my family, and others I hold dear.'

She had not had time to read the letters, but could tell by his face that she had guessed correctly.

'You Middletons always were a traitorous bunch,' he sneered. 'You'll get no more than you deserve. Give the book to me!'

He made a clumsy grab for it, but he was unsteady with drink. Sovay evaded him easily.

'I would not hesitate to use this.' She took the gun

from under her jacket. 'So do not come any closer, Mr Fitzwilliam, or try my patience further.'

The sight of the weapon checked his step.

'You will not get away with this,' he hissed. 'One word from me will be enough to have you guillotined as an English spy!'

'I think not.'

Fitzwilliam turned to find Virgil standing behind him.

'Such accusations work both ways,' he continued mildly. 'We are none of us safe.'

'I am Irish, not English!' Fitzwilliam spat the words out. 'We are welcome here!'

'*Some* of you are, but I do not think that you are numbered among them. If you do not do exactly as we say, not only will you be reported to the local committee here – the concierge, I can tell you, is already suspicious – but every Irishman from here to New York will know that you are in the pay of Dysart and have betrayed their cause to the British Government and the Committee of Secrecy.'

Virgil was right about the Irish business. His own brother would kill him as soon as look at him. Fitzwilliam knew it. Fear flickered in his pale eyes. He lacked the temperament to be a spy. Cowardice fairly oozed from him, sheening his smooth face with a film of sweat.

'Very well.' He sat down heavily, no hint of fight left. 'What do you want me to do?'

'Simple.' Virgil nodded to Rufus who had slipped into the room. 'But first, I'm sure you could do with a brandy.'

Fitzwilliam raised the glass with a shaking hand.

'Get your man here to pack your bags. A change of mind. A change of plan. You will be gone before your brother gets back.' Virgil poured himself a drink and sat down in a chair. 'I'll stay here to make sure you are.'

Sovay left Virgil to guard Fitzwilliam. As she slipped from the building, a shadow detached itself from the doorway opposite and began to follow her.

CHAPTER 36

'What do you want with me?' Sovay turned quickly. 'I warn you, I have a gun.'

'I don't doubt it!' The man put his hands in the air. 'You wouldn't shoot an old friend, would you, Sovay!'

'Greenwood! What are you doing here?'

Sovay was so relieved to see him that it was all she could do not to throw her arms round him right there in the street.

'I've been following Fitzwilliam. I was just trying to work out a way to get in, thinking that I should have brought young Toby with me – I'm no cracksman – when who do I see turn up bold as you like? I almost thought to warn you when Fitzwilliam came back in a tearing hurry, but reasoned that you and the Yankee could look after yourselves. And I was right, it seems. Nice piece.' He nodded towards where she had secreted the pistol. 'Where did you get it?'

'Virgil gave it to me. I was just about to shoot you with it. Don't you know better than to creep up on a person like that?'

'Did you get what you were after?' Greenwood fell into step beside her.

'How do you know we were after anything?'

Greenwood gave her a look.

'Yes, we did.' Sovay smiled her satisfaction and her large eyes glittered with excitement. She really was remarkably handsome; Greenwood frowned at lost chances.

'What are you looking so glum about?' she said, looking up at him.

'I was cursing myself for being such a gentleman.' He took her arm. 'We would have made an excellent pair, Sovay. I should have had my wicked way with you when I could.'

She laughed. 'Too late now.'

'How so?' Greenwood's grin was mischievous. 'Who've you met?'

'That's not what I meant!' Sovay looked away, glad that it was dark enough to hide her blushes. She quickly changed the subject. 'What are you doing here, anyway?'

'Oldfield sent me. I'm working for him now.'

'Are you mad?' Sovay stared at him. 'It's a wonder you weren't arrested as soon as you opened your mouth.'

'I'm an educated man!' Greenwood looked pained at her implication. 'I can speak French as well as Fitzwilliam. Beside, I'm travelling as an Irishman. Patrick MacManus of County Monaghan. Oldfield got the papers for me. What was Fitzwilliam carrying?'

'Letters from Dysart to Robespierre. You can take them back with you, along with the other evidence that we have gathered. There will be enough to discredit him. I'm sure of it.'

'What will happen to Fitzwilliam? He cannot go back to England.'

'Oh, no,' Sovay laughed. 'Once he's packed his bags, he's off to the coast, in one of Virgil's barrels if need be. From there he'll be taken to America to be kept out of the way until Dysart's defeated.'

Greenwood's tone grew serious. 'That won't come too soon for Gabriel and the others.'

'What is happening to him?' Sovay asked, seized with guilt that she had been too caught up in the moment to ask for news from home.

'He's in Newgate, holding up tolerably well. I do have happier news,' Greenwood smiled. 'Lydia is to marry Skidmore, although she will not set a day. She wants you to be there.'

Sovay saw the little church at Compton, all decorated for a wedding, and her throat grew tight with longing.

'I will be there,' she pledged. 'I will be her maid of honour. And Toby, what news of him?'

'He's 'prentice to a locksmith in Clerkenwell. A good, honest fellow, a friend of Dick Chapman's. He should keep him on the straight. He's still all afire to go to America when his time is up.'

'I'm glad he does well.' Sovay smiled at the thought of him, of all of them. 'I miss them, Greenwood.'

'Come back with me now, then,' the Captain urged. 'Why put yourself in further danger?'

'No.' Sovay shook her head. 'I cannot leave Papa and, besides, I have other business here.'

Greenwood did not press her further. He was wise in the ways of the heart, and from the look on her face, he guessed what that 'other business' might be.

In the morning, Greenwood was gone, taking the letters and the documents forged by Lefere. Sovay felt a great sense of relief and exultation. There was enough evidence to discredit Dysart completely.

Although they were set about with dangers here, their enemy at home would be soon defeated. She felt a change in her mood, her spirits lifted by the first feelings of hope that she had experienced since arriving in France.

The day was warm already, and would undoubtedly grow hotter. She dressed in her lightest gown to prepare herself for the glaring heat of the dusty city streets and resolved to go to the Luxembourg to see if there was any news of her father.

Hugh was accompanying Fernand to the Convention, and Virgil was conducting Fitzwilliam to Le Havre, so she would have to go alone. She pushed open the heavy front door. The courtyard was bright with sunlight. A scrawny yellow cat dozed in the corner under the shade of a fig tree. A tangle of geranium flowers straggled down from pots on a windowsill, their petals scattered over the cobbles, like drops of crimson blood. Sovay stepped out of the street entrance, the door clanging behind her. She had made this journey many times before and set out confidently, cutting through the mass of small streets, but it was easy to get confused in the twists and turns and she found herself on a main thoroughfare that she did not know.

She was met by a throng of people, all going in the same direction. Men, women and children, their faces set and expressionless, apart from a look of stony purpose, as if they were fulfilling some duty set upon them. For such a large crowd, they made almost no noise. There was nothing to distinguish this street from many others: the high walls on either side, the closed gates, the scrawled slogans. It could not be far from where she was living, but Sovay knew she'd never walked down here before. The scene had a strangeness to it, both familiar, yet unfamiliar, like in a dream. There was no clear threat, but she had a strong sense of premonition, enough to make her shiver in the rising heat of the day. She thought to turn back, but it was too late. It was as though she had stepped into a fast-flowing river. The crowd closed round her and took her with them. To turn back would be difficult and when she attempted it, the eyes about her sparked with suspicion.

'What is the matter, Citizeness?' one woman asked her. 'Where is your patriotic duty?'

She was towing a child, a girl of about six or seven years, who eyed Sovay with candid frankness.

Her challenge drew the attention of other women, who scrutinised Sovay with growing hostility. Sovay wondered what was provoking them so, fearing that they could read her nationality in her face and reluctant to speak, in case her accent confirmed their suspicions. They looked one to another, then the boldest swaggered forward, her face set, her curled fists set on hips, ready to challenge her outright.

'Citizeness!' a male voice boomed in her ear. 'Where is your tricolour!'

Sovay looked down in horror. Her tricolour was on the collar of the coat that she'd been wearing the night before. She'd been told never to leave the house without one. People had been torn apart, beaten to death in the streets, for not wearing the emblem of the Revolution.

Powerful male hands seized Sovay from behind and marched her away from the crowd. The women glanced at the National Guardsman and went on their way, satisfied. He took off his hat and she saw it was Léon.

'You must remember to wear this at all times, Citizeness,' he said, taking the large red, white and blue cockade from the turned-up brim and attaching it to her shoulder. 'If you are not to attract the attention of the Revolutionary Committees or get a beating at the hands of the *bonnes républicaines* who were subjecting you to such rude stares. Now, let us complete our patriotic duty.'

He held Sovay tightly by the arm and it was not long before she realised the purpose of this determined pilgrimage. The smell was enough. Rust-red ooze seeped from between the cobbles beneath their feet and the gutters ran with blood. Complaints from each successive resting place, about the blood and the stench, meant that the infamous machine had been moved to the eastern edge of the city, to the barrière du Trône. The place had been renamed Trône-Renversé, the throne reversed, but the great stone pillars that had marked this entrance to the city still soared upwards, monuments to the old regime. There was a new throne now. They were herded into its presence. Set up on a high platform, the angled blade was like a macabre canopy, the collar like a great mouth where the seat should be. The executioner and his attendants looked like butchers, their clothes and smocks drenched with blood.

Tumbrels waited in line, like carts outside a slaughterhouse. Their passengers stood bunched together, held upright by the press of numbers, collars torn away from their shoulders, hands bound behind their backs, shorn heads bowed.

The process was brutally swift, born from the efficiency of long practice. Each victim was loaded onto a board to be delivered to the blade. The head was thrust through a small aperture, known as the peep-hole, the upper part then dropped down to fit round the neck, the lever was pulled and the blade hissed down. The whole process took less than a minute from the prisoner lying down to the executioner holding up the dripping head for the crowd to see. The head was dropped into the basket below, the body tipped into a waiting cart, ready to be taken to a mass grave hastily dug in the grounds of a nearby convent on the Rue de Picpus.

Sovay had been brought up on a farm and was well used to seeing animals slaughtered, but the gush of blood from the neck, the hot coppery stench of it, was truly shocking. Even harder to bear was the stoical dignity and frail fortitude of the waiting victims: strangers stood shoulder to shoulder, a mother held her weeping daughter, a father clasped his son, a priest administered the last rites, who could stop him now? A nun sang the *Te Deum* in a wavering voice that grew stronger as her time came nearer. The crowd grew quiet and still as the executioner's assistants printed her white habit with blood. Sovay would have turned away with the pity of it all if Léon had not held her steady. To turn from the scene would be to give herself away, would be seen as unpatriotic.

There was little cheering. The few desultory cries of triumph from the claque, who were paid to applaud as each head was held up, were not taken up by the rest of the crowd

'Why would they cheer?' Léon said. 'The aristocrats are all dead, or fled. These poor devils are shopkeepers, printers, locksmiths, lacemakers, waiters, servants, poor priests, sisters dragged from their convents. Enemies to somebody: a vindictive neighbour, a member of their local Revolutionary Committee, or deemed guilty by association with a relative or friend who has come to the attention of Robespierre and the Committee of Public Safety. Ordinary people. Like them. Perhaps they begin to feel the icy kiss of the blade on their own necks.'

'If they do not hate them, then why do they come?'

'Who knows?' Léon shrugged. 'Some are curious. Fascinated by the actual moment of death. For others, it is a kind of relief. It is not their turn today, even though it could be tomorrow. For me. For you. We are none of us safe. Enough,' he said abruptly and began to lead her away. 'The show will be over soon, anyway.'

A row of women occupied a stand of benches, needles clicking. Their attention, at least, was avid. Léon's eyes flicked towards them.

'The notorious *tricoteuses*. Do not look too closely at them. They are here each day, knitting liberty caps, or stockings for their menfolk fighting in the wars. Who knows what they knit, or why? Perhaps they are like Penelope and unravel at night what they knit up during the day. Perhaps they are like the Fates and when they stop, so will this madness. Either that, or the last thread will be snapped and we'll all be dead.' He looked at her, suddenly noticing how pale she'd grown. 'Are you all right?'

Sovay nodded, not trusting herself to speak. She did

not want to show weakness, but the scenes at the guillotine, the heat of the day, the stench of the blood, threatened to overwhelm her senses. He led her down a quiet side street and found shade under spreading plane trees that surrounded a small square. Sunlight fell through the leaves, making dappled patterns across the cobbles. They stopped at a small café and sat at a rickety table. Léon ordered wine. A woman's voice called out, pots clattered in the kitchen. There was a smell of herbs, thyme and rosemary, from the pots by the door. Sovay found solace in the very ordinariness of the scene. The horror was still going on, along with other crimes, small and large, across the beleaguered city, but here life continued as it always had done, as it would do again. The wine came with a basket of bread. Léon poured a glass for her, urged her to drink.

'It did not begin like this,' he said after a while. 'Dealing death to ordinary people. We did not start the Revolution to make war on our fellow citizens. For you to react like that –'

'I'm sorry,' Sovay apologised for allowing herself to be overcome.

'Not at all! It shows how far we have come that we tolerate such barbarism.' He shook his head. 'The things I have seen. The things I have done. In the Vendée, in Lyon. All in the name of that same Revolution.' He passed a hand over his eyes as if to wipe away the memory that existed inside. 'The slaughter you have just witnessed. Civilized compared with it. People blown to pieces by cannon fire, tied in long lines and fired upon with rifles, bound together naked and thrown into rivers, sent out in boats drilled full of holes. All done in the name of the Republic . . .' His voice tailed away and he looked up, his green eyes dull and full of suffering, whether for himself, or for the victims, it was hard to tell. 'There's blood on my hands, too, Sovay.' He looked away from her, down at his long fingers spread on the table. 'I am a soldier. I follow orders, or that's what I told myself. I no longer have a God from whom I can beg forgiveness. All I can do is hope to make reparation. That, one day, the people will forgive their misguided son.'

He drained his glass and poured more. He drank in silence. Sovay did not know how to break his brooding contemplation. No words of hers could bring solace or comfort, so she sat quietly, waiting for him to speak again.

'Tell me of your home,' he said eventually, as though remembering that she was there with him. 'What is it like there?'

She told him about Compton, how much she had longed for adventure, but how much she missed the measured normality of that life now.

'Do not seek excitement, lest you find it.' He laughed. 'I, too, come from the country. From Gascony. I was sent away as a small boy, to attend school here in Paris, but I never felt I belonged here. My heart was elsewhere, walking in the fields, hunting in the woods, fishing in the streams. I have faced death many times, and know that Gascony will be the last place I visit in my mind when it comes time to leave this life behind.'

'Will you go back?'

He smiled. 'Maybe sometime, when all this is over. I will take you there!' He took her hand. 'You will come with me! Although our lands are gone. Foxes look out of the chateau. There will be not much to see.'

'Your family have all gone?'

'To America, yes.' His laugh was bitter. 'The others to an even better place. I have no one. Nothing. I live on my soldier's pay. When I get it. Like my men.'

'Why did you not leave, too?'

'Because I believe in the Revolution! I still hold to those first ideals!' His green eyes lost their pebble dullness. 'If you were there at the beginning, you would understand. To be there was to see the world split apart and a new one emerging. To see everything change. For ever.' He looked at her, his eyes hard and bright, like polished agates. 'To want equality, freedom, for all men – and women. How can that be wrong?'

'I have heard the same words all my life, from my father, my brother, and I never doubted either, but to see what we have both just witnessed . . .' She wanted to believe still, but the memory of the guillotine made her shudder.

'It is hard to live through these days, it is true. But they are *days* only. They will soon pass. In the life, the history of a nation, what are days, weeks, months, years even? What began here, in 1789, will affect the whole world for centuries to come.' He leaned forward, his green eyes intense. 'What is happening now is an anomaly. It is a diversion, not part of that great movement of change. It has to stop. In the name of the Revolution. All this killing has to stop.'

'Is that why you have returned?' she asked.

'Partly.' His reply was noncommittal. He threw

some money on the table. 'But not my only reason. We will talk while we walk.' He took her arm as they crossed the square. 'This morning, my men picked up an English spy trying to leave the city. There was a scare in St Germain the other night, now there are English spies everywhere. We are besieged by them.' He looked down at her, eyebrows raised in unspoken enquiry. 'This particular fellow will say nothing of his mission, but the papers he carries have your name on them, Sovay.'

'Where is he?'

'At my headquarters. I will take you there. It is not far from here. Just across the river.'

The streets were still deserted, one side in shadow, the other in bright sunlight. They turned a corner to see a group of men were approaching. In the front were a burly pair of *sans-culottes*, in striped trousers and liberty caps, who walked with fixed purpose, eyes on the street, stout cudgels at the ready. The two behind them were dressed as gentlemen. The smaller one was exquisitely turned out in a sky-blue coat with lace at his neck and immaculate white stockings. Underneath his dazzlingly white wig, his small features were pinched in concentrated thought. He wore green eye glasses which caught the sun as he looked up at his taller companion who was, by contrast, dressed in black, blond-haired, extraordinarily good-looking and very young. As soon as he saw them, Léon put his arm round Sovay, pulling her close, as if they were lovers.

'Saint-Just and Robespierre,' he whispered in her ear. 'Do not stare.'

'Citizens!' he said and stepped out of the way to let them pass.

Deep in conversation, they did not return his greeting. Robespierre did not look up, only Saint-Just glanced in their direction. He had the face of an angel, with eyes as blue and empty as the sky.

'Robespierre does not live far from here,' Léon said. 'In the house of Duplay the carpenter on Rue St Honoré. The family worship him. The place is a fortress. He is guarded day and night, doubly so since that girl, Cécile Renault, tried to kill him with a fruit knife. He sees conspiracy everywhere. Renault and her whole family have paid the price, but his eyes are in the wrong place. The threat will not come from the widows and servant girls the tumbrels bear every day, but from some of those most near to him. The tigers are beginning to fight. He has succeeded in uniting good men and bad against him. Idealists like your friend Fernand have been joined by rogues and scoundrels who fear they will be next. Who will go first to the guillotine? We have an expression: *he who sows the wind reaps the storm*.'

As Léon and Sovay continued along the narrow street, a man in uniform appeared round the corner accompanied by a tall, dark-haired man dressed in civilian clothes.

'*Merde!* Hanriot and Carnot! They are all out today!'

'Who are they?'

'Carnot is on the Committee of Public Safety. Hanriot is Commandant of the Guard. I'm not supposed to be here. I'm dead if he sees me!'

He dodged into the sharp shadow of a doorway, pulling her after him. He swung her round so that her back was to the street and held her in a passionate embrace. His skin was rough against her cheek and his mouth tasted of wine. Sovay felt as though she was falling. She put her arms round his neck, weaving her fingers into the thickness of his soft, black hair. When, at last, he released her, she was slow to return to her surroundings, as if she was gradually resurfacing through shimmering layers of water.

'Have they gone yet?' she whispered.

He looked down at her, smiling. 'Oh, they went a long time ago,' he said, and gently replaced a lock of her long, dark hair, 'but I fear others may follow.'

He took her in his arms again and pressed her against the wall. This time his kisses were softer, less hurried, but more searching and no less urgent. She returned his caresses with equal fervour. Her breath came faster, the strength of her passion sweeping through her. She was not aware of time passing, their embrace might have lasted hours or only a moment, but when he finally let her go, she knew that she was his, body and soul.

They went on together, arms round each other. Nobody looked twice at them, or pursed their lips in disapproval. Paris was a city for lovers, even the Revolution could not change that.

They crossed the river and walked along the quays before turning into one of the side streets. To Sovay, Paris was still somewhat of a maze, and looked different during the day, or she might have realised that she was near where she and Virgil had been the night before. Léon was taking her to his personal headquarters: some old noble family's grand hôtel, seized by the Republic. A red flag flew next to the National Guard tricolour and *Propriété Nationale*, inscribed over the gate, obscured the ancient, weathered coat of arms. Two guardsmen stood, pikes crossed over the entrance. They jumped smartly to attention when they saw Léon and drew the pikes sharply back .

Sovay and Léon walked under the wide arch with its big swinging lantern and on into a paved court-yard. A flight of steps led up to an imposing front door. Above it, a shield showed a lion rampant, remarkably unweathered and not obscured by Republican paint.

'Welcome to my family home,' Léon said, and laughed.

The inside resembled a barracks. All grand accoutrements had been stripped away and off-duty guardsmen lounged around drinking wine and smok-ing pipes. Some gossiped together, while others played cards. A particularly lively game was going on in the corner, with loud exclamations of triumph followed by good-natured disagreement. As they came in, one of the guardsmen shouted, 'Remove this fellow, Léon, before he takes us for everything we've got!'

'Not yet!' one of the other players objected. 'Not before we've had a chance to win some of it back.'

Their opponent stood up and made a mock bow. 'Thank you for your time,' he said. 'And your money.'

He laughed as he made a show of counting the sheaf of black-and-white *assignats* that he had collected before folding them and putting them into his pocket. His smile died when he saw Sovay.

'They caught me,' he shrugged. 'I'm sorry for it. Is there somewhere that we can talk?'

Léon took them into the room he was using for his

office.

'This used to be my mother's drawing room.' He looked around with faint nostalgia. 'It has changed a bit from those days.'

The elegant furnishings had been removed, replaced by plain wooden chairs and tables. The primrose-and-white striped wallpaper was torn and marked with greasy fingerprints round the door and a grimy stripe at shoulder height. Various weapons: pikes, guns and swords, lay in boxes or stacked against the sides of the room.

'I've been thinking,' Greenwood started.

'Not like you,' Sovay smiled, but he did not smile back at her.

'I'm serious, Sovay. I've had a look at the letters.' He patted his pocket. 'Virgil is right. There's enough to condemn Dysart, but he's far from stupid and no one is more alert to changes around him. At the first whiff of suspicion, he will run for the coast. If he escapes, you will be in considerable jeopardy.'

'I am aware of that,' Sovay said quietly. 'I'll take my chances.'

'No,' Greenwood shook his head. 'Come with me now. You have done enough.'

'But it is not safe for me in England. Dysart is not defeated yet.'

'I will get you out of the country, to Switzerland,' Léon interjected. 'You will be safe there with others who have fled from Paris.'

'No! I will not leave while my father is held prisoner and Hugh faces who knows what dangers.'

'Hugh can look after himself.'

'What about Papa?'

'There is nothing you can do for him.' It was a brutal message, but Sovay knew the truth of it. 'Would he not want you to be safe?'

'Of course! But what am I to be kept safe for? The only people I care about in the world are here! Without them, my life will mean nothing. I am proscribed in my own country. I do not want to go back to skulk and hide, or to wait in another country until it is safe. When will that be?' She turned to face him. 'You did not run away. You stayed, even though your life has been in constant danger, to fight for what you believed in.'

'That is different!' He took her by the arms. 'I am –'

'A man! Is that what you were going to say? I will not be treated differently because I am a woman! Anyway, this is not about me. The most important thing is to get Greenwood away.'

'Because I am a soldier – that is what I was going to say.' He shrugged his defeat and turned to Greenwood who had been watching the exchange with frank interest. 'She is right. You should go. The local Committee here is most zealous. Their leader is a Jacobin crony of Robespierre and he dislikes us being in his *Section*. We need to get you away before he gets wind of your presence. I will disguise you as one of my guardsmen.'

'Good luck, beautiful,' Greenwood whispered as he prepared to leave with Léon. 'I told you it would happen,' he said in English, nodding towards Léon. 'I do believe you've met the man for you!'

'What is he saying?' Léon saw her blush and frowned at Greenwood.

'Nothing,' Sovay said. 'Just telling me to keep safe.'

Just then, a guardsman appeared at the door.

'Excuse me, Captain,' he said, 'but Dupré demands to see the English spy . . .'

'Tell him to clear off,' Léon growled. 'He has no business here.'

'I'll be the judge of that, Citizen.'

A little man, his chest puffed with his own importance, strutted into the room, a soiled liberty cap like a rooster's cockscomb perched on top of his large head. He was not alone, other members of his Committee crowded in with him, all here to see justice done.

One of their number stepped forward. Lefere. He pointed to Sovay, almost choking in his eagerness to make his accusation.

'Her! That's her! The English spy!'

Dupré looked up at the two National Guardsmen standing before him.

'Good work, Citizens. I'll take care of her from now on.'

As he took her by the arm, Léon reached for his sword. Greenwood stepped forward to join him. They were prepared to cut these men to pieces to save her. Sovay could see it in their eyes, the hard set of their jaws, and what would happen then?

She put a hand out to each of them, stilling their sword arms.

'Thank you, Captain. Guardsman,' she looked from one to the other, willing them not to jeopardise themselves. 'But I cannot impose on you further.' She turned to the men who had come to take her. 'I am ready.'

CHAPTER 37

The place they took her to resembled a tavern, stinking of spilt wine, stale sweat and tobacco smoke. Dupré swept ends of sausage and crusts from a rough table for the waiting dogs to snarl over and the Committee took their seats. Sovay was not allowed to speak in her own defence. Her papers were dismissed as fakes. She was accused of being the daughter of a *Milord Anglais* and, de facto, a spy. Her appearance was used as supporting evidence. They squinted at her, pronouncing that she had an English look about her. At a time when a person could be arraigned for merely appearing aristocratic, failing to prosecute the Revolution with enough vigour, or thinking the wrong kind of thoughts, it was enough to condemn her many times over. She stared at them in mute defiance as they went through the motions of deliberation, scribbling on scraps of paper, heads together. They were as capable of administering justice as a troupe of gibbering apes. She found their posturing tiresome and just wanted the charade to end. She was guilty. She would appear before the Revolutionary Tribunal. When that would be, they could not say, but whenever it might be, it would be a formality. As far as these men were concerned, her life was over.

Two officers of the Paris police appeared and she was pushed into a carriage. One policeman rode inside, but he did not speak or answer her questions.

She looked out of the window. The slogans, scrawled in dripping paint across the walls, seemed written in blood: *L'Egalité, Fraternité, la République ou la Mort*. She was beset by sudden apprehension, wondering which way they would go. Back across the Seine could take her to La Force, the scene of the worst of the September Massacres. She sank back with relief as the driver urged the horses, turning away from the river.

As they bounced over the rough cobbles, she thought of Léon. He would have cut that man down as soon as look at him. What would have happened then? He would have been arrested for interfering in the Committee's Revolutionary duty, Greenwood with him. She would still have been arrested. Dysart would have won. What she had done was for the best. He would save Greenwood, make sure Hugh knew of her arrest. But still . . . He might have done something. If this was a story, he would come galloping after her, fight the gendarmes, sweep her up into his arms, take her . . . Where? She had no idea. Some vague place of safety.

But this was not a story, it was real life. He was a man, a patriot, a soldier, strong and fearless, but he was just as powerless as her. Nothing that had so far happened brought home to Sovay the hopelessness of the situation, the helplessness of everyone in the face of these violent forces of unreason. Their destination began to gain superstitious significance. If they arrived at the Luxembourg, then there was hope for him, for her, for the both of them. If they were destined for some other dismal fortress, then all was lost. Looking out of the window again, she caught a glimpse of the huge towers of Notre Dame, the great cathedral now devoted to the worship of Reason. Sovay closed her eyes against the irony of that and offered a silent prayer to the deity who used to reside there. The Conciergerie, the most feared prison of all, was next to it. The only way out of there was by tumbrel. The coach slowed. She forced herself to confront her fate, but found they were held up by the press of people in the narrow streets. They were not going there after all.

'Luxembourg.' The policeman interpreted her apprehensive glances through the window. 'That's where you are going. You were supposed to go to the Conciergerie, but I owe Léon. He saved my brother's life at Verdun. I changed the order for him.'

❧

So Sovay was delivered to her place of incarceration. The receiving officer scarcely looked at her. She was one of a whole line of people waiting to be processed. He took down her details and she was dismissed as he passed on to the next. She was taken into a room, stripped and searched. She stood in her shift, determined not to show her humiliation while any shred of dignity and what little money she had was taken from her. She was allowed her clothes back with a curt 'Cover yourself, Citizeness.'

From here, she was taken into a public room full of others who had just been brought to the prison. People of all descriptions, from the ragged to the well-dressed. Nobody spoke. Everyone seemed sunk into their own misery. Even the children were quiet, looking round in slow bewilderment or clinging to their mothers. Sovay sat down and waited. For what?

She could not guess.

When the intake was complete, the prisoners were divided, men from women, and taken to their places of confinement. The palace's apartments had been divided up and converted into cells. Some were tiny cupboards, barely large enough for one person, others were more like dormitories. She asked anyone she saw if they knew of her father, of Dr Thery. The guards ignored her enquiries, or told her roughly to keep quiet. The prisoners were just as indifferent, either too wrapped up in their own misery to speak to her, or afraid to talk to anybody, lest they be suspected of conspiracy. Despair sucked at her spirit. How would she ever find her father in this vast place? That she might see him, that they might be united, had been her only solace. At length, she gave up and lay down on the straw pallet which was to be her bed. She stared at the decorated ceiling high above her, a peeling, cracked and stained vision: plump cherubs peeping from behind billowing pink and white clouds, set against the blueness of the heavens, and wondered when she would be under the sky again.

She must have dozed, trying to escape into sleep as many around her were doing. She started awake as a hand shook her shoulder, although the touch was not rough and the voice that spoke was gentle.

'I'm sorry to startle you, mademoiselle.'

She looked up into a pair of tired grey eyes. The man looking down at her was obviously a gentleman. His clothes were stained, worn and frayed, but they were of good material and he wore a grey wig upon his head.

'I am Dr Thery,' he said. 'Are you the English girl

just brought in? Daughter of John Middleton?'

Sovay nodded.

'I've been looking for you, but with so many prisoners . . .' He looked at the rows of sleeping forms littering the floor. 'Come with me. I will take you to your father. You know my daughter?'

'Yes, she has been giving us news of him.'

'Your messages have been a great comfort. I'm allowed more freedom than other prisoners,' he explained. 'They let me do what I can to help the sick. Send out for medicines. Not out of any sense of humanity. Do not think that. They do not want people to cheat the guillotine by dying too soon.' He gave a little hollow laugh. 'Although they have been known to cut the heads off the dead. They keep a close eye out for poison, sharp instruments. They make sure we are fed and even allow some exercise. They want us to be as healthy as possible when we meet our deaths.'

Her father was in a small room on his own. There was little in it except a table, chair and a bed. Sovay was glad that he was asleep when the doctor took her in to him. She would not have wanted him to see her face when she saw him, or the tears that sprang into her eyes. He was so changed that, at first, she thought the doctor might have brought her to the wrong man. He had lost so much flesh that he appeared a mere husk of himself, his body scarcely swelling the thin blanket that covered him. He always wore a light brown wig and it was a shock to see his own hair, pure white, a sparse scattering on the pillow. His face was a greyish colour, apart from two hectic spots on his cheeks. Prominent blue veins showed through the thin skin on his temple and forehead. His mouth was open slightly, his jaw sagging, and if it had not been for a slight movement in his chest, she would have taken him for dead.

'You find him much changed,' the doctor said.

Sovay nodded, unable to speak.

'He has been gravely ill but he clings tenaciously to life, mademoiselle. It will give him fresh heart to see you, although we must be careful given the circumstances. The shock, you know.' He patted her hand. 'Perhaps they will allow you to stay and nurse him. Sometimes they allow families to be together. I will see what I can do. Meanwhile, sit here quietly and wait for him to wake naturally. He has been told that you are coming. You must have at least one friend on the outside.'

He went away then and left them. Sovay did as he said and sat by her father, taking his hand in hers. It was smaller than she remembered, shrunken like the rest of him down to bone and skin. She didn't know how long they sat like that, his fingers interlocked with hers, but the little light that came in from outside had almost faded when she felt his grip strengthen. His eyes remained closed but tears seeped from the corners, pooling onto the filthy striped ticking of the pillow.

'I didn't expect to see you again, Sovay,' he said, his voice the faintest whisper, like corn stalks rubbing together.

'Don't cry, Papa!' She was on her feet in an instant, leaning over him, brushing the wisps of hair back from his forehead.

'It breaks my heart to see you in here,' he looked up at her, his eyes full of anguish, and began to sob bitterly as he turned his face to the wall.

'It is the shock,' the doctor said when he came back. He examined her father quickly, putting his ear close to his chest. 'His heart is steady, if a little weak in its beating. He has lapsed into natural sleep so we will let him rest.' He led her away from the bed. 'I have good news, mademoiselle; you will be allowed to remain here with him. A guard is bringing you a pallet.'

Sovay slept on the floor of his cell, caring for his every need. She kept the room swept and clean, and made sure that there was fresh water. She collected food from the dining hall and fed it to him in tiny spoonfuls. Day by day, she fancied he became a little stronger. Sometimes, he seemed near to his old self.

'Mr Thomas Paine is in here, you know,' he said to her one day. 'He is working on a book, Thery tells me, called *The Age of Reason*. He is a great hero of mine. I would very much like to visit him when I am fit and well.'

Sovay promised to arrange a meeting, but she did not know when it would be. Mr Paine was sick with a fever and her father's recuperation was painfully slow. Signs of recovery were often followed by relapses when his mind would wander and he was unable to rise from the bed. He slept much of the time and often, on waking, he thought he was home at Compton and would ask how she did and how her day had been. Sovay would make things up about what she thought would be happening now: how the crops were ripening towards Lammas; how pretty the hedgerows were, and the cornfields studded with cornflowers and red with poppies; how well the gardens looked now it was July. He would grow wider awake and his eyes would flicker round the tall room with its high dark walls and go to the window, boarded and barred. He knew well where they were then, but talk of home comforted him, so they kept up the pretence, hour after hour, until she almost imagined that they were there and she would walk out of his sick room to pass on orders to Gabriel or Stanhope, or to listen to Lydia talk of the latest gossip from the village as the day cooled and she dressed for dinner. Sometimes, her longing was so great that she couldn't speak of it any more. Then, he would pat her hand and tell her he was tired and he would like to take a little sleep.

Sovay would leave him to slip into dreams of Compton and go out into the corridor. Sometimes the doors were unlocked so that prisoners could take exercise, or mix a little in society. The prison had its own rituals and, although discipline had been much tightened, at certain times of the day the prisoners congregated to look out of the windows that over-looked the Luxembourg Gardens.

Sovay remembered when she had been part of that sad parade loitering below. Day after day, many came in vain, not knowing that their friend or relative had long been moved to another prison. The next time they would see them was in a tumbrel. Sovay went with the others and peered out as eagerly as they did. It was the only glimpse of the outside world, the only bright moments in the succession of dull days. From in here, it seemed shocking to see people strolling about in the sunlight, walking under the shade of the trees. The prisoners beside her teetered on tiptoe, laughing, shouting, screaming and waving to people below who could neither see nor hear them, but who trusted that they were there.

She went faithfully every day; sometimes to see Hugh, sometimes Virgil, sometimes both together. They would stand for up to half an hour, staring up at the window in silent vigil. She derived great comfort from this, but suffered almost equal anguish. If one was missing, she feared for the other and vice versa. She dreaded the days when neither appeared at all. Whoever appeared, she always told her father that it was Hugh. Each day, she searched the crowd for another, and had almost given him up when there he was, in his distinctive uniform of dark blue and white, his highly polished boots silver in the bright sunlight. His gold epaulettes glittered and the decorations swinging from his lapels shimmered as he swept off his hat and bowed. He stayed for several minutes, staring upwards, his hand on the pommel of his sword, his heavy, handsome face unsmiling, his thick brows drawn together.

'Comme il est beau!' The girl standing next to her grinned. 'Is he your lover?'

'Yes,' Sovay replied, almost without thinking, and continued to stare back at him. No word had passed between them, but she knew it to be so. She kept her eyes upon him until it seemed that the prison walls had melted, the other people, the trees, the gardens themselves had faded to nothingness and they were the only ones left whirling in an eternity of time and space.

She was so lost in the intensity of his gaze that she failed to realise the purpose behind his appearance. He had come to deliver a warning.

◆➤◆◆

There was another ritual, as unvarying as the parade. Every evening, at around six o'clock, all talk ceased, all movement stilled, silence spread round the prison like a rippling wave. It was as if the building itself were holding its breath. An officer walked through the public rooms where the people stood frozen like statues; the silent corridors echoed to his slow, measured step. As he walked, he read from the sheet he held before him, the 'Evening Paper', the names of those who were to appear the next day before the Revolutionary Tribunal.

Sovay heard his voice and stopped what she was doing. Her father sat up in bed, his ears straining, his face puckered in concentration. It was a quality of listening that everyone adopted, as if sheer intensity of concentration could change what the guard was going to say, or make him go away. One of his feet dragged slightly behind the other. Every night, Sovay tracked his halting step as he went past them and on up the corridor. One evening, he stopped outside their door.

'Middel-ton!'

Sovay and her father looked at each other. The moment they had most dreaded had come. Her father struggled up and swung his legs out of the bed by gripping them one at a time. He could scarcely walk but he was reaching for his breeches.

'Help me, Sovay!'

'No, Father. Stay where you are. I will go to enquire.'

She opened the door. Her father had taken up his sticks and was coming after her.

'Which?' she called. The guard was already past them. 'We're both Middleton. Which one of us is it?'

'What does it matter? Me! Take me!' her father shouted.

The guard ignored him and traced his finger back up his list.

'It says female here.' His fingernail was blackened and broken, she noticed, as he pointed to her name written in gothic script. 'It is for you, Citizeness.'

CHAPTER 38

A number was chalked on her door and in the morning that number was called. Sovay went out, her head held high, her shoulder wet with her father's tears. She had said her goodbyes to him and, although they would never meet again in this life, she did not look back as she left the cell. She needed all her courage for the ordeal ahead.

Sovay was taken from the Luxembourg with about thirty other prisoners to appear before the Revolutionary Tribunal. Prisoners were now tried in *fournée*, batches, in the same way that they were herded to the guillotine. They travelled in a long, covered cart drawn by four horses. There were people of every age and condition, from a little servant girl who looked no more than a child, to an old man of eighty or more who still wore a soiled wig and rags of velvet that marked him as an aristocrat. These were people of every sort and class but they had one thing in common: once they had appeared before the Tribunal, they would be dead within twenty-four hours. If there was a lesson in uniting the nation, this was it. United by their shared fate, all differences of degree, age and status melted from them. Laundress comforted countess and vice versa, servant shared bread with his master. Sovay had to smile at the irony of it. She offered her scrap of kerchief to the little servant girl and asked her name.

'My name is Minette,' the girl answered as she

wiped her tears away.

'Why are you here?'

The girl looked at her dumbly. She had no idea.

Sovay put her arm round the child and held her close until her shivering stopped.

They were taken to the hall of the Revolutionary Tribunal where they were put together with people from other prisons, some of whom, it was alleged, had been part of the same conspiracy, even though they had never seen each other before. They were directed to their places on the ranges of benches reserved for prisoners. Since 22 Prairial, the number had been expanded so that the accused could be tried a hundred at a time.

Sovay looked around from her place about halfway up the tier of benches. The hall bore some similarities to a courtroom, in that there were clerks, a jury, but in other ways this was markedly different. There were guards everywhere; the judges sat at a long table in the body of the court; there was no witness stand, because there would be no witnesses, and what dock was large enough to accommodate a hundred? The jury came in and sat down on the right-hand side of the judges' table. Again, this had the semblance of justice, in that they were a jury, but the jury was always made up of the same people, all Jacobin friends of Robespierre or other members of the Committee of Public Safety.

They were told to stand and the judges filed in. There were five of them, all formally dressed in black with white wigs under tall, black hats which were crowned with great black plumes. They wore the tricolour like a badge of office, on the bands of their hats, the rosettes in their lapels and the sashes across their chests. They stood and bowed to the court, their president at the centre, some kind of official insignia swinging from a tricolour lanyard round his neck. They sat as one as he rang a small bell to signal that proceedings should begin. The noise was tinkling and slight and sounded odd in the sombre room, more suited to the ordering of tea, than the deaths of so many.

They had been followed into the room by Fouquier-Tinville, the prosecutor. Hated and feared in equal measure, this was the man who had sent hundreds, if not thousands, to the guillotine. Most eyes were on him not the judges. A tall man dressed in black like the others and swathed with tricolours. He wore black gloves and a black wig under the nodding, funereal plumes. He looked around and held out his hand for the charge sheet. He began to read in a monotonous voice, as if his task had become tedious and wearisome. Proceedings had begun.

Each prisoner was asked to stand, their name and the charge against them read out. At this point any semblance to proper court procedure ended. There were no defence lawyers, no witnesses, even the prisoners were not allowed to speak up for themselves. Any who did were silenced by the president with a peremptory *'Tu n'as pas la parole'*, it is not your turn to speak. Any who persisted were turned out of the court room and condemned in their absence. And condemned they were and quickly. The proceedings went on apace. The charge was read, the jury gave a verdict of guilty, the Tribunal conferred, the president announced the sentence. 'Death.' In every case.

The charges varied: conspiracy; hoarding; being a

suspect, suspected of being a suspect, associating with people who were suspect; being an aristocrat, having aristocratic connections, an aristocratic appearance; acting in an unrevolutionary manner, uttering unrevolutionary words, thinking unrevolutionary thoughts, even grieving for those who had been sent to the guillotine was enough to land one here. The charges were relentless and most of them trivial. On what Sovay heard, most of the people of Paris, most of France, would have been condemned. The death sentence was inevitable. There was nothing you could say, nothing you could do. One spirited woman, accused of conspiracy, protested that she was not even in the prison where the alleged conspiracy took place. The president's bell tinkled, she was told to be quiet, and informed with cold impatience that 'You would have been in the conspiracy if you had been there!'

Most people heard the charge and the verdict in silence, staring forward without expression, struck by a kind of numbness that Sovay could feel creeping through her, too. She withdrew from the vicious absurdities played out before her and lapsed into a kind of reverie. Part of her remained present, watching everything, but it all seemed to be happening to someone else.

The sound of her own name startled her. She stood up and stared at Fouquier-Tinville. His dark eyes hardly registered her presence. He read out the charge. 'Proscribed person, English spy and enemy of the Republic.' He turned to the jury, expecting no answer, when there was an interruption. Virgil Barrett was standing at the bar of the court.

'This is a case of mistaken identity!' he shouted

across to the prosecutor. 'She is an American citizen. Married to me. I have papers here to prove it!'

It was a vain intervention, with no hope of succeeding, but at least she was not completely abandoned. The weight around Sovay's heart lightened just a fraction to know that she had not been forgotten.

Fouquier-Tinville turned to him. 'We have plenty of evidence to the contrary,' he said.

His hooded eyes looked towards the back of the room. Standing there was Dysart, dressed in black, with a white wig, plumed hat and tricolour sash, just as if he were a judge at the tribunal.

The president rose and bowed in his direction. 'We have pleasure in welcoming Citizen Dysart to our proceedings from the Departement of the Thames.'

Sovay was not shocked or even surprised to see him. She stared straight ahead, as hope finally died within her, snuffed out by his presence. All her fire left her, collapsing into grey ashes of resignation. She was determined to show nothing, but Dysart scented her utter defeat, as a predator smells hart's blood. His thin nostrils flared and, in a rare show of emotion, he gave her a smile of gloating triumph. *I win, you lose*, his pale, lustreless eyes seemed to say. *I get my revenge at last*.

Sovay scarcely heard as the president rang his bell.

'Guards! Remove that man from the court.' He pointed to Virgil. 'He and his *wife* can spend one last night together. Put him in with tomorrow's batch.' He announced the verdict on Sovay without consulting his colleagues. 'Death. Who's next?'

CHAPTER 39

Sovay was taken from the Revolutionary Court to another part of the Conciergerie in Paris. The prison. The most feared destination. It was the antechamber to the guillotine; all those who were to die the next day were brought here. She joined a line of other prisoners and they were marched across the great courtyard. Some of the paving stones still lay heaved up like tombstones from burying the dead of the September Massacres, and all around gaped gated dungeons, crowded with wretched prisoners from every part of France.

Conditions were very different here. The gaolers were grim and unspeaking with large mastiff dogs snarling at their heels. Sovay could not see Virgil as she waited with other prisoners outside the Records Office. He must have already been processed. She was registered by a prison clerk who rarely looked up from his scribbling and then taken to another room for the toilette. A man stepped forward, scissors in hand. He was an assistant to the executioner, here to perform the ritual inflicted on all the condemned in preparation for the guillotine. The collar of her dress was sheered off. Then he took the heaviness of her long, dark hair in his hand and began to cut. The slicing of the blades sounded like tearing silk. Sovay watched each lock curl to the floor like smoke. Her hair was cut short into the nape to allow no obstruction to the falling blade. When he had finished, the prison dampness felt cold, clammy on her neck and she put her hand up to feel the strangeness of her newly shorn state. The hair that remained felt like fur.

The process of her death had already started. She was leaving a part of herself behind, already lost to her sight, mixed there on the floor with hair of every hue and kind, to be swept up and disposed of; so much dead stuff, as she would be tomorrow. The executioner's assistant pushed the pile together with his foot and took up his broom.

The turnkey led her away from the common areas of the prison. Sovay shivered as they passed along dank, stone passages, running with water and clotted with slime. Contagion breathed from the very walls. Sovay did not believe for a moment that the president of the Tribunal would keep to his word, certain that his remark to Virgil had been just another jibing cruelty. She followed the guard with a heavy heart, sure that she was to spend her last night on earth alone, but when the man turned the big key in the lock and the door creaked back, there was Virgil waiting for her. His hair had been shorn like hers, and his shirt collar had been torn away. She flew into his arms and he held her to him. The gaoler had no difficulty believing that they might be husband and wife.

'Make the most of it!' he said with a leer as he shut the door.

Almost as soon as he had left them, they broke away from each other.

'Sovay,' Virgil held her at arm's length, searching her face for signs of change. 'How are you?'

'All the better for seeing you! What you said in that

courtroom, knowing it was certain death.' She shook her head. 'I am for ever in your debt. Or, at least, until tomorrow.'

'It was worth a try. I thought it might work. Occasionally, such things do. A case of mistaken identity . . .' He sat down on the filthy straw pallet and buried his head in his hands. 'Anything is worth a try.'

'But you have thrown your life away. For me. Why?'

She looked round at the ancient, crumbling stone of the walls carved with names, dates, prayers, rows of little lines scratched in and crossed out to measure time passing; messages of despair from all the poor wretches that had been incarcerated there. Waves of misery washed over her.

'It is hopeless!' She shook her head.

Virgil's fingers parted. His grey eyes looked up at her.

'Perhaps not entirely,' he said.

'What do you mean?'

'Things are happening.' It was his turn to stand and pace. 'Yesterday, I was at the Convention. Things did not go well for Robespierre. He went too far. He made thinly veiled threats against Tallien, Fouché, Vadier, Barère and others, implying that he was ready to move against them. The convention trembled, then rallied. Tallien and his allies are ready to join with Fernand and his moderate friends. It has come to the point where it is either him or them. I don't know what happened today but the reign of the tyrant may well be nearing its end.'

Sovay sat on the bed, listening to him, her hands

held in her lap, clutching each other for comfort. *I will not hope. I will not allow myself to hope*, she recited it inside herself like a litany. What hope could there be when people like Danton, Desmoulins, men who had been among the original leaders of the Revolution, had perhaps sat in this very cell, powerless to prevent their own deaths?

'Even if it is true,' she looked up at him, 'it may well come too late for us.' She touched her shorn neck. 'We are due to die tomorrow. The people here will follow their orders, whatever happens in the Convention. They have turned the Revolution into a great machine: once something is set in motion, it is impossible to stop.'

'Perhaps. It is on an edge as keen and narrow as the blade of the guillotine –'

He was interrupted by the gaolers making their rounds, turning locks in doors, herding people back to their cells, demanding lights out, numbering the doors for tomorrow's *fournée* with a swift chalk scrawl.

Sovay looked to the tiny scrap of light that still gleamed through the bars high above her.

'They make us turn in earlier here than in the Luxembourg,' she said. 'What day is it? I lost track of time in there.'

'Twenty-seventh of July – 9 Thermidor.' Virgil stretched out beside her. 'Come, let's get some rest.'

❦

Sovay must have slept, because she was suddenly being shaken awake.

'Hssh!' Virgil's face was close to hers. She could see the whites of his eyes in the darkness. He held his fingers to his lips. 'Listen!'

At first, Sovay could here nothing. Then, through the night sounds of the prison, a muffled shout, the scrape of a key, footsteps echoing, she heard a bell ringing, a slight sound, thinned by distance, tiny but insistent. It was joined by another, a deep toll, loud and ominous, booming through the thick walls.

'That's Notre Dame. They are sounding the tocsin.' Virgil sprang up and went to the faint patch of light that marked the window. 'Calling the city to arms.'

'What does it mean?' Sovay rose to join him.

They both listened as the rest of the gaol woke around them. Others had heard it, too. There was movement and rustling of feet through straw, the sound of running and men shouting. A cry went up of fear and lamentation. A clamour started as prisoners hammered on the doors and beat on the bars and walls with their metal food pans, fearing that they would be dragged from their cells to be hacked and beaten to death on the paving stones and cobbles outside, as others had been at the time of the September Massacres.

'What will happen?'

From above came the beat of hooves as men rode into the courtyard; the rumble of cannon being moved into place.

'Who knows?' Virgil dragged the bed over to the wall and climbed upon it, to try and see out.

'Here,' Sovay hitched her skirt. 'Let me stand on your shoulders.'

She relayed to Virgil what she could see happening. The night was fully dark. It was not long past midsummer, so she would think it before three o'clock. The grating of their cell was almost underground; her eyes were on the level of the paving stones outside. She could see the stamping hooves of the horses, cannons being wheeled about and rolled towards the gates. An officer dismounted and strode towards the entrance steps, his spurs ringing and sparking on the stones. Whatever he had come for, he didn't get it. After a few minutes he was back again, mounting his horse. The gates opened and he was gone, the cannon rumbling after him. She wondered for a moment if it could be Léon.

'What do you think it means?' she asked as she dropped down from Virgil's shoulders.

'Well, I don't think that we are all going to be dragged out and massacred. Not just yet, anyway.' He rubbed the fair stubble on his chin as he paced the room, aching to escape out into the city. 'It could still go either way, but it could be that Robespierre and his friends have been arrested. If that is so, then that officer could be trying to find a prison to take them.'

'What about the cannon?'

'Let us hope that it is not being used by Hanriot to move against the Convention. He's an ally of Robespierre. Let's hope your friend, Léon, is able to deal with him. Léon's been rallying the other battalions, so that they will be ready to act when the time comes. He's a good man, clever and courageous and devoted to his country. If anything is to be salvaged from the wreck of the Revolution, it will be by men like him.'

'Why do you say he is my friend?' The mention of his name had made her heart beat a little faster and she had found that she was blushing despite herself.

'Is he not?' Virgil smiled. 'Perhaps I am mistaken, but *he* has sworn to marry you, if we can get you out of here. The marriage was his idea. When he knew that you were to appear before the Tribunal, he wanted to go to them and declare that you were man and wife. He would see you go free or share your fate. I took his place. As you say, the gesture was near hopeless and, in the balance, his life was more important. He can do more than I to stop this madness.'

By now there was sound and movement out on the corridor. Virgil and Sovay went to listen. The turnkeys were making extra rounds, checking every lock and door. They were more surly than usual, some of them plainly fearful, their dogs barking and yelping as they picked up their masters' agitation.

Any communication with the prisoners was strictly forbidden, but not all the gaolers were on the side of Robespierre. Gradually, word began to spread by means of what the prisoners called *the whispers along the wall*. As the first light of dawn struck through into the filthy cells, the news broke to general rejoicing. They were facing a new morning; one without Robespierre.

No one was sure exactly what had happened. Some stories said he was dead, others imprisoned, still others attested that he was alive but wounded, but all agreed that his reign of terror was over. Many found it hard to believe and as the morning light strengthened towards day, they listened for the rumble of the tumbrels in the courtyard outside. But the gates remained shut, the guards did not come to check the numbers chalked on the cells and escort the occupants to have their hands bound in readiness by the executioner's assistants. The prison was still, as if none quite knew now what to do.

When the guards finally came round with the *gamelles*, the mess tins, they were uncommunicative but they unlocked the doors to allow access to the public areas.

Everyone crowded round the bars, although there was not much to see. At length, the gates opened. A carriage rolled up and the overseer of the prison returned, his face white and rigid with shock. He was accompanied by an escort of National Guardsmen. Commanding them was Léon.

He came striding down the aisle with the Governor behind him.

'I don't have orders,' the man was saying.

'*I* have the orders, Citizen.' Léon brandished the papers in his face. 'I have cannons, too. Trained on this place. If you do not release them into my custody, it will be the worse for you! Now, where are they?'

He was besieged by supplicants, all clamouring to be released from their hateful confinement.

'All in good time, Citizens! All in good time! Your turn will come soon.'

'Is it true?' someone cried. 'Is it true? Has the tyrant fallen?'

'Aye!' Léon looked round them. 'It is true. Robespierre, Couthon, Saint-Just are appearing even now before the Revolutionary Tribunal.'

His announcement brought bitter laughter and fresh cheering.

'What about the others?'

'Dead or dying, as the Incorruptible will be shortly.

He tried to kill himself but only succeeded in shooting half his jaw off. Do not worry, my friends, he will not cheat the guillotine. You will all be freed soon. My present orders are for two prisoners only.' He turned to where Virgil and Sovay were fighting their way through the press of people. 'They are to be released to me without delay.' He took Sovay in his arms. 'Especially this one!'

He kissed her and the cheering redoubled. Clapping broke out all around them, while Virgil looked on, grinning like a groomsman. Even turnkeys joined in the jubilation. The spell of the Terror was broken. The dismal walls of that grim prison had rarely witnessed a moment as joyful as this.

❖❖❖

Sovay left the prison to find a Paris transformed. The streets were full of people, showing their release, their gladness, by laughing, singing, drinking and dancing. They had endured. They had survived. The Conciergerie was close by the great church of Notre Dame. The doors were open. A steady stream of visitors, mostly women, was going in to give thanks to whichever deity, God or Reason, had prevailed.

Later that day, Sovay would go to the Place de la Révolution, accompanied by Léon, Virgil, Hugh and his friend, Fernand. The guillotine had been brought back to the centre of the city and reassembled for this special occasion and the streets were thronged with people. There were as many lining the streets and crammed into the square as had been present at the death of Louis XVI. They were here to witness the end of a different kind of tyranny.

Shouts and cheering marked the slow rumbling progress of the tumbrels across the city. A great roar went up when at last the carts rolled into view. One by one, the prisoners mounted the scaffold, were placed on the plank, as so many had been before them. The crowd seemed to hold its breath at each hissing, heavy fall of the blade, to explode into cheering at the tumbling of the head into the basket, the lazy sluice of blood.

At last, Robespierre, a slight figure, his face bandaged, his sky-blue jacket stained with blood, mounted the scaffold. His coat was stripped from him. The executioner tore the bandage from his wounded jaw and a high-pitched animal scream rang out across the huge expanse of the Place de la Révolution. A single, sharp cry of agony from one who had brought such suffering to so many. Robespierre was strapped to the plank and the blade descended. It was all over in less than a minute. The people had their revenge.

More were to die that evening, but Sovay had seen enough death. She left on the arm of her lover and did not stay to witness the passing of the various allies and supporters of the tyrant, among them the Englishman, Dysart.

Afterword

June, 1816

'And your sister never returned to England?'

'No, she never did.'

The story had begun with Sir Jonathan Trenton's portrait of her that stood at the top of the stairs. It was finishing with the miniature that Sir Hugh was showing to us now. It had taken him some days to tell and he'd kept us well entertained through the current spell of unseasonably inclement weather.

'She married Léon, the dashing young captain and hero of the Revolution. After all that austerity, Paris went wild. One long round of hectic gaiety: parties, salons, theatre, the opera. Sovay and her husband were much in demand. They called her *La Minerve*. This is a likeness taken about that time.'

The picture showed a striking young woman in a pale primrose dress, seated on a chaise longue, her head turned *à l'odalisque*, her bare shoulders and long neck accentuated by her dark, cropped curls.

'Her short hair was very fashionable. The new fashions of the *merveilleuses* suited her, those simple dresses based on the style of Greece and Rome. All very à la mode,' he laughed. 'Although she never adopted that most extreme of Thermidorian affectations: a thin red ribbon tied round the neck.'

'Is she still alive?'

'Why, yes! She lives in Venice, in a palazzo by the

Grand Canal. Now that the war with Napoleon is over, I'm thinking of visiting her.' He looked around at the company. 'Perhaps we should all go to escape this beastly weather.'